has been translated into seve~~~ ~~~~~~~~~~~ ~~~,
German and Serbian.

She grew up in South London and has also lived in Nigeria and
America. She admits to watching too many soaps and reality TV
but firmly believes they enhance her writing. She even taught a
class on it!

Keep up to date with Lola via her website: www.lolajaye.com,
and on Twitter (@LolaJaye), Instagram, and Facebook.

LOLA JAYE

Orphan Sisters

EBURY
PRESS

1 3 5 7 9 10 8 6 4 2

Ebury Press, an imprint of Ebury Publishing
20 Vauxhall Bridge Road,
London SW1V 2SA

Penguin
Random House
UK

Ebury Press is part of the Penguin Random House group of companies
whose addresses can be found at global.penguinrandomhouse.com

Copyright © Lola Jaye, 2017

Lola Jaye has asserted her right to be identified as the author of this work
in accordance with the Copyright, Designs and Patents Act 1988

This novel is a work of fiction. Names and characters are the product of
the author's imagination and any resemblance to actual persons,
living or dead, is entirely coincidental

First published in the UK in 2017 by Ebury Press

www.penguin.co.uk

A CIP catalogue record for this book is available from the British Library

ISBN 9781785036330

Printed and bound in Great Britain by Clays Ltd, St Ives PLC

Penguin Random House is committed to a sustainable future for
our business, our readers and our planet. This book is made from
Forest Stewardship Council® certified paper.

MIX
Paper from
responsible sources
FSC® C018179

For Mum, Toods & Nanno

PART ONE

PART ONE

Chapter One

Nigeria, 1958

Lanre sat in between Mummy's knees, short legs stretched out in front of her, head tilted by the force of strong fingers as they meticulously wove each strand of hair into a spiral shape around her head. Asking Mummy to read out Daddy's letter for the umpteenth time had merely been a ploy to delay the inevitable.

'Ow!' she complained as, once again, a shock of pain passed unapologetically through her body. It was swift, almost forgettable, yet a mere prelude to the next one.

'Ow, ow,' her mother teased. 'Why are you complaining like a baby? You are seven years. What would your father say of this?'

'He would tell me I must be smiling always. Even when I am having my hair plaited.'

'That is correct.'

A chicken ran past Lanre's feet, and she wished she could chase it. She often did.

'Don't worry, I am almost finished. You will soon look like a beautiful girl for your daddy.'

Lanre smiled at that. She hoped to one day be as beautiful as Mummy with her pointed nose and her long hair that, when plaited, touched the tips of her elegant shoulders.

She wished Daddy would indeed see her new hairstyle, along with the pretty dress Aunty had purchased for her only yesterday; it was blue with flowers embroidered on the side. Mummy sometimes said that with Lanre's extra-long eyelashes and pretty British dresses, she was the most beautifulest girl in their street and possibly the whole of Nigeria!

The pain lessened as Mummy worked her way through the final strands, the humidity wringing sweat from her forehead. As Mummy applied the Vaseline to her scalp, Lanre closed her eyelids and once again thought of Daddy; how his top lip curled whenever he laughed; the way his broad shoulders moved front to back when he walked towards her with his arms outstretched, like he did every time he saw her; how much she missed him. Lanre opened her eyes in time to see one of the neighbours pass by, clad in a green and black wrapper, which was folded and tucked under each armpit.

'Don't worry, the hair will soon finish,' said Mama Bimpe with encouragement. 'We all have to go through this to look lovely!'

'Yes, Ma,' replied Mummy dutifully.

Lanre did not like being interrupted when thinking of her daddy, but the front yard was open to all, graced with a multitude of vegetation that included plantains and one coconut tree, which some of the local children climbed for enjoyment. The house never felt empty, even though Daddy's absence had left a noticeable void. Neighbours filled the house separately but daily, bringing food, like fufu wrapped up in a giant leaf or sometimes soup, which Mummy did not like because she preferred to cook her own. They would sit for hours talking about adult subjects that did not interest Lanre. She was seven and not supposed to listen in on adult conversations, but she always did. When Mama came to visit with Baba (every day), they would often refer to their oldest grandchild as 'the more inquisitive of the two'. Or just a 'nosy little girl'. But this was OK; Lanre liked having a title separate from her little sister Mayowa.

Minutes later, her hair finally completed, Lanre stood in front of Mummy.

'I know you are missing your daddy,' her mother said, flicking an imaginary something from Lanre's cheek. 'The letter said we will all be together soon. Trust your daddy. He is working hard to bring us all to England. He is attending college and he is working at a job.'

'Yes, Mummy.'

Mummy's beaming smile allowed Lanre the comfort she craved. Her mother never smiled much lately. Before Daddy left, he and Mummy were always smiling together, holding hands when they thought no one was looking, feeding one another blobs of pounded yam as Lanre and Mayowa giggled their embarrassment. Mummy and Daddy were not like other married people in the area. They did not shout at one another in the road like Mr and Mrs Adjobe, and there were never any rumours about Daddy impregnating this girl or that (Lanre still wasn't quite sure what 'impregnating' actually meant, but it couldn't be good). The Cole family were essentially like white families in England, according to Mama (who had never been to England but was a very wise grandmother), which was to say perfect. In England there was no hardship and no conflict. Everyone was happy and they laughed all the time.

'Mummy, please read Daddy's letter again!'

'OK, but this is the last time today. Call your sister, come.'

'Mayo-waaaa! Mayo-waaaa!' she yelled. In seconds, her sister was walking towards them, dragging her feet across the sandy floor.

'What is it?' Mayowa's eyebrows were knotted. Her younger sister was always annoyed at something.

'Mummy is going to read Daddy's letter from England again!' said Lanre.

Five-year-old Mayowa, dressed today in a yellow dress with a white bow on the shoulder, sat beside her sister, yawning half-heartedly. Her hair was a little shorter and much harder in texture than Lanre's. Mummy often called it 'stubborn' – which was also a great way to describe her little sister, especially when she'd refuse to play with Lanre whenever her best friend Titi was away in Ondo.

Lanre clutched her sister's hand as Mummy once again read the precious letter, which had taken four weeks to arrive. At least this had been quicker than the previous delivery, which had eventually arrived minus the money Daddy had enclosed. Baba said postal theft was 'an offshoot of poverty brought on by the teefing Europeans', whatever that meant, whilst Mama blamed it on 'greedy Nigerians'.

Mummy began the letter and, once again, Lanre's thoughts drifted to the day Daddy revealed he was leaving for England. Her mummy and daddy had been sitting under the shade of the coconut tree on makeshift seats made from an upside-down table that someone with too much money and not enough sense (according to Mummy) had discarded. Lanre and Mayowa had been throwing an orange and yellow ball to one another, only to suddenly stop when Mummy had begun to cry. Lanre had been momentarily distracted until her sister had thrown the ball at her and it had bounced roughly off the side of Lanre's face.

'Why did you do that?' Lanre had complained.

'You're supposed to be playing with me!' Mayowa had replied. Mummy had quickly stopped crying and begun to laugh as Daddy had held her tight. This had been very confusing.

Mummy had explained later that she had been happy because their family had been given the chance of a lifetime, but she had also been so very sad that Daddy would have to leave. Lanre still didn't quite understand.

'When you girls and your mother join me,' Daddy had continued, 'we will have a good and happy life in England. He had placed Mayowa on his lap as Lanre had started to understand what this all meant: Daddy was leaving.

'And you will speak very good English, like the white people there. Good Queen's English,' Mummy had added.

'I don't want the Queen's English!' Mayowa had protested, before burying her face into Daddy's shirt.

'I thought that is what I am speaking now,' said Lanre.

'It will sound better than this. Better than my own,' said Mummy.

'Ah, ha, Adanya, there is nothing wrong with the way they speak.' Daddy had hugged Mayowa close.

'I want the children to be better,' Mummy had answered.

Daddy had shaken his head. 'Anyway, do not worry, my angels. We will not be apart for more than six months. Once I have enough money, I will send for you all.'

That had been nine months ago.

'Oya, Mayowa you are next!' said Mummy, placing the precious letter to one side.

Her sister groaned with dissatisfaction as Lanre glanced into the tiny cracked mirror, pleased with the results. Her daddy always commented on how pretty she looked after Mummy had finished her hair.

She missed her daddy so much.

They'd spoken only once on the telephone, four months previously, and just a few days after Mr Adelepo's rich grandchild had installed a telephone at his office almost six miles away. That occasion had been so full of joy, not least because it had been the first time Lanre had ever seen a telephone before.

Her little sister's exaggerated whimpering was silenced by the sound of a disembodied voice. 'Adanya! Adanya! Come quickly!'

Mummy let go of Mayowa's head, much to the child's relief. 'Ma?'

Mama calling her daughter's name was far from unusual, but Lanre detected urgency in her tone. They entered Mama's house, just a few doors away, and sure enough an assortment of neighbours had already gathered, all smiling greetings in Mummy's direction. The air was thick with heat and expectation. A slim gecko ran up the wall.

'I have an announcement!' said Baba, in that baritone voice. Strong lines of white dominated his beard and full hairline. His large belly protruded from his generously fitted buba. Lanre liked to poke it through the kaftan-like garment after he fell asleep on the chair. 'Mr Adelepo's granddaughter's friend has a sister in London. She returned from there yesterday and delivered this message today. A message from London!'

Mummy grabbed Lanre's hand. 'What is it? Is it my Tayo? Is he OK?'

'He is very well, of that I am sure.' He pulled from his pocket, an oblong-shaped envelope and someone gasped. Lanre recognised Daddy's handwriting immediately and so did Mummy, it would seem, because she too gasped rather loudly. Baba passed the precious envelope to Mummy, who was careful to open it slowly so as not to tear the precious written words inside.

'Do you know what it is?' asked Baba, rather knowingly.

The room was now a hub for more neighbours, friends, passers-by, in fact anyone who cared to join them. Even Lanre's best friend Titi had arrived, a development that almost thrilled her more than the arrival of the letter.

At last Mummy spoke. 'It is a ticket.' Her hand moved towards her opened mouth.

Lanre wanted to ask if there was only one and, if so, why?

'Ah no, there are three tickets!' said Mummy doubling over with laughter and yet a tear rolled down her face.

Lanre felt her legs buckle as the crowd erupted into a loud mixture of cheers and congratulations; Yoruba and English; laughter and joy.

Daddy, as always, had kept his promise. After so many months apart, they were finally going to go to join him in England!

*

The luggage was packed. A number of family members would be benefiting from the various larger items they would have to leave behind. But, as Mummy said, they would buy many new things in London. Much more beautiful things.

'I can't wait to go!' said Mayowa.

'Shhh ... Mummy is sad to be leaving. Don't let her hear you!'

Mayowa threw Lanre a confused look. 'What are you talking about?'

'I know what I mean.' Lanre was older and knew grown-up things. She was aware Mummy would miss the only home she had known. She would miss her parents being a loud call away, and miss being surrounded by people she'd known her entire life. Lanre was sure of this because she felt exactly the same way. She too would miss walking to school with Titi in the matching khaki dresses that every girl in the school had to wear. She would miss watching Mama pound yams in the large mortar in the yard, especially after Mummy had told her no one in London owned such a thing – they would have to buy it already pounded and inside a bag, according to Daddy's letter. Just last week, Lanre had overheard a conversation between Mummy and Mama:

'My daughter, do not be sad. You will soon be with your husband. This is what you have wanted for so long.'

'I know, Mummy. And when that day comes, I know I will miss you all so much.'

'As will we. Especially your father. You have always been his special one. This is why we named you Adanya: her father's daughter.'

'Thank you, Mummy.'

'You are destined for great things, my child. You were not born to stay here and amount to nothing. You will not sell tomatoes, pepe, or onion on the street. And never will your children. We did not name them after British queens for no reason!'

'Yes, Mummy.'

'I am sad to see you all go, but I do not want you to stay in this country. We are part of the British Empire, so it is right you will go and sample its fruits. Your father is thinking differently, though. He is always shouting about foreign rule this and that, and saying he can't wait until the white people leave his country! Don't mind him. I am happy you will soon be living in the United Kingdom and with all of the wonderful people!'

Grandmother exhaled with a huge smile. 'This is what I want for you and your children. They will be big people one day, and so will you. England is the right decision. It is more than I could have asked for, so stop these tears and be thankful you have been chosen. OK?'

'Yes, Ma.' Mummy wiped her eyes, and Lanre wished she could embrace her. But if she did, they'd find out she'd been listening to a private adult conversation, and that was not allowed. She would hug her on the aeroplane instead. The big frightening aeroplane she was about to set foot on for the very first time in her life.

After what would be their last meal in Nigeria for now – a delicious plate of pounded yam with two meats instead of the usual one – Lanre excused herself from the dinner table early. She wanted to be alone in the room she shared with her sister one last time. But as her bare feet trod the hard floor, she heard the collective groan of her elders as the house quickly descended into darkness. The electricity, never reliable, would probably be off until morning. She slowly navigated the short route to her bedroom, careful not to veer away from the left to avoid cockroaches that might have been scuttling around. She hated those. Lying back on the single bed, she was delighted when light from a neighbouring house illuminated her room. The electricity had returned. Although she was used to the erratic electricity supply, it was fitting that her last night in Nigeria would not be cloaked in darkness. She'd heard from a teacher at school that London had electricity twenty-four hours a day! What would that feel like? She was about to find out. Her eyes rested on the peeling grey walls. The dull heat allowed the room to shrink before her eyes as sweat beaded her forehead. She couldn't wait to be in London. Titi had already expressed her jealousy as she delighted in telling her once again of how cold it would be.

'They say it is freezing all of the time!' she'd enthused.

'That's OK; at least I will not be hot like you are here!'

Titi had not looked amused, but still followed her to the Adelepos' empty yard and into a small outhouse where Titi opened a very large white container full of bags of food at a very cold temperature. She'd dared Lanre to place her hand inside.

'Ah, that was easy!' Lanre had told her, moments later.

Titi had merely folded her arms and knotted her eyebrows. 'It was only twenty seconds!'

'I will be OK with the English weather! It is going to be fine!' Lanre had laughed, playfully nudging her best friend on the shoulder. Despite herself, Titi had not been able to stop smiling back.

Chapter Two

The lady in the smart uniform smiled and informed Mummy they'd be landing in half an hour. Mayowa had sobbed for part of the journey, and the other passengers had failed to conceal their disapproval. One even went so far as expressing his distaste that Mummy had not given her 'a good slap'. Mummy had respectfully informed him that it was not her way.

Halfway through the journey, her younger sister had fallen asleep on Mummy's shoulder. Luckily, Lanre had the window seat and was able to marvel at how small Nigeria appeared as the aeroplane had taken off into the air. Unfortunately, she hadn't learnt anything about what kept an aeroplane in the air, so this new fear only made her grip tightly onto her mother's hand and wish her daddy was there.

'Mummy, I am scared of the aeroplane,' she whimpered.

'It is OK. Just thirty minutes until we are with your father, in England.'

The word England still bought a swish to her tummy. Even though she already missed Titi, she knew that what awaited her would be worth the sacrifice. She'd heard everyone was nice to everyone in England. All of the few white people she'd seen in Nigeria had been nice to them, so it made sense they would also be nice to others in their country too! This logic carried her through the fear of the landing, which was officially announced by the captain in a clear and crisp British accent.

She turned to Mummy who had placed her hands together and was praying in Yoruba for a safe landing.

As almost everyone on board had looked like her, Lanre wasn't prepared for the sea of white faces in the busy arrivals hall. Feeling small in her favourite orange dress, she tightened her grip on the worn suitcase she carried, a gift from a second cousin. The sheer multitude of people had surprised her, and frightened her a little too. Scores of bodies milled around, noisily lugging suitcases, greeting loved ones with loud tears and long embraces. For the first time in her life, Lanre and her family were in the minority, and she suddenly longed for the home they had left behind. The safety of the area she, Mummy and her grandparents had been born into. The coconut tree. The smell of fresh plantains frying in the yard. In contrast, her younger sister cheerfully skipped along the floor, holding onto Mummy's hand.

They had landed an hour ago, and there was still no sign of Daddy.

What if he'd forgotten? What would they do? Lanre felt a tight knot in her stomach as she stared at the floor.

'Adanya.'

She looked up, and there he was.

'Tayo!' screamed Mummy as she let go of her daughter's hand and ran into her husband's open arms.

Lanre was dancing inside as Daddy let go of Mummy and stooped down, pulling both his daughters into his arms. She instantly fell into the safety of his body, the cushion of his chest and the fresh-soap scent of him. Her daddy had not forgotten them. He had come! He had come!

'Tayo, is this you?' asked Mummy, smoothing her hand over his cheek. 'Is it so?'

'Of course, my love.' He stood up and gazed into her eyes. Once again, the love Lanre's parents still had for one another was clear.

Nothing had been altered by distance or time. If anything, their love appeared to be stronger than ever. They embraced madly, squeezing one another so tight that Lanre feared there would be broken bones.

'Daddy, we missed you!' cried Mayowa, holding onto his leg. There did not seem to be enough of Daddy to satisfy each person. Lanre did not doubt they had all missed him in equal amounts. Daddy pulled Mayowa up and into his arms and with Lanre now holding onto his leg, the family of four headed outside and into the unknown, the dream of a new and beautiful life together.

Lanre slept for the entire car journey to their new home. It was her sister who nudged her awake as the car pulled up outside the building. She wished she'd worn something thicker than her thin-but-pretty orange dress.

A white man named Dave, who was Daddy's boss, bid them farewell before driving away in that noisy car. Lanre, still unsure of where she was in such darkness, rubbed her eyes vigorously as the pull of sleep still threatened to claim her again. Daddy's home was in a place called Padd-ing-ton, but it was one room in a larger house. It was bigger than her bedroom back home and sprinkled with a smiling brightness thanks to the crisp, white paint adorning the walls, and a clear light bulb.

Tiny spots rose on her arm, despite the presence of what Daddy referred to as a paraffin heater in the corner. Lanre could tell Mummy was resisting the urge to complain.

'This is where we will be sleeping. I know it is not very big—'

'Ah ah, Tayo, it is ... fine! Our room back home is smaller than this.'

'Yes, but this is all we have. This room is for us all.'

Mummy swallowed.

Inside the shared kitchen, Lanre rubbed her eyes but noticed dozens of silver-bottomed tins resting on the countertop. The cooker beside it was so tall, it was past her height!

'This is where you place the bread,' said Daddy pointing to an oblong contraption. 'It will cook it. Much better than our one stove or the pot with fire and sticks beneath it!' Daddy pulled Lanre towards him, smiling.

'Ah ah, Tayo, we did not live badly in Nigeria,' said Mummy.

'We did not. But here, we will live better.'

'Daddy, what is this?' asked Lanre picking up one of the tins.

'That, my dear, is a tin of tomato soup. It is very good. A bit like our own soup but without the pepe so it will not hurt your tongue!'

'Why are there so many of them?'

'If you look at them closely, they are misshapen.' He pointed to a small dent in the tin she was holding.

'It is still fine to eat, though?' asked Mummy.

'It is, but the factory where I work, they say they cannot sell them and we must take them home. So we have plenty!'

'What a wasting of food!' complained Mummy, shaking her head.

Daddy bent down to one of the cupboards, standing up a moment later with his hands wrapped around a long transparent container with a colourful collection of long-stemmed flowers inside. 'These are for you.'

'What is this?' asked Mummy. 'Where did you get them?'

'This is what they do here. Give flowers to a lady,' Daddy said, grinning. Mummy stared at the flowers, her eyes narrowed.

'I could not find the purple ones. I know you like that colour.'

'Thank you …' said Mummy absently.

Daddy's smile wavered. 'What is it, my love?'

'I appreciate the flowers, but I am very cold. The children are cold too.'

Lanre appreciated the admission. Daddy had said it was almost summer here; this did not feel like almost summer.

He moved over to his wife and rubbed her shoulders. 'I will buy another heater and we shall wear more pullovers. And, of course, I will keep you warm in the night.'

Lanre recognised the look that passed between her parents. It was the one that usually came before they shut their bedroom door for at least an hour. Once, when she was little, Lanre decided to investigate what her parents did in that room, but with her ear to the door, all she heard was laughter and an occasional moan. She had been confused at why laughter would be in the same mix as the sound of pain.

Mummy had placed a dozing Mayowa onto the bed and the three of them sat on the floor on top of a blanket that Daddy told her was called 'tartan'.

'I am sorry, my love, that you will have to share the kitchen and toilet with strangers and that we do not have a sitting room,' he said. 'One day, I will get us a big house.'

'Back home, we shared our house with our entire family and many of the neighbours. The people we are sharing with ... are they also Nigerians?'

'Yes, my love.'

'Eh heh! So what is the difference?'

'But we do not have anywhere to bathe. The toilet outside is very small.'

'Where do you bathe?'

'There is a place not far from here. We will go once a week.'

Mummy made a face. 'What? But Tayo, we must bathe at least once a day.'

'I will buy us a small bath for the room. For now, we will have to use the sink in the kitchen to wash ourselves. I'm sorry, Adanya.'

She took his hand. 'No, it is fine. We are all together. This is what matters, my love.'

'I knew I married the correct woman. Ajoke Buka would never have been like you!'

'Ajoke, *ke*?' said Mummy, before falling into his arms once more. Ajoke was a lady from Daddy's hometown of Abeokuta who had told everyone that one day they would be married.

16

Daddy's family had really liked her too, and so had Daddy, until he saw Mummy in a blue dress speckled with yellow flowers as she walked past, a pail of water on her head. He claimed it was love at first sight and that he could no longer remember what Ajoke Buka looked like. They had laughed about Ajoke Buka ever since.

'You wanted me because of my pointed nose. That was the real reason!'

'No, no! It was your shapely hips in that dress!'

Mummy smiled. 'Stop it, Tayo! The children can hear you!'

'I defied my parents to marry you! What do I get for that?' Although Daddy was still smiling, Mummy's had dropped.

'They have never forgiven me for that,' she said.

'They are far away in Nigeria and we are here. Forget about it all. Let us begin our lives together again.'

'I love you, Tayo Cole,' she said, her slim hands cupping his face.

'I love you, Adanya Cole.'

That night, the family of four lay in one bed. Daddy held tightly onto Mummy as she slept off the fatigue of a long flight. Lanre felt happier than she had for a long time. Her entire family were all under one roof again, and in one bed, away from the effects of a British almost-summer; away from frightening aeroplanes and in the only place she ever needed to be.

Daddy spent the days at work in the factory whilst Mummy tidied up the shared kitchen, tiny toilet and the one room they called home. And then tidied it all over again. Daddy sometimes attended college in the evenings, and it was during such nights that the room felt so empty. Daddy's presence brought life and excitement, which would lay dormant throughout the day as they waited for him to return.

The two other residents who shared their home left before sunlight and would not return until they were all in bed. The only evidence of their existence were the crumbs in the sink beside two unwashed cups.

A week into their new life, they were still yet to venture outside. Mayowa seemed content with *The Cat in the Hat* – an English book Daddy had kept for her. Every day, she sat in the corner of the room engrossed in another world, paying no attention to anything else. Lanre sometimes wished her sister would play with her more, talk to her about their new life ... anything. But for now, Lanre was happy to help Mummy clean their 'home', even if it did seem to only take minutes.

'We will have to go and buy some pepe. The food I brought from Nigeria will soon finish.'

'This means we have to go outside, Mummy,' said Lanre with a slight burst of excitement.

'Yes,' she said with a sigh. 'But you will maybe have to stay here and look after Mayowa.'

'I don't need you to look after me!' she shouted, without looking up from her book.

'Why can't we go together?' asked Lanre.

'You are right. We shall go together. Come on, put on two pullovers and you will be warm enough. Let us go!'

Lanre hadn't meant right now, but she was pleased they would finally be venturing out into the real England. Their new country. They were ready within five minutes. Lanre had already begun to sweat under the weight of two adult-sized sweaters wrapped around her body.

Mummy opened the large wooden door that had suddenly grown in size. 'OK, then ... we will go to ... the shops. Your father has told me where they are.'

'Are they far away, Mummy?' asked Lanre.

'No, they are very close.' Mummy placed one foot out of the door, as the sound of a siren sped past the house. The first time they had heard such a noise, Mayowa had jumped into Daddy's arms and immediately burst into tears. Now they were already used to the strange sounds of London, but had yet to see more than was outside their window.

'Come on. We are going!' Mummy said quickly, yet without conviction. She grabbed a hand of each of her daughters and they slowly stepped out into the street. In the area of London where they lived there were rows and rows of large brick houses that appeared to be stuck together. The pavement outside their house was full of small puddles, evidence of the drip-drip sounds of the night before. A small vehicle balancing crates of empty bottles went past in the road as a slew of people moved from one end of the street to the next. Where were they all going?

'Soooo ... let us go,' said Mummy, her eyes searching the area around them, as they remained stationary. A weak wind blew a piece of paper onto Mummy's shoe and Lanre bent to pick it up.

'Keep Britain White,' said Lanre. She had always been a good reader.

'Leave it!' Mummy snatched it from her hand. 'Let us go back inside!' she snapped.

'Why, Mummy?'

'Back into the house. Don't ask me questions!' Mummy ushered the two little girls back inside, and with a huge sigh she closed the door behind them.

Two days later and with the last of the butter scraped from the container, they finally left the flat again. Each of them was now draped in an overcoat with sleeves too long for their arms, thanks to Daddy's miscalculations. They ventured into the unknown realms of the streets beyond theirs, passing neatly aligned houses and roads were so smooth-looking that Lanre wanted to get on her knees and run her hand over the surface. There were many, many trees, but not one contained coconuts or anything that looked familiar. Lanre looked out for anyone who looked like them, but did not see anyone. At least when they turned into a street market, she was slightly reminded of back home. Traders were shouting their wares but with words she had never heard before.

'Get your ripe bananas, Cox's apples! Get your ripe bananas, Cox's apples!'

Fruit, fish, meat, the sound of singsong voices amongst the noise of a very busy London market. Mummy held onto Lanre's hand tightly, preventing her from investigating any further. She was mumbling to herself in Yoruba that this was just too much.

Mummy liked to look at the ground as they walked, but Lanre was fascinated with the many people that walked by, especially the men with their hair piled high on top of their heads. How did they get their hair to be such a shape? One of these men stopped when they walked past, his lips pursed, eyes narrow. Lanre smiled her thanks but his expression remained the same. Perhaps it was because of the weather that white people did not smile that much. Even so, having been confined to the flat for over a week, the unfamiliar sights of the world outside their room were something Lanre wanted to remember forever. She would one day tell Titi about the wide squared floor they called a pavement; about looking up at each of the large imposing buildings with curious faces peeking through the windows; about the smooth roads with a number of fine automobiles driving past, and the flashing lights on tall stalks that appeared to tell the automobiles when it was safe to 'go', and the huge, red, two-storey automobiles she had heard about but had now seen – buses, they were called. A real-life London bus, that scared her little sister with its loud bubbling sounds and clouds of smoke when it rode past. London was everything she had imagined it to be and more.

By the end of that first trip, Lanre decided that London was indeed the best thing to ever happen to her – even with the cold.

'I love it here, Mummy!' she enthused as Mayowa gave a rare smile in agreement. 'Do you, too?'

'Sometimes,' Mummy said, quietly.

Chapter Three

'I do not understand why it is we have to move,' said Mummy. Mayowa sat in the tin bath that Daddy had finally purchased, beside the bed, as Mummy gently scrubbed a nub of black soap onto her back using the course and stringy Kankan sponge from Nigeria. Apparently, English sponges were far too soft and could never rid the skin of any real dirt.

'The landlord says I must pay more rent because we are now four. Instead of paying what he is asking, I will find a flat for the same money. It makes sense. We will have a lot of space and I can have you all to myself in our own room.' Daddy kissed her playfully on the cheek.

'I don't know, Tayo.' Mummy shrugged her shoulder as Mayowa giggled over something only she found funny.

'Just think, no more having to bath the children in the room … a real bathroom inside the house! You said you don't like going to the swimming pool and bathing in their bath houses.'

'No, I do not, but this is fine,' she said.

'I know you don't mean that! You want a proper bathroom.'

'It is very expensive, though. Will we be able to afford this? It cannot affect the money we send home, Tayo.'

'My love, it is perfect. There is plenty of overtime available and my supervisor is leaving very soon.'

'What has he leaving to do with you?'

'He said he will recommend me for his job.'

'As supervisor?'

'Yesso!' sang Daddy.

'But why would they give you the big job?'

'My boss, Dave, is a good man and he seems to like me. Look at what he has done for us already. Collected you all from the airport and I didn't even have to ask him. He is a good man and likes me. I think he will accept me for the job. No, I am very confident of it.'

A lady walked by, her umbrella tilted so that her eyes remained fixed on Mummy and Daddy. Lanre and Mayowa stood with their parents in matching beige raincoats, under the temporary shelter of an awning outside a closed shop as the rain fell from the sky.

'When did she say she would meet us?' said Mummy, her voice on the edge of complaint.

'I spoke to the lady on the phone and she will meet us here in five minutes' time. The basement flat is in the next street. A very nice area. There are many shops to buy food. I know it is not a pleasant day, but it will all be worth it!'

Lanre stepped out of the shelter. She loved the feel of rain against her skin and couldn't wait for this 'snow' she'd heard so much about to also make an appearance.

'Move inside, your hair does not like the rain!' ordered Mummy. Lanre stepped back under the awning. 'You are right, Tayo. We should do this.'

He smiled warmly. 'Hopefully, we will be in a new home by the time the girls start school.'

The rain finally stopped. If their new home was to be in this area, that would be OK. Although she did not see anything differ-ent from their current street: the straight roads; identical houses; some with smoke billowing from something called a chimney and no animals running around, except for dogs and cats who actually shared homes with people! But it was people she questioned the most and their reasoning for not acknowledging them in a way that didn't include narrowing their eyes as if they had just tasted the hottest pepe on their tongue. Or moving their noses like they were smelling poo. Even when Mummy went to greet them, they would at times ignore her, or wave their hands dismissively. Lanre would never behave in such a way to another person. Perhaps she would to Mayowa if she was annoying her. No one else, though, and especially no one older than her.

Lanre had many questions resting on her tongue, but always stopped herself from asking them. Everything would be OK. Daddy always made everything OK.

The rain finally stopped and they stepped out of the awning.

An older white woman with silver hair was approaching. She was dressed in a very smart skirt and jacket with a golden sparkling object on the left lapel.

'Hello, Madam. Are you Mrs Towers?' asked Daddy with that refined accent Mummy referred to as very British and one Lanre and her sister were to mimic if they were to ever get anywhere in life. Sometimes when he was being playful, Daddy would return to the silent H's and the familiar dialect she'd grown up with.

'Yes, I am Mrs Towers.' Her left eyebrow raised, and Lanre was massively impressed with this skill.

'Wonderful!' enthused Tayo, pulling out his hand. 'I am the gentleman you spoke with today on the telephone. It is nice to meet you. How do you do?'

She looked towards his outstretched hand. 'I believe you are mistaken.'

Daddy slowly pulled his hand away. 'It is me, Mrs Towers.'

'Mr Cole?'

'Yes, Mr T Cole.'

'If it's about the flat …?'

'Indeed.'

'Then I'm afraid it's gone.'

'I thought you said it was still available, not one hour ago. My wife and I have walked in the rain with our children—'

'I said it's gone. Now, if you'll excuse me.' Her eyebrows wrinkled and her pointed nose could obviously smell the poo.

'OK, Mrs Towers, that is fair. Do you possibly know of anywhere else to rent? My wife and I must find a place soon as our daughters must start school. I would be grateful—'

'No. Not at all,' she said quickly, backing away.

'Mrs Towers!'

'I'm sorry,' she said, turning the corner.

'She was horrible!' said Mayowa.

'Do not speak like that about your elders, OK?' chastised Daddy. He rarely raised his voice to anyone, but Lanre suspected this was more to do with Mrs Towers.

'Tayo, what will happen now?' asked Mummy.

'It is OK, my love. I promise you I will find us a place before we have to go. I will never disappoint you or my children.'

They ventured back down the London street, the adults once again locked in quiet conversation. It was then that Lanre noticed the sign.

'Daddy, look!' she said, pointing to a large notice taped to a busy shop window; ONE BEDROOM FLAT TO RENT.

'Well spotted, my angel,' said Tayo. 'I will write down the phone number.' He scanned the small sign.

The six words in smaller print were less easy to read, but not for Lanre. 'NO DOGS. NO BLACKS. NO IRISH.'

'Daddy, what does it mean?' asked Mayowa.

'Nothing, my sweet angel. Let us go.' He stuffed the pen and paper back into his pocket.

'Go where?' asked Mayowa as Mummy grabbed her hand. Lanre followed behind, her mind awash with what the sign suggested.

And then it hit her. 'Daddy, do they mean us?'

'Come on, forget about it. What do you think of fish and chips? Let's go get some!'

'Yeess!' enthused Mayowa. Lanre caught Mummy's expression, who, like Lanre, was not so keen to let go of this moment.

That evening, Daddy and Mummy sat together on the bed as they ate this curious food called fish and chips, which had become their new Friday-night ritual. The sharp and unusual taste of the vinegar, which at first appeared off-putting, Lanre now found delicious and an essential part of the meal.

'Adanya, it is OK, I know you are disappointed about the flat. But the property was let. We will find something,' he said, pinching her nose. She smiled up at her husband with trust in her eyes, warm with a fresh belief in him.

But Lanre had questions. 'Daddy, what did they mean by no black, no—'

'Oh my darling, nothing bad! They were just saying that some places are not suitable for us because ... because it is too cold for what we are used to. The heating system is not good, that is all.'

'Really? Oh! Daddy, then I am glad we did not stay there. It can get very cold in England.'

'Exactly, my angel. Now eat your food, bedtime soon. I will tell you a story before you sleep. Would you like that?'

'Yes, please!' Daddy's stories were always funny and sometimes very long, but it was one of the things she'd missed most when they had been separated for so long. He told stories about growing up as an only son and the many adventures he had looking after his younger sisters. But Lanre was eight years old and too old to believe every story she heard – just like she could not believe the one Daddy had just told her about the 'to let' sign.

Mummy and Daddy celebrated with wine when he announced his new job as supervisor.

'Adanya, I know I came here to study but the money they are giving me is wonderful. I am the first black man to be given this type of job there. They are very nice to me and I enjoy my work. Perhaps I will stop my studies for now and return to it in a few years.'

'Of course, Tayo. I am happy with this decision,' said Mummy, although her faded smile spoke differently.

Mummy's smile did lift considerably though when Daddy returned home from work the next day with news that a colleague had introduced him to a landlord keen to fill a number of properties in a place called West London. Now that, Lanre could pronounce.

The day before the Cole family moved into a top-floor two-bedroom flat in Notting Hill, the sun had shined the brightest Lanre had ever seen in London and it was the best day of her life since moving to England.

'It is decorated and furnished. A lovely place,' announced Daddy as they floated from room to room. The landlord, a man with hair like salt and pepper and a stomach like that of a woman with child, had proceeded with a double take when the family first walked into his office. Lanre wondered if he too did not want blacks, Irish or dogs.

But his crooked smile was kind as he'd said, 'I don't give a hoot where you're from, as long as you pay me on time.'

'Of that, I can assure you of, Mr Andersen,' Daddy had told him, as he sat down beside Mummy on one of the chairs facing the desk.

'Rex. Just call me Rex.'

He placed a wad of papers onto the desk. Mayowa sat onto Mummy's lap, *The Cat in the Hat* securely in her hand.

'You don't look like the type to start any trouble.'

'Never, Mr Rex.'

'I suppose you heard about those Teddy boys getting into a fight with those men a few months back? Caused a massive riot, it did.'

27

'Yes, I did, sir. I keep myself to myself. My family and providing for them is my only concern.'

'Good, that's the way it should be. I don't agree with violence, but that coloured boy going with that nice white lady was asking for trouble. We should all stick to our own, don't you think? It's unnatural, really. We weren't made for all of that!'

'Mr Rex, I do not concern myself with such things.'

'Good man!' he'd said.

Now, they were finally moving in to their new home. If they'd been back in Nigeria, the move would have been effortless. Family members as well as their many neighbours would have helped them pack up and move to their new home. Luckily, their items were not plentiful but with Flat B only accessible by a small number of steps, Daddy was sweating profusely as he and his boss Dave carried each item into the flat. Dave was a good man, according to Mummy, and did not behave like a boss and, unlike the people who stared at them in the street, his interaction was only that of warmth.

Once all the items were safely placed into number sixty-three Pettyford Road, Lanre already knew the effort had been worth it. This palace, this sanctuary, was their new home and, she suspected, would be for a very long time. No more sharing with strangers. There was a separate room with two beds for Lanre and Mayowa and a beautiful white bathroom with a bath and clean tiles. Their very own bathroom!

They now lived in a very impressive three-storey building nestled on the end of a busy street lined on either side by big, beautiful green trees in full bloom. She couldn't wait to skip down that street. It was beautiful. Better than anything she'd ever seen before. She could not imagine the Queen of England living in a better street!

Within weeks the flat was transformed. The sitting room walls were decorated with green and white spiral wallpaper and a multicoloured glass fish sat on top of a cabinet beside what

Daddy called a spider plant. It didn't seem to have a purpose but Mayowa seemed to be obsessed with the glass fish, sometimes staring at it for minutes at a time. The glass cabinet was filled with glasses and plates and flowers that never died.

One evening, Daddy wheeled in a huge brown globe of the world, which he placed in the corner of the sitting room. Much to the delight of a squealing Lanre and Mayowa, the top half opened to reveal a huge hollow space, which Daddy said would be filled with drinks only adults were allowed to drink.

Mummy hummed a lot now, especially as she chopped pepe and cooked rice in their new kitchen or waited for the hot comb to heat. She had recently discovered a Jamaican food stall that sold plantains, yams and authentic Nigerian pepe (or Scotch bonnet as they were labelled). They now even owned a Hoover: a contraption that ate the dirt on the green and brown carpet and also scared Mayowa so much that she ran into the bathroom the first time Mummy had switched it on, refusing to return until the 'horrible creature' was gone.

Their home, their lives, were now bathed in a new calm in which Lanre felt safe. She looked forward to school and in the meantime was content to help Mummy around the house or listen to the wireless Daddy had surprised them with one day. A real-life working machine with a big dial for selecting the stations! Titi would be so jealous! Mummy enjoyed a show called *The Archers*. Whilst Lanre couldn't be sure what it was about, she noticed that some of the people on the radio spoke in strange accents. Even stranger than Ginny's. Aunty Ginny. Lanre was never allowed to call an elder by their first name, even though this strange white lady had insisted.

According to Mummy, Aunty Ginny, who lived in Flat A, was a widow with two boys of her own. She was always quick to offer advice even when Mummy had not asked for it. Like how to fold clothes and apply lipstick without staining one's teeth.

She'd even taught Mummy to knit.

'D'you think you'll have more kids?' Ginny had asked one day, sat nestling a mug of tea Lanre had been happy to make. Lanre had quickly realised the importance of 'a cuppa tea' in England.

'If I do, I would love to have a boy. I think Tayo would like that too.'

'I wouldn't worry about all of that; he's obsessed with your girls and who wouldn't be? They're adorable.' She had smiled towards Mayowa, sitting on the floor with her back against the green armchair that had been delivered three days ago. Daddy had announced it was to be 'Daddy's chair'.

'I wish I'd had a girl. Sick of being surrounded by boys. Even at work, all men. I suppose that's what you get for working in a butcher's shop!'

Mummy had smiled politely. Lanre had wondered if Mummy was able to follow Aunty Ginny's fast-paced English. In Nigeria they'd been brought up speaking the Queen's English and banned from talking to one another in Yoruba. Mummy said they would have more opportunities this way. But what Aunty Ginny spoke was far from the Queen's English. Still she was kind to Mummy and to them.

'You can have my boys if you like!' Ginny had said. 'Little tearaways!'

'They are very big boys.'

'Yes, they get the height from their dad. If they're this big as teenagers, I dread to think what will happen when they get older.' She had let out a long drawn-out sigh. 'One of them was caught stealing the other day! As if I don't already do enough to put food on the table. I'll let you have them both for a good price!'

Mummy had pulled out a yarn and two knitting needles. 'You joke too much, Ginny.'

With her short curled hair, and long and tight skirts that hugged her hips and behind, Ginny was the first white woman Lanre had ever really spoken to. She always smelled of a perfume called

Chanel No 5 and even drank beer! Yet, unlike some other white people, she did not stare at them for too long or ask to touch her hair. Ginny would look her square in the eye as they spoke and could reduce Mayowa into a fit of giggles within minutes: something not many could achieve! Aunty Ginny quickly became a fixture in their new home when Daddy was at work. She would sit down with Mummy and drink tea … or sip the contents of a bottle taken from the huge globe of the world.

The week before the start of school, Daddy kept saying how proud he felt of his 'two angels'. He insisted on photographing Lanre with their new Bantam Colorsnap camera. According to Daddy, this was the latest model and he was forever pointing it towards them. A smile, a new dance, freshly plaited hair – the camera would appear at the most startling of times to capture a moment in time they'd one day cherish as part of their memories.

'We have so many pictures, Tayo! Mummy's wall back home must be full with them!' said Mummy as she lay in Daddy's arms on his special green chair.

'Adanya, I can never take too many pictures of all my girls. Do you remember in Nigeria, we had none of this? I have seen just one photograph of myself as a boy. Just one!'

'Yes, you are right.'

'I want the best for my girls. I want them to enjoy the things we did not. They will go to university here. And now their British passports are on the way, they will finally have everything!'

'They will be very special children.'

'Adanya, they are already special. As are you.'

The morning of her first day at school, Lanre was buzzed with excitement at the prospect of starting a new term. She didn't even have to wear a school uniform, with Mummy allowing her to pick out a dress. So she chose a yellow one decorated with white flowers.

Daddy looked very nice in his long jacket and brown hat tipped to the side. Mummy wore a pink dress with white lapels, a small jacket and white silky gloves. Lanre noticed she was shivering underneath these thin layers and was confused as to why she hadn't worn a topcoat.

The family of four walked proudly down a West London street they had never seen before. A street full of shops that sold buttons or records. Even now, Lanre had yet to get used to shops that sold things like records. She was sure such establishments had existed in Nigeria, but not in the street she'd grown up in. There, shops were strictly for food, clothing and car parts!

Now, people would sometimes look at them, but she didn't notice it as much as when they had first arrived in England. Or maybe she'd just gotten used to it. Once a lady did start to cross the road as soon as the family approached, and when Lanre turned around, she noticed this same woman cross the road again and was right back where she started. It was clear to Lanre that some people were just plain stupid.

They stopped by a newsstand. A picture of a beautiful lady with 'Lana Turner' written in bold letters was on the front page of a newspaper. As Daddy spoke kindly with the man, Lanre remained transfixed on the image. Lana Turner was the most beautiful woman she had ever seen … even more beautiful than Mummy, something Lanre had never thought possible. Long, blonde curls tumbled down her back, her nose perfect in the middle of a smooth, white face. It was unfortunate that Daddy didn't buy that particular newspaper.

'Mummy, that is just like my name!' she said excitedly. Mummy didn't hear her as they crossed the road and headed towards their new school.

Ten minutes later, Mummy and Daddy sat in an office in front of a huge desk as Lanre stood, leaning on Mummy's shoulder and Mayowa sat on Daddy's lap. Daddy opened his newspaper.

'Tayo, he will be back soon and you are reading the paper!'

The door opened. 'Sorry about that, Mr Cole, Mrs Cole,' said the bespectacled headmaster. Lanre was curious about the circle of skin on his head, surrounded by wisps of brown hair. He cleared his throat and sat behind the desk.

'I had a little emergency to deal with.'

'That is OK, Mr Marcomb,' said Daddy.

'Now where were we? Yes, I think everything is in order regarding the paperwork. Just one other thing.' He slowly pulled his glasses from his face. 'Their names. They are a little ... how can I say this ... unusual.'

'They are fine Yoruba names. Mayowa means "to bring joy" and Lanre's full name is Olanrewaju and this means—'

'Indeed, but they are a little hard to pronounce.'

'There are harder ones to pronounce. Believe me!' Daddy laughed, as Mummy placed her hand on his arm, as if to halt his laughter.

'I think what Mr Marcomb is trying to say is that we should maybe use their English names instead,' Mummy suggested. Most Nigerian children were given English middle names as well as their traditional Yoruba names. 'Lanre's middle name is Victoria and Mayowa is named after the Queen herself, Elizabeth.'

'I did notice this on the forms. I think this would be adequate. Elizabeth and Victoria are splendid names.'

'I prefer them to use their Yoruba names,' said Daddy, 'but I understand what you are saying, Mr Marcomb. They will one day be in university and I want that transition to be smooth for my girls. I just don't want them to lose who they are.'

'University?' said Mr Marcomb.

'Yes,' Daddy replied, matter-of-factly.

'Tayo, if they use their English names, they will fit in better with their classmates,' Mummy said. 'They'll be respected more.'

Her parents rarely disagreed on anything, but Lanre felt this was more than a disagreement about names.

'I have a Nigerian name, my love. Am I not respected among my peers?'

The headmaster cleared his throat, his skin a new shade of red.

'I'm afraid your wife has a point. We did have one coloured girl here called Eyitope and no one could get the name right, not even our teachers. I think I was the only one who could because I have travelled to some of the colonies. I'm used to it. Anyway, this poor girl was teased relentlessly by the other students and I wouldn't want this to happen to your children.'

Daddy was not happy, Lanre could tell. 'Come here,' he said, waving her over.

'What do you want to be called: Lanre or Victoria?'

'Tayo, you can't ask her this, she is a child!' exclaimed Mummy.

'It is OK, my love. I want her to answer.' Daddy moved his arm round her back, tickling her just under her arm. 'Do you like your name?'

Lanre giggled. 'Daddy stop!'

'Answer the question!' ordered Mummy, somewhat annoyed.

'I do like my name ...' she began but seeing the look on the headmaster's face she had an idea. 'I saw a newspaper and there was a lady inside called Lana Turner. She is very beautiful. Lana sounds very much like my name.'

'That it does, my angel. But is this the name you want to be called here, in the school?' asked Daddy.

'Yes!' said Lanre, feeling a shock of elation at this rapid turn of events. She was actually being allowed to share the name of such a pretty lady.

'What of you, my angel?' asked Daddy to Mayowa, sat on his knee.

'Tayo, she is a baby!'

'My name is Mayowa,' she said firmly.

'Sometimes Daddy calls you May ...?' Lanre, now Lana, suggested.

'How about that then?' said the headmaster, as he looked at his watch. 'It's still her name, but shortened.'

'You want to use May?' said Daddy. Mayowa nodded her head profusely as Mummy shook hers, slowly.

'OK, that is settled,' said Daddy. 'At the school they will be called Lana and May, but we –' he turned to Mummy '– we shall continue to call them by their full names at home.'

'Would this not be too confusing, Mr Cole?'

'Not at all; as Nigerians, we have many names anyway. My own father does not call me Tayo but Adekoyejo, for instance.'

The headmaster cleared his throat. 'OK then, well, Lana and May Cole, welcome to our school!'

Chapter Four

Lana – as Lanre was now called – had hoped her first day at school would be a lot better than it was. She knew so much more than her classmates academically, and was able to answer each of the teacher's questions, enthusiastically shooting her arm in the air much quicker than anyone else. But for some unknown reason, this wasn't pleasing to the rest of the class, and the other children seemed to ignore her even more. They never seemed to tire of how 'funny' she sounded and Lana began to dread whenever she was asked to read out a passage from a book. There were only two other girls who looked like her in the entire school. But after a tentative 'hello' resulted in her promptly being ignored, Lana decided to give up on trying to be their friend. And that was OK. As Daddy had said many times to Lana and May as they both sat perched on his knee: 'You will be big people after you study hard and attend university! Friends will come later!'

Although Lana felt confident she could handle the schoolwork (at eight she already knew most of her times tables), sometimes during music and movement class, she instantly felt not of this land, especially as everyone else seemed happy to wander around in their underwear and shoes, listening to a faceless voice on the wireless.

'Sway like a moving tree!' came the voice. Such an act didn't seem to have a purpose. If Lana wanted to be a tree, she wouldn't have flown all the way to England. She was certainly not about to become a tree!

Lana had been at the school a week, enjoyed hearing her new name on the lips of the teachers, and had assumed a routine she could handle. However, as she stood in a queue to meet someone referred to as a 'nit nurse', she wasn't quite sure.

Two white girls were in front of her, the nurse sliding a comb through their hair as she inspected the contents.

'Uh oh,' said the nurse as Lana moved forward. The nurse let out a loud sigh. 'What's your name, luvvie?'

'It's Lana. Like Lana Turner.'

'Well, Lana Turner, I haven't got a comb strong enough for your hair. Already broke one last time I had a coloured kid.'

Lana had no idea what she was referring to and just shrugged her shoulders.

'Is there a comb you can bring in, Lana, love?' said the nurse, a lot louder this time.

'Yes, my mummy has one.'

'Good. I'll just have a quick look, but you will have to bring one of your special combs in next time, OK?'

'My child does not have head lice!' insisted Mummy as Aunty Ginny appeared to be consumed with overwhelming laughter.

'It's so funny!'

'No, it is not, Ginny!'

'Don't get up on your high horse, Addy; every child has to get checked for lice.'

'My children are clean!' she insisted as Aunty Ginny fell back onto Daddy's chair with even louder guffaws.

Lana didn't like Aunty Ginny sitting in Daddy's chair. By the time he returned from work, she was usually back in her own house anyway. But it seemed wrong to use the chair without him being around. If truth be told, she missed her daddy when he worked late and wished she could be with him all the time. She wished she could tell him just how much she disliked her new school; she preferred the one back home in Nigeria where she had many friends, though she missed Titi most of all.

Slowly, though, Lana began to enjoy school a little more, even without any real friends. She looked forward to the bottle of creamy milk each day, had given the nurse a wooden long-toothed comb she could use in her hair, and she now even enjoyed the strange movement class. No longer giggling to herself whenever the faceless voice consumed the room with strange commands. Lana was becoming a British person (according to Mummy, who could not be happier). By the age of nine, her accent was almost gone, aided by the radio and Aunty Ginny. She had even uttered words like 'Give over' and 'I'm alright, darling', again, aided by Aunty Ginny.

Without realising, Lana had also accepted the unusual British weather patterns as part of everyday life, enjoyed Ginny's roast beef even more than fish and chips and was rather prone to exaggerating her Britishness at school or when speaking to people in the shop. Indeed, Mummy would insist on it.

Daddy had been out for most of the day, unusual for a Saturday. When he suddenly appeared, his face was full of excitement.

'Come with me, Ginny, I will need your help. You are of manly strength!' said Daddy.

'Cheeky!' Ginny laughed, playfully punching his arm.

'Adanya, girls, close your eyes!'

'Ah ah, what are you doing now, Tayo?' asked Mummy with a smile. Over the year and a half, Lana had gotten used to Daddy's surprises: a bunch of flowers one day, new shoes for each of them or a large bar of chocolate to share. Daddy was the best father anyone could ever want!

'It is a surprise,' he said.

'Another one? Yesterday, you bought me the case,' she said, pulling the shiny circular leather case onto her lap.

'Yes, that is for your womanly things. This will benefit the entire family!'

Minutes later, Lana heard a loud dragging sound.

'Do not open your eyes yet!'

'When can we open them?' asked Lana.

'Now!'

Each eyelid opened to a large wooden cabinet placed by the wall. Mummy slid a wooden flap to the side to reveal a record player, just like the one they'd seen in one of Ginny's magazines.

'Wow!' said Mummy. Lana randomly turned the knobs at the side.

'What a beauty!' enthused Ginny.

'It is a wonderful Magnavox record player!' said Daddy. May appeared uninterested in the unfolding scene, happy to stare at the picture book in her hands: another present from Daddy.

'Where did you get it?' asked Mummy, smoothing her fingers over the five protruding knobs on the side.

'Dave graciously gave it to me. He is a good man.'

'He just gave it to you, just like that?'

'It is an older model. He has bought a new one and asked if I would like this. He knows I am very enthusiastic about modern things.'

'He must really like you!' said Ginny.

'I don't know why. I do my job, that is all.'

'Tayo, everyone likes you!' said Adanya, eyes fixated on the new machine.

'Do you even have any records?' asked Ginny.

'No. Till now we only listen to the wireless,' said Tayo.

A moment later, Ginny returned and took a black plastic disc from a sleeve.

'What is it?' asked Adanya.

'What is it? Why, Chuck Berry of course!'

*

The sun appeared with a loving glow as Tayo pointed the camera towards the children as they rolled around in the grass and offered bread to birds. The park was now her favourite place in the whole wide world, where she loved to partake in various poses as soon as the camera appeared. Lana at nine was clearly the showier of the two and as Aunty Ginny had commented more than once, 'Destined for the stage, that one. No wonder she's named after Lana Turner!'

'We did not name her after an actress. Her name is Lanre. This is just for school. We continue to call them by their names. But if you want to call them by their English names, it is Victoria and Elizabeth!' Mummy had said.

'Don't be so stuffy, Addy! Lana and May are terrific names!'

'They will become big people. Doctors or lawyers,' Mummy had retorted.

'Yes, Dr Lana Cole does have a special ring to it!' Aunty Ginny had teased.

Mummy had shrugged her shoulders and pretended not to smile.

'Tayo! Stop it! I don't want any more pictures,' Mummy now said, with another reluctant smile as Tayo pointed the camera towards her.

He smiled. 'Too late, my love, it has been taken. I want to show everyone back home how happy we are; that soon I will get a better job and we will live the high life; that you can come to this wonderful country and be happy; that your children can be happy and excel here in England!'

He planted a huge kiss on her cheek. 'I have some news, my love.'

'Look at that bird!' said May pointing at a blackbird, which stood out from the pigeons.

'Yes, it is a beautiful bird!' he said obligingly. He turned back to Mummy. 'I am in line for a promotion, Adanya.'

'When?'

'In three months. The timing is excellent. There will be a lot more money and less hours! We will soon be able to save up to buy a house. The children can have their own rooms.'

'This is wonderful!' said Mummy, albeit cautiously. 'But, do you miss home? Do you ever think about going back ... even for a holiday?'

'No, my love.'

'Nigeria will soon be independent ... it will be better—'

'There is no need. We all have our British passports. We are proper citizens of the United Kingdom. This is our home now.'

Lana rarely saw her parents argue, but one day she heard raised voices coming from the kitchen.

'You don't need to work; I am earning enough for us all Adanya and when I get the promotion—'

'They are not even paying you the same as your white friends who work there!' she spat. 'This Dave you speak so highly of does not pay you the same!'

'Yes, I know, and there is nothing I can do about that. I am a black man in a country that needed me, but, now I am here, does not want me anymore. But I will continue to work hard and be courteous. Ah ah, Adanya, why are you talking this way to me? These are hurtful words, eh?'

'Oh, Tayo. I am sorry, my husband. I just feel I should be doing something. You are so good with the girls, better than me ...'

'Nonsense! What are you talking about? You are a wonderful mother, Adanya. What is this? All this doubt?'

They joined the girls in the sitting room.

'Ginny knows people who need their dresses mended. I can do that; I was taught how to sew in Nigeria,' said Mummy.

Daddy sat in his green chair and May immediately shifted herself onto Daddy's lap. 'If it will make you happy, Adanya, OK.'

'I am happy about this, Tayo.'

He placed a kiss onto May's forehead. 'I am happy, if you are happy, Adanya.'

Lana soon got used to the number of women entering the house with bags of garments. Dresses with broken zips, men's trousers with missing buttons. More importantly, she noticed Mummy's ever-increasing smile whenever she handed over a newly mended item to its satisfied owner. The bigger of the three leather vanity cases Daddy had bought her now brimmed with sewing paraphernalia and was rarely closed.

Ginny would sometimes bring over a record and the two of them would laugh insanely as Lana tapped her feet to a beat or May moved her head up and down.

Lana's favourite singer was Cliff Jacks, though Ginny had scoffed at this, dismissing him as 'too lovey-dovey' and 'not exactly, Jackie Wilson is it?'

Lana woke up one morning to the sound of a very loud screech she'd assumed was part of a bad dream. She rubbed her eyes just as the sound got louder.

'Mummy? What is wrong?' She raced to the hallway where Mummy stood in her nightgown, facing the doorway to the bedroom.

'Go and fetch Ginny! Go and fetch Ginny!' These were screams mixed with words. She couldn't see the expression on Mummy's face, only her back.

Lana raced to Ginny's flat where Ginny appeared at the door with her hair rolled into pink curlers.

'What is it? Where's the fire?' she said with a wry smirk.

'Mummy is calling you!'

Lana knew this was a matter of urgency, but did not know why.

'Let me get these curlers out first, darling—'

'No, she needs you now, Aunty Ginny!'

May had roused from her sleep and Mummy was no longer screaming, just standing in the doorway of the bedroom, her breathing loud.

'G ... Ginny!' she managed to say.

'Stay here with your sister,' commanded Aunty Ginny. She followed Mummy into the bedroom and shut the door behind them. Lana stood in that corridor, not daring to move. Something was very wrong.

Ginny reappeared moments later, her face whiter than Lana had ever seen it.

'Erm ... girls,' she said, the door ajar behind her.

Lana tried to see past Aunty Ginny and into the room. She could see part of foot. That was Daddy's foot.

'What's happening, Aunty?' asked Lana.

Aunty Ginny gently closed the bedroom door. 'You both go to your room and I will get you later. I am going to call an ambulance.'

Alarm rose in her body. 'Why? What's wrong with Daddy?' asked Lana.

'I'm just going to ... call an ambulance.'

'Where's Mummy?'

Ginny was answering no questions as she bundled the girls into their room. May quickly began to amuse herself with a book as Lana sat on the bed in silence, locked in even more confusion. She'd always been told to do what an adult asked, yet was so very tempted to march into her parents' bedroom and ask Daddy what was going on. He would tell her. Daddy would never hide anything from her.

A full hour later, the girls were finally allowed to leave their room. Daddy and Mummy were at the hospital, apparently. Ginny's eyes were red from crying.

'Girls, come and sit with me on the settee,' she said.

Each girl sat side on either side of Aunty Ginny and she took both their hands. 'Lana, May. I'm going to need you both to be strong.'

'Why?' asked Lana.

'Is it Mummy?' asked May.

'No, it's your father. He's … your daddy's gone to heaven. He's … gone.'

Chapter Five

Mummy came back from the hospital but did not speak for three whole days.

For three days, May sat lost in a book. For three days Lana could only think of her daddy, the sight of his foot. His lifeless body, already cold.

The only time she could erase that final image from her mind was when helping Aunty Ginny with whatever they could find to do in the flat. Like cleaning the kitchen or making a sandwich. No one sat in Daddy's green chair.

At night, Lana's eyes filled with tears as she lay on the bed. Her cries silent and so unlike Mummy's, who she could hear clearly through the wall each and every night. How could this be, when she had heard nothing from Daddy whilst he had perished in that very room? Not a sound, not a whisper. Just the sound of Mummy's pain moments later.

Lana had now entered another life. The house, furniture, street, the sky all looked the same, yet would forever feel different. This horrible new world without her daddy in it. She longed to be part of that old world again, where he would point his camera in her face every chance he could. Where he would pop strawberries into her mouth promising they would make her big and strong. A world in which Mummy would speak to her, laugh with Daddy and hum songs from Nigeria, as she washed parts of a chicken in the kitchen sink. Now Mummy said nothing as she sat and gazed at the wall, at times, rocking back and forth as Aunty Ginny said on repeat, 'I don't know what to do for you, Addy! How can I help you? Tell me what to do!'

Lana continued to think about Daddy every day, except for when she needed to iron May's dress or make Mummy a cup of tea she would never drink, after which she would simply give into a strong wave of a feeling so utterly horrible. Yes, horrible, that was the only way she could describe the feeling ... it was horrible. Unable to remove that image of Daddy's lifeless foot from her mind and wondering if there was anything she could have done to help him not die.

'That number Lana gave me to call in Nigeria for the Ade ... deleepoes. Well, they've finally gotten hold of your parents. They're on the phone downstairs and want to speak to you,' said Aunty Ginny to Mummy. Daddy had been gone two weeks and Mummy had only spoken on average three times a day.

'Addy?' said Aunty Ginny, stooping down to Mummy's level on the settee. 'Addy, did you hear what I said? Your parents are on the telephone.'

'Mummy, please?' asked Lana, placing a hand onto her leg. Mummy scrunched her eyebrows as she sometimes did and Lana was just pleased for the acknowledgement of her presence. 'They want to talk about Daddy, please speak with them.'

Lana's words appeared to strengthen her enough to get up and be led by her daughter to the telephone downstairs in the communal corridor. She picked up the phone receiver and stared at it for a moment, perhaps like Lana, recalling the day the landlord had surprised them with its existence. To live in a building with a phone was something they would never have dreamed of back in Nigeria.

'We are a revolutionary family!' Daddy had said. 'We now have a phone! Oh, how far we have come!'

Mummy whispered into the receiver, its winding cord slightly tangling at the top. 'Hello?' she said.

'Adanya! Oh, my poor child, Adanya! It is your mummy here!' Her mother's voice was as loud as usual and Lana felt at ease with this sudden moment of familiarity.

Within seconds Mummy was on her knees, eyes stamped shut and emitting a sound from her mouth that was extraordinary, loud, painful and piercing. Like the sound of the neighbour's dog in Nigeria when it had connected with the wheel of a car. Like the sound of a thousand sirens racing to an emergency. Like the sound of a woman who had lost the very meaning of her existence.

In the days leading to the funeral, Lana had not witnessed Mummy take a bath or even brush her teeth. She had simply remained in Daddy's unwashed work shirt and her own wrapper.

Lana had divided herself between making sure her sister was fed and watching the door, as if she was still waiting for Daddy to return home from work. Mummy played the Cliff Jacks record many times in one day and even Lana was getting tired of it:

> *I see you every day, even though you're not here*
> *Memories of a day later*
> *I feel you in my heart, even though you're not here*
> *These are the things I remember*
> *Memories, oh oh memories*
> *Memories of a day later.*

It was Ginny who'd slowly coaxed Mummy into taking off Daddy's shirt long enough to sit in the bath. Lana had stood by the doorway and watched as Ginny had gently rubbed her back with the coarse and stringy Kankan sponge, a stillness in the air, except for the occasional sound of water and a gentle humming from Aunty Ginny.

Mummy had not flinched, eyes vacant, her face void of a smile.

'I used to hum to my boys at bath time,' Ginny had said, squeezing the sponge above Mummy's shoulders, allowing the water to trickle down her back and into the bath. 'Do you think I have a nice voice?'

'Yes,' Mummy had replied hoarsely, but without expression. Lana had just been glad she had spoken. That would mean she'd spoken ten words that day. This was good.

Gradually Mummy had begun to speak more and more. By the day of the funeral, she had almost been back to speaking as she once did. She had shaken the hands of Daddy's smartly dressed workmates and had vaguely agreed when one person or another had said, 'I'm really going to miss him.'

May hadn't said anything, which wasn't that unusual these days. She had retreated into her books. But Lana also felt mute. Not on purpose. She just couldn't think of anything to say that wouldn't make her cry. And she must not cry. She needed to be strong. For Mummy. Even when Daddy's boss, Dave, had held out his hand to her, she had merely shook his hand, nodding her head when he had said, 'Your dad thought the world of you girls.'

Everyone had been very nice and kindly enough, dressed in their smart suits, drinking, and laughing about things Daddy had said in the factory to brighten their days. He had been the factory 'joker', apparently, and very much loved by all. They had continued to express their disbelief and had said if there was 'anything they could do, don't hesitate to ask'. But they couldn't bring him back, could they? No one could.

When that cold and rainy day had begun to draw to a close, and when everyone gathered finally stopped saying how much of a 'good man' Daddy was, all Lana had wanted to do was scream. She had wanted to ask that if he was such a good man then why, why was he currently lying in an oblong box?

*

Lana was alarmed at how quickly life began to slot into a new shape without Daddy.

Within weeks, Mummy seemed to make up for her previous lack of conversation by talking non-stop as she sewed dresses for paying customers who began to appear at the door again. She would sometimes go into deep detail about the laziness of her customers before moving on to how Daddy's family were very angry at her for allowing their only son to be buried in England. They now hated her even more than before, apparently, having always wanted Daddy to marry Ajoke Buka. They also believed Mummy had turned him against his own family and perhaps that was why Lana had only seen Daddy's parents on a handful of occasions. Mummy would now repeat the Ajoke Buka story so much that Lana was now fed up of hearing it. But that was OK; Lana was just happy Mummy was talking regularly again.

'What do you think I should cook today? Ground rice or just plain rice? I know you prefer pounded yam but ground rice is the closest we will find here.'

Lana had become accustomed to ground rice in place of pounded yam. With its white dough-like texture and white colouring, it was supposed to be similar to the pounded yam they'd once enjoyed in Nigeria, but it wasn't. It was different and, to Lana, even better, although she would never admit this to Mummy.

'Chicken or fish today?' added Mummy. These questions were a little too grown up for her but Lana was happy to assist in any way she could in the absence of Daddy. Her parents had always made the important decisions together and now Daddy wasn't around anymore, it was up to Lana as the eldest to take his place.

Aunty Ginny 'popped in' each day and sometimes took the girls for walks to the park. Lana hated those walks because they reminded her of Daddy and the many times he had taken them there. Lana did want to laugh though, when Aunty Ginny made a face and asked, 'What's your problem?' to anyone who stared at the three of them for too long, a gaudily dressed middle-aged white woman with two sad little coloured girls.

'Addy, you're not listening to me. You have to start thinking about this flat!'

'Tayo took care of everything!'

'Yes, the rent was paid up to a certain point but your savings are very slim even with the whip-round from work. Then there's the rest of the funeral expenses that still need paying. There won't be much left – and you don't make enough from your sewing to cover everything. You could sell the radio, or the the record player, I suppose, to buy some time. You know Tayo was always buying things.'

'For our family, Ginny. He wanted our girls to have the best. I won't sell the things he bought for us. Never.'

'I wasn't criticising. I just mean you have to face facts. What about your parents in Nigeria?'

'They don't have any money. We were the ones sending money home.'

'Tayo's parents, then? Do they have anything they can give?'

'No! They hate me.'

'I doubt that, Addy!'

'Forget them!' insisted Mummy. Lana had never heard Mummy be so disrespectful about any elders before.

'OK, OK, perhaps you can think about renting someplace smaller, like a bedsit.'

'And live like we did when we first arrived to London? No, Tayo would not want that.'

Adanya stuck a pin into a rather short polka-dot skirt and placed it up to the light.

'You can't stay here for free, Addy. Rent will be due soon. From what you've told me, you've got about a couple of months left. Or maybe even six weeks. Old Rex is understanding when it comes to a couple of weeks, but if you don't pay—'

'I will pay, Ginny.'

'How? There's only so many dresses you can sew with two kids around. I mean I love having them and coming round, but I gotta work too.'

Silence.

'Addy?'

'I will speak to the landlord and sort it out.'

'I just think it's best to bring these things up now.'

'OK, OK, I understand.'

'Then there's the school for the girls. They can't miss much more, or they'll be in trouble.'

'No! I don't want them to go back yet. They stay here with me.'

'OK, OK, we can hold them off for a bit.'

'Soon, they will go ... but not now. I need them with me.'

These days Mummy did not sleep in the room she once shared with Daddy and instead slept on the floor beside Lana's bed. One late night, Lana awoke to the sound of May's snoring being eclipsed by Mummy's voice.

'Tayo?' she said into the darkness. A dark figure stood by the door and Lana's stomach knotted. Had Daddy come back? Perhaps her suspicions had been correct and he had not 'died' after all.

The figure loomed closer.

'It's me,' the man said.

Mummy sat up, rubbed her eyes and switched on the lamp. May continued to snore softly as Lana kept her eyes closed.

'Mr Rex?' asked Mummy.

'I was knocking but no one answered. I have a key, of course.'

'Of course. What can I do for you at this late hour, sir?'

'Let's go into the lounge.'

Lana sprang out of the bed and followed the voices. She stood by the door of the sitting room, rubbing sleep from her eyes.

'May I?' He pointed to Daddy's chair.

'I will sit there. Please, take the settee,' said Mummy, thankfully. Lana did not want anyone to sit in Daddy's chair in case he came back and needed it. But the sight of Mummy sitting in it was at least better than someone they hardly knew.

'Adanya, you've been here a while now and never given me any trouble. Your rent has always been paid in advance and on time … but …'

'I know what you will say. We are about to be overdue in a few weeks.'

'Two weeks. And I need to know what's going to happen. I'm really sorry to hear about your husband but I have to ask you about this.'

'We … I have plenty of savings that will give us extra time …'

Lana was confused; didn't Aunty Ginny say there was almost nothing left?

'What about after that? I do sympathise, love. Your husband was a good man, but I have to make sure all the rents are paid.'

Lana flinched at the sound of her daddy being spoken of in the past tense. A fresh stabbing pain pierced her flesh.

'I do understand and I will not let you down.'

'That's fine, love. I'll take your word for it. I'll be off then. Sorry to come by so late.'

'It is OK. Thank you.'

'Good night, Adanya.'

'Good night, Mr Rex.'

Lana ran back to bed and a moment later Mummy returned and immediately began to weep. Lana suspected that, for once, her tears were for more than Daddy.

They were 'potless' according to Aunty Ginny, yet Lana still didn't know what this meant. And yet bags of porridge and bags of meat began to mysteriously appear; sometimes orange juice for Lana and May, and even a box of chocolates for Mummy. Mummy mentioned she did not like accepting charity, but as long as Aunty Ginny never mentioned the 'gifts', all was well.

'I know what it's like, you know ... to lose the bloke you love,' said Ginny as Lana and May sat on the floor, listening to 'Uncle Mac' on the radio. The volume was high but, as usual, she preferred the adult conversation despite the fact *Children's Favourites* was her favourite programme.

'Bloke? Your husband?'

'Yeah.'

'It is not easy,' said Mummy.

'At any age. You're just a kid.'

'I am thirty-one!'

'A kid. I've got at least ten years on you!'

A rare smile.

'When Eddie left, I thought – how am I gonna bring up two teenaged boys by myself? But you get on with it, you know? I didn't have a choice.'

'When did he die, Ginny? You do not speak of him much.'

'Who?'

'Your husband.'

'My Eddie's not dead.'

Lana's eyes widened in surprise.

'He went out for a pint and didn't come back. Last I heard he was with some tart in North London. Same thing though. I still lost him.'

'He is alive, then?' asked Mummy.

'Hasn't seen me or the kids, not once. He's gone. Never to come back. So I do understand.'

'I see.'

'It's all the same, Addy. We just have to make the best of things and get on with it. For the sake of the kids if nothing else,' she said, her hand beckoning May onto her lap. May only seemed to respond to Aunty Ginny of late – not that Mummy had interacted much with her lately.

'Looking like your dad more and more each day,' said Aunty Ginny as May sank into her embrace. That much was true; everything about May was Daddy. The darker skin tone and even her top lip that curled whenever she laughed, which wasn't that often any more.

'Have you thought about the welfare?' asked Aunty Ginny.

'Charity?'

'No, it's money from the government … It will give you something to live on, you know, until you get on your feet again.'

'Tayo did not believe in that.'

'He'd been paying into it for a while now … see it as a bit of money coming back—'

'No!' said Mummy, making them all jump.

May moved from Aunty Ginny's lap and joined Lana on the floor in front of the radio.

Aunty Ginny lowered her voice. 'I know I've mentioned this before but surely some family back in Nigeria can help. I don't want to see you go but wouldn't they welcome you back? I thought you said Tayo's parents were not too badly off.'

'You don't understand our culture, Ginny.'

'I don't think they'd want to see you homeless.'

'Tayo's family … oh, Ginny, you do not understand. When a man dies suddenly … and with no explanation—'

'Sometimes there *is* no explanation. I know it's hard for them to accept; I mean even I still can't believe it—'

'Ginny, a lady in our village … her husband was found dead … he had not been sick. The day after his funeral, they chased her out of his house and she never returned. They took everything, even her children. Do you understand what I am trying to say?'

Mummy's broken sentences were designed to confuse the ever-listening Lana, but she understood. She understood perfectly.

'I don't believe this, Addy.'

'Tayo's parents have been visiting mine and harassing them.'

'Are they OK?'

'Yes. It is not them they want. They would take my children from me even if I could afford the plane tickets home.'

'This is awful ... are you sure?'

'Why don't you believe me?'

'I didn't say that, Addy.'

'Even if I wanted to go back home, I could not. And I don't want to. Tayo's wish was for our children to have a better life here and I will not dishonour him.'

'OK, Addy, well, I'm sure you can tell me more later. It can't be as bad as you say.'

'Ginny, it is worse.'

The landlord's deadline was fast approaching. With only one meal a day, Lana could feel Mummy's bones through her pullover as they listened to the radio.

'You are such a clever girl. You will be a doctor one day,' Mummy said, smoothing the top of her head.

'I would like to be a doctor, then I can find out why Daddy went to heaven.'

Mummy grabbed her shoulders and faced her. 'It is the evil spirits that took him. The doctors gave us no explanation, but I know. I know.'

Lana nodded her head, confused because she'd no idea what Mummy was referring to.

That night, as May, as usual, snored gently in the next bed, Lana responded to voices coming from the sitting room and stood in the passageway.

'Hello, Adanya,' a man's voice said. She noticed the strong scent of aftershave immediately, even from where she stood. Or perhaps it was her imagination.

'I am glad you could come.'

'Adanya, Adanya, Adanya,' he said, as if he would be shaking his head.

'Yes, sir ...'

Lana moved closer to the door, so she could see.

'What news do you have for me?' This time he didn't ask if he could sit down in her daddy's chair, and this felt like a punch to her belly.

'I cannot pay the next month's instalment and I was wondering if you could wait.'

'Until? Look, love, I've been in this business too long. If you haven't got a job starting in the next few days, how are you going to be able to pay on time?'

'I have been doing some more sewing jobs ...'

'That's not going to be enough and we both know that, don't we?'

'Yes, sir.'

'Call me Rex.'

'I would prefer to call you Mr Rex.'

'As you wish. So what now?'

'If I am honest, I do not know what to do.'

'Adanya, I'm not a bad man.'

Mr Rex stood up, finally out of Daddy's chair.

'I'm sure we can come to an arrangement. I know times are tough, but I can be understanding. Very understanding.'

'Thank you, Mr Rex.' Her mother's voice was a whisper.

His finger found the tip of her nose.

'You're so beautiful,' he said in a way no man apart from Daddy had ever said it.

'Mr Rex ...' she said, before his finger moved down to her lips.

'Shhhh ... It's OK. Remember what we spoke about? What I asked. We can start that now, if you like.'

Mummy inhaled. 'No ... not now, Mr Rex. My children ... perhaps when they go back to school ...'

'I understand.' He reached into his pocket and produced a piece of crumpled paper, which he placed into her hand.

'You call this number anytime. Speak to me and we can start the arrangement, OK?'

'Yes, Mr Rex.'

Chapter Six

A quick chill ran through her body as she stood on the staircase trying to listen in on a private conversation between Mummy and whoever. She'd followed the footsteps down to the phone in the unheated communal corridor, where Mummy had waited until the lady from Flat C had finished her conversation. Mummy's whispers made it hard to hear anything, with Lana running back upstairs long before Mummy had replaced the receiver. Her mind ran amok with who this mysterious person on the other line could be. Mummy had no friends other than Aunty Ginny, and she lived in the same building. Perhaps she'd been talking to her grandparents. But, if so, why hadn't she called Lana and May to speak with them?

Starting school late didn't appear to have wielded much consequence. Not many of the children spoke to her anyway, but a couple of teachers expressed their sympathy about her 'poor dad'.

Things had improved at home. Mummy was smiling again, as she accepted more sewing jobs. Mr Rex visited a lot also to check on the house and make sure everything worked properly. He even fixed the Hoover once.

Lana had long since abandoned the role of standing in the hallway to listen in on adult conversations, and wondered just what her grandmother would make of it all because she certainly wasn't 'minding her business'. That was until she heard a cry coming from the direction of the kitchen one evening. She climbed out of the bed and quickly smoothed one of Daddy's shirts over her nightdress and slotted her feet into Mummy's slippers. The door of the kitchen was firmly closed so she could not see inside. But she could hear. The sound of a chair slightly screeching across the floor. A plate or a cup toppling into the sink, perhaps.

And a man's voice. 'What's wrong with you? You said you wanted this!'

'Do what you have to do.' Mummy's voice.

Lana pressed her ear to the door. It sounded like someone being slapped, but over and over again. As well as an incessant moaning sound.

She edged backwards, her mind glazed with confusion as the back of her head hit the wall, harshly. The moaning sound grew louder, but it wasn't Mummy's voice.

That night she squeezed her eyes tightly and pressed the pillow against each ear, desperate to erase the imagined images in her head. Those sounds, just like the ones Mummy and Daddy used to make together, had scared her. Her grandmother had been right all along, 'If you don't mind your business you will find something you did not need to find!'

She would forget about everything she'd heard that night. The possible questions too harsh to bear. The thought of Mummy ... with a man, at night, and with the door closed. What about Daddy? No. She would banish it to the ether of her mind and live on like it had never happened. Besides, there could have been a perfectly good explanation for what she had heard. However, she told herself that she had no interest in ever finding out.

So when Lana happened to be awake when the door sounded late at night, she would simply squeeze her eyes tightly shut until she drifted off to sleep.

Luckily, after many months, the late-night visits began to die down anyway. Until one day, she realised it had been a very long time since the last one.

Aunty Ginny's appearances seemed to increase though. As did the whispering between Mummy and her only friend. Only sometimes, Mummy's whispers were loud enough to hear.

'I'm sorry,' said Mummy.

'Shhh ... the children will hear you!' said Aunty Ginny.

'I'm sorry,' she reiterated.

'Mummy, why are you sorry?' asked Lana once her curiosity had won.

'Nothing,' said Aunty Ginny, her hand moving in the air to effectively shoo her away.

One day, Mummy and Aunty Ginny were drinking tea together as Lana and May sat on the floor drawing.

'What's that in your hands, Addy?'

Lana turned around as Mummy's fist unfurled to reveal a ball of paper.

Aunty Ginny took the paper from her hand and straightened it onto her lap.

'What are you doing with this?' she said with a sigh. 'I told you it was all rubbish. Those Teddy boys are a bunch of bloody idiots who need to stop blaming everyone else but their lazy arses. No one listens to them anyway!'

'How can you be sure of this?'

'When we first came to England and we went out, I saw it on the floor. It was like a message,' she said, quietly.

That night, after Aunty Ginny had left, Lana retrieved the piece of paper from the bin.

KEEP BRITAIN WHITE.

*

'What's going on, Addy? Come on! I got extra shifts now and I can't look after these kids all day. I've got my boys to think of too. Talk to me, please!'

The three of them stood before Mummy who was sat on the chair with a day-old sandwich sitting on a side table. She'd been like that for twenty-four hours. Not saying a word apart from a mumbling that Lana could not decipher.

'I didn't know what to do. She was like this when we went to school, and when I returned, she was still here!' said Lana. If she'd been truthful with Aunty Ginny, she would have told her Mummy had been like this a lot. On and off for months. Not answering when one of the girls asked a question. Sometimes not eating for days. Lana had not seen anything wrong with the lack of food because Mummy seemed to be putting on weight, not losing it. Some days were worse than others, though. When she would speak about evil spirits coming to take them all away, like they did Daddy, her voice would raise and her eyes would widen, frightening May so much she'd burst into tears. Lana didn't mind getting the breakfasts and dinner ready. She didn't mind running the hot comb through May's hair even though she once singed a tiny section of her head. She didn't mind making sure they got to school on time. She also didn't mind when Mummy forgot her birthday because Aunty Ginny gave her a pretty card and a colouring set anyway. She didn't mind any of it because Mummy would usually return back to normal within days, opening up one of her vanity cases and pulling out her needles and thread. But not this time.

'It's OK, you did the right thing by getting me.' Aunty Ginny bent down to Mummy. 'Addy, please talk to me!'

The expression on Mummy's face was blank. Just like it had been before.

'Erm … OK,' Aunty Ginny said, her eyes searching the room.

'Aunty Ginny, what are you looking for?' asked Lana.

Aunty Ginny squinted her eyebrows and exhaled. 'I have no bloody idea. This is beyond me, it really is!' She turned back to Mummy. 'Addy, what's wrong. Speak to me please. Shall I call the doctor?'

Mummy grabbed her arm. 'I'm sorry, Ginny, please forgive me!'

'For what, Adanya? What's this all about?' Aunty Ginny moved her fingers over Mummy's hand. 'Please tell me what's wrong. Come on, old girl.'

'I'm sorry,' said Mummy, her eyes focused on the tears of her best friend. Her smile bringing relief to Lana, because this was a clear sign she was coming back again.

But it wasn't to last. One day the girls came home from school to find Aunty Ginny waiting for them. They followed her to a hospital just like the one they said Daddy had gone to, Aunty Ginny's shoes making a loud click-clock sound as they walked along the shiny floor. Auntie Ginny was clutching May's hand.

'Why are we here?' asked Lana. Mummy said she now sounded less like the Nigerian girl who had travelled to England four years ago. Lana sometimes wished they had never travelled to England.

'Is it Mummy?' she dared to ask, fearing that Mummy would die just like Daddy had in such a place.

'Yes,' said Aunty Ginny, opening the door to a room. On the bed was Mummy, who was sitting up and smiling strangely. Or it could have been a frown; it was hard to tell. What was unmistakable was the bundle of white a nurse had just placed in her arms.

'Addy?' said Aunty Ginny, letting go of May's hand and moving closer to the bed. 'Addy, love. Are you OK?'

Lana moved closer to the bed and immediately the slight gurgling sound was obvious. Peering into her mother's arms, she saw it; a white doll like the one Daddy had bought her just before he went away.

Mummy asked the question Lana was about to. 'Is this a baby?'

'Yes, it is. A beautiful little girl,' replied Aunty Ginny.

'What?' asked Mummy.

'Addy, love, it's your little girl.'

'I want Tayo,' said Mummy, as she gently closed her eyes with the dolly still in her arms.

Lana watched Aunty Ginny release the dolly from Mummy's weakened hold. Nine-year-old May watched aghast from the other side of the bed.

'You have a new sister,' said Aunty Ginny by way of bizarre explanation. Nothing made any sense. Lana didn't know much about such adult things but how could Mummy have had a baby without Daddy and why did this new sister look so white? Surely a baby with this type of skin was more likely to be Aunty Ginny's child?

Lana's eyebrows knotted in confusion.

'I don't know what to tell you ... I just don't know anything anymore.' Aunty Ginny placed her head in her hands.

But Lana was eager for more information about this strange baby who had appeared out of the sky and into Mummy's arms. Lana was eleven, still a child in the eyes of many, but she felt equipped to handle the truth, even if, really, she didn't understand any of this.

The next morning, she pushed open the door to Mummy's hospital room, Aunty Ginny and May trailing slowly behind. She immediately noticed that the dolly was nowhere to be seen, just Mummy lying on the bed with two white people dressed in even whiter garments holding onto her arms.

'It's alright,' said one, as the other produced what looked like the longest and fattest needle Lana had ever seen and advanced it towards Mummy's arm.

'No, leave my mummy alone!' shouted Lana, just as Ginny appeared, open-mouthed.

'Get her out of here!' said the one holding the needle in the air.

'Come on, Lana,' said Aunty Ginny. 'May ...' Lana did not understand why Aunty Ginny was allowing them to hurt her Mummy.

Mummy's eyes caught hers. 'Where are my children, please? Where am I?!'

'Mummy!' Tears sprang in Lana's eyes.

'Come on, let's go and get you and May a milkshake. You'd like that!' Aunty Ginny closed the door behind them and Lana could only feel a helplessness that threatened to topple her entire body. 'What are they doing to my mummy?'

'They're just giving her medicine to help her get better.' Aunty Ginny's voice lacked the reassurance Lana so needed at that moment. But Lana had no power to do anything else but listen to the sounds coming from Mummy's room; not unlike the sounds she'd heard that night with the man in the kitchen. Not unlike the sound she'd heard the morning Daddy had left them alone forever.

PART TWO

Chapter Seven

The tall and imposing children's home stood on a large hill surrounded by a forest inhabited by mini gargoyles, flying anteaters and a witch that devoured little children. At least this was the explanation in the book entitled *The Dwelling for Little Children*, which May had reread a dozen times already.

'There are no monsters in the trees,' said twelve-year-old Lana, sitting on the edge of one of two beds, in a small room that still felt unfamiliar. She followed the line of dust floating in a stream of sunlight angled from the window, all the way back to the side-table lamp that shone above a sleeping toddler clutching a cloth elephant.

'How do you know?' asked ten-year-old May.

'Did you see any when they drove us up here?'

'It wasn't dark. What if they only come out at night-time?'

'No one's going to get us, we're safe.'

'I read in the book that—'

'Sshh, you'll wake the baby!'

Their faces turned to the door as it creaked open to reveal a white lady with curly hair just like Aunty Ginny's.

'Hello, girls,' she said.

'Hello,' they replied in unison.

'Sorry we had to keep you waiting here so long, but there's a lot of paperwork to sort out. Soon be done.'

'Then, can we go home?' asked Lana. The woman sat on the bed beside Lana, almost squashing little Tina with her bum.

'The baby needs to go to bed. I always put her down at seven,' said Lana.

'You will not be able to go back home tonight, so let's make you comfortable for now. My name is Dee and I'm going to make sure you get settled in properly, OK?'

Dee patted Tina's chubby leg, smiling warmly and the toddler began to stir. Everyone was drawn to her youngest sister. They would often comment on how cute she looked with her pale, golden skin, those soft, brown, ringleted curls, huge beaming smile and big green eyes. Lana was always glad to admit she did indeed have the cutest baby sister in the whole wide world!

'How long will we be staying this time? This place is so far away. Why couldn't we go back to the other home we went to last time?' asked Lana.

'And we heard there are monsters in the woods!' added May.

Dee smiled. 'Now I can honestly say I haven't heard about any monsters, May. But, the place you went to last time didn't have enough room and we want to make sure we keep you all together.'

'How long are we staying this time? A week? Mummy got better quicker last time and that was only a few months ago.' Lana pulled a now wide-awake Tina onto her lap.

'Actually, it was three months ago. I counted,' said May.

Dee avoided eye contact. 'Girls, I think it's best we all get a good rest before dinner? I'll just take Tina. There's a special wing for little ones.' She extended her arms in expectation.

'Bubye!' said Tina towards Dee, as if reading Lana's mind.

'No, she's staying with us. We have to stick together. Aunty Ginny said,' Lana stated firmly.

Dee looked like she was about to insist but instead she smiled warmly. 'I understand. You can stay together. I'm sure it will be alright for now.'

Lana gripped Tina's hand tightly as they slowly headed through a long windowless hallway that would lead to a busy dining hall. Tina had only started walking two months ago, which Aunty Ginny said had been excellent progress. Apparently one of her boys hadn't started to walk until he was eighteen months old.

Inside the dining hall there was an aroma of overcooked food and rows of tables and countless children adding to the clattering of crockery. The volume decreased suddenly with their appearance. All eyes on these three new kids.

'Make yourselves comfortable, girls. Sit anywhere,' encouraged Dee as the sea of faces remained locked in their direction. There were slightly more kids who looked like Lana and May than at school, but they did not look any friendlier than the others, just indifferent; the noise quickly increased again and no one bothered to stare at them anymore. Lana placed Tina onto a chair beside an empty wooden table, and May sat beside her.

Dee leaned over the table. 'Girls, you'll have to go up to the front together and serve yourself!'

'What about Tina? She can't.'

'I will see to your sister.'

'No, I will get what she needs,' insisted Lana. 'May, please stay with her.'

Caring for Tina with Aunty Ginny's help had been Lana's entire focus ever since her mummy had fallen ill the first time, just after Tina was born.

Then, she was gone for three months, and Lana and her sisters had lived with Aunty Ginny in between both flats. Aunty Ginny had complained a lot about looking after a baby and not being able to do the day shift at the butcher's. But Lana had happily attended school, with evenings spent doing homework and looking after her two little sisters alone, whilst Aunty Ginny had gone to her night shift at the butcher's. At night, they would be left with her sons who were really tall and quite scary with their deep voices and blank stares. But they'd usually leave them alone as soon as Aunty Ginny left the house.

Each morning, Aunty Ginny had returned in a bad mood, complaining about her dry hands and peeling nail polish thanks to 'all that poxy cutting and packing'. So, Lana had been relieved when Mummy had returned because she hadn't been quite sure that Aunty Ginny would want them back!

It became Lana's job to make sure Mummy swallowed the correct pills at the right time. Sometimes she would argue with Mummy when she'd insisted, 'I don't need those pills. They are not good for me! They are trying to poison me!' When she had to go away for a second time, Lana had felt it was her fault for not making sure she took the pills on time. Luckily, Mummy had returned home within ten days.

To ensure they would never be split up again, Lana quickly became accustomed to making sure everyone and everything in her world was catered for and ran efficiently. Sometimes, when she closed her eyes and concentrated, she could still see her daddy. Photographs remained dotted in various sections around the house, reminding her of his features; his shiny dark skin and the way his top lip curled whenever he cracked a smile. He looked just like May, Mummy often said (before grabbing May by the hands and saying, 'They took him. Why did they take him?').

When Mummy went away six months ago, they had stayed in a home for the very first time. As Aunty Ginny had promised, it was only temporary and to give her a break. There was no reason to believe that this third time would be any different.

The first night at Sir John Adams Children's Home, Lana and her sisters fell into a deep slumber, despite the unfamiliar surroundings. May on the second bed, Tina and Lana huddled together separated only by a lilac, yellow and red elephant called the Puffalump. It had been a present from Auntie Ginny and Tina hated to be separated from the creature.

They were awoken the next morning by a loud piercing screech from an invisible source. Dee had warned them the alarm would go off at 7am and that was OK because Lana's mind had popped into focus even before she'd opened her eyes. She had a lot to do today, including a talk with Dee to find out when they'd be going home. She hoped they'd be back in time for tea.

The canteen buzzed with activity once again, their presence of no interest to the lines of children sitting at each table, all intent on shovelling as much food into their mouths as possible before they went to school. The porridge was rather soggy and nothing like Aunty Ginny's, but Lana ate what she could whilst assisting Tina to do the same.

'Everything OK with the three of you?' asked a very tall white woman in a generously filled suit who approached their table.

'May I please speak with the lady who brought us in yesterday? Miss Dee?' asked Lana.

'She isn't here. She doesn't work here. Her job was to settle you into your new home,' said the woman.

'We already have a home at Pettyford Road and we will be going back soon. Mummy's just a little sick, but she'll get better. She always does,' said Lana, gently smoothing a napkin across Tina's mouth.

'Lanaaaa!' cried Tina, smiling so cutely, curls bouncing around her face.

'My name is Mrs Daventry and you can direct any questions you have to me.'

'When are we going home?'

Mrs Daventry let out a puff of exasperated air. 'Your home is here now, Lana. I am rather surprised no one has informed you of this.'

'We went to a home before and—'

'This is different.'

'Why is this different?'

'Eat your breakfast,' instructed Mrs Daventry, moving away before Lana could offer a retort.

'May, look after Tina, OK?'

'Where are you going?'

'I'll be back in a minute or two.'

Lana searched the bustling room again for Dee, unwilling to accept Mrs Daventry's weak explanation.

'Excuse me,' said Lana, tapping her fingers onto the arm of a ginger-haired man with his hands behind his back, like a soldier inspecting his troops.

'What is it?' he asked without facing her. She followed his march up and down the aisle of tables.

'Have you seen the lady who brought us in yesterday? I would like to speak with her.'

'What was 'er name?' he replied.

'Dee.'

He stopped pacing. 'Starts with a D?'

'No, her name is Dee.'

'Dee ... Dee ... actually, I think I know who you're talking about.'

'You do?' she asked hopefully.

'Hair up to 'ere.' He lined his hand against his chin.

'Yes!'

'Curly?'

'Yes!'

'Dee?'

'Yes!' she said with happiness.

'She left.'

So, she had gone. The woman who looked a bit like Aunty Ginny hadn't even said goodbye.

'Anything else?' he asked.

Lana thought for a moment. 'My baby sister likes to have a mashed banana in the morning. Do you have any?'

'You want something different to eat?'

72

'Yes, for my sister.'

'Did she drink the milk she was given?'

'Yes.'

'So she's not going to starve then, is she?'

'Aunty Ginny says we must always eat our fruit and vegetables.'

'Good advice. I'll see what I can find. Anything else?'

'No, that would be fine, thank you.'

Most of the children had left the dining hall and the man with the ginger hair still hadn't returned with anything for Tina to eat.

'I'm going back to the room,' announced May.

'I'll just wait here.'

'Why?'

'That man said he would bring a banana for Tina.'

May rolled her eyes and left the table. Tina began to fidget as the canteen emptied of any distractions.

'Come on, let's go,' whined Lana. The man had probably forgotten, she reasoned.

That night, May had questions. She rarely spoke and when she did, it was to ask about things that Lana could not confidently answer.

'May, I don't know how long we are going to be here. I think we should just wait for Aunty Ginny to get in touch. She'll know.'

May's eyes clouded over. Like Lana, she clearly missed their old life. The life before Daddy went. Days out in the park and all those pictures, the laughter and the joy. Over the past year since Mummy got sick, Aunty Ginny had tried to recreate the past with trips to the park. Sometimes Mummy would even join in, though at other times she refused to get out of Daddy's green chair. Mummy did once manage to take Lana and her sisters shopping for clothes and pens. It was a rare and magical day; Lana hoped she would never forget it. They had walked along the high street with Tina in the pram, each girl holding onto the side. Mummy had bought them sweets and ice cream and the sun had lasted the entire day. That afternoon had felt so good and even May hadn't been able to stop smiling.

On other 'good' days, Mummy would tell stories as she plaited Lana's hair. She liked to reminisce about their life in Nigeria.

'This style is the Koroba. Your grandmother used to do it for me,' said Mummy. Lana no longer added, 'But I was there too!' Now, she had simply learned to listen.

As Lana lay on this strange bed, she wished she'd never complained about the plaits hurting so much. She wished she'd made sure each and every pill was swallowed at the right time. She'd do anything to be with Mummy again, experience the sensation of her soft fingers twirling her coily strands. Anything.

Lana was certain the day would come again. It had to.

The next morning, Lana and Tina slowly headed towards the dining hall without May who had gone on ahead.

'Excuse me,' she said, having spotted the man with the ginger hair in the dimly lit corridor.

'What is it?' he said with a sigh.

'I think you forgot us.'

'I did?'

'Yesterday. The banana for my little sister.'

'I didn't forget.'

'Then why didn't you ...?'

His eyes searched the immediate space around them and he moved closer, resting his arm against the wall as if to block her escape. She gripped onto Tina's hand tightly.

'I didn't forget, alright?' Flecks of spittle attacked her cheeks. 'If you think I'm at your beck and call, think again. You're at John Adams now, and you will do as I tell you to, ya hear?'

'I only asked for—'

'Did you hear me?' he hissed.

'Yes,' replied Lana, chest swelling with emotion. She hadn't expected this reaction. The heat of his breath so close and how he'd quickly morphed into one of the characters in those scary comics she'd found at Aunty Ginny's.

'Good. Now get to breakfast,' he commanded as Mrs Daventry glided by with a sincere smile. At that moment, the man again morphed into someone else.

'New recruit got a bit lost. Giving her a helping hand, poor thing.'

'She's lucky she has you to help, Stan,' said Mrs Daventry. But as soon as she disappeared further down the corridor, he turned to Lana. 'Now, I realise that people like you love bananas, but you get 'em when everybody else does, you hear?'

'Y … yes,' said Lana.

'Good. Now get to breakfast!'

She did as commanded, unable to shake off the fear lodged in her throat.

She avoided the man called Stan as much as possible, although at times would catch him watching her with an amused expression. She couldn't understand the source of his behaviour towards her. What had she said to offend him? When a letter arrived from Aunty Ginny, her confusion turned to happiness. She scanned the piece of paper, quickly.

My darling girls,

I hope you are all keeping well. I miss you all so much. Give Tina a big hug from me. I bet she's now running all over the place! May, I bet, is reading all the time. And you, Lana, I suspect are still bossing everyone about!

Take care, my little sweethearts.

I love you all.

Aunty Ginny

She read the letter again. No date of when Aunty Ginny would be arriving for them and no mention of Mummy. Already a week into their stay, Lana was hungry for answers.

'I would like to see the person in charge,' she demanded once Mrs Daventry had answered the knock.

'I am in charge and you can ask me what it is you need to know. Take a seat, Lana.'

Lana sat down on the wooden chair, in front of an imposing desk. A picture of a golden dog was locked in a frame. Mrs Daventry did not look like someone who cared for a dog.

'Well, Lana?'

'I would like to know when we are going home.'

'Home?'

'Can you tell me what day we will be leaving? I would like to write to Aunty Ginny and let her know, so that she can come and collect us on the right day.'

'I don't know what's been said, but you are certainly not going home yet. I thought I had made that clear already.'

'But we can't stay here for ever!'

'We have been notified by a Mrs Ginny Jones that you have family in Nigeria. She has given us a phone number retrieved from your mother's address book; the Ade ... leepos or something. Apparently she thought they could get a message to your grandparents.'

'Yes.'

'It would appear that the telephone line is no longer in use. As you can appreciate it is hard to get letters out there and this can take weeks even with a full address. Something you can't seem to be able to remember. This is most unfortunate.'

'I know we lived on Ogun Street.'

'Nigeria is a big country. That didn't really help.'

This was the only address she recalled because it was the street in which their house was situated. They had never spoken in terms of addresses, more, 'Go to Mama Ladi and buy some tomatoes', never 'go to Critchen Street and buy some tomatoes'. It wasn't like England! Lana was almost pleased she had been so little when they left Nigeria and so didn't know much else because, truth be told, she didn't want anyone in Nigeria found. Their home was England now and she wanted to stay close to Mummy.

'Mrs Jones also said you don't have any relatives here in the UK.'

'Only Mummy and Aunty Ginny.'

'Yes, quite. Anyway, if we locate any of your relatives we will let you know.'

She was effectively being dismissed.

'If I were you, Lana, I'd make the best of it here. Like most of our residents, you might be here for a while.'

'How long is a while?'

Aunty Ginny used to say Lana was bright for her age and understood so much, maybe a little too much. Yet at that moment she was unable to decipher much more than a strong need to be back home with her mummy and in her own bed again. Or playing with baby Tina on their settee, gazing out of the window and watching the world go by.

'I cannot tell you how long you will be here. But I do suggest you make yourself comfortable here at Sir John Adams Children's Home. You may actually find you like it.'

In the new environment of the children's home, Tina began to wake up during the night, insisting she wanted to play. Mrs Daventry mentioned a cot being available in another wing, where Tina could be with other infants. Lana flatly refused.

'I can look after her. She's not a baby anymore.'

'We have regulations, Lana. You were only allowed in the same room as we had no space in the toddler wing when you arrived. Luckily one of the girls is leaving and there will be space by Tuesday. These are the rules and you will have to abide by them, I'm afraid.'

Lana's pleas were ignored and she only began to calm down once May pointed out that Tina would only be 'down the corridor', and it wasn't the end of the world. She was right, of course. As long as Lana and her sisters remained under one roof, she'd tolerate anything.

By Tuesday, no one had arrived to take Tina away. Lana hoped they'd just plain forgotten and she wasn't about to remind anyone of this 'mistake'. She made sure to avoid staff as much as possible, keeping Tina occupied in their room. She'd be thrilled with just one more night snuggling in the bed with her baby sister, nose pressed into her hair, warmth from her chubby little body filling her with comfort as it had done almost every night since her birth.

The door flung open and the man with the ginger hair appeared.

'I'm Stan,' he said, looking towards May. 'I've been off a couple of days and I wanted to come and see how the new recruits were getting on. Welcome you an' that.'

'Thank you,' replied Lana, her voiced laced with scepticism. He seemed to have forgotten their previous encounter but she had not.

May looked up from her book. 'Have … have you come to take Tina to the toddlers' wing?'

Lana widened her eyes at her sister in silent chastisement.

His eyebrows wrinkled. 'The kid really shouldn't be in here with you but they're gonna let her stay.'

Lana's heart filled with joy. 'Really? Oh, thank you so much … Stan!' She held onto her sister a little tighter.

'Don't thank me. The old biddies here just feel sorry for you.'

'Why would they feel sorry for us?' asked May.

'What, you don't know?'

'Thank you, Stan, but we do not need anyone to feel sorry for us. We're fine,' said Lana matter-of-factly.

'Wot, even though you ain't got no mum?'

'We will be with our mummy soon,' countered Lana.

May placed her book to one side.

'That would be quite difficult considering wot's happened.'

'What's happened?' asked Lana.

'Poor stupid kids.' He shook his head slowly.

'We're not stupid!' protested May.

'Oh, really?'

'Take that back!' cried May angrily as she stood up. Stan fell into a heavy fit of laughter, his body convulsing with exaggerated guffaws. 'You stupid, dumb kids!'

'Don't call us dumb!' said May. Lana had never seen her sister like this before.

Stan moved over to May and stooped to her height, staring intently into her face. His words were clear and even, yet with a heat that could singe the very tips of their hair. 'She's carked it and you don't even know it!'

The room fell silent for just a moment.

'What does that mean?' said Lana.

'It means, she's gone, dead, and she's never coming back.'

Another silence. Lana would surely have fallen to the ground if she'd been standing. Instead, she decided he was lying just like he had about bringing Tina the banana.

'You're not telling the truth!' Lana squinted her eyes, fuelled by a fresh determination that not one of his words would touch her because they simply weren't true. May sat back onto the bed, a look of quiet disbelief etched onto her face.

'Suit yourself,' he said with a smile as he left the room.

'He's lying. You do know that, right?' said Lana.

'Yes,' whispered May.

'Carry on with your book. Everything is fine.'

That night as Tina slept cuddled up to May on Lana's bed, she slipped her feet into the red furry slippers Aunty Ginny had bought for her last Christmas, closing the door gently behind her.

She knocked twice on the door of Mrs Daventry's office.

'It's late, you'd better have a good excuse,' she said coldly from inside. As soon as she spotted Lana the lines around her mouth seemed to soften.

'Lana, do sit down,' she said in a voice Lana suspected was designed to sound warm, but simply failed.

'When are we going to see our mum?'

Mrs Daventry opened her mouth to speak, yet no sound emerged.

Now she just stared at the desk. 'Lana …'

'Please tell me, when we can see our mummy? Tina misses her. We all miss Mummy.'

Mrs Daventry moved away from the desk and approached her. 'Lana, I think you—'

'Where is she?'

'I'm sorry … we had a call earlier today and we weren't going to say anything until—'

'Where is she?' Lana's breathing was erratic and tears came unbidden. 'Where is she?' Her shoulders convulsed.

The more Mrs Daventry remained silent, the more Lana's hysteria increased.

A nervous-looking Mrs Daventry called for reinforcements in the form of Stan, who lifted the shrieking Lana off the ground, placing her roughly onto his shoulder.

'Let me down!' she called angrily. Her fists pounded his back, the struggle to break free her only concern and not the look on Mrs Daventry's face. A look identical to Aunty Ginny's the day they told them Daddy had—

'WHERE IS SHE?! WHERE IS SHE?'

To struggle was pointless, but she would continue to anyway, as Stan carried her along the length of a corridor, her cries never waning, her throat drying with the effort; this madness in her heart at a peak.

She landed roughly on May's bed and Tina woke immediately and also began to wail hysterically. May looked on at the confusing scene, but remained silent.

'Where is she?' Tears ran down her face and her nose was in need of a tissue. Stan turned away with a comment she didn't understand – 'Good job the government's put a stop to all this immigration lark. Sick of all you lot coming in!' – and shut the door behind him. Lana wanted to run after him, ask him again and again about Mummy, pound his back violently, force him to speak to her, answer her questions, but her body was spent of emotion and strength. Even new tears refused to fall.

'Where is she?' Lana's voice was much softer, quieter now, and tinged with the horrifically, painful realisation that Mummy was in the same place as her daddy.

Chapter Eight

Three little girls were dressed in the only black clothes they owned. Ten-year-old May had insisted on wearing her blue woolly hat, to accompany the black polka-dot dress, which just looked silly, according to Lana. Tina only had one pair of shoes – shiny, patent ones with a silver buckle – which had been a present from Aunty Ginny, and were thankfully black.

Aunty Ginny held onto Tina's tiny hand as Lana and May stared blankly towards this oblong-shaped hole in the ground. Lana couldn't help sobbing deeply at the sight but May simply stood watching the wooden coffin being lowered into the space. Lana refused or was simply unable to reconcile the image of her beautiful mummy with whatever was in that box. None of the past two weeks had made any sort of sense in her mind.

'It's not surprising to me,' said Aunty Ginny.

'What do you mean?' asked May, her eyes not moving from the graveside.

'Your mum ... she died of a broken heart, didn't she? Just wanted to be with your dad and here they are together again. Side by side.'

May squinted her eyes in a way that disputed what Aunty Ginny was saying. But even though Lana agreed with Aunty Ginny, she could not look at either grave anymore. She did not want to imagine that both Mummy and Daddy were there. It was too much for her mind to decipher. The pain feeling like fresh swipes of a knife slicing through her emotions. It simply felt … horrible all over again.

'Come on, let's go, girls. We've seen Addy off now,' said Aunty Ginny, her face red with emotion. Tina was unable to understand the magnitude of the moment, shiny shoes sparkling in the sunlight as she rested on Lana's hip as they slowly headed away from the graves of their parents.

'What happens now?' asked May, the first words she had spoken the entire day. Lana could not remember having a full conversation with her or even seen her sister cry since being told they would never see their mummy again. Lana had cried herself to sleep every night with Tina by her side, yet May had remained silent.

'You go back to John Adams,' Aunty Ginny said quietly.

Stan stood by a small car, an unwelcome reminder of their possible fate.

'Aunty Ginny, can we come home with you?' asked May.

'I wish you could, darling, but I just don't have the space. I'm moving somewhere smaller. One of my boys is in the army now and it will be cheaper for me to run. But when he comes home on leave, there's not going to be enough space to swing a cat.'

'We won't be much trouble. We haven't got much luggage. We can chuck a lot of things away anyway.' May held onto Aunty Ginny's arm.

'I'm sorry darling, I just can't. Maybe in a few years, yeah? Just not now. You go with that nice man Stan and get some rest.'

'But you said you loved us,' said May.

'I do. I loved your mother and I love you, never forget that!' She retrieved a handkerchief from her pocket. 'This is really hard.'

Without warning, Lana threw her tiny body into Aunty Ginny's surprised embrace. Her nostrils immediately catching the whiff of Chanel No 5 – the sweetest, most familiar smell in the world. She needed this woman to bundle them into a car and drive them back to Pettyford Road in Notting Hill. She needed to immerse herself into the familiarity of her regular life. The tree-lined streets and the sound of the milkman as he drove noisy bottles up and down the street each morning. She needed to sit in her daddy's green chair. She needed her mummy!

'Come on, girls,' said Stan, playfully tugging on Tina's collar.

'Aunty Ginny, please don't make us go back. You're all we have left. Please!' pleaded Lana, suddenly fearful of being in the car with Stan. Scared of a world without her parents. Orphans left to perish without a trace. 'Please don't make us go back there!'

Ginny's tears returned. 'I've been speaking to Stan here and he's assured me you will all be OK. He will personally look out for you all.'

'Please … don't!' whined Lana.

'I'm so sorry, love. Please don't make this harder for me. I can barely take care of me and my boys. I just can't afford it. I tried. But they said I … I did try for a while there. Please don't make this harder.'

Stan clumsily held onto Tina's hand and placed her into the car, returning for Lana and May.

'Aunty Ginny? Please don't leave us!' said Lana with tears soaking her face, chest heaving with sobs, which made it difficult for her to speak clearly.

Aunty Ginny shook her head slowly as she reached into the plastic bag Lana hadn't noticed her carrying. 'Please just take this.' Inside was a rounded leather vanity case, one of three Daddy had given to Mummy. 'There wasn't much inside so I stuffed a few photos for you. I didn't have much time.'

'Come on, girls. I know this is hard, but it's for the best. I'm sure your aunt will visit,' said Stan in a voice that sounded almost sincere.

'I don't want this; we just need to come home with you, Aunty Ginny. Please let us come home with you!'

'Stan's right, it's for the best. Please, just go with him.' She pushed the case into her arms.

'We won't be much trouble, please, Aunty Ginny. You won't even know we are there. I'll look after the girls. Cook their dinner, clean. Please, Aunty Ginny, please!'

'NO!' came the roar of a voice.

Lana turned to May.

'She doesn't want us, Lana! Now, let's get in the car and go back to the home. Come on!'

May's expression was resolute, and she was more accepting of their predicament than Lana could ever be. Confused at her sister's outburst, Lana silently climbed into the seat beside May, never turning her head to look back. If she had, the view of Aunty Ginny on her knees sobbing for forgiveness would have been what she saw.

Stan turned the knob on the car radio, a blast of rock music filling their ears. 'You little wog girls better get used to your lives now. It's all about Sir John Adams Children's Home and you're gonna be there for a loooong time!'

Lana had no idea what wog meant, but it appeared to amuse this man no end. The sound of his overblown laughter echoing throughout the journey and long after it had stopped.

That laughter was a sound that would haunt her for many more nights to come.

Lana decided that she would have to cope. With her sisters by her side, she could cope with anything. Of course she could.

Life at Sir John Adams Children's Home became an uncomplicated routine she was prepared to endure. Lights out at eight, soggy porridge in the morning, cleaning duty once a week and the two faces of Stan she would soon get used to. The other kids still stared at them – some with suspicion, others with amusement. But Lana had no intention of making friends with anyone as she'd more than enough to do looking after Tina, and, well ... she really didn't need anyone else as long as she had her sisters by her side.

The room she shared with May had no sun. May had cleverly explained that the room was simply on the wrong side to be able to catch any sunshine rays. So every morning they would endure a bleak start to the day that would only brighten once she saw Tina. With special permission Lana was regularly allowed to spend time in the toddler wing, hold her little sister and watch her fall asleep after a story or a song, just like they used to at the home she missed almost as much as Mummy and Daddy. Moments spent with Tina allowed Lana to focus less on her own grief and her brewing sense of injustice. But it was during lights out and in the stillness of everything, that the weight of their loss lay heavily upon her. That startling and confusing image of Mummy being lowered into the ground. The finality. The certainty she would never see her again.

Now that Tina slept in another room, Lana could only fall asleep hugging a pillow wrapped in a cardigan that Tina had worn recently. The smell of Tina was comforting and had the power to soothe away the horrible things Lana's mind insisted on remembering,

'Can I have a hug?' she whispered once in May's direction – a question not met with the stony silence she'd expected but the quick sound of air through teeth, from behind pursed lips. May had 'kissed her teeth' – something Mummy had never allowed them to do.

Lana vowed never to ask May for a hug again.

At first Lana didn't feel ready to look at the contents of Mummy's vanity case, she could only trace her fingers across the soft, pink, silky interior. Then shut it. It was too soon.

Days later, and, after a particularly fun day with Tina, she placed her hands inside the vanity case once again, this time exploring the tight side pockets and pulling out a receipt for groceries and a pair of socks. Thankfully, the items in the main compartment of the case were more substantial even if they did seem rather random. Like Mummy's black-rimmed reading glasses, a round, yellow, plastic fan inscribed with illegible writing, long since rubbed off by time (she could just about make out the words Happy Wedding Day. Iju, Lagos), a black address book and an envelope containing a bunch of photographs: some black and white, a few coloured. How Daddy loved to take pictures! It was still too painful to look carefully at the snaps, but she ran her fingers across the outline of each item and brought a cluster of pictures and the fan to her nose. They didn't smell of Mummy. She had truly gone. The realisation that these items were all that remained of her felt too painful to contemplate. Yet, whatever Aunty Ginny's reasoning for handing the case over, Lana was glad of its presence. Or at least, she felt that one day she would be.

The odd letter from Aunty Ginny was handed to them at certain times of the month. Mostly they described her day, what she ate for dinner, how one of 'her boys' was doing in the army. These were things Lana did not care about because all she really wanted to know was when Aunty Ginny would be arriving to collect them or even when she planned to visit. Lana refused to give up hope though, even if May had clearly done so on the day of Mummy's funeral.

For now, and in the absence of grown-ups, Lana remained the head of the family and would see to it that her sisters wanted for nothing. She would carry the hopes of Daddy who always vowed they would enjoy all the good things a British way of life had to offer. Or something like that. It was hard to remember what Daddy used to say word for word, but she'd always remember how they made her feel loved, warm and secure. And she would make sure her sisters would always feel that way too.

The day she started at the new school near John Adams, Lana was fearful of being without her sisters for the first time since arriving at the home.

'If you need me just …'

'Just what? We're in different schools. We're not twins and we can't communicate telepathically!'

May was so clever. How would she know words like this? Lana swelled with pride at having such a bright younger sister.

'I'll be fine,' insisted May, patting down the cardigan, which appeared to flood her slim frame.

'Are you sure?'

'Yes! Stop fussing, Lana!' She shrugged her shoulders defiantly. Lana wasn't at all sure if she'd be fine though.

In the canteen, Stan hurried along a number of children. 'Come on now, let's all go get in the van!'

Lana, dressed in her green school uniform, bit into a piece of toast smothered in marmalade as she headed towards the white van stationed outside the building. May had gone to the toilet and she wished she would hurry up! Lana sat by the window watching as lines of children dressed in the same green school uniform rushed towards the vehicle. She failed to look pleased when a scruffy-looking boy, with uncombed strands of thick, coily hair, placed himself beside her.

'Hi,' he said.

'Hi,' she replied with disinterest.

'My name's Clifton.'

She glanced at him quickly, recognising him from the home. 'Lana. And by the way, that seat's taken. My sister will be sitting there.'

'What type of name is that?'

'It's really Lanre – it's Nigerian.' She stretched the word laboriously. 'But everyone calls me Lana, after Lana Turner.'

'Right,' he said, unconvinced.

May walked by without saying a word and sat at the very back. Lana strained her neck to turn back. 'Don't you want to sit here?'

'Nope,' replied May.

'Problem solved,' said Clifton.

As the van exited the gates of John Adams, Lana wondered if this was how a bird felt when let out of a cage. Yet, as they drove into a town she'd never seen before, past the shops and parks and homes, she still felt less than free. Weighted with the burden of worry. Would they give Tina enough food to eat? Would they understand Tina's obsession with listening to stories she had yet to understand? Thankfully, the scruffy boy called Clifton did not utter another word for the duration of their journey, and when Stan dispatched them outside the school he disappeared nice and quickly.

The two sisters stood by the van as Stan fiddled about with a wad of papers.

'Stick with me,' whispered Lana.

'I don't need to. Anyway, what's the point? We're in different schools, remember?'

'You'll only be across the road.' May was going to the primary school across the way, while Lana, being twelve, was now in big school. 'We have to stick together, remember?'

As usual, she ignored the roll of May's eyes.

A blonde, white lady, wearing what Aunty Ginny had called a beehive, approached them.

'Lana and May are the new kids,' said Stan, handing over a wad of papers to the friendly-looking lady.

'Well, it all seems to be in order. Thank you,' she said, her voice effectively dismissing the odious Stan. This pleased Lana.

'Welcome to our school,' she said, her voice sounding a little softer.

'Thank you,' said Lana, just as another white lady appeared.

'Hello, girls,' she said with a smile, 'I'll be taking the ten-year-old across to the other building.'

May didn't even say goodbye as she followed the kindly woman.

'Follow me, Lana, and I'll take you to your class. Is there anything you'd like to ask me?'

What she really wanted to ask was how long they were expected to be here. But that was followed by that clear image of Aunty Ginny after the funeral, standing by as Stan drove them away in the car.

She was going to be at John Adams and at this school for a very long time.

'No, thank you, Miss, I have nothing to ask you.'

Although Lana assumed her Nigerian accent was long gone, she still lacked the confidence to speak up and risk being exposed by her new classmates. However, this wasn't the reason she stood out at her new school.

'She one of them? From the children's home?'

'Yes, one of them.'

'Best keep away from her then! Might catch something!'

At Sir John Adams Children's Home, she'd been one of many children who had ended up without a family ... without a mummy and daddy. But now, as soon as she left those gates, she was to be singled out, marked. She was one of the unfortunates, the discarded and the unloved, easy to spot among the mass of children belonging to normal families with dogs and half-term trips to Cornwall. Lana and her sisters were now orphans, abandoned by everyone they had ever loved.

Three days into her new school, Lana thought seriously about speaking to one of the kids and perhaps making a friend. Without May and Tina, she was alone for the entire day and it would be nice to talk to someone. Anyone. Unlike her last school, there were more kids who looked like her so the law of averages was on her side; she'd learnt about that in Maths once.

Someone had to want to be friends, whatever colour they were.

'Hello ...' she said, after finally amassing enough courage to approach two girls standing by the water fountain. One had blonde hair and what looked like real lipstick on her thin lips, whilst the other had two bunches of coily hair held up by bright orange ribbons; her skin was as dark as May's. Lana hoped the girl could advise her on what to put on her hair as it had become increasingly tough to comb. The Vaseline Mummy had left them with was useless without the hot comb, an item she wished Aunty Ginny would have included in the vanity case.

'What do you want?' said the girl with the orange ribbons. Her skirt was surely shorter than what was allowed, her knees scuffed and in desperate need of some cocoa butter.

'I'm Lana.'

'What kind of name is that?'

'It's after an actress.'

'Who cares?'

'Actually, it's short for Lanre. That's a Nigerian name,' she said, desperate to impress. But judging by their expressions, she had misjudged the level of their interest.

'That in Africa, is it?'

'Yes, it is.'

The blonde girl bent down to the water fountain as the other one spoke. 'What do you want?'

'Just to talk to you.'

'Just to talk to you,' mimicked the girl in an exaggerated accent Lana could not recognise. She turned to the blonde girl for a little understanding, but she remained silent.

'Look, just sod off you African booboo, OK?'

Lana felt confusion. This girl, with the exception of the scuffed knees, looked like her.

'I ... I just wanted to see if you'd like to be friends.'

'Are you stupid or something? I said, sod off!'

They both fell into guffaws of laughter as Lana felt drenched with humiliation. She wasn't used to such bad language. Aunty Ginny would sometimes say bad words when referring to her sons, but other than Stan, most people said nice things. But, it would seem these girls had standards and were not about to be seen in the company of an unfortunate from Sir John Adams Children's Home.

She spent the remainder of her break alone, wishing she too had a love of books like May. She'd asked May how she was settling in to her own school but May had simply shrugged her shoulders without even a response. She suspected her sister didn't care much about making friends and could always escape into her books. Lana, however, felt totally alone at school and this loneliness felt like a breeding ground for thoughts about her parents ... Daddy's foot over the bed ... Two cramped oblong boxes filled with the lifeless bodies of the two people she loved dearly.

'Want some company?'

Lana turned to the scruffy boy who'd sat next to her in the van.

'No, thanks.'

His bottom lip protruded stubbornly. 'Not as if you're fighting off mates, is it?'

'What did you just say?'

'Let's face it, you ain't got any mates!'

'It's only my third day,' she said, feeling slightly stung at his accuracy.

'You can come and hang out with us if you like. But you have to know how to play football. It's what me and the lads do every break time.'

'No, thank you.'

His lip protruded once again and her guilt set in.

'Maybe some other time, OK?'

When the white van arrived for the trip home, Lana was pleased when May sat beside her (without saying a word, of course). Lana could only gaze through the smeared window, counting down the minutes to when she would see her little Tina again.

Lana forgot to ask why they were missing school. It was a relief, because in two weeks she hadn't managed to secure any real friendships. Clifton, at first rather annoying, was now the only person she looked forward to chatting with on the van, and she had even watched him play five-a-side a couple of times – something that had bored her half to death.

The news they were to miss school raised a rare smile on May's face as Lana finally questioned Mrs Daventry about the reason.

'Just do as I have asked and be sure to be in my office within twenty minutes. Oh, and dress ... nice,' she said with a look suggesting she could smell rotting fruit.

Lana selected the pink, cotton, party dress with puffy sleeves her mother had made for her and the black polka-dot dress for May.

'I'm not wearing that!' she protested.

'Mummy made it for you!'

May insisted on her blue, cotton skirt and orange blouse, tied at the neckline. Lana suspected she would have chosen the original dress if only Lana hadn't suggested it first!

Twenty minutes later, Mrs Daventry led them away from her office and into a bright and airy room filled with welcoming clutter like framed black and white photographs of babies wrapped in the arms of smiling adults, neat rows of books on white shelves and colourful plastic balls nestled in the corner.

Why had they never seen this room before? Tina was sat on a multi-coloured mat beside a woman with brown hair whom Lana had also never seen before. A skinny, bearded man perched on a chair opposite them, smiling towards her little sister.

'Hello, again. These two are her siblings,' announced Mrs Daventry as Lana and May stood side by side like museum exhibits. 'Girls, say hello to Geraldine and Peter Morgan.'

'Hello, Geraldine and Peter Morgan,' said Lana obediently. May did not utter a word as she scratched the top of her head. The effects of a dry scalp and not the bewilderment, Lana felt. The two strangers stared at the new arrivals, their mouths slightly agape and also stuck in surprise.

Their eyes shot to Mrs Daventry. 'These ... they are her sisters?' asked the man.

'Why, yes.'

Both adults stood up as Tina ran into Lana's arms.

'Tina, what have you been doing?' she asked, face buried within Tina's soft curls.

'Play, play!' she enthused. Lana placed her hands under Tina's armpits and perched her onto her hip.

'How's my little ballerina? Missed you!' she said as the little girl giggled, resting her head on Lana's shoulder.

'This is not what we expected, Mrs Daventry,' said the woman patting down her skirt.

'I'm not sure I know what you mean.'

The couple looked towards one another again, participants in their own private understanding of what they were saying.

'What she means is ...' said the bearded man.

'They don't really look ... alike,' said the woman.

'Lana, May, take your sister and wait outside,' ordered Mrs Daventry.

The trio stood in the corridor, Tina uneasy on her tiny bandy legs. Lana picked her up and she immediately relayed the contents of her day in toddler fashion, none of which Lana really understood.

'Play, storrwee,' said Tina.

'No story right now. We have to wait here,' replied Lana.

Unable to decipher the mutterings from the other side of the door, Lana was relieved to see all three adults finally appear. The man walked rapidly ahead as the woman turned to Tina, who was in Lana's arms.

'Goodbye, my sweet,' she said tenderly.

'Bubye,' replied Tina. Her hand opened and closed slowly. Lana had taught her that.

'It was so nice to meet you,' said the woman, the tips of her fingers smoothing the edges of Tina's head. A single tear plopped onto the woman's blouse as the man turned back and walked over to the woman, placing his arm onto her shoulder and gently leading her away.

Mrs Daventry ushered the girls back to their room, explaining they could spend the rest of the day together. As confusing as the morning had been, none of that mattered as the three sisters roamed the grounds like they were its only inhabitants, daring to explore more than just their immediate surroundings. Unbeknown to them, a hilly, grassy area existed around the back of the building where residents were permitted to roam. This new discovery sent each girl into a joyful frenzy. Tina giggling wildly at the peculiar sight of Lana and May each rolling themselves down a grassy hill as she clapped her hands in glee. Three sisters rushing about with abandon, the onset of rain doing nothing to subdue their excitement. Within these moments, it was easier to forget the circumstances that had brought them to John Adams. Lana herself was unable to remember the last time she'd felt so free and joyful – when she actually felt like a twelve-year-old girl.

The glorious weirdness of that day soon washed away as life continued at the pace Lana had recently become accustomed to: May on her bed, face up and lost within the pages of a book; stolen moments with Tina and strolling the grounds of

Sir John Adams Children's Home until Mrs Daventry would appear, announcing their time was up for the day.

Lana didn't think to wonder why, each day, Tina was allowed more and more time with her sisters. An extra hour here and there. She never questioned it. She would just enjoy it.

When on yet another day Lana and Tina had played past their allotted time, May offered her opinion. 'They're up to something.'

'They're just being nice, May,' said Lana as she smoothed a comb through Tina's soft curls.

'No one's nice here.'

'Yes, they are, May.'

Now, two hours past their allotted time, Mrs Daventry inevitably arrived for Tina.

'She's probably a little tired now, aren't you?' said Lana, planting a kiss onto Tina's forehead.

'No!' said Tina, in response to Mrs Daventry taking her hand. 'No! Lana!'

'It's OK, I'll see you tomorrow. OK?'

'No!' she replied stubbornly.

'If you go with Mrs Daventry, I will give you a treat tomorrow,' said Lana, smothering Tina's face with an abundance of kisses.

Tina smiled mischievously and Lana knew she'd gotten through to her.

'Bye, Tina,' said May, getting up to gently ruffle her little sister's hair.

Tina's hand opened and closed like a duck puppet. 'Bubye,' she said in that glorious childlike voice that Lana adored.

The following day, after school, Lana waited for Tina to be brought to her. By seven Tina had still not arrived.

'I wonder where she is? It's lights out in an hour,' said Lana.

May lay in her bed staring up at the ceiling. 'Why don't you stop moaning and go and find out?'

'Coming?'

May leapt off the bed and followed her sister through to the now familiar route from their room to Mrs Daventry's office. The dark, almost airless, trek was marked only by the soft tones of children and the deeper voices of staff members, and that forever present smell of rhubarb and custard mixed with bleach (the only way Lana could describe an odour she would forever associate with Sir John Adams Children's Home).

'Mrs Daventry, where's our sister?' asked Lana.

Mrs Daventry beckoned for Lana and May to sit down. Two chairs stood facing her desk as if they had been waiting for them.

When Mrs Daventry spoke, she did so with a finality that sounded both chilling and heartbreaking all at once. 'Tina has gone.'

Lana looked towards May.

The inside of her tummy lurched. 'Where?'

'She's gone and I'm afraid ... I'm afraid ... she isn't coming back.'

Chapter Nine

When she first heard the words, Lana feared Tina was in the very same place as Mummy and Daddy.

A somewhat clearer explanation soon followed, yet she found it hard to comprehend the words.

Tina had been adopted.

To a nice couple.

She was in a nice home with a new mummy and daddy.

It was for the best.

Lana hadn't asked why she and May had not been adopted also. Those questions would sit at the back of her mind, ready for another day. At that moment, all she could allow herself to feel was a confusion followed by a numbness that started in her chest and travelled through her entire body. When the numbness had gone, the tears still did not arrive, just questions, but not the obvious ones.

'What about the Puffalump?' she asked.

'What?'

'She needs her Puffalump, it's her comfort. You have to make sure she has it Mrs Daventry, please.'

'I …'

Then everything went silent.

Lana couldn't remember when she'd started or finally stopped crying. Perhaps it was when her throat became hoarse and her eyes bereft of tears. Or when Stan pulled her away from Mrs Daventry's office as she desperately grabbed onto the chair, pulling, tugging, fighting her way out of an invisible trap. The chair screeching across the floor, a photo frame smashing against the ground, again with no sound. A horrible man whom everyone seemed to like, marching her away yet again through that cruel, dark corridor and into her room. Chucking her roughly onto the bed where she immediately curled into a foetal position, shoulders heaving as she wailed silently into the skin of her forearms.

'Don't you touch her!' bellowed May, standing square in front of a smiling Stan, hands balled by her sides. The sound had returned. 'I said, don't you touch her!'

With no idea where her sister had been during those last horrible minutes, Lana was glad for her presence.

'Oooh you're a feisty one.'

'Get out!' screamed May, loud enough for the entire building to hear.

'Pleasure,' said Stan.

Minutes or an hour later, Lana spoke. 'May, what are we going to do?'

'What we always do.'

May was sat on her own bed, staring into an empty space as Lana began to shake with the intensity of another round of sobs, pressing her face against a pillow that still smelled of her little Tina.

That had been two days ago.

Lana's whole world now felt as if it had crumbled into nothingness. Tina, her darling baby sister, was gone. Lana's heart filled with sorrow every time she pictured her face. The last time she had seen her.

She now walked slowly with her eyes fixated on the floor. Her entire world cloaked in darkness and doubting she would ever notice the sun again.

When two days turned to three, Lana merely began to get used to the tight knot that regularly appeared in her belly. She'd no interest in talking – to anyone – or to open her eyes or to breathe again.

Even though she'd refused to speak to any staff, no one had actually approached her with any updates about her sister; like Daddy and Mummy, Tina had simply ... gone.

At breakfast, one of the other kids leaned over the table and said, 'We heard about your little sister ... that's bad news, man. But at least she's in a better place than this stink hole.'

She remembered someone saying at Daddy's funeral that he was in a better place. Hadn't Aunty Ginny even said it about Mummy? And on day four of Tina's absence, Lana thought she too should perhaps go to a better place.

Mummy had died of a broken heart and gone to be with Daddy and finally, Lana understood why.

Why did it keep happening? If she couldn't keep her sisters together then maybe they'd be better off without her. May probably wouldn't miss her; Aunty Ginny no longer cared. Maybe if she too just went to sleep and never woke up ...

A knock on the door.

'Who is it?'

'Me,' said a boy's voice.

'Clifton?'

'Yep, I just wanted to see if you were all right.'

'I'm fine.'

The door opened and Clifton appeared. She instantly felt a rush of self-consciousness what with her snotty, red-eyed appearance.

'If you want to come watch us play football later, you can,' he said grandly. 'You could even play ...?'

'OK,' she said with a hiccup.

'Try not to cry too much,' he said clumsily as he perched on the end of her bed.

'Thanks, I'm trying ...'

'Good. OK, well, I'll see you around.'

She nodded her head, watching his back as he left, and, for the first time in days, decided she was going to try not to cry anymore.

The first Saturday without Tina, Lana awoke with an anticipation of a very difficult day ahead. May wasn't particularly responsive and her lack of talking had actually gotten worse since their baby sister had been taken away. She now spent even more time immersed in her books and at breakfast she still ravenously ate every last scrap on her plate, whilst Lana had been unable to eat a full meal for days. It was as if her sister no longer cared about Tina.

Outside, the morning sky was unapologetically dull. Lana headed towards the area at the back of the building that she'd since found out was called Grassy Green. Predictably, various John Adams kids now occupied the area that was once a playground for Lana and her two sisters and one of the last places she had truly felt happy.

She sat down on a patch of grass as more and more children filled the area around her, yet she still felt like the only girl in the world. She wondered where Tina was at that very moment. Who had taken her? Was she happy or crying out for her? Would her new parents tell her stories?

'Hi,' said Clifton, sitting down in the space beside her on the grass. His hands remained stiffly inside his pockets as he shifted from side to side.

'It's easier if you take your hands out of your pockets,' she teased.

'Yeah, thanks.'

'You're welcome.'

'I brought you this.' He reached back into his pocket and retrieved a shiny red apple.

She smiled.

'I saw you at breakfast and you hardly ate anything.'

'Thanks.' She felt a burst of warmth at this small kindness. It meant everything.

'That's OK. I'm sorry your little sister went away. Everyone's talking about it. How you were crying and everything. My mum went away too. I know how it feels.'

'Where did she go?'

'Who knows? All I know is, she doesn't want me.' His smile was empty, a style she had used on many occasions, so she understood. Clifton's appearance by her side suddenly allowed her to think about someone else's anguish, a reminder that a painful history in John Adams was not exclusive to her. Others were suffering too.

Clifton explained that he'd been a regular children's-home resident since the age of three and was at a loss to explain just why each of his mother's boyfriends seemed to hate him.

'P'raps I got bad breath,' he joked.

'When did you last see her? Your mum?'

'About six months ago. She writes me now and again, but not much.'

'Letters are good.'

'I'd prefer to see her though. Last time I'd been back about three months and she said we could be a family again – even bought me some really good stuff!'

'That's nice,' said Lana, wishing she could remember the last toy Daddy had bought her. Maybe if she thought hard enough, she could.

'You can play with some of my stuff, if you like …'

'I don't play with toys anymore, Clifton.'

'I meant games and that … I have Snakes and Ladders. Everyone likes that game!'

'That would be nice. Thanks for the apple.' She smiled warmly, grateful her thoughts had been distracted, if only for a moment.

Ignoring the huge grass stains destined to appear on her bum, Lana listened as Clifton explained the best way to score a goal and his dislike of the English teacher they shared and why he'd always hated peas. The boy talked – a lot.

'This place isn't that bad once you get used to it, Lana,' he said tearing at a handful of grass.

'Don't do that, you're killing them!'

'Grasses don't live!'

'So, how do they drink the rain when it comes down? Explain that.'

Clifton looked thoughtful before squinting his eyes as a blanket of sunshine appeared defiantly above them. 'I dunno.'

He grabbed another clump of grass, flinging it into the air and green strands tumbled around them like confetti.

'Hey!' she called as Clifton giggled quite loudly.

Lana decided he was a strange boy. Yet, as a steady swarm of young residents skipped by or just wandered aimlessly around them, she decided that for a boy, he was OK and, simply put, apart from May, the only friend she had.

Chapter Ten

May picked up an overstuffed duffel bag brimming with exercise books, a weathered pencil case and a freshly washed PE kit. She glanced at herself in the tiny compact mirror, glad it was too small to reflect the state of her hair. They weren't allowed hot combs at John Adams apparently and with only being able to purchase Vaseline in the local shops, her thick strands had suffered years of neglect. Lana would gather her hair into a large plait every other day, sometimes insisting on one either side of her head. This wasn't ideal for May, but at least it looked half-way tidy. She threw the mirror onto her bed and sped towards the white van she'd steadily grown to hate. The white van, otherwise known as the moving advertisement of her rubbish life.

She hated when her sister Lana always insisted on sitting with her during the journey, when all she wanted to do was deal with the collection of thoughts in her head. May was always thinking, or reading, or both. She'd no real time to entertain people who lived outside of the pages of a book because they were just as fake. At least characters in a book never pretended to be real. Besides, she'd have to learn to navigate this world without Lana one day, anyway. Their age differences meant Lana would be the first to leave John Adams.

With May already planning ahead for when Lana would have to abandon her too.

Lana had already started the process, like today, sat next to the boy who liked her. Clifton his name was. May had simply walked past them and to the back of the minibus where, thankfully, the space beside her remained empty as Stan pulled out of the prison-like gates of Sir John Adams Children's Home. The short journey was, as usual, a newsreel of life outside of those gates: a high street dotted with shops including a chemist, butcher's and greengrocer's; women pushing kids in prams across dirty pavements; a small misshapen lake with ducks and toddlers throwing bread, reminding her of when she'd been a part of something … a family of four with a mummy and a daddy. Each weekday morning, the van passed each scene like a film, a fantasy, tantalising her with a way of life she'd never be a part of again.

Stan stopped the van outside of the school building and each child tumbled out of the vehicle as he voiced his usual displeasure. 'Steady! The school ain't going nowhere!'

A newer kid, a girl with brown pigtails called Jessica, smiled up at Stan and said; 'You're so funny!'

'I'm just telling it how it is. Have a good day at school, you hear?'

She often wondered why so many people seemed to adore this slimy, disgusting man. Or perhaps his derision was solely meant for her and Lana and the other coloured kids at John Adams. Nothing made sense. Nothing had ever made sense in her life.

'See you later,' said May as Lana and Clifton stood by the bus.

'Will you be OK?' said Lana, just like she did every single morning.

'Lana, I'm fine.'

'Maybe you can make friends with the new girl.'

'No, thanks.'

'Don't be like that!'

Lana's rosy view of the world was annoying. She wasn't the one being called 'Eggy Mayonnaise' behind her back, a name imaginatively thought up by the school idiots, once they found out the long version of her name.

'I don't care, Lana,' she whined.

'OK, if you need me ...'

'Yeah,' she replied sarcastically, wondering once again why this boy hung around her sister so much. May wasn't into friends and only spoke to Jessica, the new girl with the brown pigtails, because they'd been paired up on Jessica's very first day at the school.

Later, with the school library closed because of a small leak, May reluctantly joined Lana and Clifton by the netball court.

'We don't usually see you at break time!' said Lana.

'I'll just go then.'

'No! So how was your morning?'

'Like any other day,' she replied, looking towards the ground where a sweet wrapper moved in time with the wind. May resented Clifton's presence. Perhaps this was because she wasn't used to interacting with boys, Stan being the only man she regularly had to endure. Or perhaps, she simply found Clifton strange and almost lapdog-like in his obvious worship of her sister. Pathetic, just like Stan, but in a different way.

'Like any other morning ...' she reiterated absently, yearning to follow the sweet wrapper as it flew off into the ether. Her mind was already out of school and back at John Adams. Her fortress. Her home.

Once back through the iron gates of John Adams, May headed to the one place she had ever felt true peace.

'Hello, there, I've been expecting you! It's arrived,' said the familiar voice. As usual, May released a lungful of air and instantly felt her body relax.

At one time her bedroom had been the place where she could shut out the world and simply enter into a new one through the pages of a book. But when Tina left, Lana began to invade that space, using it to sob like a baby and constantly ask questions – 'Why did they take Tina? Please tell me, May!' – she could not begin to answer.

Her old haven had become Lana's crying pit and May had needed somewhere she would not be reminded of everything she'd lost. She needed somewhere she could lose herself; a place that did not remind her of Tina. Even the grassy area around the back of the building was now tainted with the memory of what had been a really fun last day. A stark reminder of what she would never have again and would much rather forget about. So, when she stumbled upon a door marked 'Library', May assumed it a mistake. No one had mentioned Sir John Adams Children's Home having a library! Or, perhaps this detail had swept across their lips during the rushed 'introduction' she hadn't bothered to pay attention to, safely wrapped in the belief they would only be staying the weekend.

As she stepped inside, a dull light reflected upon shelves of books slightly obscured by an empty trolley. She could only gasp in awe at the breathtaking sight before her: glorious books, laid out in alphabetical order. Fifty or sixty, more than she had ever seen in one room. Hardbacks, paperbacks, magazines and even a newspaper.

A miniature counter held a small typewriter and a collection of pens. And even though the room was windowless like the corridors, a musky smell permeating the air, to May it was the most wondrous sight.

She had stumbled onto something magical.

'Hello?' she'd called.

'Oh, hello?' A head had appeared from behind a door she hadn't noticed.

'Can I help you?'

'I'm looking for some books.'

'You're in the right place,' the woman had replied, walking around the counter, patting down her skirt and smiling warmly.

'As you can see, we don't have much, which works as we hardly get many of the children in here. I don't think they even know I'm here most of the time ...'

'I see ...' May had said, her eyes wide. Books were her refuge, her joy, and so many were here just waiting to be read and devoured.

She'd accidentally found a seemingly lost treasure just off of one of the dark soulless corridors of John Adams. This was shaping to be an amazing day, she'd thought.

'When the weather's nice, the kids prefer to play outside, rather than come in here for a good book. They see it as another extension of school.'

'I've always loved books.'

'That's so refreshing to hear! I can tell by the way you speak and your enthusiasm that you read a lot.'

'Really?' May wasn't used to compliments but had been pleased with this particular one; further proof that she sounded nothing like the little girl who left Nigeria many years ago. 'What books do you have?'

'Only a small selection as you can see.'

May followed behind her.

'What are your interests?'

'The books I've read over and over again are fairy stories.'

'So you like fairy stories then?'

'No, I didn't have a choice. They were all I had left from home. Fairy stories are for kids.'

The woman smiled. 'I like them.'

'I don't believe in fairy stories anymore.'

'OK, what about Roald Dahl? He is fantastic.'

'He's for kids.'

'Lewis Carroll?'

'Again, for kids.'

'When you get older, perhaps you will see them differently.'

'I doubt it.'

'I'm Mrs Branbury, by the way.'

'Hello, Mrs Branbury,' she'd replied dryly, desperate to get to the books. Being Mrs Branbury's only customer could possibly mean a relentless barrage of questions and attempts at conversation. May had hoped her standoffish responses would register because she hadn't come for chitchat. She'd just wanted the books.

'Okey dokey, now let's see what we have here for you.'

Sat between two shelves and a trolley, May had comfortably flicked through the pages of each book, deciding that, if the first two pages didn't grab her attention, she'd merely move onto the next.

'When you find the book you want, you won't be able to stay there, May. You will have to take the book back to your room.'

'It's not as if there's anyone in here,' she'd protested.

Mrs Branbury's left cheek had twitched slightly. 'OK, then. Just this once.'

From that moment on, May had become a frequent visitor to the tiny library, if only to remove herself from the clutches of doom that was Lana. Mrs Branbury ordered in regular copies of *Bunty*, which May also devoured, even though Mrs Branbury quietly insisted they were 'too old' for her.

Within a month, May had read all the 'half-decent books' at John Adams library, so by the time she started at the secondary modern school Lana was already at she was more than ready for the fully stocked school library that eclipsed John Adams. Who needed friends when you could spend all your break times in the sanctuary of a library, immersed in the company of hundreds of books?

Back in her room, May peered excitedly into the first page of the new book, *A Wrinkle in Time*, that Mrs Branbury had ordered when the door creaked open.

'Hello, Miss Cole,' sang Stan. She'd had to get used to Stan walking into her room unannounced. May had long ago decided to choose her battles wisely and not protest any little game the Ginger-Haired Man would inflict on her on any given day.

'I said, Hello,' he reiterated.

She placed her book to one side. Her back was up against the wall as she stared towards him. She would do this until he got the message: stare him out. It was a game she had long since tired of, but would continue to play until he left.

'You really think you're something don't you?' he began. She didn't fail to notice the menace in his voice but her eyes simply remained strong in their resolve.

'Do I?' she said confidently. The Ginger-Haired Man was clearly in a bad mood today, so she would have to play carefully.

'I bet you do after the results you got in your Eleven-Plus.'

'What about it?' She had taken the written exam some months back but hadn't heard anything else about it – and she'd ended up in the school across the road from her primary school, the same as Lana and every other kid from John Adams.

'Seems you did really well.'

May felt temporarily lifted at this news. She'd found each question quite easy at the time.

'They probably never told you the results because there's no point. Someone like you is never going to one of those fancy grammar schools anyway. No one from a place like this would ever be able to do that!'

This information, although a little confusing to May, did feel like it needed further investigation. For now, she needed Stan out of her room.

Stan parted his ample, crisp lips just as the door tentatively opened.

'May?' said Lana.

'What?' she snapped, unwilling to echo the relief she felt at her sister's presence.

'Me and Clifton thought you might want to hang about with us.' She gazed at Stan with suspicion. 'Are you alright, May?'

Stan reached for the door and Lana deliberately stepped between him and her sister.

'See ya later, girls.'

'He's such a pig,' enthused Lana as soon as Stan left.

'He certainly is that.'

'If he's been stirring up trouble with you again, we will have to report him.'

'Who would believe us? Everyone thinks he's an OK guy. Anyway, I'm fine. He doesn't scare me.'

'Are you sure?' asked Lana, her voice laced with tenderness.

May suddenly felt bathed in a feeling of warmth she hadn't expected. It felt so unfamiliar, she couldn't quite decipher a suitable response. 'I'm sure, Lana. Don't go on about it!'

'We'll stick together you and me, OK? I'm your big sister and I will always look out for you.'

'Yes,' she replied with non-committal shrug. May was old enough to be aware of her sister's misplaced notion that she should step into the shoes of their parents. Although warm memories of their father had long since blurred with time, what she remembered about their mother certainly wasn't all gooey and mushy. Her last memories of her were of being ignored most of the time before she had left them for good.

As for Lana, they were sisters, yes. But a team they would never be, because May stood alone. It was bad enough the staff at John Adams telling her what to do and when to do it, whilst the other sorry messes (including her sister) felt happy to fall into line. She would continue to stand her ground and follow her own rules.

'Mrs Daventry,' she said sternly, as she stood in front of that infamous desk in her office.

'Yes, May.'

'Why didn't anyone tell me I got a good score on my Eleven-Plus?'

The older woman's face turned a crimson red. 'Well ... it ... it wasn't deemed necessary at the time.'

May sat down without being asked. 'Why? If I got a good grade, maybe I would have got into a better school than the one I'm in. I read somewhere—'

'You are mistaken, May. You attend a perfectly good school and I am sure you are excelling in your subjects like domestic studies and English.'

'Yes—'

'Good, then. Then there is nothing more to discuss. I must say at your age it is rather unusual to be discussing education. Are you not more interested in music? Rock and roll and such?'

'Music does not interest me.'

Mrs Daventry let out an impatient sigh. 'Wait a few more years and you can discuss this with your teachers. I'm sure they will be able to steer you in the right direction.'

May doubted that any of the teachers at the school would be steering her anywhere but out of the door. They were all the same and just like most people in her life – unreliable.

Chapter Eleven

May soon forgot about the whole Eleven-Plus saga having decided she would find a way to achieve a goal that had been planted into her mind a long time ago. She wasn't sure where this need to attend university had actually come from but suspected it may have come from her father. But that was a lifetime ago and now there didn't seem to be an ounce of encouragement, not even at school. Indeed she was being steered towards a 'good trade', like being a secretary, especially if she was unlucky enough not to find a husband, something which was very possible due to the short supply of coloured men in the area, according to one of her teachers.

May continued to be a loner and she knew most of the other kids – and teachers too – considered her slightly weird, but people's perceptions of her was of no concern. She continued to find her happiness and solace in the secure pages of a book. She was secretly educating herself on all matters of the world when those around her appeared too lazy or disinterested to bother.

She'd recently heard a few classmates whispering about a book, which had been banned from the school library. One of the girls had obtained a copy from her older sister and had been passing the book around all morning. As their English teacher

113

attempted to pass on her knowledge of verbs and nouns her class had never appeared more disinterested as many of the girls failed to hide their giggles.

'This book is so amazing,' whispered a girl sat behind May.

'I can't believe we finally got our hands on it!'

'Wasn't there a trial about it a few years ago? Is it THAT bad?' said another girl.

For the first time in her life, May wished she'd made some friends. Even Jessica had now given up on a friendship. She never wore pigtails anymore, her hair swept into an untidy ponytail, and never really spoke much to anyone. Just like May.

At the back of the classroom, endless titters and giggles followed, with May finding herself in that unfamiliar position of actually wanting to be a part of the commotion.

'Whatever is going on back there, stop it now!' said the bewildered teacher. May whirled around quickly enough to catch a glimpse of the title of the book: *Lady Chatterley's Lover*.

As a treat, residents of Sir John Adams Children's Home were allowed a lie-in on a Saturday, bacon for breakfast and a trip into town. The first Saturday of the month, May headed straight for the bookshop and placed the controversial book by D.H. Lawrence onto the counter. She's made an effort in the last few weeks to casually befriend the horrid girls, just to get a glimpse of a few pages. The words had been tantalising enough for her to want to embark on one of her most costly purchases, placing two months' pocket money onto the bookshop counter with confidence.

'How old are you?' asked the bald-headed shopkeeper.

'I'm twenty-one,' she lied. At thirteen she was taller than most of her year with a sophistication in her voice she knew surpassed any of the unruly kids at the home. She could just pass for older. She hoped.

'You from John Adams?'

'Of course not!'

'I can look out of the window in, say, thirty minutes and see that big white van pull up and ...'

'OK, OK, I am. But I'm old enough to read this.'

'Being from that place you're probably not. And I don't like the thought of you using government money to buy such books.'

'It's my money.'

'The home gave it to you didn't they? So it's government money. Our money.'

'Are you going to sell it to me or not?'

The bookseller sighed. 'You know what? It's not a banned book anymore so I'll let you have it.' He slipped the precious book into a brown paper bag. 'But don't tell anyone you bought it here.'

May should have been insulted, but kept quiet, recalling the need to choose her battles wisely. She forced herself to smile and asked for the other book she'd been saving up to buy.

May chose to stay in her room during the next trip into town, which was an easy decision. The meagre pocket money she'd been putting aside in her bottom drawer for weeks had dwindled rapidly with the purchase of her new books. But no libraries stocked the type of books she now wanted to read. Books with adult themes. She couldn't afford to buy many, though, as she needed as much money as possible to fund her life outside of John Adams. Having decided she would stay on in education to fulfil her ambition of attending a university, she still had five years to go. Her sister Lana was set to leave in three years if she too stayed on in education or learned a trade. For May it would have been tempting to just leave school and John Adams at the age of fifteen, but education was important. And she would attend university.

A few chapters into her new book, the knock at the door startled her.

'Guess who?' said the voice.

When the door opened, she wasn't surprised to see Stan glaring at her.

'I thought you'd be in town,' she said with disdain. She sat up and placed the book to one side.

'Not yet. The van's waiting outside. I came to see why you weren't on it.'

'Mrs Daventry already knows why.'

'I ain't Mrs Daventry, am I?'

Stan moved closer to the bed and May shifted up, her back firmly against the wall.

'Don't be scared. I just wanted to see you were OK. I'm nice like that. Ask anyone.'

'Thank … you,' she said submissively, simultaneously hating herself for this switch in demeanour.

'You are a pretty little thing.' His sausage-like finger brushed against the side of her forehead. 'You know, for a wog.'

And there was that word again. A word she'd heard for the first time as Stan drove them away after her mother's funeral. Instinctively she knew it was a similar kind of word to the one mentioned in *To Kill a Mockingbird* – nigger – and she often wondered why he just didn't say that.

'Yes, growing up very nicely,' he said in a way that made her skin feel cold. She knew what was on his mind; she'd seen the look in the faces of men in town. Even the beady eyes of the bald-headed fool in the bookshop seemed to rest on her chest when he spoke to her. She'd noticed the changes in her body too; the way her hips now were rounding out and this new monthly menstruation quickly explained away in class as 'women's troubles'. Lana had once tried to explain it all to her, but she'd quickly dismissed her attempts as too embarrassing. Besides she'd found out all she needed to know from books in the library.

Her skin twitched.

'You little wog,' he hissed.

'I did hear you the first time,' she said, nonchalantly. She hoped that one day his words would no longer be able to sting her.

'Good. As long as we're clear on what you are, we shouldn't have any problems. You sort get too many big ideas. Really glad old Enoch Powell put you all in your place. He's going to help make England great again!'

Choose your battles, May.

'Sometimes I think you forget who you really are, what with all those fancy books you read.'

Choose your battles.

Without a further reaction from May, he finally turned to the door. 'I'd better get back to the little bastards before they start acting up. But I'll most certainly be seeing you later.'

He left and May exhaled slowly, angry at her own reaction to him. It took a while for the fear to leave her body even after Stan had left the room. Her heart rate had accelerated to a point she could almost hear each heartbeat and tears seemed desperate to make an appearance, despite her silent protest. She bent over the bed, hands rummaging crazily amongst various boxes and bags until she felt it. The one item with the power to ease all the bad feelings away: a medium-sized toy made of cloth. And as she held the cuddly toy close to her chest and fell back onto the pillow, she felt the warmth of her father, Aunty Ginny and the memory of a time when all she wanted to do was dance or be covered in kisses. The cloth of the toy wiped away her tears. Lana had presumed that it had been found and sent on to Tina. And May would never confess to having it because she would just take over like she always did. Like she had with Tina.

What comforted May the most, was the smell of her beloved little sister that still lingered on the surface of the ugly multi-coloured elephant, the Puffalump.

May decided that the weakness she had shown to Stan would never be repeated.

She was taller than all her classmates now, and 'big and black', as she'd once overheard herself described by one of her classmates. May felt it only fair to give them what they wanted, so she kept herself to herself and if anyone asked so much as a stupid question, they would feel her anger. She may have been powerless at John Adams, but at school she would call the shots when it came to her life.

It was of no surprise when she heard on the school grapevine that a girl by the name of Nicola Rhodes wanted to fight her. Nicola was 'big and black' like her but her skin was slightly lighter. She always wore her hair swept into a neat bun that May secretly envied.

'So Eggy Mayonnaise, you're from that place for loonies,' said Nicola just as May bent to tie up her shoelaces, an act temporarily placing her in a very vulnerable position.

'Is that a question or a statement?'

'You're a loony! So, not a question, just fact!'

'Takes one to know one, right, Nick?' she replied brazenly, her eyes now slits of growing rage.

'What did you just say?'

'You heard.'

'Think you can talk to me like that with your dry, picky hair all over the place? I should really slap some style into you!'

'You don't scare me.' She stood to her full height, and if Nicola was scared, she wasn't showing it.

'Good,' said Nicola.

The sense of a fight brewing appeared to attract an uninvited audience of acne-faced kids whispering and cackling their delight.

'You're a stupid cow! Get away from me!' said May, knowing full well this was the last thing Nicola would do.

'You little bastard! No mother and no father!'

The moment those hateful words left Nicola's lips, May could no longer see her, but instead she saw a smirking ginger-haired man who'd taunted her for three whole years. Rage eclipsed any common sense or promises to choose battles. This was it. Now was the time! The crowd grew as she was blinded with adrenalin. What followed was a quick, unthinking response as her right hand formed into a fist and connected beautifully with Nicola's cheek. The assembled mob clapped and voiced their appreciation and encouragement as the two girls fell on the floor and traded jabs. By the time it was over, a clump of May's hair, along with Nicola's shoelace, lay entangled on the playground floor.

The promise of a week-long detention and letter home was met with a shrug of May's shoulders but Nicola broke down in tears at the news, a move that, for a split second, allowed May to feel envious of more than her neat hairdo. A letter 'home' for May meant just another piece of paper placed with all other bits of administration in Mrs Daventry's office, none of which meant anything to anyone. If she so wished, May could embark on a shoplifting spree, stand in the middle of the town square and scream every obscenity she had ever learned over the years, and, still, no one would care. Her punishment would be swift and then she'd move on. No mother to reprimand her, no father to chastise her. Who really gave a damn about her anymore? Lana seemed to have given up on her. And where was Aunty Ginny when Stan slipped into her room to taunt her? Aunty Ginny was with her real children snuggled up in Notting Hill without a care in the world, believing the odd letter made up for what she had done the day of her mother's funeral.

The fight with Nicola had showed her peers that she was 'tough' with an ability to handle anything they threw at her. This new, uncovered sense of self further fuelled May, allowing a rare sense of hope for the future. She now dreamed of taking over the world and never being held back.

At school they were learning about the suffragettes, but she'd no desire for any of that. She preferred the stories of the many men she read about in her books, or even the men who wrote the books. She wanted a life like them: of freedom and power; to live in a world where she could be whoever she wanted to be and never be held down like her mother had been.

One day, she, May Cole, would become bigger and better than anyone could ever have expected. Not that that was difficult as no one actually expected anything from her. The stigma of a childhood spent in a home generally erased any expectations from teachers that she would ever do well, as did the colour of her skin. She'd clocked their worn expressions as they pretended to teach, convinced their ending to her story was the only one.

But her story hadn't even been written yet.

May Cole was going to be someone.

'Aren't you on cleaning duty tonight?' asked Stan, as usual, strolling into her room minus the invite.

'I thought it was Lana's turn,' she said, without looking up.

'Look at me when I speak to you!' he said, snatching the book from her as it shut. This act allowed May's anger to simmer just below the surface, ready to boil over at any moment, regardless of the consequences.

She obeyed slowly and mockingly. 'My sister is scheduled in today. It's my turn tomorrow. Now, if you don't mind, I have things to do.' May took the book back from him without asking for permission and attempted to locate the previous paragraph, fully aware this would provoke an angry response from Stan.

'You think you're so smart, don't you?'

'No, I don't.' I know, she thought.

'It's a waste of time someone like you trying to be all academic. None of you kids will amount to anything much, so what's the point?'

May located her paragraph, continuing the pretence, experience informing her that Stan would soon tire of his tirade and leave.

'Murderers, thieves and drug users, just like your parents. There's nothing waiting for you kids outside of here.' He waited for a response. May remained silent.

'Did you hear what I just said?' he pushed.

'Yes,' she replied with deliberate nonchalance. Stan was not going to win this.

'You and the rest of the pieces of shit in here will never amount to anything. You should do us all a favour and top yourself, like your mother.'

May began to play a Chuck Berry song in her head, knowing full well that Stan, in his frustration, was trying to rile her. 'So what's the point of all this, then?' he continued, his words quickening with frustration. 'All these books, reading?'

'I like to read.'

'Why?'

'I just do.'

'What's the point?'

'It's something I like to do. Now if you don't mind—' Before she could finish, Stan grabbed the book back from her weakened grip, her response too slow to prevent the ugly sound of a page being ripped away from the bind. And then page after page after page snatched from its home and desecrated. Precious words flying to the ground like feathers in the wind. When the violence finally ended, she was unable to speak. Stan's forehead glistening with sweat and triumph, himself spent as if he'd used up every ounce of energy to violate her sanctuary: her one light in a world filled mostly with darkness.

He beamed a corner smile and left the room quietly.

She stared at the torn pieces of her book. Stan was not going to win this.

He would never win.

After the book incident, Stan's torment became confined to the odd stare, with no more unannounced trips to her room. She wondered if he sensed that he had gone too far but she feared he was just biding his time. When she spotted Stan with Jessica in the hallway, his hand gripping her shoulder, May couldn't help feeling relieved that he'd found someone else to torment.

At school, rumours flew around about a possible rematch with Nicola Rhodes. The last few months serving as a way to build up a momentum of frenzy amongst Nicola's cronies.

The last day of term seemed like the perfect opportunity for most fights at school. Symbolic or just shrewd, considering teachers were less likely to be bothered just a day before the summer holidays. As predicted, May felt a firm tap on her shoulder just as she was about to step through the main doors.

'Meet Nick by the shed in five minutes, or else,' said a blonde nightmare of a girl with a further shove.

'May, come on, the bus is waiting!' shouted Lana in that annoying little shrill voice of hers. As usual, the bus stood a few yards from the school gate. Missing it would spark a major security alert, like the time one of the John Adams kids wandered off on the Saturday trip and three police cars searched the local town for over an hour.

May approached the bus and weighed up her options. She could answer Nicola's war cry, get the fight over with and perhaps face a clean slate next term. Or she could get on the bus and return next term to the increased wrath of Nicola and her gang, along with the more humiliating title of 'chicken', all the recent bravado washed away as if it had never happened.

Pick your battles, May thought, as she got on the minibus, already ignoring the future jeers of the other students.

Chapter Twelve

Few events ever brought brightly coloured ripples of excitement into the gloom of Sir John Adams Children's Home. The occasions when a kid got to go back home or was found a new family were incredibly rare.

Usually the brightest part of a kid's stay was when they were legally allowed to escape the care system and venture out into the world on their own. But other spots of sunshine came in those moments when a letter or a package was handed out to those lucky enough to have been remembered.

Lana and May had been at John Adams for four years now and had only received a handful of letters from Aunty Ginny. Sadly, during the last year Aunty Ginny had not sent anything. The disappointment was, at first, crushing for Lana, as each week residents were handed letters and a scattering of parcels. She still hoped one day to hear something from Aunty Ginny or even the couple who'd taken Tina. Or maybe even a childishly scrawled attempt from Tina herself. Had she forgotten them already? But, as more and more months passed, so did any real expectations. Then, one week, after Clifton was handed a jasmine-scented letter from his mother – the first in many months – Mrs Daventry called out her name.

'There's something here for you,' she said with a look of surprise.

'I can't believe it!' cried Lana, unable to care if she sounded rather pathetic.

The smoothness of the envelope felt exquisite between her fingers, this perfect rectangle. Sighing deeply, she held the letter to her chest.

'Hurry up and open it, then!' encouraged Clifton as if it could disintegrate. As much as he was her best friend and perhaps understood her more than anyone else, Clifton Joseph, with his somewhat irregular letters from a mother who at least was still alive, could never understand the magnitude of what she felt. Or the huge excitement threatening to engulf her entire body. Or the mass of expectation already heaped upon this letter.

'Can I meet you in the canteen later? I just want to read it with May, by ourselves.'

'OK.' If Clifton was hurt, he did not show it. Lana raced to her room where May predictably lay on the bed consumed with a book.

'May, May!'

'I'm reading!'

'We got a letter!'

Lana moved over to her sister's bed and placed the letter within the space between them.

'From who?' asked May, as she turned her attention to the envelope.

'It looks like Aunty Ginny's writing,' said Lana.

'I'm surprised you remember what her handwriting looks like. We haven't heard from her in ages.'

Lana's resolve remained steadfast. She wasn't going to allow May to spoil this moment. 'Maybe she's found Tina and wants us all to live with her again!' Lana enthused, knowing how unlikely it sounded but unable to stop herself.

'She doesn't even know Tina's gone!'

'She might know now!'

'Just open it.'

Lana carefully slid her finger inside the tiny opening of the envelope, pushed upwards and pulled out a single piece of paper.

Dearest girls,

How are you? I am so sorry it's been such a long time since I have been in touch with you all.

I think of you all constantly. My three girls: Lana, May and Tina. You must all be getting big now. Does Tina still have those lovely curls?

Everything is fine here. My boys are growing up fast and my eldest is doing really well in the army now. I'm hoping it will knock some sense into the big oaf!

I want you to know that I have never forgotten you. I think about you all every day. I hope I will see you all, one day soon.

I love you all.

Yours,

Aunty Ginny

Lana placed the letter onto the side table, beside the lamp.

'Oh well. Just as I thought, a pile of rubbish,' said May.

Deep down she knew her sister was right. Not one mention of coming to take them away or even visiting, yet, worst of all, Aunty Ginny clearly still had no idea about Tina's adoption years earlier! Any daydream ever conjured up in her mind had now been forced into the darkness along with any hope of ever seeing her little sister again. She now wished Aunty Ginny had never sent the letter. At least then a seed of hope would have remained, however minute.

'I thought she would have said a bit more,' said Lana.

'I didn't. I'm surprised she even bothered to write.'

At that moment Lana Cole craved some form of affection from her sister; anything to acknowledge a shared sadness. But, as always, May was already lost within the pages of a book, her mind far away from the pain Lana was feeling.

A cloud descended above her as Lana went in search of her only true friend in the whole wide world. She headed to Grassy Green around the back of the building, where she often met Clifton for a chat or to just 'hang around'. As they had both just left school last year at fifteen, their time together was limited as he was now training to be a mechanic and Lana was learning typing at college.

'I was wondering where you were,' said Clifton in that gruff, textured voice she was now getting used to. He'd also grown many inches taller and now kept his hair in a neat cut. He was also beginning to get noticed by some of the girls at John Adams.

'Oh, Clifton,' she said shakily.

'What's the matter?' He moved closer to her, wiping away the single tear moving down her cheek. She felt the warmth of his hands on her back, the pressure pulling her closer towards him. Her head fell into the crook of his neck, his words soothing her soul.

'Lana, don't worry. Everything's going to be alright, OK?'

'No, it isn't,' she said.

Clifton cupped his hands on each of her cheeks, gazing straight into her eyes and those extra-long eyelashes. 'It will be, I promise.'

She was about to ask, 'How can you promise that?' yet her mind went immediately blank as she felt the pressure of his lips suddenly press against hers.

'Clifton!' she said quickly, springing back as if electrocuted.

'I'm sorry, Lana!' His eyebrows widened, hand covering his mouth. 'I'm really sorry, I just wanted you to feel better!'

Clifton needed to be told clearly and strongly that what he had done was wrong and should never be repeated. And she would have, too – if the tiny ruffles of excitement poking about in her belly would just leave; and if the thought of kissing him again hadn't sent waves of heady pleasure coursing through every cell of her body.

That very night, instead of being consumed with the disappointment of Aunty Ginny's letter, thoughts of Clifton's kiss wouldn't leave her mind. She'd nothing to compare it to, thereby concluded it had been good. Very good. The pressure had been a little hard, but his lips soft and firm all at once, just before she'd pulled away. She wondered how long Clifton had been thinking about kissing her or if it had been spur of the moment, only happening because he'd felt sorry for her. Would their friendship survive this? Were they now boyfriend and girlfriend? She'd known Clifton for four years and had always viewed him as her – at times annoying – brother and, at best, a true friend. Yet, she'd noticed the way other girls would stop conversations mid-sentence as he confidently walked by with his long legs and sweet smile, their eyes moving over every inch of his lean body.

They'd once been play-fighting and she'd felt his 'thing' harden against her knee. The play-fighting never happened again.

But a kiss between friends changed everything.

Their usual meetings on Grassy Green soon turned into secret rendezvous where they would stare at one another and lock mouths endlessly. They held hands under the canteen table and stole private moments together whenever they could. Now, Saturday trips into town, once spent loitering around shops they couldn't afford, became time spent at a bus stop kissing, talking and kissing some more. Lana and Clifton began to discuss a future together, far away from John Adams, where they would share a quaint little flat by the sea. Clifton would be part of a mildly successful band whilst Lana would bake all day.

Even Tina's birthday, generally a difficult twenty-four hours for Lana, felt somewhat easier with Clifton literally holding her hand for the majority of the day.

Both were adamant nobody should uncover their secret; these feelings, these sensations were so precious and all that mattered to Lana. She'd never felt so loved or so complete in all her life. This was it for her. She didn't need or want anything else – not even parents. She had a boyfriend now, one who promised to never, ever leave her.

Lana looked forward to spending weekends with Clifton, having planned matinee trips to the cinema, walks in the park and lots and lots of kissing.

But then she began to notice a firm shift in his behaviour. He started missing a lot of their daily meetings on Grassy Green because of this sudden need for almost non-stop football practice. The change was stark, with Lana determined to uncover the truth, if only she could get to spend more than five minutes with him!

'Can I talk to you please?' asked Clifton, running towards her as she headed to her room after dinner. 'Grassy Green, tonight, after lights out?'

She should have been short with him, yet was unable to hide the flurry of excitement at the thought of being alone with him again.

The evening air felt brisk and she considered returning for her cardigan.

'Lana,' said Clifton in almost darkness, a single ray from the home illuminating his smile.

'Clifton?'

'First off, I just want to say, I'm really sorry about the way I've been with you. Really, I am.'

'It's OK.' She quickly remembered the friend he'd once been: holding her in a headlock in the common room; giving her his last piece of chewing gum. She longed for those times again and if he wanted to break up with her, of course she would cope, as long as they remained friends.

Friends who kissed from time to time.

'Well?' she said expectantly.

Clifton stared at his shoes. 'I like you, Lana.'

'I like you too.'

A few spots were camped out around his chin, above that, tiny tufts of hair growing in an arch above his lips. He was irresistible.

'No ... No, what I mean is ... I ... I ...' he stuttered.

'What? We know we like each other, Clifton! We've been going together for months.'

'I know, and being with you is the best.'

She wanted to sing out with happiness. He'd clearly been too embarrassed to express his feelings all this time!

She brushed her hand against his, and felt an immediate stab of hurt as he pulled away.

'I have something to tell you, Lana.' He spoke with just a hint of finality as his eyes searched her face. 'My mum wants me home.'

She faked a smile. 'That's great.'

'She's not drinking anymore, and, well, she's ready ... ready to be responsible again, I suppose ... don't you think?' Clifton searched her eyes for an ounce of reassurance.

'Sure, yes, I think so. I'm really happy for you. But what about your training at the garage? That's why you stayed on here, isn't it?'

'I stayed on here because of you.'

She swallowed. She wanted to be happy for her best friend but inside she felt a mixture of emotions all bubbled together to make an inedible soup of envy and abandonment.

'Are you going to go, then?' She knew the answer; it lingered in the air, hovering above them like a dark cloud.

'Yes, Lana. I have to go.'

'Of course,' she said, biting her bottom lip.

'If it works out ... you know, I'll be staying there ... with her ... for good.' He squeezed her hand softly whilst confirming her worst fears. She attempted to turn away, blinking back a treacherous tear, her shoulders starting to heave.

'I won't be able to visit for a while because I don't see Mum bringing me out here. But I'll write. We'll keep in touch for sure.'

'No, you won't!'

'Don't, Lana.'

'You're leaving me. You said you'd never leave.' Lana spoke with an odd mixture of disbelief, envy and resolution.

'Lana, I love you,' he said for the very first time. By now, Lana had only ever known the word love to be synonymous with being abandoned. Why had she been stupid enough to think Clifton would be any different? Her hands balled into fists as she swiped at her slippery tears. They'd shared their dreams and loved each other with an innocent passion not known by either before. Where would she go from here?

'I love you too,' she replied finally. 'But that doesn't really matter, does it? It never does.'

Weeks later they embraced once again as the white minibus waited for its lone passenger. Clifton Joseph looking so much older than his sixteen years and dressed in his best trousers and red shirt.

'I love you, Lana Cole,' he said, as Stan sounded an impatient horn. The residents of John Adams had said their farewells the night before at a leaving party decorated with balloons, streamers and looks of envy among those to be left behind: this child was leaving because a parent wanted him.

'I'll write every day,' he said.

'Every week should be fine,' she said untruthfully. They embraced again and this time she did not want to release him.

The bus sounded another impatient horn. 'Come on. I'm only giving you a lift as a favour!' said Stan.

'Got to go.'

'Yes, of course.'

'Your mum will be waiting,' said Mrs Daventry creeping up from behind. Hand in hand Lana and Clifton walked to the mini-bus and stole one last taste of each other's lips.

'Love you,' they said in unison.

And then he was gone. Another person she had loved and lost, probably forever.

Chapter Thirteen

Since returning to school after the holidays and finally winning the Nicola Rhodes rematch, May's reputation preceded her, with 'Eggy Mayonnaise' banished to the realms of history.

May was now able to command a certain level of respect among her peers, with multiple offers to join various cliques – all of which she refused. As a result, any real friendships still failed to materialise, but what with another spurt in height and the aloofness to match, her reputation was secured.

Far better to be feared than pitied.

The stray cat she'd discovered roaming the grounds one evening after dinner was the only kind of friend she wanted. At first she'd ignored his incessant meows. But by the second night his appearance had forced her to turn back into the dining room where she scooped leftovers from a random plate into a handkerchief.

The animal lapped up the food gratefully and, unbeknown to her at that moment, he would expect the same treatment each and every night.

'Why do you keep stealing food?' asked Lana.

'Keep your voice down, it's just some manky black and white cat.'

'You have a cat? Where? How?'

'He hangs around out back after dinner. I don't know where he's from.' She resented having to include Lana in her secret, and felt a stab of jealousy as the cat purred in and around the space between her sister's feet.

'He's lovely!' cooed Lana as she brushed her hand across his dark coat.

'He's OK. A bloody nuisance if you ask me!'

'Do you think he belongs to someone?'

'Why do you keep asking me stupid questions? I don't know!'

Feeding the cat every night became a routine. May and Lana's little secret. She was OK about sharing him as it had finally given Lana something to smile about since Clifton had left. She had wondered if Lana would now leave John Adams early because of Clifton's departure, and was surprised when Lana grabbed her shoulders and said, 'I stayed on in this revolting place because I wanted to learn a good trade but mainly because of *you*, May. When will you understand that you're the most important person in my life? I have to look after you and I can't do that from the outside!'

This had made her smile inside, yet outside she had merely shrugged her shoulders.

'This year is most important for May,' said Mrs Lincoln, one of the better teachers at her school, as yet another social worker feigned interest at yet another façade of a parents' evening.

'These are really good results,' she said, stifling a yawn.

'May has been an excellent student with perfect grades, even though we were initially concerned with her lack of social skills and her behaviour.'

'That's right … yes, so what are the predicted results then?' The social worker glanced sneakily at her watch, perhaps under the impression no one had noticed.

'We expect these very high marks from May to continue. As you know, she has continuously scored highly in her tests. All As.

'Oh, right …' she replied clumsily. May knew the woman hadn't read anything about her; they rarely did. The last social worker had at least pretended to care.

May scanned the large gymnasium area. Once the setting for the regular humiliation of PE, it was now unrecognisable as children, parents and teachers intermingled, and a plethora of loud voices produced one large incoherent echo. Instinctively, her eyes shifted to the door where a boy from another class stood aimlessly, holding the hand of a tiny little girl with curly pigtails and a huge smile.

The social worker scanned the document. 'Well done, Martha … I mean May …'

May allowed the slip to wash over her, smiling falsely as she led the idiot to the next table. Where they would be told much as before, adding: 'May is top of the class in her subject and has shown a willingness to listen and learn. If this carries on, I see no reason why she won't do well in life.'

'Shame she can't go to Oxford!' said the social worker, followed by an unwarranted fit of laughter.

'Well, if her start in life had been different, who knows what she could have achieved.'

The social worker then pretended to be overly interested when the teacher added a line about her 'aloofness in class' and appearing to be moody all the time.

'She was born in Africa, is that right?' asked the social worker. A fact she perhaps should have read in May's files beforehand, May thought.

'Yes, Nigeria.'

'D'you think that has something to do with why she's like this?'

'I'm not sure what you mean, Miss—'

'They're not very civilised there, are they? You know, in the colonies?'

Both the teacher and May stared back at the social worker blankly, before May added, 'Nigeria is actually independent from the United Kingdom now.'

'Oops, silly me! That's why I didn't get into Oxford!'

Thankfully, the social worker refrained from opening her mouth any further.

As the adults continued to talk about her like she was not even present, May's gaze wandered back to the little girl with the pigtails. She looked just like Tina, the little sister she hardly thought about anymore, or rather how she imagined Tina might look now. Same smile and those chubby little legs she once loved to squeeze playfully. A man had joined the family and was all smiles as he blew loud raspberries onto her cheeks.

May closed her eyes and slowly pushed any further thoughts of Tina from her head, just as she heard her name.

'May? Are you listening? Mrs Wright here was just saying what a good pupil you are.'

'Right … yes … thanks.' May needed to be in the present. The now. Her grades were good and by next year they would be even better and enough to lead her straight into the path of a better life. Despite what she was told, she would end up at university – not Oxford, perhaps, but somewhere in London. And she would then go on to earn the level of status she deserved. The only thoughts pushing her out of bed each morning were those of a future away from John Adams. Indeed, this was all she and Lana now spoke about.

'I'm leaving in two years and will set up a really nice flat for us and then you will have somewhere to come to,' said Lana.

'That sounds like a good plan.'

'I'll have got a job and will some hopefully have made some friends and all you will have to do is slot yourself in. I can support us both while you carry on with your studies. So in the meantime, keep your head down at John Adams, stay out of Stan's way, and you'll be out of here less than two years after me.'

'That sounds so long. Two years without you here!'

'Miss me, will you?'

'I didn't mean that. I just meant …'

'OK ... let's call it a year and a bit. Sound better? You will get out of here a year and a bit after me.'

'A year and a bit.'

The idiot social worker dropped May off at John Adams just in time for dinner. Stan was waiting in the dining hall.

'How was parents' evening? Oops, sorry, you don't have any parents, do you?'

Stan was whispering tightly in her ear as she moved the food around on her plate. Most of the children had finished and the majority of the tables were empty. 'You do have a white aunty though, but oops, she didn't want you either! Isn't that right?'

After a brief hiatus, Stan's words of torment had only recently started up again. But what with her brilliant grades and Lana's support she now had a clear and realistic plan for her future and no longer needed to fantasise about battering Stan over the head with a chair leg. His words held no power, no meaning. Her mind occupied with a rosy future that would be hers in just a matter of time.

Patience.

That night as usual, the black cat was waiting for her with that annoying meow.

She unravelled the handkerchief, the cat moving hungrily as the bits of food fell to the floor. She sat on the ground and waited for the cat to finish.

'Satisfied?' she said. Its pink tongue moved over its mouth. She knew the cat didn't really care about her. As long as she provided the food, he would come. And that was OK with May. More than OK because at least she knew where she stood with the cat.

May hoped that at sixteen, her growth spurt had halted at five feet eleven. Yet she began to notice further changes. Her skin had now settled into an even, dark-brown complexion, an ample head of strong, textured, coily hair now tameable thanks to some hair oil Lana had managed to buy from a girl at John Adams who had an aunty who lived in Brixton (apparently that was the place to find such things). May enjoyed the looks she received when she wore her hair in a large afro bound together by a multicoloured hairband. Her body was long and she was tiny-waisted with broad shoulders that fiercely contradicted her tender years. A set of hardened eyes only added to the illusion of maturity.

Apparently, May was beautiful. Not in the way reflected back from the magazines her sister read, or what they saw on the television, but she assumed it must be true to some extent because Mrs Branbury often said so and every male student at the sixth-form college seemed to constantly gawp at her – especially when she turned up with a full afro, flared denim slacks and a T-shirt displaying just a hint of belly button. The same old men in the street who gawped at her with lust were probably the same ones who also thought of her as a wog or a coon and had agreed with the 'Rivers of Blood' speech she'd read with a disgusted Mrs Branbury one afternoon the year before. To receive both lust and hate from one person felt very confusing, and just another reason why she found it hard to think of herself as actually beautiful.

Luckily no boys had attempted to ask her out. She just couldn't understand the fascination her classmates had with boys. They were such a useless distraction. Even Lana's flirtation with Clifton had caused nothing but heartache. She'd been closely aware of their little relationship, even though they'd attempted to keep it all a secret. May had kept quiet, knowing it would soon end, which it had.

Time quickly funnelled through to the month of Lana's eighteenth birthday, when May began to count down each and every day.

'Anyone would think it was your release date!' said Lana. The suitcase lay open on the floor, various items of clothing sprawled out on the bed.

'You going means I only have a bit of time left here too and I can't wait!' smiled May, feeling truly happy for the first time in ages.

'Do you want this? It will be shorter on you.' Lana held up a burnt-orange embroidered ankle-length dress.

'No, thank you!' replied May as if insulted. 'Are you going to buy all new stuff with the money they give you?'

'No, of course not. It's not that much and I'll need it to help furnish the flat. I have to be sensible. Plus I'll need to find a part-time job whilst I finish my course.'

'You'll find one.'

'I don't know how easy it will be. I've seen the news. Not many people want to give us jobs.'

They both stared at their laps for a moment, united with thoughts of their father and what he had sacrificed to live in England so he could give them a better life. But for all he had done, they'd still ended up at Sir John Adams Children's Home.

'Make sure you paint our new home a good colour,' said May, breaking the spell of gloom with a rare hope.

'Green OK, your ladyship?'

'Why green?'

'Green and white like the Nigerian flag! I hope Tina likes it too ...'

'Tina?'

'Yes, Tina, our sister. Remember her?' replied Lana sarcastically.

'Lana ...'

'I'm going to try and find her. As soon as I get settled. No, before that! I can at least try social services and see what they can tell me!' Lana sounded excitable but there was no way May could find it in herself to feel the same.

'Lana, she's seven years old now. She's with her new family, whoever they are. Why would you want to interfere? She probably doesn't even remember us. Besides, who's going to give you, an eighteen-year-old John Adams kid, any details just because you asked?'

A single tear ran down Lana's face. 'You see, this is why I never speak to you about her.'

'Then don't, because I don't want to hear it.' With an effort May softened her voice. 'Look, just write to me with your address when you're settled so I can look forward to something that can actually happen, OK?'

'OK,' Lana sniffed. Droplets of tears resting on her long set of eyelashes.

The subject was changed.

'I really don't want to leave you here,' said Lana.

'It's only for a little while, don't fuss! Just get yourself sorted with a two-bedroom and I'll be right behind you.'

'Even if I only get a one-bedroom, we'll just make the sitting room a bedroom!'

'That will be my room!'

'No way. It will obviously be bigger so it's mine!'

Laughing with her sister, although unfamiliar, felt pretty good to May, as if streams of sunlight were entering her soul in that dark room. She told herself that waving her off was far from the sad occasion Lana made it out to be. It was actually a good thing because it allowed May's own release to appear more real. She was one step closer to finally leaving John Adams herself and starting on the journey of her own life. She'd never admit to missing her sister, but May knew that with every fibre of her being, she would.

Chapter Fourteen

Standing on the brink of adulthood, Lana had never felt more lost and inadequate.

The excitement of finally being released from Sir John Adams Children's Home, six years after first arriving there, was overshadowed by the overwhelming reality that she would most certainly be alone for the first time in her life. She was about to be let loose into a world riddled with the same dangers that had claimed Mummy, Daddy, Tina, and even Aunty Ginny, who she'd not heard from for months. Lana had written two letters and was now ready to believe that Aunt Ginny just wasn't intersted. May, on the other hand, not the most active participant in her life, had nevertheless remained a constant and comforting backdrop, and thoughts of embarking on a world of flats, bills, jobs and food shopping without her, felt scary.

'I am so jealous right now!' sang May happily that last weekend before she was due to leave. Lana couldn't remember her looking any happier as she lay on her bed looking up at the ceiling – and that hurt.

'Your turn soon,' said Lana.

'I know and I can't wait!'

'Are you going to be OK?' asked Lana, not for the first time.

'You don't have to worry about me. Stan's an idiot. No one messes with me anymore – just look at the size of me!'

'You'll be six feet in no time!'

'Don't say that! Seriously, you go ahead, set up that flat and I will join you soon. OK?'

'OK. And at least you have the cat!'

May smiled. 'That manky thing?'

'You *know* you love him, don't pretend. When you're with him it's one of the only times I see you smile!'

'I smile a lot of times.'

'No, you don't. Even when you're reading a book, you're always concentrating. This cat has been good for you.'

'Whatever you say, Lana. Not everyone is as soppy as you.'

May was trying to be dismissive but her sister wasn't fooled. The cat had done something Lana never could. It had reached her sister in ways she had failed to over the years and that was OK. When May finally joined her in their own little flat in just under two years' time, their relationship would be able to heal without the interference of Stan, and the authorities ... without the iron gates of Sir John Adams Children's Home. Maybe after a few months they could look for Tina together ... if Lana hadn't found her by then.

'May, I've been wanting to talk to you about something for ages and now I'm leaving ...'

'Spit it out,' said May, sitting up.

'Have you ... have you ever wondered who Tina's father was ... is?'

'Nope.'

'Really?'

'Yes, really. Who cares?'

'I do, sometimes. Especially now I'm older.'

'Maybe it's written down in that manky address book Ginny gave you! I don't know!'

'You know I don't like to look at that much ... it hurts me.'

141

'It's just an address book.'

With our mummy's precious handwriting, she wanted to say.

'The only men in the book are Dave, daddy's boss ...'

'Yes, I know who Dave is!' spat May.

'... the insurance guy, landlord. Bills and things.'

'What difference would it have made to us who he was?' May asked. 'Like everyone else, even he disappeared!'

'Don't tell me you haven't wondered who it was.'

'No, never. But if it makes you feel any better, I'll have a think ...' May placed her finger to her chin in an exaggerated thinking pose. 'Hmmm ... it could have been Dave, or the milkman. Anyone. Again, who cares? Whoever it was clearly wasn't a nice man. So, let it drop, Lana. You really know how to put a dampener on things. We're supposed to be celebrating and here you are wanting to dig up the past!'

'I suppose you have a point.'

'Just focus on the fact you're finally getting out of John Adams!'

For once her sister was right. The identity of Tina's father was irrelevant now. All that mattered was leaving John Adams, setting up a home for May and eventually finding their sister.

That night, after dinner, the girls set off to find May's 'secret' friend. Although the cat technically belonged to May, Lana wanted to say her goodbyes and perhaps stupidly whisper in its ear, 'Take care of my little sister.' So they waited for him to appear as usual, this time with two lots of tasteless fish wrapped in a white handkerchief.

An hour later, he still hadn't arrived.

'Let's go back to our room. We don't want to get into trouble,' said Lana.

'This isn't like him,' said May.

'You said yourself that he doesn't always come. Maybe someone else is feeding him too and he's got a better offer.'

'Yes, maybe. OK. We'll check back tomorrow. Bloody cat, we'll have to ditch this fish!'

The next morning as they headed to Saturday games, Stan was in front of them, carrying a blue plastic bag in his hands, and smiling vindictively.

'Want to know what's in the bag?' he asked.

'No,' replied May.

'Aren't you a little bit curious?' he said.

'No, we are not,' said May rudely.

Lana wished she would just toe the line with him at times. It would make life so much smoother.

'We're going to be late for games,' said Lana.

He pushed the plastic bag closer towards them. 'Look inside. It will only take a minute.'

Lana peered into the bag and gasped. There was no mistaking what was inside.

'Your turn,' he said to May. 'Look inside.'

The quick swell of emotion Lana felt surprised her. Inside the bag was the sweet stray cat; they hadn't even named. And yet her tears were for all the people they'd lost and the hope that had died with each of them. Her tears were also for May who had lost a friend just before Lana was about to leave. Who would look out for her now?

'Have you nuthin' to say, then?' asked Stan.

'Yes. Can we go to games now?' said May.

'Want to go and have a good cry like your sister? Or do you want to help get rid of it?'

'No, I'm fine, thanks. Why should I care? It was just a manky cat. Do what you want with it.'

May's hardened demeanour still had the power to shock her. And at that moment, Lana doubted she would ever understand her sister.

The next morning, Lana expertly banished any further thoughts of the cat from her mind to focus on the very important event ahead. Only one more day remained until she could finally leave the gates of Sir John Adams Children's Home for the very last time.

'You look very dapper,' commented Mrs Daventry as Lana stood in front of her desk during the exit interview. Her back straight, shoulders erect, and eluding an aura of confidence she wasn't sure was real, Lana listened as Mrs Daventry repeated instructions already given to her by the social worker. When she added what a pleasure it had been to have Lana's presence at John Adams, she stayed silent, there was no way she could ever return the compliment.

'If there's anything you need, Lana, don't hesitate to call us.'

'There is something you can do for me,' she said assertively.

'What is it?'

'Tina.'

Mrs Daventry's gaze shot to the ground.

'You remember my sister?'

She returned Lana's gaze. 'Yes, of course.'

'I'm eighteen now and I'm leaving and I want to find her. I'm legally old enough to look after her.'

'I'm not sure what you're asking, Lana.'

'You had her adopted, illegally probably, and I want to know where she is.'

'That is a very serious allegation and one that is without any foundation.'

'I just want to know who took her. A name, anything.'

'Even if I knew, I couldn't tell you, and I don't. That is dealt with by another department.'

'Then give me the name of the department, a telephone number, anything?'

Mrs Daventry bent over her desk and scrawled onto a piece of paper. 'This is the name of the department. You'll find their number in the phone book.'

Lana placed the paper into her pocket.

'You're wasting your time, Lana. If you want my advice, use your energy to furnish your flat, find a nice coloured boy, get married and have a child of your own. Get on with your life. Wherever

Tina is, she's a happy little girl with a better life than she would have had here or with you. You just go on and try to be happy too.'

In the evening, staff laid on a few soft drinks and crisps for the residents in order to say 'goodbye' to Lana.

'Good luck, Lana!' echoed from all corners of the room and there were tears, hugs and promises to stay in touch. Lana's cocktail of emotions ranged from bittersweet to fear to excitement.

'Are you going to see Clifton when you get out?' asked May.

Lana could only smile. Despite her fears that he might forget about her, Clifton had written often. Their letters had been fun – brief yet frequent – and the thought of seeing him brought a fizz of excitement to her tummy. 'Maybe. I hope so. I don't know yet!'

'I take that as a yes!' said May, rolling her eyes.

Mrs. Daventry passed around a bowl of crisps and Lana whispered into her sister's ear. 'Let's get out of here.'

'Shall we go to the pictures? A pub? Oh wait, we're still locked up!' mocked May.

'Let's go to Grassy Green.'

The night air sent chills through her entire body and she was tempted to shuffle in closer to May as they sat awkwardly on the edge of the grassy hill. This would be her last night at John Adams.

'So, this is it!' said Lana, her throat suddenly tight. She'd been determined not to get upset again.

'Don't start crying, Lana. This is a good thing. The start of something big. The start of our proper lives. I feel really good about this and you should too.'

'I don't want to leave you.'

'We've been through this, Lana. Stop being so weak!'

'I'm not!'

'You most certainly are! All you have to do is get things sorted on the outside and I'll be there in no time. A year and a bit, remember?'

'A year and a bit. It just sounds so long.'

'It will fly by. So will you be contacting Aunty Ginny?' asked May, expertly changing the subject.

'I've got Aunty Ginny's address from her last letter, so we'll see. I really just want to find Tina and Aunty Ginny doesn't know where she is. Anyway, I have a name of a department I can look up in the phone book to start my search. I can't believe how negative old Daventry was being.'

'I agree with her for once. Leave it be. Focus on our flat and our future.'

'You know I can't do that. I have never been able to do that!'

'I don't think we're ever going to see her again, Lana. I'm just being honest.'

'You don't know that.'

'She probably doesn't even remember us. Have you thought of that? She was so little when she was adopted ... and perhaps her family haven't even told her we exist!'

Lana had never thought of such a possibility, having always stayed safe in the memories of Tina as the little baby who had relied so heavily on her.

Maybe everyone but Lana was right.

Lana turned her face away, now gazing into the darkness that rested upon Grassy Green, refusing to be bathed in May's negativity. With every ounce of her being, Lana knew she would one day see Tina again.

The day to leave had come, and Lana was headed towards a waiting car as a sporty blue vehicle drove into the grounds.

'The suitcases are all in the back. Good luck,' said Mrs Daventry.

'Thank you.'

'Where's your sister?'

'She's in our room ... she doesn't really like goodbyes.'

'I find that awfully rude. This is not about her!'

Lana smiled in response to Mrs Daventry's incorrect evaluation of her sister. May was a complex individual whom many found difficult to understand, but she loved her sister with everything she knew to be real. And May loved her back. She knew she did. Lana was confident of that.

An excitable social worker headed towards them, waving a folder in the air. 'Got all the paperwork sorted, now let's hit the road!'

'Bye, Mrs Daventry,' said Lana, knowing she would not miss the formidable woman who'd not even blinked when telling her the news that Mummy had died or her sister had been taken. Lana had never forgotten those moments and finally waving goodbye to her would in some way ease some of the harshness of those memories. Perhaps.

Luckily Stan was nowhere to be seen as Lana stepped into the car behind the social worker.

'Wait!' called Mrs Daventry. 'One moment ... come back!'

Instinctively, she looked beyond Mrs Daventry and spotted him immediately.

Clifton Joseph in a flowery shirt, blue waistcoat and the widest flares she had ever seen.

'Clifton?'

His long legs strode confidently towards her, arms outstretched. Lana couldn't believe what she was witnessing as she moulded herself into his body, resting her head against his chest.

'I don't believe this. What are you doing here?' she jumped up and down excitedly.

'I thought you'd be happy to see me!'

'I am. You pick your moments though – I'm leaving.'

'I know and I'm getting you out of here.'

'What?'

He shook his head and sighed. 'Don't you remember our little talks on Grassy Green?'

'There were loads.'

'How we were going to run away from here?'

'With matching sports cars or horses? There were so many daydreams, Clifton.'

'That's correct, but today, Lana Cole, I'm going to make one of them come true. How about the sports car, but only one?' He took her hand and Lana was disappointed at the lack of fizz as the tips of their skins collided.

'There you go! It's a Frogeye Sprite, just ten years old, good as new and waiting for you,' said Clifton, placing his hands on the bonnet of the car. The roof was down, the shiny gold exterior shining in the sunlight.

'It's beautiful … but how could you afford this?'

'It's my stepdad's. We've been working on it for a week and he let me take her out.' He pulled open the door. 'Shall we?' he asked with a bow.

'Is my stuff going to fit?'

'Let me worry about that!'

The social worker and a smiling Mrs Daventry joined them.

'What's going on, Lana, are we heading off?' said the social worker.

'No, thank you. I'm going to catch a lift with my best friend Clifton, if that's alright?'

Having loaded Lana's meagre belongings into the small boot, Clifton moved off deliberately slowly, leaving Mrs Daventry and an open-mouthed social worker behind them. The building where she had lived for the latter part of her childhood was slowly disappearing from view and she was already beginning to feel lighter.

As they exited through the large gates, she said, 'Drive a little faster. I want to get away from here as quickly as possible.'

'Right on!' shouted Clifton as he revved up the engine.

When Clifton turned onto the motorway, Lana knew that whatever romantic notions she'd ever felt towards him were now neatly swept away in the past. Clifton was her best friend and she loved him, but just as that: a friend. He would assist her on her road to freedom, having tasted it before her, and they'd continue to share their dreams, laugh at each other's clothes choices and even decisions in love. But that was all they would ever have. There would be no romance. She had to concentrate on setting up home for May and on finding her other sister.

A new phase awaited Lana Cole, away from John Adams and away from everything she'd known over the last six years. She had finally been set free. She was now an adult and free to look for her sister so they could all be together again.

'You alright?' asked Clifton.

'I'm great!' she said, smiling confidently towards the window and the road ahead.

Chapter Fifteen

May lay on the bed, staring up at the ceiling of the room she'd called home for over six years. She'd just finished a novel by a new writer named Jackie Collins. It was a very different book to her normal reads, but entertainment and escapism were in short supply at John Adams.

Opening this particular book invited her into a world that was sexy, outrageous and loud, leaving her infused with the idea that money, and lots of it, was what she would have. Her life would be filled with the finer things in life, like the softest of mattresses and holidays in exotic locations like Hollywood. Most importantly, she would never have to answer to anyone as she lapped up the freedom being wealthy would afford her. She would be safe.

Her eyelids closed, and her mouth curved into a smile. May loved such moments, when she could truly travel within herself and allow the dreams of her own making to flow effervescently into her being. Ever since Lana had left just one month earlier, May would quickly wander away from the pain of this loss by dreaming of a better life with the sister she missed more than she could ever have imagined.

Lana had written only once in a month. She'd sent money for a book and a promise to visit 'very soon'. May understood. Lana's hands were clearly full, what with trying to finish the secretarial course and trying to find a decent job to support them both. She was currently in a flat on a rough estate, in a place called Peckham. Indeed, May would be allowed her own flat upon leaving and hoped she could persuade Lana to move in with her. Thankfully, Lana hadn't mentioned anything about looking for Tina.

May was pleased that Lana's bed still had yet to be filled, loving the solitude of being alone.

'What do you want?' she said, without looking up from the book as she sat on top of the bed.

'S ... sorry,' said Jessica, standing by the door.

'You made me jump, that's all. I thought you were someone else.'

'Who?'

'No one important.' She placed the book to one side. 'Well?'

Jessica had never had the audacity to enter her room unannounced before. That was Stan's thing.

'I'm sorry to bother you, May.'

Now she realised why they could never have been friends. This skinny kid was a shivering wreck. Weak.

'It's done now. What can I do for you?' she said with sarcasm.

Jessica moved closer and May noticed the bags under her eyes.

'You can sit on Lana's bed,' she said.

'I ... are you and Stan ... friends?'

'Certainly not. Next question.'

'I ... because. He's my friend. Well, I thought ...' Jessica averted her eyes to the ground and May thought she'd spotted a tear, but couldn't be sure.

'What?' she said impatiently. The last thing she needed was Jessica crying all over her.

'I ... nothing,' she said sharply, as she stood up. She shook her head vigorously and it was then that May noticed a dark bruise on her neck.

'Are you sure you're all right?'

'I'm fine. See you at school,' she said, rushing out.

May shrugged. 'Suit yourself.'

Five minutes later, just as she was getting back into her book, she was interrupted yet again.

'What now?'

'Is that a way to talk to your superior?' asked Stan, closing the door behind him.

'It's you.' Her calm voice did not match how she felt inside, her heart quickened with nerves and her brow began to moisten. Ever since Stan had killed the cat, she'd sensed a new determination in him, fuelled even more by Lana's departure. He'd continued his campaign of secret taunts whispered into her ear as she waited in line for breakfast or lunch, sometimes threatening to destroy every single book she owned. He'd even let himself into her room once whilst she'd been at school. She'd known this because of a stain that had suddenly appeared on the top of her bed. She wasn't sure what it was, a drink or even urine, but, without further investigation, she had bundled the top sheet into the washing basket and taken it to the laundry.

'First one sister then another. All gone now.'

'I know,' she replied with as much sarcasm as she could unearth.

May avoided eye contact and instead searched through the lines of the hardback she'd been reading; an instrument for escapism, but now a possible weapon. The side lamp illuminated the pages, but, she hoped, not her fear.

'What do you want, Stan?'

'Nuthin'.' He sat on the edge of the bed, the impact moving her closer to him.

Their eyes were level. She felt the sensation of his breath flicker against her nose.

'If you want to rip up another book, go for it,' she said. 'But it's not mine, it's from the library.'

'Meow!' he said mockingly. 'Missing the moggie yet?'

'Is that all?' she said.

'For now.' He stood up. 'For now.'

He left the room, but as a chill ran through her body, May was certain that whatever this was, it wasn't over.

For now.

Yet, hadn't he already reached his limit by killing the cat? There was nothing more he could actually do to her, was there? He had definitely crossed the line the day he did that.

May had peered inside the bag after her sister and noticed the specks of red against black fur immediately, as well as the slight stench of something once new, now old, and not of this world anymore.

Stan's smile had curled with satisfaction. Her sister was trying not to cry.

She'd noticed the cat's white 'bib', now a crimson; the tiny pointed ear her sister had once called 'cute' was now caked in a slick red-to-black thickness. She'd hoped the end had been painless, like Daddy's.

'Have you nuthin' to say, then?' he'd asked, his rancid spittle landing on her forehead.

'Yes. Can we go to games now?' With the back of her hand, she wiped him away from her skin.

He had continued to goad her, and she, in turn, had refused to react. She would never give him the satisfaction of her true feelings.

Now she pushed those thoughts away. They were never helpful. Like her mother, father and Tina, any thoughts of the cat needed to remain banished from her mind. As did any lingering concerns about Jessica, whatever they were. She had to remain focused on her future. It was all that mattered. So it was with a huge smile on her face that May drifted off and into a lovely sleep that night.

She didn't hear the footsteps. A large clammy hand was placed over her mouth. Her eyes sprang open. She was unable to scream or to tell him to stop this; she could only sink her teeth into his hand. The same hand that immediately slapped her clean across the jaw and then covered her mouth again.

Her body locked. She was rigid. She could only question him in her mind: Why?

He straddled her, his eyes widening in the semi-darkness. She stared up at him, a wide catatonic stare. Why? She detested the disgusting hardness against her leg, the weight of him pinning her firmly into the grooves of the bed.

'I've waited long enough, don't you think? Ever since the first day you came in here, all uppity, thinking you were better than everyone, with all those fancy books, when all you are is a wog with big ideas. Always thinking you're better than the rest of us. That bitch of a sister always around you. She's gone now. Who's gonna protect you now, eh?'

She wriggled stiffly underneath him, fear rising from her stomach. His knee shifted between her legs and she willed herself not to pass out, her eyes pleading with him to stop this. *I'll be good, I promise. Just don't do this. Not this. Not this.*

'I've waited long enough for you, little girl and this is gonna happen.'

She stamped her eyes shut, submitting to the feeling of nothingness, a preparation for what was to come. She was dimly aware of a door slamming elsewhere and then, in one quick action, she felt her body released from his grip, a weight lifted. Then she opened her eyes and quickly shifted up.

Stan was stood in front of her with a wide grin, the front of his trousers, just below his stomach, pitched up like a tent.

'Not today though. Too many people about. Maybe tomorrow or the next day. You won't know when. It will just happen and you'll love it.'

As Stan left the room, May reminded herself to breathe again. Her heart rate slowly returning to normal.

She sat on the edge of the bed.

Fear was now replaced with a blinding anger. She had to make sure she was better prepared next time because Stan would be back. Of that she was sure.

Morning came all too quickly after a sleepless night. In the canteen an exhausted May placed a dinner knife under her sleeve, returned to her room and secured it under the pillow. She was now in no doubt of what Stan had been planning. She'd seen the determination locked in his eyes, and felt the insane strength of his arms. She needed to tell someone, but who? The staff at John Adams were useless, united in their trust of Stan and indifference towards the people in their care.

She thought about Lana. May had received one measly letter without an address or phone number. Like everyone else, her sister had betrayed her. Any previous promises about writing regularly or at least phoning had been a lie.

May's heart rate accelerated, tiredness and fear mingling to form an entirely different person to the one she'd been just twenty-four hours earlier. She turned to the mirror, staring at her own face. While she'd seldom been happy at John Adams, she'd once known what it was to smile, truly smile, to watch her top lip curl involuntarily like her dead father's; to feel the warmth she knew could exist in her heart. But that had been a very long time ago. Casting her mind backwards to the odd memories of her mother, she did not recall a single cuddle that hadn't come from the arms of a white lady named Aunty Ginny. Yet, even Ginny had betrayed her, refusing to take in three little girls when they'd needed her the most.

From underneath the bed, she pulled out a grey sack she used for PE.

No one could be trusted, only herself. She was all she had in the world and May needed to get away from the home now before Stan carried out his wicked aim. She'd been patient, planned ahead and enjoyed her daydreams of the future, but time had moved too slowly and nothing had prepared her for what had almost happened the night before. She needed to leave as soon as possible but desperately needed Lana's address. Unfortunately, Mrs Daventry was the only person who could give it to her and she was away on leave until Tuesday. May would have to wait until then to ask for her sister's address, though whether it could be retrieved from Lana's social worker was another question.

May packed as much into the sack as she could and counted out the money saved over the years as well as what Lana had sent. She placed it into the side pocket. She would have enough to last a few weeks – although this was an assumption because May had never before had to survive in London on her own.

'Shouldn't you be off to college?' asked Mrs Branbury, as May appeared at the doorway of the library.

'I'm on my way now. I just wanted to say hello because I haven't seen you in a while.'

'You've hardly been in at all. And why should you, with those fancy libraries at sixth-form college? I can't blame you.'

'I wanted to say thank you, Mrs Branbury. Thank you for ordering all those books for me all those years ago. You have no idea how much you helped me.'

'It was my pleasure, May.'

'Well ... I just wanted to say thanks.'

'You are very welcome but what's this all about? You're not leaving us yet, are you?'

'No. Not yet,' she lied.

Mrs Branbury moved from around the counter. 'Anyway, if anyone should be doing the thanking, it should be me!'

'You? Why?'

'I've been here a few years now, as you know, and in that time it's been hard to get some of the kids interested in books. You made me look forward to coming into work, May. You were a joy and a pleasure.'

In recent years, May had never recalled anyone referring to her as a pleasure.

'I'd better get going now,' she said awkwardly.

'You do that. Get those good marks and make something of yourself. I know you can do it.'

That night, again, she did not attempt to sleep. So when Stan opened the door to her room at around 2am, she was alert.

'Ahh, you're awake. Good.'

'What do you want?' She felt underneath the pillow. The knife was still in place.

'Nothing. Just to check on you.' He walked over to the bed and sat down beside her. 'I'm sorry about yesterday. Dunno what come over me.'

She scooted back and closer to the wall. She never trusted Stan when he was 'nice' – it was almost worse than when he was horrible to her. She hated the vulnerable position he put her in but for now the knife remained under the pillow.

'It's OK. Please, just leave it.'

'You said please. You never say please and thank you. Not usually. I s'pose that's the only reason I wanted to bring you down a peg or two. I hate it when people think they're better than me.'

This was all very weird, but there did seem to be a shift in Stan's demeanour. Even his voice sounded different. Softer.

'I like you, May,' he continued. 'I really like you. Ever since the first day you came in here. So beautiful.'

'When I was ten?' She tried not to sound sarcastic.

'You weren't ten to me. You're just someone ... I liked. But you didn't like me back. Why couldn't you be more like Jess? Friendly.'

Jessica?

Stan's words felt very confusing. At least when he was being mean to her, she understood. But this was sounding more like a grown man asking her to be his girlfriend and it felt plain weird.

'Anyway, I just wanted to say sorry. That's all. You know, for giving you a fright yesterday and ... and the letters.'

'What letters?'

'You don't have to worry, I will get them back for you. The other letters your sister sent. I promise you I didn't read 'em.'

'You took my letters?' Her confusion slowly turned to anger. She needed those letters. She needed to get her sister's address.

'Sorry ...' he whispered, placing his hands upon hers.

She pulled her hand away, both fear and anger mingling inside of her.

'What's wrong?'

'My letters, you took them?'

'I told you I was sorry.' His voice was changing into that of the old Stan she knew and hated.

He traced his fingers across her arm.

'Don't touch me!'

'So, you still don't think I'm good enough for you, eh? Even after all that?'

Before she could answer his hand was stamped against her mouth, this time tighter than last time. She could hardly breathe. She didn't want to breathe, because this time she knew what was about to happen as her head smacked back against the bed.

She needed the knife. But it and the pillow fell to the ground as Stan restrained her with his entire body, his knee pressed against her chest so hard she couldn't speak. He wriggled, sliding out of his trousers, his hand firmly on her mouth, her entire body rigid with fear. The weight of him pressed down on her chest. If only she could pass out. She hoped that whatever was going to happen would be quick. She thought about her daddy. He would never have let this happen. He would have saved her. She closed her eyes and then felt an ease of the pressure. Just a bit. She opened her eyes and Stan had shifted whilst fiddling with a trouser leg that would not slide over his shoes. A chance.

158

It all happened quickly. Her suddenly free hand clutched the lamp. The sound of impact as the top of the lamp landed on Stan's large head.

He fell backwards and crashed to the floor without a sound.

She shot up.

'Oh no!' She spoke underneath shaking hands.

The room was dead quiet. A line of blood ran down the side of Stan's lifeless face as she stood over him, trembling.

'Oh no,' she reiterated.

She began to absorb the realisation of what she had done and she knew what she had to do. May stepped over Stan's body and reached underneath the bed, pulling out her PE sack. She placed more items inside and took one last look at Stan lying on the floor of her bedroom, lifeless.

So that night, and a lot earlier than expected, May Cole ran out of the gates of Sir John Adams Children's Home with a PE sack, two plastic bags and the belief that she had just killed a man.

Chapter Sixteen

May was now back in London.

The reality of what she'd done finally hit her as she stepped off the bus in an area called Peckham; an area where Lana lived, according to the one letter Stan had allowed her to see.

Stan.

She could not allow herself to think about him and what she had done.

The driver said they'd arrived at the bus station. Peckham was clearly a vast area and nothing like the small town nestling outside the imposing gates of John Adams. This was a sea of people, of all different colours, swarming around like bees. Her sister could be anywhere. She could be nestled inside the flats behind the row of shops or in the street behind the post office. May spent almost an hour pacing the worn pavement, eyes alert for any sign of Lana, her shoulders aching with the weight of the bags. Finally she settled inside a crowded cafe offering warmth, tea and a chance to rethink.

Luckily, she had written down Ginny's address in Brighton before Lana had left. At the time her anger towards Ginny was on high, but as many of the heroines in her books had taught her, 'always be prepared'. So, May had slipped the address into the bottom of the PE sack as a way of being just that. What the address brought was options. Whatever her feelings about Ginny, she would at least have a bed for the night – guilt would secure her that at least.

She felt the reality of depleting funds once she'd handed over the train ticket money at the station. She hadn't realised just how much it would cost. Day trips with John Adams had involved a quick head count before a number of loud, gum-chewing kids piled onto a train and onto whatever beach town they would descend on to 'frighten' the locals. She'd never really taken note of the price of things – except books, of course. Perhaps Ginny could help her. Go with her to the police, and tell her side of the story. No, she could never go to the police. No one would believe her side of the story.

The train journey to Brighton included excited day-trippers discussing their plans for the day, a toddler hurrying up and down the carriage as a harassed mum gave up the chase. Once at the station, though money was still her primary concern, she purchased a pair of cheap, overly large sunglasses that covered a lot of her face even though the weather was overcast. She couldn't afford to be recognised. She unfurled the address from her coat pocket, approaching the first person she saw. The directions were clear and according to this stranger, Ginny lived a twenty-five-minute walk away.

As she walked to Ginny's home, the frenzied screams of seagulls made her jump, as she likened the sound to sirens. Were the police on the lookout for her? She set down the PE sack and plastic bags for a moment to allow her arms a rest. The waft of sea air floated into her nostrils and she felt instantly calm. She decided there and then she would forgive Ginny. Apart from the fact she really needed her at that moment, May genuinely wanted to make amends. A part of her quietly looked forward to laying down roots with someone who had actually known her parents and had been such a huge part of her childhood.

'I could get used to this,' she whispered as a gust of sea air caught in her nostrils. Instead of referring to seaside life, her confession had more to do with the release she felt in being prepared to embrace Ginny after so many years.

Ginny's sunny, lilac front door was a welcoming sight, with a potted plant on either side. The chime of the doorbell coincided with a hungry growl of her tummy. She heard hurried footsteps bounding down a flight of stairs before the door was opened by a worried-looking white man who looked somewhat familiar.

'Hello, can I speak with Ginny Jones, please?'

His eyes rolled over her body, yet not in the same way as the men in the street. Not in the same way as Stan.

'She isn't here,' he said, eyeing her and her belongings suspiciously.

'Do you know when she'll be back?'

'No.'

'I've come a long way …'

'I don't really care how far you've come, she isn't here,' he said with an eerie calm.

'Are you her son?'

'One of them. What of it?'

'I remember you when you were younger. It's me, May, one of the kids at Flat B Pettyford Road. You used to babysit us …? Well, sort of …' She hoped his eventual recognition would allow him to soften.

'Yes, I remember. And I also remember how much stress you gave my mum. She doesn't need any more of that now.'

May averted her eyes.

'All she ever did was spend her time getting bothered about you lot. Looking after three kids who weren't even hers.'

The way his eyes blazed aroused a fear in her. He may not have harboured the same intentions as Stan but he was certainly filled with a similar contempt.

May backed away from the door.

162

'Can you please tell her I came around? I'll only be in Brighton today. I'll be by that fish and chip stand near the station. Blues, it's called.' She perhaps shouldn't have told him that, in case he called the police.

'That it?'

'Yes, that's it. I just want to speak to her. Five minutes, that's all.' May hated herself for the plea to her tone, but this was a means to an end.

'OK!' The door slammed against the hinges, so sudden and so vociferous, her hand opened in shock and one of the plastic bags fell to the ground.

Blues Fish and Chip shop prepared an incredible greasy platter of fish and chips, which fuelled her zapped energy and depleted even more funds. The various cups of tea consumed as she waited caused her to want to use the toilet, yet she was too frightened to leave the table in case Ginny arrived.

She never did.

That evening, as the lights lit up the vibrant area of Brighton beach promenade, May was bereft of any ideas. She would have to get back on a train and head off.

To where, she did not know.

Unlike the train into Brighton, the journey back to London had been full of thoughts and no concrete plan. Refused to be led astray by the fear that existed miles away and within the gates of John Adams, she reminded herself of the money nestling inside her purse. Money meant options. She knew that from the books.

Tiredness crept in as the train bounded into London territory. Her thoughts had already mutated into what felt familiar and comforting; a new hatred towards Ginny's son and then to Ginny herself, who'd clearly been in agreement with him because she hadn't even bothered to show up at Blues Fish and Chips Stand. May had risked everything to meet her and, as usual, had received nothing in return.

The tears appeared without warning. Memories of her little sister, Tina, ripped away from them before May had even had the chance to say goodbye. Lana. The cat. Her parents; mother Adanya and a father who had disappeared long before. She turned to the train window, just so the passengers wouldn't see the shame of her tears. Perhaps they should have seen them though, because as the train pulled into Victoria station, May vowed to herself she would *never* feel the sensation of hot tears again. She would *never* embrace the weakness it took to cry. No one on this earth would ever get close enough to hurt her again.

Never.

Arms laden with bags she'd been carrying all day, May started walking the streets near the station. As soon as she saw the cloudy front door lit up with a neon sign reading VACANCIES, she made a quick decision to go in.

Behind a worn wooden desk sat a bouffant-haired woman, a cloud of smoke swimming above her and the sound of The Kinks wafting from the wireless.

'Can I help you, love?' she asked, stubbing the cigarette in an ashtray decorated with a drawing of the Queen.

'I'm looking for a place to stay. Just for a couple of nights, maybe three.'

'Make your mind up. I get really busy here at the weekend so it's best to book in advance.'

May searched the empty space, crumbling décor. 'Two nights will be fine for now.'

'Have it your way. It's not as if anyone else will take someone like you. You're lucky to find me. I don't judge.'

For one moment, May assumed she meant 'a murderer'. 'Someone like me? What do you mean?'

'You know.' She ran her finger over her own hand. 'Coloured girl, like you.'

'Oh … yes … yes, I am very lucky,' she said dryly.

'Name?'

A bolt of shock hit her. May had not been prepared for the question, assuming she'd hand over the money and that would be the end of their transaction.

'Name ...' said May, stalling for time.

'Yes, everyone has one.'

'Cole, It's Ma—' she began, with thoughts of John Adams and Stan. She was underage. And the police would already be looking for her.

'Your name is Ma Cole?'

'No ...' She thought about the other name on her birth certificate, Victoria. 'Vic—' It would be stupid to use one of her actual names as the police could easily trace her. An imagined image from a character of one of the books she'd read a few months ago sprang to mind. Eve: a woman never to be crossed. 'Eve ...'

'You sure now?'

'Yes, it's Eve Cole,' she said confidently.

'I don't care what name you give me,' the woman said, scribbling onto the page of a large book. 'Something to put on the records is all I need because as long as you're paying me up front, I don't care.'

May placed her bags onto the floor of the small-yet-neat room, her new name rolling around her tongue.

'Eve.'

She liked it. It had been a mistake to give her real surname but it was too late now.

The busy sounds of the street outside and the incessant flash of a neon light didn't bother her much and without the strength to undress or wash, she flopped onto the surprisingly comfortable bed and closed her eyes into a dreamless sleep.

The next morning, she would awaken to a new life and would only answer to the name of Eve Cole.

Chapter Seventeen

Lana stared in shock at the woman before her, her lips quivering with disbelief. 'Excuse me ... what did you just say?'

Mrs Daventry evaded eye contact as she spoke again. 'We assumed May would be with you.'

'Well, she's not!' The panic rose steadily.

'I see ...'

'Why didn't someone telephone me? I don't understand this.' Once again, she was in the very same place as before and this woman yet again was reeling off another dose of gut-wrenching bad news.

May had run away.

'She left two days ago. The police have been notified ... we were in the process of writing to you.'

'So you're telling me that my sister May just upped and left? No way. She would have said something to me!' Lana felt a lightness in her body and leaned onto Mrs Daventry's desk for support. 'How do you even know she's run away? I mean, I was going to take her out for the day as a treat. Buy her a book. She might not have run away. How do you know?'

'A few of her belongings are gone. She's taken her PE sack, we think.'

'She has a suitcase, why didn't she take that?' asked Lana unnecessarily.

'I do not know, but she also had a violent altercation with Mr Alford.'

'Mr Alford?'

'Stan Alford. Luckily he has recovered fully and doesn't want to press charges. He, like the rest of us, just wants to see her returned here safely.'

May violent? That wasn't her. She'd got into one or maybe two fights at school, yes, but May was such a careful and clever person. Always thinking and planning ahead. None of this made sense.

Another half an hour passed, with Mrs Daventry unable to say anything Lana deemed worthwhile. The police would be in touch apparently.

'Please give her this when ... if she comes back. Please.' Lana hastily scribbled her new address and phone number onto the pad resting on the desk.

'We will certainly notify you when she returns,' said Mrs Daventry in a voice bereft of any confidence.

Her previous letter to May had merely contained up-to-date pictures showing the progress of the flat – their flat – and some details about an impromptu visit and trip to London to show her the property in its newly decorated state. Clifton and Lana had spent all week transforming the flat into something much more homely and inviting: placing pictures on the walls and a second-hand lamp in the corner of the living room that would one day serve as May's bedroom. She had planned to spend the rest of the time getting May acquainted with their new neighbourhood, including the local bookshop, followed by a night bereft of sleep as they basked in the excitement of seeing one another for the first time in months.

Why hadn't she phoned and asked to speak to May? Lana hadn't been overly concerned with May's silence after writing the letters because May was like that sometimes. Perhaps she'd been planning to run away for weeks. The whole situation with Stan didn't make sense – what if he had tried to hurt her?

She could go over every possibility in her mind and nothing would change, her worst nightmare had reoccurred and Lana was unsure if she'd ever be able to forgive herself.

May was out there alone, possibly afraid, and the only person to blame was Lana.

Burdened with guilt, Lana searched her mind for possibilities of where she might have gone, given May had the address of the new flat yet still hadn't shown up there after two days. There was only one possibility and that was Aunty Ginny.

Clifton promised he would drive her to Brighton after work, but Lana had already missed May – by days, it seemed – and she wasn't about to make that mistake a second time.

The train deposited her at Brighton station, a newly purchased map safely tucked under her arm. She found the address she had for Ginny easily and was confronted by a cheerful lilac door, noticing the leaves on the potted plants standing either side had started to turn brown. A cool breeze swept across her face as she rang the doorbell twice. She was impatient. The panic surrounding May's disappearance had not allowed her to analyse the possible impact of seeing Aunty Ginny again after all this time, because this strangely didn't matter now; her main concern was locating her sister.

'Can I help you?' said a middle-aged white woman, her head stretched out of the window next door.

'I'm looking for Ginny Jones. Is she here?'

'The lady with the sons?'

'Yes, that's her.'

'No, they're not here. They all left and packed up this morning. Didn't even say goodbye.'

'Packed up?'

'Had suitcases, so I assume they were going on a rather long holiday. Not that I like to pry.'

'Do you know where they went?'

'There were enough bags for a long stay, but I assume they're coming back. I didn't go out and ask them, I'm not nosey like that.'

'Were they with a girl ... who looks like me?' she said as tactfully as possible.

'No, dear. Just Ginny and the two boys.'

Lana felt the crushing weight of disappointment as she headed in the direction of a pebbled beach. She passed by Blues chip shop, and inhaled the delicious aroma of fish and chips. Wetness splashed against her feet as she gazed out towards the endless horizon covered by sea. Her sister could be absolutely anywhere.

Lana had been back at the flat a few minutes when she recalled numerous television shows like *Dixon of Dock Green* and *Z Cars*, that always seemed to imply that every missing person would always head to a scene of importance, a favourite spot or simply a place they had once felt happy.

She pulled her coat back on and headed straight to number sixty-three Pettyford Road.

The tree-lined street hadn't changed much over the years; it was just somewhat busier, with more cars on the road than she remembered, and a slew of new shops.

She glanced up at the windows of their former home into what had been the living room, and saw the outline of unrecognisable furniture; a dog-eared teddy bear lay misshapen in the corner of the window. Somebody had changed the curtains, and this one simple act brought fresh pain. Everyone and everything had moved on. It was as if Daddy had never breathed within these walls; as if Mummy had never gasped at that first sight of snow as the four of them gazed out of that very window. She walked to the park they used to play in, her heart heavy as she found a bench nearby and sat down. She waited. And waited.

As darkness descended she knew it was time to leave the place where she'd spent half of her childhood.

The trail had turned cold; another sister was gone. Lost, perhaps forever. Lana was alone.

Chapter Eighteen

Eve – no longer May – slept for almost fourteen hours, waking with yet another hungry growl from her belly. She rifled through the hastily packed PE sack and retrieved the pack of biscuits she'd bought at the train station.

She went downstairs, where the smell of cooked breakfast hit her.

She watched as the landlady placed two bowls of scrambled eggs and sausage onto a tray.

Eve approached her.

'Excuse me. Is there anywhere around here I can find work?' she asked after a moment.

The landlady saw her eyeing the food. 'You could have had breakfast if you'd paid the extra. Even at this late hour.'

Eve continued to gaze longingly at the food. The sausage coated with a film of glorious fat, the eggs yellow and fluffy.

'I was hoping you'd tell me where I could find a job.'

'If you find one, tell me so I can leave this place.' The landlady smoothed an ample amount of butter over brown toast. When Eve failed to utter a polite chuckle, she continued. 'You've got a few places down the road, offices that need cleaning. I suppose you can ask around. There's also a couple of department stores who might need people, though I'm not sure they'll want you front of house, if you know what I mean.'

'I know what you mean,' Eve replied sarcastically.

'How old are you?'

'Eighteen,' lied Eve.

'You shouldn't have too much trouble then,' she said, before moving off with the tray of food.

'I can help you out?' said Eve, following the landlady to the table where she placed two plates of food in front of one man. 'I'm sure there's stuff you need doing around here.' She could only cringe at how close to begging she sounded.

The landlady began to clean a nearby table. 'If you're that desperate, I have a friend who's looking for help.'

'That would be great!'

'I'll jot down the address. Tell him Mrs Harris sent you, OK? It's about half an hour from here if you're slow.'

'Thanks.'

A light of hope flickered in her mind as she stuffed the crumpled piece of paper into her pocket.

Twenty minutes later she stood in front of a dilapidated building, her hope slightly dimmed. With no doorbell or knocker, Eve pounded a fist onto the hard wood door and waited until it opened.

A smartly dressed man with a suspicious gaze and overgrown stubble appeared.

'Can I help you?'

'Mrs Harris sent me,' she said, feeling rather silly. Surprisingly, he nodded his head and opened the door wider to allow her inside. What she saw was a total opposite to the exterior. It was clearly a bar with an entirely different ambience of dark lighting, soft leather sofas lining the walls and full of squishy colourful cushions, surrounding low-level coffee tables. She followed the man into a back office where on the wall a large multicoloured framed photo of a dreadlocked little boy looked down at the brown shiny desk. There was a fuschia vase with neatly cut roses filling the room with a glorious scent and the sound of Jimi Hendrix was on low.

'Mrs Harris said you had some work going?'

'I'm always looking for people. I run a few bars in the area, not just this one. What are you looking for?'

'Bar work would be good,' she said, merely because he'd mentioned it first.

'Got any experience?'

With the possibility of being asked to fix an exotically named cocktail by way of a test, she decided on honesty. 'No, I don't.'

'Never mind. We can get you trained up.'

'Really?'

'Yes, really. I like your look, the afro. Very now. Would you like to start tonight?'

'Yes, please!' She hadn't meant to sound so eager or desperate, but with funds depleting and a seemingly endless rumbling from her belly, she was.

'Get yourself back here by nine tonight and someone will take you through the ropes, get you started, OK?'

'Thank you so much.'

'Don't thank me yet.'

As he explained the wage system – heavily reliant on tips – Eve wanted to sing out loud with happiness. Of course her future did not lay in the bar scene, but this would be a step leading to where she needed to be. And appeared a million miles away from whatever she had done within the gates of John Adams Children's Home.

'See you tonight!' she said confidently.

Dressed in her best outfit – tight bell-bottomed jeans and black sparkly shirt – Eve waited in the staff room for a lady named Belinda.

'Eve, is it?' said the woman, who was dressed in a figure-hugging mini dress with a bright gold chain hanging from her scrawny neck. Eve wondered if she'd ever eaten in her life, as her shoulder blades protruded prominently through the fabric.

Her blue eyes were striking, though, and highlighted by thick kohl eyeliner.

'My name's Belinda but I go by the name of Bell, without an E. It's easier and I don't like the customers who drink here knowing my name.'

Bell led her back down the stairs through to the darkened room. The bar sat in the corner as low music played from a record player attached to siren-like lights, which reflected on a wall decorated with psychedelic colours that seemed to move with every beat.

'This is it!' announced Bell as if presenting the Crown Jewels. 'Most of the punters won't arrive just yet. For now you've got your early birds. Well, you know what that's like.'

Eve had never even been to the local pub, let alone 'known what it's like', but she just nodded.

'You just wait till it gets to midnight,' said Bell.

Eve was rapidly trained on the easiest drinks to mix as well as the correct way to dry a glass to avoid smears.

'You'll do a bit of everything. Clearing the glasses, washing up – even cleaning the bog if we ask you. One day you might make it to the till, but, for now, this is it. Oh, and the top floor is off limits to you, OK? Stay away from the top floor.'

'Yes, OK.'

'Anything else you want to ask me, just let me know.'

'That's great, thank you,' Eve muttered, uncertain if Bell could hear her over the pumping base of the music, which had recently increased in volume.

Eve worked until 3am on the first night and then until 4am on Saturday, and thus began her routine. She would sleep during the day, waking for lunch, before preparing for the evening shift. Her tips were small, the hourly wage meagre, but by the end of the month she might save enough to pay Mrs Harris upfront for another four weeks.

First to admit they'd nothing in common, Eve still felt uneasy whenever Bell was away from the bar. Quite frequently she'd disappear for half an hour or so, leaving Eve alone with a sea of people twice her age and experience. On a usual day, she'd begin her fifteen-minute break with whatever bar snacks she could tolerate, sitting obediently in the dedicated staff room upstairs, a room directly below the 'forbidden floor'. She'd seen Bell gain access to this mysterious section of the building on more than one occasion, with May's curiosity heightened a little bit more each day.

Stay away from the top floor, she told herself.

One day, as it usually did, the service lift opened on the top floor. Unlike those other days, Eve decided to exit the lift into the nondescript corridor. She noticed the door marked 'Private' almost immediately and stood staring at it. Her curiosity was live, but she wasn't going to jeopardise a good job so she turned back to the lift and pressed the button.

The sound of her name startled her.

'Eve? What are you doing?'

Bell had come up the back stairs.

'The lift came straight up and I got out. Sorry.'

Bell smiled, raising her eyebrows. 'You know the top floor is out of bounds.'

'I know. Sorry.'

'Bored, were we?' asked Bell.

'It won't happen again. You can trust me.'

'I know I can. Usually the girls say they made a mistake and thought it was the second floor ... but you told me the truth and I like that.'

Telling a lie just hadn't occurred to her.

'I think for you, for someone like you, it's hard because you want bigger and better things. I can see it in the way you walk ... and those eyes. Hidden inside is so much more. You're just like me.'

Bell's sharp perception of her was surprising. In a seedy club in London, this woman had clocked Eve's potential.

'I wasn't sure if a young girl like you could cut it, but perhaps you can,' said Bell, scrunching her eyebrows.

Bell moved in closer. 'Apart from the customers you see downstairs dancing to Jefferson Airplane and all that, we also have another set of clients who don't actually come for the music. Those willing to spend a bit more. An elite set, if you like. You know, posh types. They don't want to mix with people in the bar and they need something … you know, a bit more exclusive. Maybe we could have you work up here. I can't promise anything.'

'That would be really good,' enthused Eve, already envisaging the larger tips.

'I'll see what I can do then.'

Bell instructed Eve to dress casually and said that, yes, the flared jeans would be OK – Eve's bubbly personality was all that was needed to succeed on the top floor anyway. Eve briefly wondered about this 'bubbly personality'; Bell clearly didn't know her at all but she decided to try her best anyway.

On the top floor she followed Bell into a darkened room. Hypnotic music sounded from the speakers, too low to cause a pulsating beat in her chest, but loud enough to make the chatter inaudible. A group of men sat on centrally placed sofas, a small number of beautiful women served drinks on trays. The curved bar in the corner was covered with bottles of alcohol as an intermittent swirling light cast its multicoloured glow over the room.

'Don't go to them, you wait for them to call you,' Bell instructed.

Bell was beckoned over by a thin man in a suit. She bent down to whisper in his ear, returning a moment later with an order of drinks. This looked easy enough.

A larger man in a striped tie waved his hand in Eve's direction. Bell nodded her head with encouragement and Eve moved over to his table.

'Can I help you?' she said.

'I can't hear you!' he shouted quite reasonably.

She bent down and leaned in towards his ear. 'What can I get you?'

'Vodka and orange, and whatever you are having.'

Eve recalled the club's no booze rule for staff and was happy to turn it into a tip, as instructed.

She returned with the man's order and he patted the seat beside him. As she'd seen many of the girls do the same, she sat down on the chair opposite him.

'Are you new here?' he asked.

'Yes,' she replied, just as the tempo of the music rose.

'Nice to meet you.' He placed a large hand over hers.

'Thanks.' She moved her hand away, eyes searching the room for Bell.

'Who are you looking for?' His voice sounded slightly irritated.

'Bell.'

'She's probably in the other section.'

'There's another section?'

This seemed to amuse the man. 'Yes, through that door. There are so many little sections in this club.'

He pointed to an area behind the bar. 'Why don't we both go and look for her?'

Eve was desperate to find Bell, to placate the sudden insecurity of being surrounded by strangers, by men. So she followed him through the door and into a darkened corridor where she was hit by a strong smell of smoke. Not cigarettes, but a substance that was unfamiliar.

'I don't think she's here ...'

'She is, through there.' He headed towards another door. She wanted to turn back to the party room, but, as if in a trance, followed him into the room as the background music became almost like a pounding whisper.

Though the light was dingy, she could see the room was scarcely decorated, with a double bed under an unidentifiable painting. The man was staring at her, that much she could tell, as confusion washed over her. She began to feel as if she was being held underwater.

'Don't be afraid. Bell told me about you. Told me to look after you. First time and all that.'

Bell had mentioned her? Why? And first time for what?

The man switched on a lamp, the light highlighting a scarcely furnished room with a bed and a startled expression on Eve's face.

'Don't be scared. Sit down and get comfortable.'

She now noticed how posh he sounded. Her body stiff as he placed his hands onto her shoulders, gently leading her towards the bed.

'Sit down, I don't bite,' he said.

'I …'

'You really should have taken that drink when I offered it.'

He sat beside her on the bed and placed a hand onto her leg.

'I should be getting back,' she said. Her heart was beating fast.

'Why?'

'Bell …'

'Bell's busy. Don't worry about that old hag. I like you.'

Before she could utter a response his hand was behind her head pressing her face onto his lips, crushing her, stifling her words.

'Get off!' she managed.

'This won't take long.' His hand tore at her blouse and she quickly felt his cold hand connect with her skin beneath it.

'Get off me!' she roared, pushing him roughly away.

'What's going on with you?' he said, eyes ablaze with anger.

'Leave me alone!'

'What?'

She made for the door. She needed to get out and find Bell. This man had wanted to do what Stan had planned and she'd die before she'd ever let that happen. She would even kill – she'd already proved that.

The door was jammed and wouldn't open and panic rose in her body.

'Help!' she screamed.

'Stop! Shut up! I wasn't going to hurt you, stupid bitch!' he said, now equally panicked.

The door flew open and Bell appeared.

'I'm out of here!' said the man, pushing past Bell.

'Bell, I'm so glad you're here, he tried … he was going to … I don't think you should let him get away!' Eve's breaths came in spurts, the adrenalin refusing to disperse.

She clutched her stomach, unable to grapple with the relief of seeing a friendly face. 'Call the police!' cried Eve without thinking. Of course she couldn't talk to the police; she was on the run after all. 'No, I mean … you don't have to call them, just make sure he never comes back here. Please. He's really dangerous.'

'You silly girl,' said Bell with a sneer.

'What?'

'Are you stupid?'

'But he was going to …'

'He was going to have a good time with you, pay you well for it and now you've frightened him away. You do know he's one of our regulars, don't you?'

'Regulars? What are you talking about?'

'Did you think you were up here just to serve drinks?'

'Yes … what … yes, like downstairs.'

'You're as stupid as you look, then. I knew you weren't as old as you said but I let that go because I thought the punters would like it and you'd make a lot of cash. Last time I try to help anyone. I'll never make that mistake again,' said Bell, shaking her head.

'You wanted me to …?'

'Go home, Eve.' Bell's heels clicked in her wake as she left the room.

Frightened the man would return, Eve grabbed her belongings from the staff room and ran out of the building as if being chased, only daring to feel safe once back inside her room in the B & B. The shock of what happened meant she needed time to feel calm again, for her breathing to settle and to not think of what had almost happened with the man in the bar; to not think of what Stan too had almost done.

When she awoke the next morning, her mind was less foggy and she felt clearer in what she needed to do.

Daylight had stripped the club's building of any power, the peeling paint now much more visible.

'Who is it?' shouted a voice Eve recognised.

The door opened to reveal Bell, looking as skinny as ever, the traces of last night's make-up still visible on her haggard face.

'What do you want, Eve? Come to get your job back? I don't think so.'

Eve wanted to tell her that was never going to happen but forced herself to be polite.

'I've come for my money, that's all.'

'Money? What money would that be?'

'I worked five shifts this week …?'

Bell closed the door behind her and stepped into the street, invading Eve's personal space.

'You have got to be kidding me.'

'I just want the money I am owed.'

'That punter you embarrassed? Well, he won't be coming back in a hurry so we're down a lot of cash because of you.'

'That's not my problem. I just want the money you owe me,' she repeated.

Bell was moving dangerously close to Eve. 'We're even. Now get the fuck out of here!'

Being so close, Eve felt the full rage in Bell's voice, yet this was not even mildly equal to what was building inside of her.

The obscenities rolling from Bell's mouth, unable to cause a flinch because she'd heard them all before, especially the ones about Eve's skin colour. Bell could not and would not intimidate her.

'You owe me money and I would like it now,' said Eve firmly.

'What, are you going to call the police? I doubt that. Now, you just go on home or I'll get two of the lads to remove you. They start their shifts soon.'

Her mind flashed to the two burly bouncers employed by the club. Huge bulldog-type thugs who she suspected would think nothing of physically manhandling a girl. As for the police, Bell was right ... she couldn't risk that for more than one reason.

As she turned and walked away with a straight posture and a roll of her eyes, anyone looking on would know she was better than Bell. Better than the situation she'd found herself in. No one needed to know she didn't have a penny to her name and within a few days could be out on the streets again. She was Eve Cole and she would find a way out of this current predicament.

She had to.

'You'll keep, Bell,' she said loudly. An empty threat? No. She was just going to choose her battles wisely; Bell would keep for another day.

Instead of looking for work, Eve remained in the room – hers for another three days – with thoughts turned towards Stan, hating him more than ever before and hating herself for still allowing him the power to drive her thoughts. She was nothing like the heroines she'd read about in favourite novels; they overcame adversities and triumphed. She was not even fit to utter their names. She was weak ... a kid from a children's home who no one actually wanted, not even her own mother. She was a nothing.

That night she wondered what death would feel like. Would she be at peace or would the same worries that stalked her carry over into eternity?

Quickly, a memory appeared: that of Daddy, Lana and May happily dancing in the snow. It may have been the first time they'd ever seen snow. But that feeling, as large cotton-wool buds fell from the sky and landed on the tip of her nose, had felt like she was being bathed in magic.

She closed her eyes, and the dark corners of her mind comfortably caressed the possibility of falling asleep and never waking up, just like Daddy.

Chapter Nineteen

Lana sat in a half-furnished flat on a dodgy south London estate deemed dodgy by the locals.

Since moving into the notorious Grogan Estate, she'd regularly clocked the police presence outside the local newsagent's, and the boarded-up flats on the ground floor. The small gangs of children loitering in every corner clutching bottles of cider failed to intimidate her in the slightest because they simply reminded her of the kids at Sir John Adams Children's Home. The small cockroaches running along the sink of her kitchen, and the iron bars attached to her front windows and doorway were less welcome. But being inside her first real home since the age of twelve meant she was grateful for the warmth of the radiator, comfortable second-hand armchair, and to be able to get up when she pleased, eat when she wanted to, without the constant noise of a busy dinner hall … allowed to truly be the adult she had always been.

This was supposed to be the most exciting time of her life, yet the pain of May's disappearance weighed heavily on her soul.

When first told that May had gone, she'd called John Adams Children's Home daily as well as liaising with the welfare service and the police. Yet there'd been no sightings of her sister. The painful realisation that no one cared about a sixteen-year-old black runaway soon became clear to her.

The ensuing weeks were mostly spent moping around the half-finished flat, still hoping May would turn up, unable to settle her mind on much else, the excitement of her first home drowned out by worry.

The only person with the power to lift her spirits was Clifton. His weekend visits in the past, always fun, now served as a lifeboat to keep her from drowning in her own depths of despair. He prepared his 'special breakfast' of cereal, fruit and cream in the morning and baked beans on toast for dinner, and insisted that she eat when she insisted she couldn't. He would refuse to leave until every last morsel of food had disappeared. Never one to engage in emotional heart to hearts, his bad jokes and attempts at forcing her to smile mostly worked.

And now, after three months of tapping into the strength and presence of her best friend, Lana began to pull away from the negative and dare to imagine a life where hope still lived.

'I'm going to find Tina,' she said.

Clifton's expression dropped. 'I thought you were going to try and get on with things.'

'I never said that included giving up on Tina. May's disappearance knocked me for six but, instead of moping about it, I want to find Tina. At least then, I would have one of my sisters back.'

'Lana, this is …'

'Important to me, Clifton. YOU know how important this is to me. So please, please don't tell me not to do this!'

The social worker wasn't much help.

'Lana, like I told you when you rang, there is nothing you can do,' she said, her eyes on the clock. As if Lana hadn't noticed her do that twice already. The office was a mess with papers and books strewn across the desk, a small typewriter with a sheet of embossed paper still inside. 'Tina has been adopted and you no longer have any rights. You're not her parent, you're just her sister.'

'There must be something!'

'She's almost eight years old now and with a family. It's better for everyone if you just get on with your life.'

By the age of eight, Lana had already travelled to a new country and begun a new life in England. She'd loved to dance, was so very inquisitive about her surroundings and enjoyed dressing up in pretty dresses. What was Tina like? Did she even remember her older sisters?

That night, at home, she relayed the encounter to Clifton, hoping to get him to be as outraged as she was.

But he took her hand and stared her square in the eye. 'The social worker's right. You don't have any rights and if they won't tell you who she was adopted by it's going to be impossible to find her.'

'I'll hire a private investigator.'

'With what?' His voice was loud as his eyes remained fixed on her. He held her shoulders, gently. 'Lana, stop this. You have to stop this. You don't have any money. You're about to be nineteen. You have your whole life ahead of you.'

She shook her head slowly as the tears began to fall. 'I can't go on, not without my sisters!'

'Yes, you can. I will be with you every step of the way. I'll help you fill out the forms for jobs, college, whatever you need to help you get on with your life.'

She wiped a tear from her eyes, angry at Clifton for not being on her side ... angry that he was the second person that day to tell her to get on with her life.

'Nice one for *just* getting into polytechnic,' enthused Clifton, as Lana handed him the offer letter.

'Studying has never come easy to me, but I scrape by,' she said, unable to match his elation. She could only think of her sisters. This was usual whenever something good happened, because she simply wanted to share her news with them. Let Tina know she had a 'clever' big sister; compare notes with May on their academic achievements. But over the course of days and weeks, she had begun to participate more in her life, her future.

'It will give you something to look forward to and get you closer to a career.'

'I miss them,' she said, wanting to rest her head on Clifton's greasy shirt. He'd been working all day at his stepdad's garage.

'I know you do.'

'And I'm going to see them again, I promise you. Getting some decent qualifications will get me a good job and I'll be able to afford to find them.'

'I know. For now though, you're doing the right thing by concentrating on the future. Getting good marks and being the best you can be.'

'May always planned on going to university,' she said, again, ignoring Clifton's attempts at a pep talk. 'It's what Daddy always wanted for us both. He told us often enough!'

'How do you know she won't? At this minute, she's probably got her head stuck in a book preparing to take over the world!'

At that very moment near the centre of London, Eve stood under a makeshift shelter as rain plummeted onto the plastic sheet above her head.

The crowds were thinning due to the weather and a feeling of dread began to set in. Less people meant less money. She didn't know how long she could do this for, yet had to admit her life looked a hundred per cent better than it had just three months ago.

That night in her room, when the thought of death had taken on a comfortable inevitability, she'd walked into a urine-infested phone box and dialled the number of Sir John Adams Children's

Home. Before she could further consider what she was about to do, she had to know. She *needed* to be told that final piece of news so that, in some way, it would validate what was currently moving through her mind.

She asked to speak to Mrs Daventry. It was time for a confession and a verbal goodbye to a woman who had been privy to the destruction of a life that, by all accounts of her memory, had started off all right. A warm home. A family. Now she had nothing and was tired of fighting. When the woman – whose voice she thankfully did not recognise – kindly explained she was off until Monday, Eve had almost hung up. Then she heard the next sentence:

'Would you like to speak with Mr Alford? He's second in charge.'

She took a sharp breath. 'Mr Alford?'

'Yes, that's right.'

'Stan Alford?'

'Yes, that's correct.'

She replaced the receiver immediately. Stan was alive. A sad day for humankind but a good one for her. She hadn't killed him. He hadn't died. His life had not ended. At that moment, as a loud avalanche of tears flooded out of her and she slid down the glass of the urine-infested phone box, Eve, with every heave of her chest, felt the onset of a rebirth. The knowledge she had not taken a life had now presented her with the chance of a new one. She had teetered on a ledge but was suddenly ready to go back inside and at least make an attempt at starting again. She would give it her best shot. No, she would give it her *all*.

And so the following morning arrived with a fresh outlook on life and a promise to take on the day with a new vigour and zest. The Bells and Stans of this world would never win. Eve Cole was determined to continue on her journey of becoming somebody one day and to finally live the life she deserved.

She'd stumbled upon a street market that very afternoon. A hive of stalls selling jewellery, food and clothes and Cockney stallholders shouting their wares over an aroma of fruity scents. She'd stopped at a stall to admire a T-shirt with a colourful, stringy image of Jimi Hendrix emblazoned on the front. A bit too psychedelic for her but very hypnotic and she couldn't stop staring at it.

'Name your price!' said a rather dishevelled yet fashionable-looking white woman with yellow and purple hair.

'I'm just looking, thanks.'

'Story of my life! No one wants to own original art anymore!'

The T-shirts did appear unique.

'I would if I had the money.'

A young man appeared, grazing his fingertips over one of the T-shirts.

'Nice, right?' said Eve.

'Yeah, it's alright.'

'Alright? It's original art. You won't find that anywhere else and the lady who designs them ... let's just say, when she's famous in a few years' time these will be going for triple the price!'

'You think so?'

Eve winked at the man, as if they shared a secret.

'You know what, I'm going to take one for me and one for the wife.'

'Good choice!' said Eve, as the owner took over the transaction.

'That was really nice of you,' she said. 'I'm Atlas.'

'I'm Eve.'

'Very nice to meet you, Eve. You've definitely got the gift of the gab.'

'Thanks ... I think.'

'I owe you one.'

'You wouldn't happen to know where I can find a job?'

'How about here? Twenty per cent cut on all the shirts you sell?'

'Really? That could work!'

'Don't look so grateful, it's not as easy as you think.'

Eve had started her new job the following day and managed to earn enough for two bags of shopping. By the weekend, she'd accumulated enough to pay for another three days of bed and board and had renegotiated her percentage to thirty per cent.

Now, three months later, Eve stood under the shelter of a plastic sheet covering the T-shirt stall, knowing the recent rain showers would be a problem. No one bought T-shirts in the rain.

'Atlas, is there any way I can have an advance on my wages?'

'Advance on what? You earn what you sell, you know that. Sorry, love.'

Eve hoped Mrs Harris would be more understanding. Since being 'fired' from the club, Eve had felt her contempt with each look and each word. Yet, she'd refused to leave and a few enquiries had led her to discover just how expensive other B & Bs were in comparison.

'Eve, I need the rent up front or else you're out. You know the rules,' said Mrs Harris, clutching two bottles of beer as she walked up the stairs that evening.

'Old dragon!' hissed a voice as Eve walked into the 'living' room – a space filled with ripped seats and a wooden television that only played BBC1 and was only allowed on after 7pm.

'I'm Melanie, by the way,' said the girl. 'Want some gum?'

Eve stared at the girl's dirty fingernails. 'No, thanks.'

Melanie's face, her whole appearance, appeared unkempt, unclean even, and as if she'd been in a fight with a lump of mud.

'Trouble with the rent, then?' asked Melanie.

'Everything's fine.' Eve hoped to erase any illusion this girl had of them being the same.

'Maybe we can go out sometime, hit a club?' she pressed.

'No, thank you.'

'OK then, maybe you'll like the sound of this. What if we share one of the twin rooms? We can split the bill and that will save us cash. How about it?'

'I don't even know you.'

'What does that matter? It's about saving cash. We're probably the same age, both girls. I just hope you don't snore like Bob in room twenty-six. Do you know I can hear him through my walls? Just another reason for me to move.'

'No thanks.'

'OK, just a suggestion. Keep your very big hair on!'

Eve shot her a look.

'No offence. The Jacksons wear their hair like that and I'm a fan!'

Eve could only hope that Melanie would receive her standoffish nature in the manner in which it was meant. She'd no time for friends, especially people like Melanie. Besides, her main objective had to be making money, keeping a roof over her head and finding enough food to keep her alive. She'd be fine once the weather improved and the money from the stall increased.

For now, the priority was to get away from the overfriendly Melanie.

Eve was certain the library she had spotted last month would be a good hiding spot. She'd been meaning to go for weeks, but the need to make money had overshadowed even her need for books. But as soon as she stepped inside, it felt like home and she stayed longer than planned, having only spent a few minutes looking at the job classifieds and spending the majority of her time leafing through pages of novels.

'I'd like to take these out please,' she said grandly, placing three hardbacks and a paperback onto the counter.

'Can I see your library card please?'

'I . . . I don't have one.' The excitement of wall-to-wall books had dulled her of any common sense. 'What do I need, to join the library?'

'Two utility bills.'

'I see.'

'Don't you live in the area?'

'I do ... but I'm under eighteen.'

'That's alright then. Just get your mum to come along with the bills and then I can sign you up.'

'OK ...'

'Or your dad?' the librarian added more kindly.

'I'll just return these to the shelves,' Eve said.

She placed the smallest of the books on the windowsill behind the bookshelf, hoping to return to it another day.

Each day after a stint on Atlas's stall, the library was Eve's destination. If she wasn't allowed to take any books out yet, she would stay in the warm and dry, reading for hours, bathed in utter contentment as she allowed the stories to transport her into a decadent world of money and power – all of which would be hers one day. Of course, she still trawled through the classifieds, but the recent improvement in the weather had allowed her to feel a little bit more secure with Atlas and the market stall for the time being.

'Where do you disappear to every day, then?' asked Melanie. Eve stared blankly at the television, hoping this kid would leave her in peace. All day, she'd been shouting at passers-by, trying to sell T-shirts and the last thing she wanted to do now was talk to a silly little girl she had nothing in common with.

'I have a job,' said Eve.

'All day?'

Eve wondered why Melanie seemed intent on becoming her friend. This weakness just made Eve despise her even more.

'Whatever you do, must be good. Or else you wouldn't have stayed so long, right?'

'Right,' she replied dryly.

Melanie soon tired of the effort, leaving Eve to doze off on the sofa. Sounds from the corridor startled Eve awake minutes later.

'Ohhhh!'

'Are you alright, Bob?' she called quietly as the old man from number twenty-six slumped against the staircase. He'd often turn up drunk, yet this time his groans sounded more like pain. She stooped to help him up.

'Let's get you upstairs and inside,' she said almost reluctantly. The thought of being alone with a man in a room repulsed her, yet, with him possibly being in his seventies and in such a drunken state, she was sure to be in the most dominant position. She opened the unlocked door to his room, leaving it wedged open with one of his shoes – just in case – and lay him on the bed. He uttered the first of many 'Thank You's' as she noticed one of the side drawers was wide open, revealing a ten pound note. Bob fell asleep quickly. Her eyes shot back to the money.

She bent down to the drawer to close it but her hand unconsciously drifted inside where she felt the sensation of a number of bank notes. She couldn't be sure but there was possibly hundreds of pounds there at least. Why was Bob staying in this dump if he had funds? she wondered, before a snort from the man himself startled her. She gazed at the money again, grabbing at a note and then another, until a cool hundred pounds nestled against the palm of her hands. Another snore. Eve turned to the door, then back to the drawer full of money. Exhaling, she placed each note back into its original hiding place. And that night, she walked out of room twenty-six with a strange feeling of frustration and ... satisfaction.

No matter what her circumstances, Eve Cole was no thief.

The next morning, Eve awoke with a sharp poke on her shoulder. After opening her eyes abruptly, she had already swiped her assailant across the face before realising who it was.

'You cow!' screamed Mrs Harris, dabbing at her rapidly reddening cheek. 'That's another good reason to sling you out!'

'I'm sorry, Mrs Harris,' she said, sitting up, horrified at her violence.

'You will be.'

'Why did you wake me up like that?'

'I want you out of here, today,' she hissed.

'It was an accident!'

'You stealing two hundred quid from one of my guests last night was no accident and I will not have it, you hear? I run a respectable establishment! That poor man's savings – what have you done with his money?'

Eve rubbed at her eyes, the morning haze now taken over by a harsh reality as she realised that her room had been searched while she slept.

'I haven't stolen anything!'

'I want you to pack your things and get out. By noon. Or else I'll call the police! I should have gotten rid of you ages ago when you showed me up in front of my mates over at the club. You're nothing but a criminal!'

Ignoring the irony in this statement, Eve knew that if she came into contact with the police she could be taken to prison. She may not have killed Stan, but she had busted open his large head!

'Don't do that. No police.'

'I won't if you go by noon. If it was up to me, I would have called the constable ages ago, but Bob stopped me. Silly fool is probably up to no good!'

'Bob?'

'Yes, Bob. You were seen helping him into his room last night. Disgusting, taking advantage of a drunken old man.'

Eve immediately began to gather up her clothes with the tiring thought that she'd have to find somewhere else to live. Three days of paid-up board wasted and she only had a few pounds left in her pocket.

She picked up the PE sack and small case she'd purchased from the market and Melanie appeared.

'Off then?'

'I suppose you heard,' said Eve.

'Yeah, shame that.'

'I'll survive.'

'I'm sure you will.'

Eve made her way to the door, then suddenly stopped. 'It was you, wasn't it?'

'Prove it.'

Eve smiled, a mixture of contempt and admiration for the girl she'd merely seen as an irritant.

'How did you—?'

'I saw you take the old man into his room. You left the door unlocked. Stupid that.'

Melanie walked away with a slight tilt to her walk, perhaps aware that Eve would not take the allegation any further. She also knew that if it came to believing one teenage girl's word against another, Mrs Harris was far more likely to believe the white girl. Though perhaps she and Melanie were more alike than Eve had dared to believe. Just two underage girls attempting to navigate a life on the streets.

By noon, Eve once again found herself standing beside her belongings with nowhere to go. Luckily, on a Wednesday the market was closed, so she'd use the time to plan her next move.

She walked the streets searching for another B & B or hostel she could afford until the cloak of night began to fall. As well as her cash supply, her options were also depleting. Most of the places had no vacancies, or said they didn't when she appeared at the door. When her fruitless search brought her to the darkened pavement outside of Reed's Department Store, she noticed a woman wrapped in a threadbare blanket sleeping in the doorway. Careful not to disturb her and hoping she wasn't about to take anyone's spot, Eve, with her bag as an uncomfortable pillow and her coat as a blanket, rested her body in the doorway next to the unnamed woman who didn't even stir for the rest of the night.

Very early the next morning, Eve opened her eyes abruptly. The chitter-chatter of the road sweepers mixed in with a calm and yet eerie atmosphere only this time of the morning could bring, was something she'd never get used to.

The second night was only slightly easier because she knew what to expect. By the third night it had almost become a routine – one she couldn't let continue.

Before the break of the sun, Eve was up and standing in front of a mirror in a smelly public toilet splashing cool water onto her cheeks. She purchased a plate of soggy chips and a mug of tea at the cafe nearby – the cheapest thing on the menu – where the waited until it was time for work.

'What's with the luggage?' asked Atlas on the third day.

'I'm off to my cousin's after work.'

'What, every day this week?'

'Something like that.'

'In between places then?'

'I'm not sure what you mean.'

'You sleeping rough? That's what I mean.'

'No, I'm not,' replied Eve firmly, wondering why this woman wouldn't just mind her own business. Eve's job was to sell her poxy T-shirts and nothing more.

That afternoon, the steady flow of customers was in direct correlation with how long the sun shone. During a lull, Atlas 'casually' mentioned the name and address of a hostel offering bed and board for the night, to the first twenty people in line.

Eve rushed to the hostel straight after work and was met by a burly man who informed her, albeit kindly, that she was too late – she'd need to be standing in line by 5.30pm to possibly have a chance.

The next day Atlas complained about Saturday being one of their busiest days and leaving early was usually not an option, whilst the thought of possibly losing her best salesperson may just have convinced her to be more understanding to Eve's request.

'You're lucky,' said the man at the door of the hostel when she got there. 'You're here on time, so it looks like you'll get a bed for the night.'

Eve opened her mouth, before closing it again. Tempted to ask him to please define the word 'lucky'.

Yet, that night, Eve was unable to sleep. While the harshness of the bunk bed was still a luxury compared to the cold doorway of Reed's Department Store, she found it difficult to settle in a large room with twenty-four no-hopers. The coughing, farting and general mumbling, along with someone crying in their sleep, begging for their mother, was more than distracting. The lingering odours ranging from stale alcohol, sweat and urine, seemed to permanently float around the room and were also major distractions! As was the lack of hope permeating the rancid air. Eve told herself she was nothing like anyone in that room. Perhaps she was being unfair by judging them, embellishing their stories to suit her needs, but she'd no choice. She could not afford to care about their stories, or to ever think she was like them. Unlike them, she was going to get out of this predicament. She was different.

At around 3am, tiredness allowed Eve to finally drift into an uncomfortable sleep, her eyes popping open just five minutes later. Her senses were sharp, her sleep light and she was able to sense the presence of a man standing too close to the bed.

'What do you want?' she hissed. The dorm rooms were meant to be single sex but clearly this man wasn't into following the rules. The dimmed lights allowed her to notice his smiling lips.

'Thought you might have something to eat.'

'Do I look like I do?'

'Shut up, I'm trying to sleep,' said a voice from somewhere.

The man quickly moved off in another direction as Eve noticed her heartbeat had accelerated. The rational side of her knew he could not have hurt her in a roomful of other women, whilst the less rational part decided she would prefer to sleep in the cold doorway of Reed's rather than return to the hostel.

Eve sold fifteen shirts the very next day, a record even for Atlas.

'I don't know what your secret is, but you've got it!'

'I just tell people what they want to hear.'

'Well, keep it up! You could make us thousands!'

Eve was finally able to pay up front for a B & B near the stall, slightly more expensive than Mrs Harris's and just as dowdy and soulless. But with every turn of the key in the door to her own room, she immediately felt safer than she had in days.

Chapter Twenty

Eve walked tentatively through the revolving doors of Reed's Department Store and into a spectacular buzzing area of activity. Men in suits straightened their ties; women, wearing name badges and uniforms that tightly nipped at the waist, expertly rearranging shiny bottles of perfume. Eve joined the handful of early-bird customers to be intoxicated by the smell of wealth and opulence. The promise of what is, and what could be, meshing beautifully in her midst.

She ignored the tall security guard continually clocking her each and every move as she walked past sweet-smelling perfumes without being offered a spritz. Then onto the womenswear department where she was faced with an oasis of expensive soft-flowing fabrics she knew would one day be a staple in her own wardrobe.

Moving her fingers along a rack of silk blouses and thick real-wool jackets, she refused to feel anything less than indignant regarding her own clothes. They were cheap, market-bought essentials, yet she wore them as if they'd cost thousands. Even when she'd slept in the doorway of this very store, leaving before the first set of deliveries at 5am, she'd ensured no one would ever have known her brief homeless status by appearance alone. Her posture had remained upright and her lips curved into a dignified smile.

The security guard hovered in the corner of her eye and she gave him a fake smile. One day, she would work in Reed's or at least a similar store in terms of prestige and central heating! With winter fast approaching, she'd no intention of spending another cold season working in the market, jumping up and down on the balls of her feet to keep warm as passers-by glanced her way with pity.

The next phase of her plan would begin before Christmas.

Over the summer months and into autumn, Eve had saved enough money to rent a tiny single room in a flat above a family-owned cafe tucked away on a treeless street. There were three other rooms in the flat and four other flatmates she had no intention of getting to know. Her room consisted of a single bed with no headboard, a tiny table and a chest of draws. There was no wardrobe, and the small window was dirty with dingy disintegrating nets and dusty old curtains. She'd immediately stripped the bed and replaced it with linen purchased from the market stall a few yards from Atlas. She cleaned everything she could; the net curtains she'd ripped down and washed with her hands in the sink and she'd beaten the worst of the dust from the velvet curtains, surprised to see they weren't bad quality. She bought a simple lamp, which she placed on the tiny table beside the bed. It had a dull glow, reminding her of the one at John Adams ... the one that had turned into a weapon.

Despite her best efforts to keep her own room spotlessly clean, lying in bed at night she couldn't ignore the intermittent scratching sounds from the floorboards. 'It's your imagination,' she repeated to herself on loop, unwilling to imagine any sort of wildlife living within her midst. She would also ignore the mould growing inside the shared fridge, ensuring the section marked 'Eve' would be wiped down with disinfectant every single day.

Eve's new routine had evolved; work at Atlas, reading in the library and then onto Reed's Department Store just for a browse and sometimes stretching to buy the smallest, cheapest item from the food hall. An overpriced fizzy drink shipped from America, a soft-centred fondant from a French patisserie or a foreign jar of mayonnaise – such items representing one treat she allowed herself each month: tokens of luxury to remind Eve of where she was and where she was heading. She didn't have to be a shrink to know why the mayonnaise was so important to her.

So, one of the flatmates couldn't understand her level of anger when Eve caught her dipping into the jar of French mayonnaise.

'My section of the fridge is clearly marked 'Eve'! Didn't you see it, you idiot?'

'We always share each other's sauces and that!'

'This isn't bloody Hellmann's, it's French!' she said totally pointlessly as the girl stared back at her blankly.

'I used a spoon.'

'I don't care!' Her voice was laced with violence. 'Don't you ever touch my stuff again!'

'You should have said that then!'

'I'm saying it now!'

The table beside her bed was where she wrote the application for Eve Cole, the name 'May' banished to the past just like the jar of mayonnaise she'd tipped into the bin straight after the altercation. Although she'd been answering to Eve for some time now, seeing it written on a piece of paper, ready to be placed into official hands, somehow validated this new existence. May Cole was truly a name from the past that needed to be filed away in her mind, never to be revisited, buried amongst a clutter of memories including her father, mother, Tina, Lana and Ginny, too, and all her memories of number sixty-three Pettyford Road. Although her birth month remained the same, she also added five years onto her age, just in case.

Eve stated Atlas as a referee, unsure if she'd even agree to it, now that her meal ticket was in the midst of leaving. But the inclusion demonstrated a history of work and, with the addition of a home address and a telephone number, the application was ready to be submitted.

She entered Reed's Department Store, smiling at the security guard who was now used to seeing her virtually every day. One of the smartly dressed, yet overly made-up, perfume ladies directed her to the fourth-floor personnel department where she proudly handed in her application.

'We're only recruiting for warehouse staff at the moment,' said the spotty girl behind the desk, holding Eve's application by her fingertips like it was a used sheet of toilet roll.

'Thank you, the warehouse is fine,' replied Eve.

'Have you put your telephone number down?'

'Yes, it's all there.'

'I see from here that it's your birthday today.'

'Yes.'

'Happy birthday,' she said dryly.

'Thanks.'

'We'll be in touch. Or not.'

'Thank you.'

Chapter Twenty-one

Lana Cole was handed the certificate up on the small stage where she caught a glimpse of a beaming Clifton cheering her on loudly from the audience. It was times like these – the good times, not only the bad – that Lana really missed her parents. She hoped that they'd have been proud of her. She hoped their sacrifices had been worthwhile.

Her newly acquired certificate in office management finally led to her getting a job helping to run a medium-sized health centre with a busy reception. She'd started as an admin assistant but soon worked her way up through the ranks. She enjoyed assisting vulnerable young families who came in on a daily basis. Chatting with the elderly patients and simply going above the call of her administrative duties whenever possible. Clifton said she liked to be needed. Perhaps he was right.

Weekends were spent with Clifton and his friends, or walking around the huge park behind the Grogan Estate. The 'concrete jungle' or 'sink estate' she'd called home for three years was now her haven. Despite its reputation, Lana had never witnessed anything more horrific than a young boy telling an older man to 'Shut up!' The bars on her doors and windows were simply pointless.

In the early years of a new decade Lana Cole was a twenty-one-year old with a job, a home, the occasional date with a friend of a colleague, a best friend named Clifton and one constant nagging belief: one day she would find her sisters and they would be a family again. Such thoughts never left her. Whether typing up notes at work, undergoing an excruciating first date or flicking through Mummy's address book and the photos that had been left in the vanity case all those years ago, her two sisters were never far from her mind; May and Tina continued to be her sole reasons for living.

An increase in her salary meant Lana had finally succumbed to redecorating the living room. The green and white spiral wallpaper had been placed onto the wall rather haphazardly by Lana and Clifton. The black chesterfield sofa made of cloth was second-hand but looked as good as new. The tall-stemmed lamp that curved at the top, highlighted a low-rise oblong-shaped wooden cabinet that had a space big enough for a set of books – just in case May ever came to stay. When she was finally able to afford the Pioneer record player, the first record she placed onto the turntable was Cliff Jack's 'Memories of a Day Later'.

> *I see you every day, even though you're not here*
> *Memories of a day later*
> *I feel you in my heart, even though you're not here*
> *These are the things I remember*
> *Memories, oh oh memories*
> *Memories of a day later.*

The tears that followed were not entirely unexpected as she had memories of dancing around a wooden-boxed record player with Mummy and Daddy many years before: a yellow dress with lace embroidery; Aunty Ginny's hearty encouragement; a wide, opened globe of the world that dispensed alcohol; the laughter of adults intermingling with the giggling of two little girls. How she missed those days.

'This is such a cool machine,' enthused Clifton, pulling the transparent cover away from the record player. 'Can't say much about the choice of song. Don't you have any Jackson 5?'

'Did you bring what I asked, Clifton?'

'Yep, in the bag.'

'Great.'

'You been blubbing again?'

'No,' she lied, taking out a bag of multicoloured birthday candles, which she would place onto the shop-bought cake, a small token done twice a year to remember each of her sibling's birthdays. Today would be Tina's tenth.

He placed his arm around her shoulder. 'No more tears, alright?'

'I'm glad you're here.'

'Where else would I be? This is a weird tradition between us now. I have to be here.'

'I hope it didn't mess up your plans.'

'Joanna can wait until tomorrow, can't she?'

'And who's Joanna?' She scrunched her face playfully.

'Erm …' he said, scratching his head, now covered in a full head of hair just like that of his heroes the Jackson 5. She wasn't sure how he was able to keep it that high when he worked mostly under cars! Indeed, working in a family business – his stepfather's – afforded him such luxuries.

Family.

'Tell me more about Joanna.'

'She's a nice girl. What more can I say?'

'Clifton Joseph, they are always nice girls right up until the day before you dump them!'

'I'm still looking for my "one", aren't I?'

'No, you're not.'

'Nah, you're right. I'm a twenty-one-year-old guy, I am *not* looking to settle down just yet!'

'You're just weird.'

'I'm weird? You can talk. Celebrating birthdays for sisters who don't even bother to show up!'

Lana would never take offence at his words. Out of everyone, Clifton understood her and this journey so far, never one to roll his eyes as she reeled off yet another sister-related story, forever opening his arms to an embrace whenever she needed to let her tears flow. Clifton Joseph: the only person who, apart from one blip, had remained a constant in her life.

Chapter Twenty-two

Eve was always keen to stay away from the pointless chatter among the warehouse staff. Her main objective was to do her job quietly and efficiently and without being bothered about nonsensical stuff. The work was strenuous at times, what with the heavy lifting and she would often leave work with a sore back and aching arms. The dust particles attached to every fibre of her clothing and clung to the edges of her hair. Yet, she'd always complete each task with a smile, even when the mostly male workforce relied on improper conversations to get through the day.

'OK, here's a joke I made up: what do you call a woman in one of them miniskirts, ring on her finger and a roasting tin in her hand?'

'Wot?'

'My wife!'

'Hahahaha!'

'I got another one: what do you call a girl in a miniskirt, no ring on her finger and a roasting tin in her hand?'

'Not your wife?'

'Nah, a bloody tart with an appetite!'

'Hahahaha.'

When one of the idiots actually had the audacity to ask her out on a date, Eve's imagined response was to slap him hard across the face, yet a hurried 'No, thank you,' sufficed.

'I know people say we shouldn't mix. But the world's getting a lot more accepting now, you know. So, you know, if you don't want to go out with me because I'm a white bloke and you're coloured ...' She winced at the word 'coloured'. She'd never liked that term because it somehow implied she had been one colour and then filled in with a felt-tip pen. She much preferred the term 'black' that some people used.

'I mean, it's the seventies, time to move with the times and all that. Why not give me a chance ...?'

'Because you're an idiot,' she wanted to say, 'and I really don't fancy those.'

'I can't see anyone else asking you out around here,' he added sulkily, once he realised his chat-ups were going nowhere.

'I'll live,' she said.

'Suit yourself.'

Eve Cole was at Reed's Department Store to work.

Eve Cole had a plan.

Whenever she was sent to deliver packages to the main floor of Reed's Department Store, she'd do so with an excitement nestling in her belly. This was a glimpse into another life and one she craved – so close and yet out of reach all at the same time.

But she was patient.

Slowly walking up the stairs and into a sweet-smelling utopia away from the dusty boxes and filthy mouths in the warehouse, she felt like Alice stepping through the looking glass, though she had hated that book as a child.

When, after eighteen months of warehouse duties, Eve dropped an updated CV into the hands of the personnel department on the fourth floor, she was told not to bother until she had been employed in the warehouse for at least two years. So, six months later, she finally felt prepared for the next stage of her life. Having worked at Reed's for so long, she was a known hard worker, with no punctuality issues. And she hoped this brief history with the company would allow her modest yet well-put-together look at the high-fashion sales assistant interview to be overlooked. Unlike floor staff, warehouse personnel were not given a clothes allowance – so Eve turned up wearing what she could afford to buy: a pair of black, flared trousers and a white shirt with ruffles at the neckline, both bought from the market.

'Thank you for coming today. We will go over the interview notes and inform you of our decision,' said the interviewer.

'That would be fine.'

'But do bear in mind that your shop-floor experience is zero, and we do like our girls to be familiar with sales.'

Eve thought about drawing his attention to her successful sales experience at the market, clearly stated there on her CV and perhaps mentioning Rebecca Whatsherface, who, after six months in the warehouse, had been transported to the shop floor. Or Amanda Whatever who she saw every day in the staff canteen, fresh out of school with 'zero' experience, who now served customers in the shoe department. The difference between her and them? Both Amanda and Rebecca were white.

'I understand. Totally,' she said.

The evening after the interview, she sat on her bed with the small window open, allowing the nightly greasy aroma to filter in from the cafe downstairs. She dared not think about what an increase in wages would mean for her. She could afford a flat of her very own for a start – a studio, of course, having already assessed rental prices in the area and produced a chart calculating all incomings and outgoings. Life would be a lot easier. She was hopeful of that.

Eve spent the next week thinking and planning as if the job was already hers, living in the future. This was the only way to cope, to get on, to live.

When she did finally receive notification from the fourth floor, this came via one of her warehouse colleagues: 'Aye love, looks like you're leaving us. You're wanted in the la-di-da section upstairs. Well done, you made it out of here!'

Eve quickly realised that working with customers on the shop floor wasn't what she looked forward to each day. The clientele was basically uppity, and most customers were in need of a personality overhaul, but through smiles and promises to 'order that item in a ten', Eve worked each day armed with a determination to rise up the ranks and one day become a manager. Like the heroines in her books, starting at the bottom was imperative: a means to an end. In her mind she was already at the top and was figuring out how to restructure the store now she knew its inner and outer workings. Two years in the warehouse had not been a waste.

Eve would not stop until she made the big decisions, until everyone answered to her, but, in the meantime, she needed to find a smaller-sized tunic for the woman in dressing-room cubicle two.

'I'm sorry,' she told the customer, 'we don't have that size but we do have it in blue.'

The customer let out an impatient sigh. 'Will you be getting any more in?'

'No, I'm afraid not.'

'Can you check again?'

'Madam, I'm afraid we don't have any more sizes. What's on the rail is all we have and we won't be getting any more in, I'm afraid.'

'Why ever not?'

'It's the end of that line. But I can show you something similar—'

'No, I need that one!'

The customer stormed back into the cubicle, pulling the curtain angrily.

Eve still had a full ten minutes until her lunch break, so decided to approach the elderly lady searching through a row of floral blouses.

'These are lovely, aren't they, Madam?' Eve said to the back of the woman.

'They certainly are. Do you have them in—' She stopped just as she turned around and faced Eve.

'What was that you needed, Madam?'

The woman's expression changed. 'Nothing. That's OK.'

'Let me know if you need anything,' said Eve.

Seconds later the elderly woman had asked Tara, one of the other sales assistants, about the floral blouses. No surprises. It wasn't the first time this had happened and wouldn't be the last.

'That last customer was such a rude cow,' whispered Tara, minutes later as they both sat down to lunch in the staff canteen. 'Fancy not wanting to be served by you,' she said, with a sympathetic smile.

'I know,' said Eve, rolling her eyes.

'Anyway, a few of us are going out for drinks after work today. Interested?'

Eve, keen to draw a distinction between work and her personal life, had not been interested the first time Tara had asked her just over a week ago.

'I'm a bit busy tonight'

'Are you shy, is that it?'

'Not at all. I'm just busy.' The words rolled easily off her tongue. She would be very busy that night with a pen and paper, plotting ways to advance up a career ladder that frankly wasn't designed for the likes of her: orphan; children's home; immigrant; young; female; black.

But nothing would ever hold her back. Her life would advance each day until she was finally able to live life on her own terms.

Tara and everyone else soon tired of asking Eve to join them at the pub or wherever else they spent their Friday and Saturday evenings. This striking, tall, young woman who hardly ever smiled was instead grabbing every bit of overtime available and working each task as if her life was dependent on its success.

And to Eve, it was.

Her look had evolved too. With the generous staff discount she'd been able to buy a few key pieces of the season that merely accentuated her beauty. Like the crushed-velvet trouser suit with gentle flares and the lamb-trimmed swing coat that accentuated her long legs. Eve was not interested in how she looked in the way the likes of Tara seemed to obsess over. She merely had to look the part in order to get noticed in a world dominated by fashion.

'Eve, I'm really impressed with your work here. Don't think it's gone unnoticed,' said Mr Hadley, manager of womenswear. Eve was very glad he'd noticed – she'd been clever, ensuring she folded the jumpers a little more delicately whenever he floated past during one of his floor tours; an extra touch of sickly-sweet sweetness to a rowdy customer if he was in earshot; an extra false smile as they crossed paths in the staff canteen.

When she was finally summoned to his plush leather-infused office a few days after his comments, this did not surprise her in the least.

'What do you know about press evenings?' he asked, sat behind a desk like a king surveying his kingdom.

'This is where you showcase the season's looks to the newspapers and magazines?'

'A very important occasion and a big deal for the store. Would you like to work that night?'

Eve had to suppress a bubble of excitement threatening to surface. 'That would be great.'

'Good. As I said, this is a big deal for us and we only ask our best staff to be on hand.' He got up and walked around the desk. 'You are more than ready for this.'

'Thank you so much, Mr Hadley.'

He proffered his hand. 'It's my pleasure.'

He held onto her fingers gently. 'I know when someone is keen and you're the best of the lot.'

'Thanks for seeing that, Mr Hadley. I try to work as hard as I can,' she said, wanting to kick herself for sounding so gushy.

Eve's excitement temporarily transported her away from the moment and she failed to notice their hands remaining entwined for longer than necessary.

'You'll be briefed by your supervisor in a few days.'

As Eve headed back onto the shop floor, she recalled the many heroines who had used their looks to get ahead. In Eve's world, men, dirty men, had always affirmed her attractiveness and beauty, and she'd recently pondered whether she should use this to move further and quicker up the work hierarchy. But as usual, her conclusion to that particular question was a firm 'no'. Then there were those hidden moments when she would question her so-called attractiveness. Her hair was as hard as cold lard when newly washed, her skin as dark as early night, her lips full and wider than what was normal. She looked nothing like the other female members of her team. She looked nothing like the female sales assistants who had been allowed onto the tills immediately, while she was still waiting to be trained up. But whether she was attractive or not, Eve had long ago prepared herself to work harder, much harder than anyone else in her position.

Everything would happen as she expected.

All she needed to do was continue with her plan.

The evening of the press launch, the staff were instructed to wear a piece form the collection they were showcasing that night. Eve chose a black puffy-sleeved blouse and a burnt-orange, pleated, flared skirt. Orange was as far as she would go with colour; Eve would wear black all day and every day if she could. Her hair was gathered away from her face and scooped into a large orange hairband, framing her lightly made-up face. A set of neon rubber bracelets dangled from her wrist.

'You look sensational!' enthused Mr Hadley.

'Thank you.'

'Very good! You ladies are so good at showing off the latest merchandise! I'm afraid I'm just sticking with the traditional male suit!'

A sales assistant walked over and whispered into Mr Hadley's ear and his face turned a strong crimson. 'I don't bloody believe this!'

'What is it, Mr Hadley?' Although not her assigned responsibility, Eve had checked the entire plans for the press evening. She'd also ensured each outfit had been steamed, the toilets cleaned and made sure the record playlist was appropriate for each section.

'Cynthia has gone down with measles!' spat Mr Hadley. The woman in charge of the set-up and running of the entire evening was contagious and not allowed to leave her bed.

'This is a disaster!' he said. Mr Hadley was now a lone angry figure among a swarm of staff moving about aimlessly. Without a leader, everyone was suddenly rendered mute and void of memory. The DJ had arrived and no one even knew where he should set up.

'Can I make a suggestion?' asked Eve.

'What?' snapped Mr Hadley.

'I've been working with Cynthia and I know the plans, what she wanted, everything. We have a copy of the timetable for the evening, all we need now at this moment is for someone to put that plan together.' It was simple really. Eve being the only member of staff not to give into panic, had begun to think logically before anyone else could. 'I can do it.'

'If you think this will work ...' he said sceptically.

'It will be fine, Mr Hadley, you'll see.'

Mr Hadley nodded his head in agreement and, with clipboard in hand, Eve strode confidently to the Ladies where she promptly threw up into the toilet bowl.

The press evening was a success.

The jealousy that followed was of no real concern to Eve. When Cynthia – and even Tara – threw snide comments just loud enough for her to hear, a once-buried instinct almost pushed her to confront them. But Eve was smart enough to look beyond that moment and instead picture the wonderful journey ahead.

As predicted, she was offered several more opportunities and responsibilities within Reed's based on that one successful press night. She continued to offer herself up for overtime without being asked and her responsibilities soon began to eclipse what she'd been originally hired for. Yet, despite remaining on a sales assistant's pay scale, she was satisfied. For now. She was determined to build her work history and, when the time came, leave for a more prestigious role, unless, of course, Reed's Department Store agreed to her terms.

'Amazing, you're still here!' said Mr Hadley one evening. He used his thumb to rub at a smear on one of the mirrors beside a row of skirts.

'I'll be finished soon. I just wanted to make sure everything was shipshape for the morning,' she said.

'If only all the girls here were as conscientious as you.' He appeared just outside the changing room cubicles as she cleared away hangers and sweet wrappers inside.

'You have such a lovely smile, Eve,' he said.

She walked past him, her body tense.

'Really nice to see every morning,' he continued, following behind her as she straightened up a row of dresses. In the handbag section just a few yards away, she spotted one of the older sales assistants neatening a row of box-shaped handbags. At least they were not alone.

His voice was now a whisper, for only Eve to hear. 'You're always keen to work late. Now, don't tell me it's all for nothing.'

'Mr Hadley, I ...' She took one step out of his way, her heart rate accelerating.

'Eve, I'm just complimenting your work ethic. Why are you running away from me? I don't bite ... unless you want me to ...'

'I have work to do,' she said, an edge creeping into her voice.

His eyebrows scrunched as if to question why she wouldn't want a man almost old enough to be her grandfather.

'Is that so ...'

'Mr Hadley, you're clearly propositioning me whilst I'm trying to work. Please don't do that and all will be fine.'

'How about after work? We could grab a drink somewhere.'

Eve rolled her eyes, her patience was disappearing. 'No, thank you, Mr Hadley.' As each word left her lips, she envisaged Stan, Nicola Rhodes, Bell, the nameless man from the club ... all had stood in the way of her progress.

'Why are you being so stupid and why are you intent on fucking up your career?' Gone was the nicely spoken manager, in his place a guttermouth with equally dirty morals.

'I work hard!'

'Yes you do, but you're clearly not willing to go the extra mile. You do know it was me who allowed you to get out of the warehouse and onto the shop floor?'

'I didn't know that.'

'There was no way you or anyone like you was going to get to be front of house. I put in a good word for you and this is the thanks I get.'

They stood face to face as if in a square off, his lecherous gaze moving over her entire body.

'I'm willing to give you another chance now you've had time to think about it.' He folded his arms expectantly.

She moved closer to him; the whiff of his aftershave was stronger than she'd realised.

He closed his eyes slowly and the tip of her lips flickered against his ear. Her voice was hoarse but clear. 'Go. To. Hell!'

He stepped aside, adjusting his collar. 'You do realise you're finished here, right?' He turned on the heels of his feet and was gone.

When Eve called in sick the next day, she was instantly believed, having never taken a day off before. She couldn't stay away forever but needed the time to plan her next move.

She sat on her bed the entire day with a pen and paper, her doodling leading to nothing, her mind unable to create any new avenues. She would have to face the truth; she was being sent on her way yet again and left without a plan or a direction.

She wasn't sure how she'd cope with this setback but she had to remain steadfast. She'd faced worse before. She could do this. She had to do this.

The next day when she finally walked back into work, the world seemed a duller place. Her dreams, once the source of sunshine, were now diminished with the thought of her expected sacking at the hands of yet another odious man. She would begin her shift as normal and just wait for the inevitable to happen. At least she had some savings this time, a cushion against homelessness. She would be OK until the next job.

A full week passed and no one summoned her to personnel during that time. Apparently, Mr Hadley was on holiday, so at least her firing would wait.

She was sat in the staff canteen nursing a coffee on the day she was finally summoned to personnel by a gleeful Tara. Her entire body moved with an acceptance of her fate as she dragged her feet along the floor with eyes fixated ahead.

A man and a woman, both unfamiliar, sat behind a desk and welcomed her in.

'Please sit down, Miss Cole,' said the man.

'You are probably wondering why you are here,' said the woman.

'Not really,' she mumbled.

'It's about Mr Hadley.'

Eve nodded, while thinking, Can we just get this over and done with? I really don't see the point in prolonging all of this. I know it's his word against mine.

'It has taken quite a while to compile all the statements. As you can imagine, this is very embarrassing for the company.'

'Statements?' She was in more trouble than she thought. How had she miscalculated this so badly? Had they also found out about the assault on Stan?

'As you may already know, we are seeing everyone Mr Hadley worked closely with.'

'W ... why? I thought it was his word against mine and you'd ...'

Both turned to one another and then back to Eve.

'No, you have a voice. As do all the young women who have come forward.'

'What other young women?' Slowly, the crossed wires started to align with one another.

'We are currently investigating a number of allegations of harassment made by female members of staff against Mr Hadley. We at Reed's will not tolerate such behaviour. We are a family firm with excellent morals and values,' said the man.

'One of your co-workers said she witnessed Mr Hadley making inappropriate remarks to you too,' the woman added. 'We wanted to know if he'd ever ...' She cleared her throat. 'Taken advantage of his position ...?'

Understanding dawned and Eve averted her eyes.

The woman from personnel reached out to pat her hand, then said, 'So please, in your own words, do tell us what happened.'

After Mr Hadley's departure, Eve and a number of female employees were promptly offered training schemes and advanced up the career ladder. Perhaps this was a way of buying their silence, or perhaps their work and dedication had finally been acknowledged as equal to the men. Eve suspected the former, yet simply did not care.

At the age of twenty-one she made sure to take every training course they were willing to pay for, do every hour of possible overtime and was careful to 'befriend' only those who could advance her career even further. She was now well on her way to fulfilling the dream of acquiring power, wealth and security – everything she needed to ensure she'd never, ever be a victim again.

Chapter Twenty-three

Eve sat on the leather chesterfield sofa watching the six o'clock news report on Concorde. Now it had been running for a few years, perhaps she should take a trip on it one day, especially as she travelled a lot for work. She stifled a yawn. It was already 11.30pm and she'd been home an hour, having taped the news story on her new video cassette recorder, which few others could possibly own yet.

Thanks to a hefty discount and generous salary, Eve's two-bedroom flat contained everything she'd ever need – or didn't actually need, but wanted. A far cry from a cold, dark doorway of a department store or putting up with the likes of Mrs Harris just for a warm bed. Now, thinking of those days simply fuelled her determination to succeed further. Even if long working hours meant no time for listening to music on the top-of-the-range music player or watching videos for that matter. Most of her time was spent at Reed's Department Store working her arse off, something she actually really enjoyed, especially as she now got to travel, to see other parts of the world as she acquired new products for the store.

Despite the travel, though, her favourite moments were still the ones spent in store swanning into each department, discussing new lines and altering shop displays. In almost two years, she'd nurtured a reputation of being a firm but fair boss, not to be messed with. She never accepted social invitations unless they were work related and would often chastise any sales assistant caught gossiping on the shop floor. She was Eve Cole, who now drove a Jaguar XJC, had tasted caviar and foie gras (and hated them both) and was regularly referred to as 'Madam' or Miss Cole – so far away from the scruffy little girl called May who everyone seemed to despise. Perhaps everyone still did. Either way, she didn't care!

On a typically busy day, Eve's diary would begin with an early meeting and then a tour of the entire floor. When the area manager visited, her workload doubled. Like her colleagues, she was keen to impress the portly man, yet, just this once, her attention was captured by the presence of a thin, birdlike woman appraising a sky-blue poncho made of sheer chiffon.

'Mr Nolan, can I leave you in the capable hands of Charlene here?' she said, almost thrusting one of her sales assistants into his path. 'Charlene, please show Mr Nolan to menswear and electronics where the store manager is waiting. I will meet you all there in, say, twenty minutes?'

Without a chance for either to respond, Eve headed to one of the security guards and whispered discreetly into his ear. Within minutes, Gary the security guard began to escort the thin woman away from the display and towards the exit in full view of customers.

'What's going on here?' asked Eve as she approached them.

'This idiot says I can't shop here,' said the woman.

'Did he say why?'

The woman looked from the security guard and back to Eve.

'Well ... he reckons ...'

'He reckons what ... Bell?'

The woman looked at her, surprised, and her skin switched to crimson. Her eyebrows knitted into confusion. 'That's OK, I'll just go. I don't need this.'

'No, wait,' said Eve, placing her hand onto the woman's bony arm. 'What did he say to you? I'm a senior buyer here, perhaps I can help.'

'I said it doesn't matter.'

'But it does. It matters to me.'

'Do I know you?' she said, as if she already knew the answer.

Eve simply smiled. Her satisfaction growing the more Bell seemed to squirm uncomfortably, desperate to leave. And as Bell sauntered away, hot with humiliation, Eve's tiny piece of revenge was complete.

'I can't even be sure it's her, Gary ...'

'No worries, Miss Cole. I prefer you to be wrong than anything kicking off when Mr Nolan's about. She won't be allowed in here again. I will see to it.'

'I saw her one night lean over a car and jump in and she was covered in bright make-up. It was obvious what was going on. We run a clean establishment here, don't we?'

'Certainly. And, as I said, she won't be back here again. I gave her a good talking-to. Right embarrassed she was.'

'I'm sure she was,' said Eve with a smile.

Gary was just a long line of men who more than admired Eve from afar. She remembered the teenager who used to walk around the department store, dreaming of one day working there. How far she had come.

The cliché of being 'lonely at the top' did not penetrate in the ways some of the novels had implied. She was satisfied even without the inclusion of a family, friends or a man in her life. Fully aware of what and who her beauty and meticulous wardrobe could attract, she still couldn't think of one good use for a man. She'd sometimes agree to a dinner if they'd met abroad (confident he was unlikely to appear on her doorstep in London) but such opportunities were thankfully rare. She hated to stay up late anyway as sleep was the elixir that pushed her motivation to greater lengths each and every day. Similarly, acquaintances were also kept to a minimum, with Eve choosing never to indulge in relationships termed as friendship. She needed no one but herself and she liked it that way.

By the age of twenty-three (albeit twenty-eight on her CV) Eve had finally reached the end of her association with Reed's. It was time to move on. A headhunter made the transition easier by mentioning just how much a rival company, confidently just called The Department Store, was impressed with her meteoric rise. They were very, very interested.

She met with the headhunter, Phillip, and within one hour of that meeting, he called to say her hefty terms had been agreed: twenty per cent increase in salary, company shares and the option of working from home one day a month. The Department Store, often visited by kings, queens and movie stars and unrivalled as the best in high-end retail, wanted Eve Cole. *They* wanted *her*.

An hour after the contracts were signed, Eve sat in her car and rested her forehead onto the steering wheel. This career move could possibly see her become the most powerful black woman in the retail industry.

She exhaled slowly. She'd done good, yes.

But she still had a long, long way to go.

PART THREE

Chapter Twenty-four

Seven years later ...

'It's like May just disappeared off the face of the earth,' said Clifton.

'Something like that,' replied Lana.

Not for the first time over the years, Lana was discussing her sisters with her best friend. Unlike those other times, he was finally taking her quest more seriously, not least because Lana was finally on the verge of making the once impossible dream possible.

After hitting a brick wall with the social worker when she'd first started looking, Lana and Clifton had mapped out a five-year plan, which had clearly overrun.

With a second job, Lana was to save enough money to embark on a full-time mission to find her sisters. The money was mainly for living and search expenses so she could devote an entire year to the search during a work sabbatical and to fund any unexpected expenses, like an extra-high phone bill, taxis, train tickets. Clifton had hinted that she could just leave her job to claim welfare, but she quickly dismissed that idea with a terse, 'My daddy would be ashamed of me if I did that.'

When Lana found extra work at a cafe five evenings a week, she was often too exhausted to function effectively at the health centre the following morning. It was only grainy images of Tina that kept her going, or the sound of May's voice in her head. Now, she was just grateful for the unexpected day off due to a tube strike as she lay wrapped in a duvet on her sofa with Clifton, her feet lying across his knees. They hadn't spoken for a while, as Lana was often too exhausted to even pick up the phone. She'd never known tiredness like this before.

'It's so close I can taste it, Clifton. Just a few more months and I'll have all the money I need to make a start.'

'You're doing too much, Lana.'

'Not long to go now. A few more months.'

'You don't want to kill yourself in the process.'

'I'm fine. I might go back to the bank and ask for a loan to cover the last bit.'

'You were a bit too honest last time. "Miss Cole, what do you need the money for?" "Err … to find my sisters!" You should have said, to buy a car or something.'

'Well, at least this time it will be smaller than what I originally asked for a few years back and now I should have built up a better credit rating, so that's a plus.'

'Shut up for a second, will you?!'

'What?'

'Listen, I can help.'

'You're already helping.'

'I mean with money.'

'How?'

Clifton's existence in her life had been the one positive legacy of the Sir John Adams Children's Home. He understood her, and her journey, and Clifton had known at least one of her sisters and that reason alone allowed him to stand out from the others she called friends. But when he reached into his pocket and handed her an envelope, she was about to realise just how important he was to her journey.

'What's this?' she said.

'Just open it!'

She stared towards the cheque with the words 'four thousand pounds only' written in a black scrawl she recognised with startling familiarity.

'Clifton, I don't underst—'

'It's for the "find your sisters fund".'

'Where did you get this from?'

'You don't need to concern yourself with that.'

Her mind recalled a trip to the car dealership just under a year ago where they had stood fawning over a second-hand BMW 3 Series.

'This is the money you were saving for your dream car. No, I can't.'

'Yes, you can. I mean, me with a BMW? How cliché!'

'Clifton, no, I can't take this!'

'I can wait for the dream car. You shouldn't have to wait for those girls any longer and that's that. Just do as you're told, woman!'

'I . . . I don't know what to say.'

'Makes a change.'

As she rested her head onto his shoulder, a shudder of excitement moved through her at the thought of telling her manager she'd be going on that sabbatical.

'Thank you, thank you, thank you!' she said, planting kisses on each of his cheeks.

'Oi, oi, stop that or Denise will get jealous.'

'Who's Denise? Another floozy?'

'You know I don't go out with floozies.' He smiled.

'Seriously, thank you so much, Clifton, and whoever this Denise is, she's one lucky girl!'

Lana's colleagues inevitably tried to persuade her to change her mind.

'A year out of this game and anything could happen. They won't hold your job open for you. There's loads of students who are willing to work for half the wages!'

'I don't care about all of that, only my sisters.'

'What will you do for money? Give it some more thought, Lana!'

I have been thinking and saving and contemplating and wishing for almost twenty years, Lana thought.

So after three months of working her notice, recruiting her replacement and a handover period, Lana was finally able to walk out of the health centre she'd worked in since leaving college. The relief she felt was immense. She vowed only to look forward and remain positive as to what lay ahead. She was embarking on a journey that had lived inside her for so long and was now about to become a reality she both feared and desperately needed.

Tina had been cruelly snatched away from her whilst still only a baby.

May had been left to languish in Sir John Adams Children's Home, only to mysteriously run away just months after Lana's release.

Lana had twelve months' worth of money to live on, a small contingency fund for expenses, a vanity case with a few pictures, a pair of black-rimmed glasses, a plastic fan and a worn address book.

Lana was ready to complete the journey that had begun in Nigeria way back in 1958, and even before that, because her story and that of her sisters had started with the love affair between her parents – Tayo and Adanya Cole – in the balmy streets of Lagos, in a country she hardly remembered but would one day hopefully visit again.

For now, she would go in search of her sisters and finally be reunited with the missing pieces of her life.

Chapter Twenty-five

Lana stood at the bottom of the steps leading to number sixty
-three Pettyford Road and exhaled.

Until that moment she'd only visited twice after they'd been
taken to the children's home that last time: once to look for
May soon after her disappearance; and then randomly when
she had just wanted to feel close to the family she had lost.
She hoped that, like before, the building, the street and the
memories would infuse her with the strength needed for the
many challenges that lay ahead. Some would say it was just a
building, but to Lana it was so much more than that. It was a
home that had gently wrapped itself around some of the best
years of her life.

And also, some of the worst.

Daddy had found that flat for them. He had danced around its
rooms with them, lifted her high up in the air and laughed with
them. Sixty-three Pettyford Road was more than just a building –
it had once been everything.

She pulled Adanya's address book from her bag. The address
of the landlord, Mr Rex, was clearly legible under a table of
'rents paid and owed'. Her heart rate quickened at the sight of
his name, as it had always done during the handful of times she
had leafed through the book.

She headed in the direction of the landlord's house, following the path Daddy would have taken on many occasions to pay the rent until that burden had fallen on Mummy. However, she could not remember ever following Mummy to Mr Rex's house.

Lana stood in front of the sprawling semi-detached double-fronted residence with its impressive newly restored bay windows. Like number sixty-three, it had three floors. However, because it hadn't been converted into flats it had remained one big beautiful home.

The sound of a barking dog punctuated the silence.

'Can I help you?' said a thin woman with silver hair, quickly descending the steps, clutching the tiny yapping dog under her arm.

'I was just admiring your beautiful house.'

'Thank you,' said the woman suspiciously.

'My family used to know the people who lived here in the sixties.'

The woman's eyes became heavy with suspicion. 'Name?'

'My name?'

'No, the people you claim to know.'

'Mr Rex. He also owned the house me and my family lived in, not far from here. I was wondering if he still lived in this house?'

'If you mean Rex Andersen, he died a few years ago, and his wife moved abroad. I have no idea where she is now. What do you want with them?'

'Nothing. Nothing at all.' Lana moved away just as the dog's yaps increased.

'So my first day of investigations didn't go too well,' Lana told Clifton, filling him in.

'What were you doing at the landlord's anyway?'

'I thought I might as well go, seeing as though it's near my house – the old house, I mean. Plus I wanted to retrace Mummy's steps. There's so much I still don't understand about her. What

230

happened? And ... I guess I just needed to feel close to her. Do something she would have done. Sounds silly, right?'

'No, it doesn't. I won't pretend to know what you're going through. You have lost so many people in your life.'

Lana hated the thought of being an object of pity, but maybe that was her lot in life: the poor little orphan girl.

'Just know that you will never be alone,' he said sincerely, 'I'll always be there for you.'

'I know. Now stop being soppy and let's get back to business.'

'Yes, boss. So what else did you find in the address book?'

'It's years old, so half the numbers don't exist anymore.'

'You said there were some addresses in there too?'

'And lots of doodling. Mummy liked to doodle, apparently.' She smiled.

'Didn't you say she also used some of the pages as a diary?'

'Yes, but things like rent due and accounting stuff.'

'I'm sure you'll find something, a clue, anything.'

Lana didn't want to tell him about the fresh wounds that reopened each time she had leafed through the address book over the years, hence why she had only ever done so a handful of times. The difficulty in turning each page and her absolute disappointment upon placing the book to her nostrils only to discover it no longer smelled like Mummy had been too much to bear.

After Clifton left to meet Denise, Lana sat on her bed with the evidence laid before her. The random nature of the items meant Aunty Ginny had gathered them up hastily and without much thought, desperate in her guilt to give the poor little orphan kids something. At the time she'd first received the case, Lana had quickly banished it to the bottom of the wardrobe. Now, twenty years later, it was all she had left of Mummy: a paltry set of items she hoped would lead her back into the past so she could finally live in the future she craved.

*

Lana wrote a short and concise letter to John Adams Children's Home. It had been a hard exercise, what with the memory of how badly they had handled everything to do with her life and their nonchalance as she pleaded with them to tell her where they had sent Tina. What with May's disappearance from their care, she could only hope they would be willing to help her with the documents she needed. They owed her that much at least.

With the letter posted, Lana tasked herself with telephoning every non-professional phone number in Mummy's address book. She could not recall Mummy having any friends other than Aunty Ginny, so she doubted it would take very long.

By the time she'd worked through to the letter C, her ears had been subjected to the now-too-familiar 'dead' dialling tone many times, but she would carry on; she was not about to give up.

The address and telephone number for Aunty Ginny was, of course, for Pettyford Road, but Lana could only smile at the 'G' page of the address book that was entirely devoted to Mummy's best friend. Doodles of daisies surrounded her name; an IOU for three pounds signed by Ginny and an 'I Love Ginny she is my best friend' scrawled in childlike writing. Lana wondered if she herself had written this because, simply put, Aunty Ginny had been her best friend too. Despite attempting to visit her in Brighton when May first disappeared, an anger still burned for the woman who'd once meant so much. She would have to stem these feelings long enough to find out what she could about her sisters, as Lana strongly believed that Aunty Ginny could also be the key to a huge chunk of information.

She flicked through the pages, determined to go back to them later. For now, she just wanted to look at the letter T.

Sure enough, T for Tayo, along with the address of their first one-room home in England, committed to paper. Theirs was a love that burned even when husband and wife were still oceans apart. The section overflowed with writing: my one true love; Mr

Tayo Cole, my husband. The terms of endearment were warming, but it was the handwriting that overlapped these words that sent a chill through her body.

Dead forever. Traitor. Hateful wife. *Mo nife re*. Adulteress. *Odale*. Wrong. *Asewo*. Evil. *Iku*.

Some of the Yoruba she could recall from her childhood. *Iku*, she knew, was death.

'Nice ride. Drives well,' said Lana, her mind still on Mummy's writings, which were a hint to her state of mind at the time. Unlike before, she now studied it with a meticulous eye. Angling for any clue that could make her search a little easier. She was still only at the letter G, really, and she wondered what else she would find on the remaining pages that could help her. Perhaps she wasn't equipped to deal with the journey ahead. Perhaps some of the money she'd saved should have gone into some sort of counselling. The doctors were always talking about that at the health centre these days. But it was too late for all of that now. She had started and needed to remain focused on the bigger picture: finding her sisters. Mummy was dead now and she could no longer help her, no matter how much Lana deeply wished she could.

'Who needs a BMW?' said Clifton, snapping her back to the present. 'This old banger's great and will get us to Brighton in no time.'

'What?'

'You alright?'

'Just thinking about the words in the diary.'

'As I told you earlier, you are not to blame for anything that happened.'

'I know, I just wish I could have noticed she was losing her mind. Or something.'

'Oh right, because you're a qualified psychiatrist. Oh, and let's not forget what decade it was. It's not even fantastic now for black people, but the 1960s? Come on, Lana, you have *nothing* to feel guilty about. You were just a little girl.'

'I know ...'

'Now, can we focus on the task at hand? You're really killing this road trip, you know.'

She smiled. 'How long to go now?'

'About fifteen minutes.'

When Clifton manoeuvred the car into the street named on the crumpled piece of paper, Lana felt a strong pull in her tummy.

'I'll drive off and give you some privacy, once I see who opens the door.'

Either side of a lilac door, two plants still hung from terra-cotta pots. Not much had changed since the last time she visited Aunty Ginny's home in Brighton. She pressed the doorbell and waited.

'No one's home!' she shouted towards the car.

'Now what?' said Clifton.

'I'll wait for them.'

'They could be ages!'

'That's OK. I'm by the sea. You go along to your mates and meet me back here say ... five o'clock?'

An hour later, her hunger had crept up by surprise. She headed towards Blues Fish and Chip shop where a delicious aroma tantalised her, instantly reminding her of the Coles' Friday ritual.

Half an hour later, her stomach full with food and anxiety, Lana pressed the doorbell of the lilac door and was quickly startled by the echo of a baby's cry. Instantly, she knew Aunty Ginny did not live there anymore.

The door opened, revealing a woman with hair in need of a brush and her pink shirt desperate for an iron. In the crook of her arm was a baby.

'I'm sorry to bother you,' said Lana, her voice immediately eclipsed by the wail of the tiny infant.

'Sorry, love, you'll have to give me a minute.'

The door closed and she wondered if the woman would ever come back. Three minutes felt like ten and Lana moved away from the door, unsure of whether to wait some more or press the doorbell again, fearful of disturbing a sleeping baby. It was hard to get a baby back to sleep. Tina had been difficult around that age.

After five minutes, the woman reappeared, child clasped to her chest and suckling contentedly.

'Sorry about that. New mum,' she said with a smile.

'No, that's OK,' said Lana, feeling sudden pangs of guilt at the intrusion. 'I'm looking for a Ginny Jones. She used to live here a few years ago and she has two sons.'

'They would have been here just before me.'

'Yes, possibly! Do you know where she might have gone? Did she stay in the area?'

'Let me stop you there, love. This is a council property and I don't get to hear anything about the previous tenants. They go their way and I go mine. That's how it works, I'm afraid.'

Lana was desperate not to give in to defeat at such an early stage. But this was hard.

'I'm sorry, love.'

'That's OK,' Lana said sadly.

'Oh, but why not try the neighbours? Next door's been here longer than me and she might know something.'

'That's a great idea,' said Lana.

She was in luck; the lady next door was home.

'Ginny was a bit of a flighty one when she moved here. And those boys ... so unruly.' The woman had bouffant, blue-rinsed hair and an immaculate line of berry red on her lips. 'She wasn't really my type of person, if you ask me. But each to their own.'

The woman had been so kind and accommodating once Lana had reminded her of their first meeting many years before. Tea and biscuits followed as well as a dossier on what sounded like the entire street.

'Ginny stayed away a few months that time. I remember her son going into the house to pick up the letters and he even managed to say hello without cracking a smile. A miserable so and so that one. Then a huge van pulled up and took the rest of her belongings away. One of the sons got married, I heard. I can't imagine anyone marrying such an oaf. I think he was in the army. As I said, Ginny wasn't my type of friend, always a bit over made-up, but she always had a wave for me each time she saw me. That was nice.'

'Did she say where they were moving to?'

'That's the thing, Lina ...'

Lana let the slip pass, not wanting to interrupt at this crucial stage.

'I expected her to at least say a goodbye. We were polite like that with one another. But I never saw her again.'

'So, since I was last here ... since I saw you, you haven't seen her?'

She shook her head, eyes drenched in pity. 'I'm sorry, dear.'

Lana wished she had written a line of questions in preparation, fearful she would think of something later or tomorrow.

'Oh, actually, I have remembered something.'

'What?'

'How red his face looked.'

'Whose?'

'When the van came to collect Ginny's belongings, I stopped the son and I remember his face. Red, it was. Like he'd been crying. Yes, I remember it clearly because I had never been used to him like that. I'd always seen him as a bad 'un really, but that day he was just like a little boy.'

Lana did not want the words to leave her lips. 'D ... do you think she died?'

'I don't like to speculate. What I will say is, if she or those boys stuck around this area, someone will know. It's not exactly London, is it? Everyone knows everyone's business. Not me, though. I'm not like that!'

'Of course,' said Lana, biting on a biscuit.

'Let me have your number and address, dear, and I'll ask around. Someone at the club may know something. You never know.'

'The club?'

'I sometimes go to a get-together with the other ladies. Play bingo and have a natter – not to gossip, mind. Someone might know something there.'

'Thanks, I would really appreciate it.'

Lana placed her arms tenderly around the woman and whispered goodbye.

Stepping out and into the cool Brighton air, Lana realised she'd also said goodbye to her bitterness towards Aunty Ginny a long time ago. The thought of Aunty Ginny being lost to her forever produced a pain, which surprised her. She'd pray Aunty Ginny was still alive and if she was, would do everything in her power to show her forgiveness and that she still possessed a love for her which had never truly gone away.

The address book lay open at H where Mummy had scrawled 'nice lady' along with a phone number. Lana placed the phone receiver to her ear and waited for the now-familiar dead tone. But the sound of a ring tone, followed by a real-life voice, startled her.

'Hello,' reiterated the woman's voice.

'I know this sounds silly, but I found this number next to the words "nice lady" in my mum's old address book. I'm so sorry, I know I'm not making any sense.'

'Calm down and start again,' said the voice, slightly Caribbean-accented and soothing in its tone. 'Let's start with your name.'

'Lana. My name is Lana Cole and your number is in my mum's address book. I have no idea who you are so forgive me as I don't know your name, or whether she was even referring to you.'

'What was your mother's name?'

'Adanya. Adanya Cole.'

Lana heard a gasp.

'Yes, I am the person you are looking for.'

Chapter Twenty-six

A picture of Adanya Cole staring at the camera lens in total surprise lay on the coffee table between Lana and Clifton; one of Daddy's surprise snaps.

Lana was still reeling from her meeting with Hortense, a calmly spoken woman who, without a flinch, had told Lana of the exact location she'd first met Mummy. Lana had ingested the news as calmly and as quietly as possible, after which she had walked home in a daze and managed to phone Clifton, who, within the hour, was leaning against her iron-gated doorway.

'You didn't have to come, you know. Weren't you going to the pictures with Denise?'

Her eyes remained transfixed on the photograph.

'I was, but that isn't important. Are you OK?'

'I've been so naive, Clifton.'

'What else did she say?'

'She said she wants to see me. That what she has to say isn't for the phone.'

'There's more?'

'Of course there's more. You don't drop a bombshell like that and leave it there. You don't say, "I met your mother in a high-security psychiatric hospital and, oh, goodbye!" She rested her cheeks in each palm. 'I'm sorry, Clifton. I'm a little on edge and, if I'm honest, fearful of what she will tell me.'

Hortense was a petite retiree with braided hair, who exuded the calmness of someone Lana would not have associated with a tough mental ward.

'Working as a mental-health nurse isn't for everyone. I didn't think it was for me when I came here from the Caribbean all those years ago. But many of my contemporaries were doing it. The pay was a little more than traditional nursing and I soon found out why.

'I saw hundreds of people come and go in those wards. Unfortunately, the more black people arrived in the country, the more they would come for a week or two. Sometimes more. In that job it was easy not to get attached to anyone; most were too … what do you say … far gone? Your mum was different though. She was just like me.'

'What do you mean?'

'She just missed her country.' Hortense smiled warmly. 'Oh, how I missed my country, still do. But seeing this lovely girl was very saddening and heart-warming at the same time.' Hortense's eyelids gently clouded over as she continued. 'Sometimes her eyes would shine as she told me the story of her mum and dad and chasing the chickens with her brothers.'

Lana caught her breath at the first-ever mention of her grand-parents from someone other than her parents.

'We used to live near them, and they had a large coconut tree in the yard!' said Lana, excitedly.

'Yes! And apparently a lot of the men wanted her in that street, but she only had eyes for Tayo Cole, your father.'

Lana smiled warmly. She hadn't prepared herself for any of this. Another human being echoing stories she had seen with her very own eyes.

'She was her dad's favourite,' Lana told her. 'Named Adanya because it means "her father's favourite"!'

'That's right. Wow. I do not need to test you to know if you're her daughter. You know plenty and you look so much like her. A very beautiful girl.'

'Thank you,' said Lana sincerely.

'There were three of you, is that right?'

Lana nodded her head mournfully, the recent joviality threatening to be lost. 'Did she ... did she ever ...'. The words felt trapped.

'Did she ever talk about you? Yes. All three of you.'

Lana could only see darkness as her eyes clouded over.

'Sometimes she spoke about the baby but mostly it was her two big girls. "The oldest one thinks she is the mother," she would say.'

Lana's teeth rested on her bottom lip.

'She said the second child was very quiet and looked too much like Tayo. I think it hurt her ... I'm not sure. Forgive me, my memories are a bit hazy but not because of my age ...'

Lana smiled warmly.

'But because of time.'

'You've been very helpful so far. You see, I didn't know she'd been in a high-security psychiatric hospital.'

'Really?'

'Aunty Ginny would just say "hospital". And as I got older, I kind of knew; I just didn't want it to be real. Hospital sounded much better.'

'I understand that. You were all so young and it was a different time then.'

'I could have handled it.'

'The baby ...'

'Tina. What about her, do you know something?'

'I remember Adanya mentioning her a great deal when she was in a really bad state. Just this and that. I can't remember much of what she said. I suppose it was all part of her sickness.'

Lana wished Hortense could recall every single detail of her mummy.

'So, do you think Mummy, Adanya, may have been suffering from post-natal depression?'

'I don't know much about that ... do you mean the baby blues?'

'Yes, I suppose I do. A lot of the doctors at my surgery talk about it.'

'Are you a nurse, then?'

'No, I run a health centre reception.'

'Maybe you should go into nursing.'

'I thought about the medical profession. It just never happened. But at least I work in a health centre. That's close enough.' Lana wanted to stay on track because there were so many emotions building up inside of her.

'In those days and even now,' Hortense continued, 'when a person loses some of their mind, a stamp is placed onto their head, like this.' She placed a palm to her forehead to illustrate the point. 'That word will continue to describe how the world sees them. Forever. I fear this happened to your mother, dearest Adanya.'

They had a much-needed cup of tea then, after which Lana was finally able to explain the nature of her quest.

'I don't know how I can help much. They've closed the hospital down now, thankfully. A dreadful place.'

'Really?'

'Yes, it's been closed for years.'

Lana swallowed. 'No, I meant was it that dreadful?' She thought of Mummy, languishing in a place that resembled a lunatic asylum from those horror movies Clifton used to make her watch.

'I don't know what they would have done with her records or if that'd be of any use to you,' said Hortense, effectively refusing to answer what Lana already knew. 'Besides, what is the point of dredging up what happened? She had her own reasons for doing what she did. Maybe the demons were too much for her or she missed your dad – only she knows why she took her own life.'

Lana's eyes widened as the sharpest of pain took hold of her entire body. 'What did you just say?'

'You didn't know ...?' asked Hortense.

Lana's gaze fell to the floor as a spiral of sounds rushed to her head.

Mummy had killed herself? No, she'd died of a broken heart. She'd missed Daddy so much, she'd died of a broken heart!

'Oh darling, I'm so sorry!'

It was some time before Lana could get her words out. 'Are ... are you sure, Hortense?'

'Yes, I am, my darling. This is something I will never forget. I'm so sorry.' She took Lana's hand. 'Sometimes it is better for us to believe certain things to get us through life. I will say this, though: she would never have left you if she'd been in her right mind. She was a mother first and loved the three of you so very, very much.'

Lana rushed home and did not bother to call Clifton as promised. She was unable to eat the dinner prepared the night before and fell into a fitful sleep. The pillowcase was soaked with her tears as contradictory and broken thoughts played out in her mind.

Her beautiful mummy had taken her own life.

Her beautiful mummy had loved her very much.

Nothing made sense.

Lana had to carry on. Dwelling on every bit of new information would only slow the process and she now had just under eleven months to find her sisters. By putting this new and very painful information about Mummy to one side, she was determined to continue in the search for her sisters. She had no choice.

Tina, by the mere act of her adoption, would appear on legal papers and files, if only Lana could get access to them. May, however, had just unceremoniously disappeared. A fruitless search of public telephone books and the electoral register produced nothing. Not one Mayowa or May Cole was listed in the United Kingdom. During a number of chaotic seconds, Lana did wonder if May was dead.

Clifton quickly swatted such thoughts with a terse, 'We'll find her, Lana. It will take a bit of time, but we'll find her.' She valued Clifton's optimism when she, at times, found it difficult to locate her own.

They spent an afternoon calling up all the Victoria Coles in the UK with none of them sounding anything like May. Not even the three who hung up with a 'You've called before! Stop calling this number!' Indeed, this wasn't the first time she'd gone through the phone book in recent years.

While Lana hoped May just had an unlisted number, Clifton unhelpfully suggested she could have changed her name altogether.

'You wouldn't happen to have a magic wand?' asked Lana, closing the telephone book for the second time that evening.

'Give me time!' he joked.

The emotional journey so far, and all that would surely come, would not have been remotely bearable without Clifton.

'I'm taking you out of here,' he said. 'You've been flat out for days and you need a break. Come on, fix your hair up and we'll go.'

'Where to?'

'The pub with me and my girl Denise. I think the two women in my life need to meet.'

'Has she said something? I hope this isn't another Misty situation.'

'Misty was a psycho who couldn't understand I just wasn't into her. Denise is different. We've been together a while now, as you know, and let's just say it's serious.'

'Serious?' she said, playfully pressing the tip of his nose in between her fingers.

'Gettoff! And yes, it is. Very. Looks like she might be the one.'

Lana placed her hand to her chest. 'Wow, I've never heard you say that about anyone.'

'I'm in my thirties now. It's time.'

'Then I most certainly have to meet her.'

Denise was in a ra-ra skirt and Dr Marten boots, whilst Clifton had turned into a different man. He now opened doors and even assisted his girlfriend with ordering some crisps and pork scratchings. What with all that and the hand-holding under the pub bar, it was finally confirmed that Clifton Joseph was in love.

'Does she look like the girl from Bananarama or what?' Clifton said, as Denise headed to the toilet.

'Which one?'

'I mean her whole image and that … sexy.'

'You really like her, don't you?' Lana was so wrapped up in her own life, she had failed to see the direction the life of her best friend had taken. 'I'm so sorry for being a rubbish friend.'

'You're never that.'

'I'm glad you're happy.'

Denise reappeared. 'Hey, babe.'

'Hey there, babe.' Clifton stood and planted a kiss onto her cheek.

'It's so great to finally meet you,' said Denise. She'd a slight northern accent, which allowed for a friendlier delivery, thought Lana.

'So, tell me what you guys got up to at John Adams.'

Lana hid her surprise that Clifton had confided in Denise about their brief 'moment'.

'Oh, well, that …'

'She means is it anything like the whole St Trinian's thing?' said Clifton, delivering a firm kick to her left shin.

'John Adams is a children's home and not a posh boarding school,' corrected Lana.

'Sorry, I didn't mean …'

Clifton moved his palm onto the back of Denise's hand. 'Babe, let's leave it.'

'Sure, of course,' said Denise, smiling solemnly towards her boyfriend and sharing an intimacy Lana had no access to. The third-wheel feeling had truly appeared and she really just wanted to leave and take another look at the phone book. Check out some variations of names her sister may be answering to.

That night as she lay in bed, the reality of losing Clifton hit her. Someone as amazing as Clifton would only have been available for a limited amount of time anyway, and she'd always known that. Yet, existing somewhere in her mind had been this tiny unexplored assumption that he was simply waiting for something to happen between them again, even though he had been the one to effectively put an end to their teenage romance. But, Lana could never be interested in a real relationship with any man until her sisters were found. However, in the meantime, Clifton had met his princess and Lana told herself she couldn't be happier for him, yet she was just a little sad for herself.

Chapter Twenty-seven

Without a reply from John Adams, and nothing else from Hortense, Clifton agreed it was time to visit the scene of their childhood.

It was time to return to Sir John Adams Children's Home.

This would merely be a fact-finding mission with no residue emotions allowed – and this is what Lana told herself as they edged closer to the building where she had been housed, fed and clothed, and was also the original setting for most of the miserable things that had infected her life. During the car journey the two friends spoke few words, both sets of eyes fixed on the road ahead.

They stopped at a roadside cafe where Lana was finally able to voice what was going on in her mind as she sipped on a steaming hot coffee. 'It's going to be weird seeing the old place, again. For both of us.'

The elderly waitress placed a bacon sandwich on the table in front of Clifton. Lana was too nervous to eat.

'I keep thinking about the trips back to see Mum and me having to listen to yet another dude telling me how to tie my shoelaces,' said Clifton. He lifted the sandwich to his lips. 'These days ... sometimes ... I mean, me and Mum are fine now, but that place reminds me of a time I'd rather forget, if you know what I mean. When all she really cared about was the booze, her men and not me.'

The emotional welts of John Adams still remained visible after many years and Lana imagined moving to Clifton's side of the table and placing her arms around his shoulders. They were two people sharing an incredibly emotional journey and for once they needed one another. For once, this wasn't one-sided.

And then she thought of Denise.

'Eat up and let's do this!' she said.

The large gates, once so imposing, swung pathetically against a feeble wind. The lack of signage in town should have alerted them to what they now faced: a dilapidated building even more soulless than before.

'It's empty!' said Lana, fearing yet another dead end to her enquiries. The building was a saddening sight; their childhood home now reduced to a mass of sprawling moss and peeling paint.

A man in green Wellington boots walking an energetic terrier approached them. 'Can I help you?'

'Yes, mate,' Clifton replied, 'we were just looking for the John Adams Children's Home.'

'This is what's left of it.'

'As we can see. When did it close?'

'Some years back. Apparently they're going to knock it down and build fancy flats. Best thing for it, if you ask me. Used to house a load of undesirables. Delinquents, the lot of them.'

'Do you know where the files and everything went?' asked Lana, his last statement unable to penetrate the hardness of her desperation.

'I wouldn't have a clue.'

'Were the children moved to another home? Where would they have been taken?' asked Clifton.

'Sent to other homes, I suppose. Or fostered. I have no idea. Are you looking for somebody in particular?'

Lana, her body void of stamina, leaned against the bonnet of the car as an image of a little girl with ringlets in her hair began to fade from her mind's eye.

'That's OK, maybe we'll go into town, find out some more there,' said Clifton.

'Good luck,' said the man, letting his dog off its lead and following it in the direction of Grassy Green.

'You OK, Lana?'

'Yes ... let's just hurry up and get into town.'

Any nostalgic memories failed to appear as they drove past the same rows of shops recalled from her youth.

In front of them, a butcher weighed a pound of mince, which, for Lana, conjured up thoughts of Aunty Ginny. The butcher told them the nearest library was almost three miles away in the next town.

'They will probably have what you need there. Files and that.'

The librarian stood beside the microfilm reader as Lana and Clifton scanned the newspaper article from 1980 displayed on the screen: 'JOHN ADAMS HOME CLOSES AMID REPORTS OF ABUSE'.

Lana's and Clifton's quick glance to one another signalled a silent and painful understanding. Lana felt sick.

The librarian provided further articles that communicated similar stories about the situation at John Adams: the allegations, the investigations, the arrests. Each article, headline and picture gradually making it difficult for Lana to run away from an uncomfortable possibility about her sister May.

The home had told her years before about the 'altercation' with Stan just before her sister had run away. With just under two years left until her release and jeopardising a place at university, it had never really made sense. And now with this new information, Lana hoped it would never, ever make sense. May's reasons needed to remain an enigma because the truth was just too much to bear.

'Can I ask what all this is about?' said the librarian.

'An adoption. I want to find out who my little sister was adopted out to after she was taken from John Adams.'

'Hmmm ... best to try social services. They open on Monday. Come back then.'

'I tried them when I turned eighteen and a few years after and they weren't very helpful.'

'Something tells me,' Clifton said, 'that in light of what happened, they might just be a little bit more accommodating now, don't you think?'

Again Lana did not want to think about what may or may not have happened to her sister at the hands of Stan or anyone else, but she would have to. One day.

Clifton drove in the direction of the B & B recommended by the librarian. Lana's eyes flickering between open and closed, exhausted with hopelessness.

'It's going to be all right, Lana. We're not giving up.'

'I just don't see social services giving me any info about an adopted child just because I ask for it, do you? Especially as Tina left before all the ... trouble.'

'Let's just hope May left before all of that started.'

'Clifton, what if it had been going on when we were there?'

'I mean ... I never saw anything,' he said, eyes remaining on the road ahead.

'You and I were so wrapped up in one another. What if ...?'

'What?'

'What if all that saved us was that we had each other? I know Stan was a bit rude around May but ...'

Lana wanted to change the subject. Fast. She did not want to think of May in any sort of abusive situation as this possible truth could destroy any ounce of hope and strength left in her body.

Clifton steered the car into a side street. 'Lana, maybe it's a good thing Tina was adopted out. You know, before ...'

Lana had never before rerouted her thinking regarding Tina's departure. Comfortable in its negativity, she'd never actually allowed herself to think of it as the right outcome.

As Clifton turned into the tiny car park of the B & B, she knew it would soon be time to mull over his words as a way of finding peace amongst the bombshells they had unearthed. And she needed peace. If only to get through the night.

'I only have one room left, I'm afraid,' said the lady behind the counter.

'I'll take it,' said Lana. 'You may as well go home, Clifton.'

'I'm not leaving you up here by yourself, no way.'

The landlady led them to the room. The simplicity of the space did nothing to hide the starkness of the huge double bed beside a side table and telephone.

'I don't have a change of clothes or anything. I didn't realise we'd be staying until the morning,' said Lana.

'Disgusting!' joked Clifton.

'What about you?'

'I'm a man. It's different.'

'Now we have to figure out who's taking the floor,' said Lana.

'We've slept on the same bed before, Lana. Remember when I used to sneak into your room at John Adams? We didn't do anything, then.'

'Denise?'

'Is she my first girlfriend?'

'No, but—'

'Then stop it! We're best mates. I'd never cross the line with you and you know that.' Clifton looked visibly hurt. 'I already phoned Denise and told her we were here. I even gave her the room's direct number.'

'OK, OK, but no farting.'

'No farting,' he said, quietly brushing off her weak attempt at an apology.

Lana found it difficult to get to sleep whilst Clifton snored contentedly beside her. The deadness of quiet alarmed her, she was so used to an errant car alarm or a siren. She was forced to think about what they had uncovered so far. And then she was able to quietly, cry herself to sleep.

The shrill of the phone startled her out of a deep sleep and into the glare of an early-morning sun. One eye closed, she reached over to the side table and retrieved the phone. 'Hello?'

'Who is it?' asked Clifton.

'I don't now. They hung up.'

Clifton rubbed at his eyes, sitting up slowly.

'I feel so grotty,' she commented, stifling a stubborn yawn.

'That's what happens when you wear your clothes to bed! At least I stripped down to my boxer shorts! Shall we go and catch breakfast? It's almost nine.'

'I don't think I can eat.'

'Did you and your husband like the room?' asked the landlady.

Clifton had left to make a call.

'We're not married,' said Lana.

'In my day, couples that weren't married didn't share rooms. But that's your business.' She spoke with a smile.

Clifton appeared. 'I just called Denise.'

'How is she?'

'Really angry. She said she called the room this morning and a woman picked up.'

'Oh no, that was me half-asleep! Call her back and tell her!'

The landlady looked on as if she'd been validated in some way.

'I had to tell her we shared a bed.'

'What did she say?'

'Think about how it sounds.'

'Oh.'

Lana's heart ached as she watched him head off in front of her, his gait hunched with sadness. She would have to start leaning on him less, that much she knew. Clifton had been her rock for so long and it was time she at least began the process of loosening the ties.

At this point, though, there was nothing she could do to help him and Denise. She had to remain focused on the task at hand as she sat in a half-full waiting room. The tall, glass windows allowed her to clock Clifton in a phone box outside and watch his attempts to appease a clearly irate girlfriend.

'Lana?'

She looked up at the smartly dressed woman standing over her.

'I'm so sorry you had to wait so long. Monday is a very busy day.'

Lana followed her into a tiny cubicle where they sat facing one another.

'You'd like to find out about John Adams, I am told.'

'Yes, as I wrote down earlier, I was a resident between sixty-three and sixty-nine. I started out with my two little sisters. One was adopted and the other ... ran away. I wrote it all down for you.'

'This is a unique request, Miss Cole, especially under the circumstances.'

'The abuse, you mean?'

'A lot of bad feeling still exists around the issue of John Adams. It is all very controversial. As well as people in this department having lost their jobs, there's a huge turnover of staff in social services anyway, so I doubt many of those who worked here during that time are still contactable.'

Lana swallowed.

'I did manage to dig out some info though.'

'That's great!'

'While you were waiting I took a look at the John Adams file. It's very extensive and a lot of it has been taken away as part of an ongoing criminal investigation and there's no way you'd be allowed to see these files unless you were filing a criminal complaint. Even then it would all have to be dealt with by lawyers first. It's all a very lengthy process.'

'Surely you can tell me something about Tina.'

'Miss Cole, I simply cannot discuss individual cases. Firstly, you have to prove who you are.'

'What do you need me to bring? I will do that and come back another time.'

'Miss Cole, I don't—'

'What if they'd taken Tina away illegally? It seems the place was run by idiots and abusers after all. I could then file a criminal complaint and then I'd have to see the files.'

'Miss Cole, I don't want to waste your time so it's best I inform you of this now. The young lady you are referring to was, according to what I have seen, never adopted. There was no adoption.'

'You mean you can't find the papers?'

'Miss Cole, your younger sister was never adopted.'

'She didn't just disappear!'

'She was released into the care of your father.'

Confusion. 'He's dead!'

'I'm so sorry, of course ... I meant that her biological father came to John Adams and claimed her. That's all I can tell you with any certainty.'

'But—'

'I really must get back.'

Lana felt winded, sucker-punched.

'Are you OK? Would you like me to get you some water?'

'No ... I ...' All the secrets of her childhood that she had subconsciously tried to rewrite were one by one turning on her and slapping her hard in the face. Mummy died of a broken heart. Mummy fell in love with a kindly white man no one else had met, a man who knew he would never live up to Daddy's memory and had quietly slipped away before finding out about Tina.

To an eleven-year-old, that story had seemed realistic and palatable in the absence of any real explanation from the adults in her life. Now as a grown woman, an adult herself, it was time she faced up to the truth.

Tina's father had kept in touch with Mummy. Tina's father was known to them.

'I can't tell you any more than that, Miss Cole. I have already said too much.'

Lana closed her eyes, trying to figure out when her tipping point would come.

Chapter Twenty-eight

'What's wrong with you? You said you wanted this!'

'Do what you have to do.'

Lana shot up from the nightmare. Her forehead slick with sweat. It was 2am. She sunk back against the pillow and thought once again about that time she had pressed her ears against the door of the kitchen and heard sounds that sounded like Mummy, but also that of a man – the only other man she remembered from their old life; the only man it could be who had possibly travelled all the way to Sir John Adams Children's Home to claim his child. Tina.

Perhaps Mummy and this man had planned this once she knew she was going to take her own life. No. Mummy wasn't well and would never do anything like that. Just as she wouldn't have gone with another man willingly.

'What's wrong with you? You said you wanted this!'

'Do what you have to do.'

Each possible explanation for what occurred all those years ago sounded unbearable. There would be no respite for Lana. Just cold, hard truths she had so far uncovered with many more to come.

Later that morning, fresh out of the shower and wrapped in a towel, Lana pressed play on her answer machine. A short message from Georgina – an old work colleague – informed her about joining her for after-work drinks: 'It would be lovely to see you. We miss you!'

Beep.

Lana reached for the tub of cocoa butter.

'This is Hortense … the nurse. I have some news for you … I have remembered something and I think it may be of importance.'

Lana's haste in getting to Hortense was met with an ease that felt frustrating; Hortense liked to take her time.

'I have prepared some food for you. Ackee and saltfish.

Lana wasn't hungry. She just needed to know what Hortense had remembered.

Hortense placed a plate of what looked like scrambled eggs and vegetables onto the white plastic side table.

Lana exhaled. 'I'm really sorry, Hortense, but I'm not particularly hungry at this moment.'

'You look very tired.'

'It's been a rough few hours. Please tell me what you have remembered.'

'I remember Adanya saying something to me. It was during one of those times she felt OK. We would talk about our homelands together and our children. One day she was speaking of Tayo and then said she had betrayed him. She kept saying sorry; she said that a lot during her episodes. I don't know why I did not remember this before.'

'Did she say how she betrayed him?' Lana's heart rate quickened.

'I knew she had three of you and I thought they were all from her husband. Then she kept saying she betrayed her husband with another man. And then she would go into her madness again. Talking, talking, talking. She felt very bad; I could see it in her eyes. She said she had betrayed him and borne a child.'

'Did she say his name? This man?'

'Yes, his name ... his name was like a name you'd call a dog.'

'Rex.'

'Yes, Rex ... I think that's what she called him. I'm not even sure if this is at all relevant.'

'It is. And this news basically corroborates what, deep down, I have always known.'

She stood in front of the large, sprawling house, her heart pumping fast.

'You again. What do you want?' said the woman standing at the door of Mr Rex's former home, the tiny dog, this time unseen, yapped incessantly in the background.

'Sorry to bother you.' She was far from sorry.

'It is almost nine o'clock at night,' said the woman curtly.

'I know it's late but I need to know more about the people who sold you this house. I really have to trace them.'

'I don't think that's any of your business.'

'I need to know. Please.'

'What makes you think I know where they are?'

'Last time I was here, you said the husband had died.'

'Yes.'

'So what happened to Mr Andersen's wife? Did they have a child with them? A little girl with ringlets?'

'What is this all about?'

'Please, tell me that!'

Her expression hardened. 'I'll have you know you are trespassing.'

'You must know something, please. I have to find Mrs Andersen. I need to know where she went after he died.'

'If you don't leave my property, I will call the police.'

Lana felt her only true lead slipping away. 'Please, I beg you. I don't mean any harm. I'm just trying to find my little sister Tina.' Lana could see a line soften in the woman's expression.

'Anything, please. If you could just let me know what area they moved to?' Then she could at least check the electoral register.

'Mrs Andersen remarried.'

'To who? What was his name?'

'His name was Jennings and he was a diplomat with a posting to Spain, Madrid or Barcelona or something. I know he was very well-to-do.'

'Barcelona or Madrid?'

'Barcelona. Yes, that's where it was. Now I suggest you leave or I shall most definitely be calling the police.'

A library search produced an address of the British Consulate in Barcelona. With no other information and no further leads, she only had a couple of options, and one was to write to them. But who knew how long it would take to get a response? Having waited so many years, Lana's impatience was growing at an alarming rate. She phoned the long number quoted and, as she suspected, an answering machine message informed her they only took emergency enquiries over the phone, and at a specified time.

Of course, flying to Barcelona was a silly idea and would devour a chunk of her savings, lead her hundreds of miles away and possibly into a wild goose chase. But what choice did she have?

She would need advice before embarking on such a big move and Clifton would know what to say. However, they hadn't spoken since the trip to John Adams.

She picked up the receiver and placed her finger into the dial. She then exhaled and replaced the receiver. They needed space, time apart. It was just another reason why a trip to Barcelona could not have arrived at a better time.

Chapter Twenty-nine

Apart from a life-changing visit to England, Lana's only other long-distance trip was a ferry journey to Calais to buy beer and cheese with Clifton. This time, her trip was charged with a more urgent energy. This time, she was searching for her sister.

Tina had clearly led a charmed life: the stepchild of a diplomat, no less, with all the trappings to go with such a role – private school, plush toys, multiple languages spoken. Tina was probably an accomplished and happy young woman, and such thoughts went some way to lessening Lana's sadness at being unable to watch her grow into the confident young woman she had surely become.

Lana gazed out of the tiny oval window, watching cotton wool clouds mingling with a pretty blue backdrop. Clifton would have tried to talk her out of jumping on an aeroplane. He'd have told her to think it all through, to stick around and gather more evidence, reminded her that Tina was now a grown woman who might not even be in Barcelona any more. Lana chuckled to herself. This internal monologue with Clifton just proved how dearly she missed him.

Lana completed two crosswords and feigned interest in the man sitting in the aisle seat, droning on about the difference between Catalan and Spanish, feeling more alert than ever as the aeroplane landed. Excitement vibrated through her entire body as soon as she stepped through the airport doors. There was a chance, even if only a slim one, that her sister was breathing this same air at that very moment. Perhaps she had walked the same route as a child and, hopefully, much more recently. Her tummy swished with excitement as she climbed into a taxi. Instead of looking out at her new surroundings, her eyes remained fixed on the guidebook, absorbing useful phrases and some basic knowledge of the city. A man dressed in a smart black and white uniform opened the taxi door outside the hotel, greeting her in English. Welcome sprays from an elegant fountain sprinkled her like tiny confetti, and stone animals watched her every step. The receptionist handed her a key and wished her a pleasant stay, and Lana followed her luggage and a bellman to her room.

Choosing to forget the real reason for the trip, if only for a minute, she rushed to the balcony and slid the glass doors open. The sun shone on the view below, representing what a holiday should look like: the sharp edge of a small rectangular swimming pool: a woman in a blue swimsuit listening to a yellow Walkman, sipping a multicoloured cocktail; a large man belly-flopping into the pool and spraying the woman with water. For a brief moment Lana yearned for such a utopia, before reminding herself of her task. She was not in Spain on holiday, but rather on a fact-finding mission that could actually lead to finding her little sister Tina. She on the brink of something amazing.

After a much-needed nap, Lana slid into the back seat of another taxi. The consulate was fifteen minutes away without traffic. As the car rode down the busy streets, headed towards Avinguda Diagonal, 477, the sky quickly became overcast, as if reminding her that this was not a sightseeing trip. She tried to ignore the brash and varied Gaudí architecture she'd read about, as well as the gothic and mysterious structures, and glass windows with cute pastries on display. Her aim was to get to the consulate as fast as possible, as if Tina was waiting there, willing her to hurry up and find her.

The car came to a stop.

'This is the place, Señora,' said the taxi driver.

'Here?' she said, waving the paper in front of him.

'Yes, Señora.'

She paid him, then stepped out of the car and felt slight spots of rain against her face. She hurried into the building.

'Can I help you?' asked the receptionist.

'I'd like to speak with the ambassador or a diplomat, please.' She wrinkled her forehead.

'Or an assistant, or just someone who can give me some information. Please.'

'Do you have an appointment?'

'No.'

'You must make an appointment to visit with the consul. What is the information you require?'

'I'd like some details about one of the diplomats who used to be stationed here. You know, a forwarding address or something. I know they move around a lot, but, of course, he could still be here.'

'This is highly confidential information. We deal mainly with travel issues and not what you are asking.'

'Who can I speak to, then?'

'You need to make an appointment.'

'OK, that's fine.'

'It will take six weeks for an appointment. And even so, it is unlikely you will be given such information.'

'I don't have six weeks here. I just need a name and an address, that's all. Can I just speak to someone now?' The words stumbled from her mouth clumsily and without authority. She had stepped on a plane without any real research, eager to have something to show for a line of investigation that had so far produced nothing.

She had been too eager. She had been foolish. And now she had failed before she'd even begun.

The receptionist appeared unmoved.

'Please, I've travelled all the way from England. I can't leave here empty-handed. Please help me!'

'I think you shall leave now.'

From the corner of her eye she noticed a man leaning over a white sculpture, a brown cloth in his hand, his eyes staring towards her.

'OK, I'm sorry about that. I can come back tomorrow.'

'As you wish. The rules will remain the same.'

She turned towards the door, noticing the man slowly walk away from the sculpture. Imagined or real, she felt a silent communication form between them. The tilt of his balding head and the widening of his eyes were a definite and coherent instruction.

Outside, her suspicions were confirmed.

'Señora, you want information about a diplomat?' he said.

'Yes, please, do you know anything? A Mr Jennings, he used to work here.'

He placed his finger to his lips as if to quieten her.

'We go and talk,' he said.

Inside a quiet little cafe, the man – whose name she still didn't know – sipped on a coffee as she impatiently nursed an orange juice. Her nerves were on edge and she was afraid she had wasted a sizable amount of her funds on a wild goose chase. If only she'd talked it through with Clifton first. He would never have let her fly all the way to Barcelona!

'Many diplomats and their family living in a place called Pedralbes.'

'Oh, thank you! Thank you so much!'

He pulled a pen and paper from his pocket and scrawled what looked like an address. 'Give to taxi. Ask for Ramón. He is a gardener, my brother. He knows many diplomats. He can help you.'

'A gardener?'

'Yes, he also use to be *cartero*.'

'Huh?'

'You know ... how you say ... send letters.' He gestured with his hands as if throwing an imaginary object into the air.

'Letters? Postman?'

'Yes, yes!'

At last, she had a lead.

'What is your name?'

'No important,' he said, waving his hand in the air. 'I soon retire, I don't want trouble!' He smiled.

This man had risked a lot to help her.

'Why are you helping me?'

'You look like you really need to find this person of yours.'

'She's my sister.'

'Sister, is good. You should find her.'

'Thank you. I just ... I miss her very much.'

'Ah, Señora, this is very difficult,' said Ramón. They stood in a courtyard in front of a huge colour blast of exotic flowers, similar to those she'd once seen in Nigeria. Or at least they appeared similar. Behind them, a neat set of terracotta-coloured apartments – shadowed by huge trees and overlooking a large communal swimming pool – was eye-catching, as was the row of luxury cars parked yards from the security gate. If Tina had ever lived here or anywhere in the area of Pedralbes, she would have grown up surrounded by luxuries Lana could only dream of.

'I use to work delivering letters for the residents of Pedralbes for many, many years. Twenty years!'

'So you would have met them! The man, the diplomat, he came with a wife and a child, or possibly more than one child,' she explained.

'Many with children.'

'This child ... she was a little bit like me ... but not much.' Lana, unconcerned with how silly she may have sounded, pointed to the skin on her hand. She was determined to leave the country with something, a clue, anything. She could not go back to England empty-handed. 'Oh, and his name is Jennings! Let me spell it for you ...'

'No, it is OK! Jennings ...' The gardener scrunched his eyebrows and then smiled. 'Yes, yes, yes, little girl! Hair, like this.' He whirled his finger around, denoting curls.

'Yes, that's right.'

'Jennings! Very good man. He come here with his wife and his child. She look, erm ... *mulata* ... yes? Just a little bit. Not usual like this. Yes, yes! They were here for long time. But they gone now.'

Of course they had. She felt the familiar pangs of defeat begin to creep in.

'What was her name? The little girl's name?' asked Lana, using what felt like her last ounce of hope.

'She have name like my sister.'

'What is your sister's name?'

'Christina,' he said. 'They call her Tina.'

Lana dragged her suitcase through the arrivals lounge as she headed towards a WHSmith. She'd missed England so much and planned to catch up on UK news whilst munching on a good old British packet of crisps. The trip hadn't been an amazing success, but at least she'd spoken to someone who had known Tina and her 'family'. Clifton would probably argue that there was no evidence she and the gardener had been talking about the same person – but what if they had? This was a lead and she would think about what to do with it after she got home. She scooped up two bags of salt and vinegar crisps, pulling out the in-flight magazine she'd taken to read at home.

'Take your time, Madam,' the sales assistant reassured her. The magazine was open on an article entitled 'Today's Woman', along with a picture and a caption: 'From Warehouse to Boardroom – FASHION'S FIRST BLACK FEMALE MEMBER OF THE BOARD'. At that moment, her hand luggage fell from her grip, scattering across the floor by her feet as her gaze remained fixed on the magazine.

'Are you OK there, Miss?'

Lana rubbed harshly at her eyeballs and yet there it remained, as clear as the Spanish sky she'd left behind.

'Miss?'

FASHION'S FIRST BLACK FEMALE MEMBER OF THE BOARD.

May.

Lana sat on the cool hard surface of a plastic chair in arrivals. The kind sales assistant had taken the correct money out of her purse before directing her to the nearest seat. She'd remembered calling Clifton from one of the phones in the hall and ignoring his gasps as she reeled off where she'd been. He'd told her to 'sit tight', but Lana had insisted that she would make it home; he could meet her there. For now, she needed to stop and regain her breath.

Unlike Tina, Lana had last seen May as a teenager on the brink of adulthood and would recognise her in a line-up of a thousand people. There'd been no mistake.

Her sister May lived in London.

Her sister May was a successful businesswoman.

Her sister Mayowa was now Eve Cole.

The taxi deposited her into the bleakness of the underground car park.

'Sorry, love, but I can't take the case up the stairs and leave my car here. This estate is a bit rough.'

She lugged the suitcase up each step, wondering if she was dreaming. Perhaps she was losing her mind like Mummy. She bent to pick up the accumulated junk mail and bills lining the front of the passageway and noticed Clifton's handwriting: Where are you? Call me?

Half an hour later, Clifton arrived to find her sitting on the floor of her green and white lounge, looking at the 'Today's Woman' article.

'Why didn't you tell me you were going away?'

'Clifton ...'

'You could have picked up the phone? You had time at the airport. You've been gone a week and I had no idea where you were!'

Her mind was a hazy mist.

'What the heck, Lana? You went to Barcelona? You could have found the number for the embassy here and just called them!'

Clifton sat beside her. She handed him the magazine.

'But then I wouldn't have seen this.'

'No offence, but I prefer the comics.'

'That's ... that's my sister,' she said hoarsely.

Clifton turned to the magazine in his hands.

'That's my sister, May.'

Slowly the recognition in his eyes matched hers.

Chapter Thirty

Eve Cole rubbed at her eyes, fatigued by lack of sleep and the glare of the computer. The soft, leather, swivel chair, specially flown in from Italy, suddenly felt uncomfortable against her back. Why she'd asked for such a machine she would never know. Perhaps it had something to do with always testing the boundaries; checking how much they wanted her.

I want a computer even though no one else in the company has one.

Of course, Ms Cole. Anything you want.

'Ms Cole, that report you requested … it's been done,' said her assistant, Lee.

'Where is it?'

'I thought you'd like to see it in the morning … it's gone eight.'

Eve resented her staff thinking they could dictate when her workday should end, but they weren't forward-thinking like her. Their lack of ambition was quite pathetic, really.

'Bring it in to me and you can go home.'

'Yes, Ms Cole,' he said.

By nine o'clock, her tiredness began to render the process useless and Eve gave up for the night. As always, she was the last to leave – her work ethic, which bought her respect, had also bought the car she drove into her security-gated apartment. As she'd told the pesky reporter for that 'Today's Woman' article, such a lifestyle depended on hard work and dedication. Eve was never happier than when she was knee-deep in work; all that decision-making and knowing that what she said mattered. She'd never been one for partying or socialising. Any time away from the office was spent either at home or at a work dinner. She travelled the world on expenses and dressed in the latest fashions, usually for free or heavily discounted. Eve Cole was living the dream, emulating the many heroines she'd once read about as a young adult, and finally escaping the hellhole that used to be her life.

'What hellhole was that, Ms Cole?' the inquisitive reporter had asked.

Eve had simply smiled and said, 'Oh, you know, the regular things.'

She switched on the lamp, opting for a quiet ambience. Eve craved quiet. She'd accurately connected this to having been subjected to living arrangements reminiscent of a zoo. The sound of noisy children, cutlery and bellowing staff; dirty B & Bs and sharing toilets with drug users and thieves – and that time she'd slept in a shop doorway. The stench and sounds had never left her. And she was glad of that, because it remained a constant reminder, something she needed to ensure she never went back.

Eve padded around the clean shiny lines of her apartment, the second home she'd owned and certainly the grandest. The soothing sound of water running into her sunken bath never got old. Neither did the knowledge that even if she lost her job tomorrow, she would be able to live the same lifestyle without another one for at least five years.

Eve knew how to invest and did not spend on frivolities. Many of her luxuries were free anyway – like the smooth black robe delicately dripping from her shoulders, a gift from the Donna Karan company during her last trip to New York, and the real lambs' leather house slippers, also free, from a little-known Italian designer the store had recently decided to stock on her recommendation. She sank into the warm bathwater, smiling at the rush of satisfaction. Her day tomorrow would be just like today – a certainty that immersed her in comfort and a feeling of absolute warmth and security.

At eight o'clock the next morning, Eve walked into her office with Lee rushing up behind her.

'Ms Cole—'

'What is it?'

'The meeting for ten has been cancelled.'

Lee shut the door behind him and sat opposite her desk, lowering his voice.

'Ms Cole, I was told by reception that a lady has called asking about your diary.'

'What?'

'Apparently, she wanted to know when you would be in the office.'

Eve had learned never to show any weakness. 'Have you told security not to let anyone in to see me without an appointment?'

'No ...'

'Then do it now.' She smiled gently, but her voice clinging to a warning that sloppiness would not be tolerated. Human resources held onto a long list of candidates who could step comfortably into Lee's job at a moment's notice, such was her reputation. Anyone with any sense and ambition wanted to work with Eve Cole.

She returned from a lunch meeting to find Lee waiting for her anxiously.

'Ms Cole, a lady came in to see you but, as instructed, security told her to call and make an appointment.'

A prick of alarm shot through her body. The woman had actually come to her office.

'She left a name and a number you could reach her on.'

Eve let out an air of nonchalance. 'What's her name?'

'Lana Cole.'

She remained expressionless, her body rigid save for a flutter of her eyelashes.

'Thank you, leave it to me,' she said.

The fear of going to prison after she had pelted Stan with the edge of a table lamp had all but vanished as she became more powerful. The fact she hadn't killed him and he'd still been working at that prison was further proof that she would be safe. But that hadn't stopped her from feeling a little apprehensive at the article's release. There was always a possibility that someone would see beyond the slight name change and short haircut.

And it was always going to be Lana.

Eve had prepared for this moment ever since the interview had wrapped, but hadn't realised just how hearing the sound of her sister's name would make her feel inside. The way the insides of her stomach twisted into a tight knot.

Eve beckoned Lee into her office.

'Take the number, call her and arrange a meeting.'

'The lady who came?'

'Just do it, OK?'

'Yes, of course.'

'Thank you.'

'How long would you like me to schedule the appointment for?'

'Half an hour should do it. We haven't much to discuss.'

*

As Lana was led through the shiny foyer and into a brightly lit office, she felt a line of tension leave her body.

Her sister had not only survived, she'd survived well.

'Hello.' The voice came from a tall figure emerging from an opened door, beautifully manicured hand outstretched. Lana repositioned her arms to receive the handshake instead of the hug she'd envisioned in her many daydreams.

'Hello,' said Lana, breath momentarily caught in her throat. Her younger sister stood well over six feet tall with heels, her beautiful face and stature emitting an insanely powerful and commanding aura.

'You look just like Daddy!' enthused Lana, yet Eve's expression remained unmoved. This wasn't the way Lana had imagined this day. There was something anticlimactic about it all. Here, standing in front of her, was May, her sister!

'I can't believe it's you!' said Lana breathlessly, her excitement betraying her. 'I can't believe it – I've finally found you!'

'Couldn't have been that hard. I'm all over the business pages.'

They both sat down on rounded orange sofas, facing one another as if in therapy.

'Great piece by the way.' Lana would not question why the article had read as if Eve had been born at seventeen. Why there had not been any mention of herself, Tina or their parents.

'So, May—'

'My name is Eve now.'

'Of course. That's part of the reason it was so hard to track you down!'

'I can imagine.'

'It's really good to see you,' said Lana, desperate for words that would thaw the gigantic block of ice wedged between them. 'You seem to be doing all right for yourself.'

'If by "all right" you mean growing professionally every day, then yes. As well as fashion, I am involved in other ventures.'

'Like what?'

'This and that.'

'Oh, I see. As you can see, I know nothing about fashion.' Lana was unsure as to how the conversation had turned to her dress sense.

'Would you like my assistant to get you a drink?'

'Eve, I thought I'd never find you and now—'

'You did a good job, it seems.'

'Not really, I mean if I hadn't seen your picture in the magazine. Wow, I still can't believe it. Let's just say you're a hard person to track down even when I had your number. You must be very busy and fed up of people wanting to see you without an appointment, I get that.'

'I knew it was you,' she said simply.

'When I called the first time?'

'Yes.'

The words ran through her like a blunt knife.

'You didn't want to speak to me?'

'I don't see the point in any of this. It's all in the past,' she said, looking towards the tiger print on the wall. 'What is the point of dredging up stuff that happened so long ago? Sometimes it's best to let things stay where they belong – in the past.'

'I wasn't expecting this,' said Lana, placing her hand on her heart, hoping she wouldn't feel it break.

'If you were expecting the whole family-reunion bit, then I'm sorry to shatter your illusions. I'm a different person now. I'm happy and I really don't want to rehash the old days. It doesn't really read well, does it?'

'You're my sister,' said Lana, her voice cracking.

A tense moment followed, with Lana assuming she'd at least shattered some of her sister's armour.

'I have a meeting in fifteen minutes. I really must go.'

They both stood.

'Can I wait for you?'

'That won't be necessary, Lana.'

'So this is it?' Hot tears obscured Lana's vision.

'I'm not sure what else there is to say. Don't cry.'

'Tina! You haven't even asked about Tina!'

Eve's nostrils flared, her eyes widening. 'What?'

'You haven't even mentioned her name.'

'OK, I will meet with you again. Come to my house on Saturday and I will be less busy. Lee will give you the address.'

'Thank you,' said Lana, grateful for the chance to hold onto her sister in whatever capacity she could, happy for another moment in her company.

Chapter Thirty-one

Eve's home, located in what used to be a brewery, overlooked the Thames and felt a trillion miles away from Lana's council estate.

'I was just finishing some work on the computer. You can take a seat.'

'You have a home computer?'

'Yes,' she said, as if everyone had one. Her sister's space may have been decorated to exacting modern standards with its real wood floors and fancy furniture, but the kitchen, like everywhere else, looked very unlived in.

'I invited you here because the office was too hectic and you deserved my time. But that part ... that part of my life has gone. You must understand that.'

'You can't just wash the first half of your life away.'

'Yes, I can.'

Lana noticed the stiff demeanour subtly beginning to crack.

'Our parents seemed to manage it,' said Eve.

'Our father died and Mummy was ill. That wasn't their fault!'

'Do you know that when she was around, she never once put her arms around me? Ginny was more of a mum to me. It was like my own mother hated me!'

'That's not true.'

'My memory isn't as selective as yours.'

'She wasn't well … she …' Lana wanted to leave the news about Mummy until another time. If there would ever be another time.

Lana gazed towards the coffee table, which was covered in glossy oversized books and magazines.

'Are you married?' Lana asked.

'Because that's supposed to define me, I take it?'

'No. I meant …' Lana had merely wanted to prick the uncomfortable silence but had only made the awkward situation worse.

'Lana, I truly feel this is a waste of your time and mine.'

'But we're sisters!'

'I exist alone.'

'That's not true. You have me …'

'Like I did when you left me at the home?'

'I was coming back for you, to take you out. Surprise you with a trip to London to see the flat, your home – but you'd gone! Why didn't you wait for me, or at least come to me?'

'I didn't have your number.'

'What? But I sent you …'

'It's a long story. Let's just say, I had to leave.'

Eve's words left a question mark floating in the air as she headed for the kitchen, returning with two cups of tea.

Smoothing down her short hair, Eve exhaled. 'Remember Stan?'

'At the home, yes. They said you had a fight with him.'

'A fight? Let's just say he wasn't very nice to me.'

'He was horrible to everyone.'

Eve began to blink rapidly. 'That he was. And he seemed to get worse when you left. He even hid your letters from me. And much worse.'

Lana closed her eyes. 'May, I'm—'

'Eve, my name is Eve!'

Lana moved closer to her sister, unsure of how this would be received.

'Don't. I don't need your sympathy.'

'Eve, I am so sorry, if I'd known—'

'What? What could you do? You were gone, starting your new life. I had no one to turn to.'

Lana resisted the urge to take her sister's hand and bury it in her palms. Instead they sat in silence, just inches apart.

'You don't have to be alone any more. You have people: me and Tina ...'

'You've found Tina?'

'No, not yet, but I will. It's only a matter of time.'

'What do you know about her?' Eve was back in business mode.

'I don't know much about her and, to be honest, the trail has gone cold. I thought she might be in Barcelona.'

'Barcelona?'

'I went all the way over there and met a nice gardener who gave me a little bit of information like a name and a few dates, but nothing much else.'

'Sounds expensive.'

'I will use every penny I have to find her.'

Eve turned away and then spoke. 'I can help.'

'Really? You want to help me find her?'

'I have the funds to help you. How much do you need?'

'No, that's not why I'm here, Eve.'

'Money is all I can give, if I'm honest. It's all I am willing to give.'

'Then you keep it, because that's not why I'm here. I want you. I want my sister back!'

'If you won't take money, at least accept the services of a private investigator one of my companies has used in the past.' She moved over to the computer desk and opened the side drawer. 'Here's his card. Tell him my name and then give him all the information you've gathered on Tina. He will bill me personally.'

The reality of finding Tina edged nearer, coupled with the real possibility of losing Eve all over again.

'I ... I will call him.'

'I suggest you do.'

'But ... but what about us?'

'There is no us, Lana. This is all I can give you. Please, just accept that.'

'What's she like?' asked Clifton.

'Tall.'

Lana's chest felt burdened with the weight of her sister's decision not to be a part of her life. This was not supposed to happen.

'You must be so thrilled to have her back!' He stalled the enthusiasm as Lana's face became a map of pain, the feel of his arms around her doing nothing to stem the mounting emotion.

'She doesn't want to know me, Clifton. She's not interested!'

At that moment Lana was unconcerned about the promise to 'stay away' from her best friend Clifton. She needed him more than ever as the familiar chimes of abandonment echoed in her ears.

'I'm staying tonight,' he said firmly.

'You don't have to do that.'

'Yes, I do.'

Lana was grateful for his company, his presence and his friendship. 'I'd really like that, Clifton. I really would.'

Lana awoke the next morning to the busying sounds of colliding cutlery and the clanging of plates.

'What's going on here?'

'I made you some breakfast.'

'I'm not hungry.'

'Well, I am. Your sofa is so uncomfortable!'

'Special cereal, is it?'

'How did you guess?'

'What about Denise?'

'I wasn't aware she wanted some.'

'You know what I mean!'

'Are you serious right now? Drop it. As I keep telling you, she isn't Misty.'

Misty was a former girlfriend of Clifton's and the only one to ever voice her jealousy towards Lana. Clifton and Lana often laughed at that recollection yet, lately, she'd become sensitive to the memory.

Clifton placed the cereal–fruit–cream concoction onto her lap. For years he'd proudly prepared this dish for her. For years she hadn't the heart to tell him just how disgusting it tasted.

Once Clifton had left, she lay on her bed and, for the first time since beginning her search for her sisters, yearned for the familiarity of her job, for the hours spent in the midst of other people's problems, too busy to dwell on her own.

Her eyes rested on the ceiling, loneliness threatening to grip her. Eve's refusal to become a part of her life – coupled with the real possibility that Clifton would soon be gone and swept up in the arms of a new life with Denise – frightened her. Life could not have looked any bleaker for Lana Cole. She wondered about Mummy and Daddy again. Her parents. The two people who'd loved her fiercely and yet, through no fault of their own, had also left.

Perhaps Eve was right to be so cold and loveless. She truly was the clever one. It was too late for Lana, though. She could never be like Eve. Lana wanted to love; she was born to love; she needed to love. Yet, therein lay the problem: there seemed to be no one left to love.

Lana dialled the number of the private investigator, feeling less than hopeful with the scant information she'd gathered in Barcelona. It all would have been a waste of time if not for the article ...

'You've got some of the real father's details. We have a name for the diplomat so he will be easy to trace and you've given me a rough timeline of events. I have enough to be getting on with for now.'

'That's … great!'

'Now leave the rest to me. I will call you when I have more info.'

The investigator called back within ten days to tell her he'd found Tina.

Her baby sister lived in London, just a few miles from where Lana had lived her entire adult life.

Chapter Thirty-two

The tree-lined street in St John's Wood evoked a feeling of aspiration and hopefulness, and Lana hoped this was a prelude to what lay ahead.

'How may I help you?'

The Asian woman dressed in a black and white maid's uniform elicited a reaction Lana could not control. She closed her mouth as soon as she realised it was open.

'I might have the wrong house. I'm looking for a Mrs Jennings.'

The woman looked at her squarely. 'You have the right house. Who may I say is at the door?'

'Tell Mrs Jennings my name is Lana Cole.'

Less than half a minute later she returned, this time opening the huge door to reveal a vast black and white tiled hallway leading to a grey spiral staircase. Mrs Jennings stood at the bottom of the staircase, under a dripping bronze chandelier. She had clearly once been a beauty, but time and the stresses of life had taken hold.

'Miss Cole,' she said steadily. Her hair was immaculately styled and her lilac trouser suit carefully pressed.

Lana followed her through a set of double doors, her eyes curiously searching for photos of her sister. A painting of a wide-hipped woman sitting on a horse and an unidentifiable figurine were the room's only decoration. She sat down on one of the blue striped armchairs.

'This is a nice chair,' said Lana.

'It's Louis the sixteenth.'

The maid – an actual maid – closed the doors behind her and the mood changed.

'Lana. I've been expecting you.'

'You know who I am?'

'Yes. Unfortunately, I do.'

As an invisible grandfather clock warned of another hour, the women began a conversation twenty years overdue.

Ten minutes later, Lana could only communicate that she didn't wish to be rude but hadn't embarked on this journey to listen to a woman's regret at not adopting all three children. She was here to see her baby sister.

'Mrs Jennings. Is she here? Is my sister here?'

'No, dear, she isn't. You will meet her, but before you do, I need to let you know my side of this story.'

'The private investigator told me everything.'

'What did he say?'

'Enough. And looking around here and seeing where you lived in Barcelona, I see that Tina had a great life, a charmed life, and for that I'm grateful.'

'There are things you don't know, Lana.'

Lana rolled her eyes with weary frustration. She'd been on such a long journey, both physically and emotionally. Now, being so close to the end had only raised her anxiety levels. She needed to see her sister, now.

'What I have to tell you will only take a moment. Listen before you judge me. Then and only then will I give you my daughter's address.'

Chapter Thirty-three

London, 1948

As a twenty-five-year-old spinster, Sarah Donald's heart had finally been taken by a slightly older half-Swedish man, whom her mother merely tolerated because of his rapidly growing property portfolio.

His willingness to finally get her daughter off the market was also a huge plus, even though Mother had always encouraged Sarah to look for a British husband with impeccable breeding and a traceable family. But even though he was 'a little rough around the edges', Rex's sizable income, and thus his ability to look after her daughter, overshadowed such specifications, and a marriage was soon approved.

Rex and Sarah Andersen remained happy for the first few years of their marriage. However, the more money he made, the more his attraction to mistresses less concerned with his marital status he became. Sarah's mother advised her to sit tight and tolerate this behaviour, as long as he remained discreet. A baby would help. Wasn't it time? They'd been married for years now and what was taking so long?

When Sarah suffered her second miscarriage, doctors confirmed that carrying a baby full term was possible but they would need to make love on a continual basis – a rather difficult feat when her husband spent most nights without his wife. Rex Andersen's indiscretions were no longer discreet when, years later, he fathered a child by one of his tenants – a coloured woman. His confession arrived one evening via a potent mix of alcoholic fumes and cigarette smoke. That night, a humiliated Sarah bundled anything she could into a bag and fled to her mother's.

It was her mother who advised her to return.

She was nearing forty and who would want her? She was to claim the property, money and position that were rightfully hers and to not under any circumstances leave a space open for another woman to slot into.

Especially not a coloured woman.

Sarah reluctantly returned home to a drunken yet remorseful Rex. Her reel of demands were met immediately and without argument: separate beds and separate lives.

They co-existed, Sara's seemingly moral high ground over a shrunken and regularly intoxicated Rex merely hiding the pain she constantly had to fight against: another woman had produced something she'd been unable to match. She was nothing; surplus to requirements.

Boredom and distrust evolved into a need to be involved with the businesses. At least then she could feel useful again, whilst protecting her financial future.

One day, Sarah decided it was time to meet their entire pool of tenants. One by one, over tea and biscuits, she discussed their tenancies and if they were happy with the services they had received. Ginny at number sixty-three Pettyford Road was a talker, telling Sarah almost everything there was to know about the coloured neighbour by answering her carefully thought-out questions. When she left Ginny's flat, she saw that the door to the other flat was ajar, so she entered. The coloured woman sat in a chair, her eyes blank yet fixed on the corner of the ceiling.

'Hello?' said Sarah. The words 'you home-wrecking whore' hovered on her lips. The woman did not flinch. An infant in a pram basket gurgled by the television. Two small children were asleep on the sofa.

'Hello?' she reiterated. The oldest of the children sprang off the sofa.

'Can I help you?'

The child's use of proper English was a surprise to Sarah.

'I am here to speak to your mother about the rent.'

'Mr Rex comes for that.'

'I'm collecting it from now on.' Sarah thought it bizarre to be continuing a conversation with a child, whilst the adult remained seated in a chair staring at the wonders of a peeling wall.

'How old are you?'

'Nearly twelve. Well, sort of.'

'What is your name, child?'

'Lana. And that's May and that's Tina. Mummy will be better soon and she will talk to you.'

'That's OK,' said Sarah, her curiosity pulling her towards the pram.

What she glimpsed inside saddened her. The sleeping innocence of a child born into a web of lies, adultery and now, perhaps, even madness.

She shut the front door behind her. This was the woman Rex was besotted by? A thin, insane, coloured woman with three children? Sarah's mind began to explore the familiar route of self-loathing and disbelief. Had she been that bad a wife for Rex to prefer that?

She decided to stamp on the cloud of self-pity for now and walked to the nearest phone box to make a call.

As Sarah realised, it was hard to hate a woman with no ability to fight back. And when the ambulance arrived, she merely stood beside Ginny, both of them watching with sadness etched onto their faces.

'I didn't know it was this bad. I'd kept my distance today because I was so tired with all the shift work. Just wanted a break ... and now this.'

'I'm sure it's not your fault,' said Sarah.

'I wish I could take them on. I have tried. Looked after them as much as I could because I didn't want them to go into a home. Now this. She's lost it. Really lost it, this time.' Ginny sobbed as Sarah looked on, determined not to be pulled in emotionally. This woman had wrecked her own family, after all.

As time moved on, Sarah's mind was never far away from those children ... and Rex's baby.

As Sarah collected the rents as usual, Ginny unwittingly kept her abreast of the woman's progress – of which there wasn't much. Rex grew tired of apologising, preferring the bottom of a booze-filled glass, and never mentioning his child. Sarah became transfixed on the plight of the three little girls languishing in a children's home whilst she sat in a huge house, as lonely as the day she was born.

When the poor coloured woman took her own life, Sarah decided to ask one last favour from her worthless husband.

'I want the child.'

His reddened face and uneven posture turned away from the vodka bottle long enough to ask, 'What the fuck you on about, woman?'

'I want the child. And you are going to get her for me.'

It wasn't difficult to arrange a meeting with the right people and suggest a blood test to prove paternity. The woman had been certified mad when she'd agreed to the 'father unknown' status recorded on the child's birth certificate anyway. Easy to contest in court.

Within weeks they were allowed to see the child and this became the day Sarah would never forget. Rex had never been a handsome man, but the child ... this child was the epitome of beauty, from the first toe on her feet to the very last strand of curly hair on her head. A rush of immediate love found a home in Sarah's body. She'd yearned for a child for so long and at last she had found her. In a certain light, Tina could possibly pass for white. Possibly. As long as they never lived anywhere with too much sun, she'd be fine. The hair was worrisome though … so curly! But with the right styling, no one would ever guess … and if they did, Sarah would not care! It was too late. She'd already fallen in love.

When Rex died six months later, Sarah and Tina began life as a twosome. She had hoped to sell Rex's entire property portfolio and move away with her daughter. But after learning of her husband's unscrupulous business dealings and massive debts, she was advised to sell off all assets immediately, barely keeping the roof over their heads.

It wasn't long before Sarah's mother offered her usual brand of advice. 'You'll just have to meet a man who can look after you, is financially stable and willing to take on another man's child. A half-caste one, at that!'

Within a year, Sarah was married to an old flame – a diplomat, much to her mother's delight. Finally, her life became a whirl of love and excitement as the family travelled the world thanks to various overseas postings, little Tina and a loving husband finally making her feel complete.

'And that's my story. The story. Tina's story. I will tell her everything tonight.'

The revelations had hit Lana like a lead weight. As clear as day, Mr Rex Andersen had taken advantage of a poor defenceless woman at her most vulnerable.

Mummy. Their mummy.

This had been no affair, as if she'd needed any more evidence. Mr Rex Andersen was absolute scum.

Lana placed her face in her hands and inhaled. She hadn't been able to help Mummy, but from now on she would be there for her sister.

'I will contact Tina in the morning,' said Lana.

'No, please, give me two days.'

The maid appeared. 'Can I get you anything?'

'No, it's OK, Susan.'

The maid 'Susan' eyed Lana suspiciously before closing the double doors behind her.

'Just two days,' reiterated Mrs Jennings.

Emotion threatened to spill out and into the room. Lana needed to keep it together. She was so close … so close to touching her sister again … to hearing her voice again.

'That isn't going to happen, Mrs Jennings. I want to speak to Tina.'

'You must give me time! Just two days, please! You must!'

Lana's voice rose to a shout. 'Why should I?'

'Because Tina knows nothing about any of this! She doesn't even know that you or your sister exist!'

Chapter Thirty-four

The five-foot-five blonde surveyed her reflection in the full-length mirror.

Mother often commented that, at age twenty-two, she should be wearing clothes that accentuated her figure, even if she did insist on dressing too old for her age.

'You must always keep your husband interested,' she would say. 'Men like Mark are easily distracted.'

At the muffled thump of a car door shutting outside, she glanced at her watch. She had just ten minutes to make a fifteen-minute journey to Samantha's nursery. How she hated tardiness, but avoiding the gossip at the gates as parents waited for home time was a perk she enjoyed. She really had nothing in common with these women and their empty, miserable lives.

Or maybe she did, and that was the point.

She picked up the car keys from a crowded dressing table and almost collided with one of Samantha's beloved dog-eared teddy bears near the door. It used to annoy her when school friends at one of the many private day schools she'd attended as a child spent time planning wealthy futures with moneyed men, where their sole purpose in life would be to look pretty and well maintained. She would always excuse herself from such discussions, secretly despising their lack of ambition and drive – and yet a few short years later, here she was doing just that. She'd fallen in love at nineteen with a man thirteen years older – sophisticated, well read – and had never looked back, although sometimes she wished she had. She wished she had slowed down and taken her time, if only to sample what it would be like to travel the world as a singleton, or indulge in tomfoolery with a group of girlfriends. Of course, she did not regret her marriage or her child. She just wished she had waited.

Raising her daughter was the most rewarding act she'd ever experienced. From the moment she was handed to her in the hospital – this gorgeous creature with her curly, blonde ringlets and a strong nose like no one in any of her immediate family – she experienced a love stronger than she'd ever felt in her life. Yet, as time went on, she began to experience a secondary emotion that sometimes swept over her as she watched her daughter sleep.

A need for more.

She wasn't even sure if these needs could be met by profiting from the joy of baking, which had crept up on her recently during Samantha's first birthday party. She'd baked two dozen fairy cakes, which had disappeared as quickly as she could place them onto the balloon-decorated table. An odd feeling of contentment followed remarks such as, 'You should really be selling these,' and her favourite: 'Ever thought of going into business?' Of course she had. Many times. Last month, she'd thought about applying for a job at an art gallery where Mark knew the owner. She'd also started a novel once Samantha started nursery, but hadn't actually written more than ten pages. So many ideas for a career had begun and ended in her head. Yet the idea of running a little cake shop seemed to linger and this had to mean something.

Mark, of course, had completely dismissed the idea. 'Who's going to pay more than fifty pence for a fairy cake, anyway?'

Her mother curtly echoed this dismissal. 'You should be happy with the joy of a child and a man who can financially provide.'

She was lucky, wasn't she? What more could she want?

Her life was ordered and offered no beautifully packaged surprises. She also expected none. So when her mother had called, citing absolute urgency, her mind had immediately imagined a myriad of horrific scenarios. The last time her mother had sounded so frantic was the day her stepfather had died.

Quinton Jennings had meant everything to Tina. Unable to remember her adoptive father, Rex – a Scandinavian businessman who'd died when she was a toddler – he was the only father she'd ever known. He'd taught her to tie shoelaces correctly, paraded her in front of smiling 'important' guests as she clung shyly to his leg and regularly told her she was the most precious thing in his life. They shared a tightly bonded love which fiercely guarded her from the harshness of being unable to make any lasting friendships as they travelled the globe. He was her world and she his. And when he died, she was fifteen years old and whispering on the cusp of womanhood. The abyss of grief had held her away from the lure of college, university or having fun, with all meaning gone from her life. Death had brought clarity and Tina realised how poor her relationship with her mother was. They rarely spoke and when they did they would disagree on almost everything.

Falling into the arms of Mark seemed like the most natural thing in the world. He was older, kind and listened to her talk about the father she'd lost. Her mother approved of Mark's family and career aspirations despite the age difference and when they were engaged, married and pregnant all in the space of a year, her mother was as thrilled as Tina was exhausted.

That evening she had ignored a call from her mother, who she knew hated speaking into the answer machine. So when her mother actually left a message, this told her of the urgency.

'I'm off to Mother's,' she said, as Mark picked at the meal she'd prepared the night before.

She'd received two more calls from her mother, assuring her she was alright but urging her presence now.

Mark nodded nonchalantly.

'Before I forget, Samantha and I would like Gita and her mum to spend Saturday with us.' She slipped into a comfortable, over-sized cardigan, her tight-fitting dress now drowned by wool.

'Why?'

'Because she's a child and it's nice for her to play with friends. And I get some female company too!' She hadn't meant to sound sharp, but her nerves had resurfaced as she once again attempted to work out why her mother had been so insistent she come over.

'She's too young for all that.'

'Oh, come on.'

'You leave her at a nursery for a few hours a day. Don't you have time for female company then?'

'It's only a couple of hours and after I've cleaned—'

'My dear, let's talk about this another time,' he replied firmly. She opened her mouth to speak, before realising there were more pressing matters. Namely, getting to her mother's. She would return for round two later and resume the disagreement – while making sure his anger never rose above a certain level, because, when it did, Mark would not talk to her for days; he would not even a glance in her direction. It was a rebuke so painful she would eventually be forced to back down and make the first move.

Their relationship hadn't always been like this: a constant battle she fought alone. In the beginning he'd been so in tune with her needs, she'd been able to open up to him about Daddy Quinton almost immediately after their first date to the opera. Mark would listen attentively, never making her feel as if she was talking about her dead father too much. Other people made her feel like that. Her mother made her feel like that.

Tina used the key she still owned to enter her mother's home and the realisation hit her that there was no one actually left to die. Her family consisted of just her mother, Mark and Samantha. This could only mean that whatever her mother had to say couldn't be that bad.

'Tina, did you hear what I just said?'

'What?'

'Tina?' Mark repeated, with a noticeable hint of irritation. Tina had left her mother's the night before in a haze of confusion and driven around aimlessly before returning home to a snoring Mark. In bed beside her husband, her mind and eyes had remained alert, recalling the way her mother's lips had moved to the rhythm of words so alien to her ears and understanding.

Sisters.

Sisters?

Her body had remained on autopilot as she completed her usual Saturday tasks that morning: tending to Samantha, cooking, cleaning – all whilst unwilling or unable to process what her mother had told her.

Sisters.

'Tina?' said Mark, eyes rising from the newspaper over in the lounge section as she stood over the kitchen sink. Samantha sat in her red and white highchair at the table, scribbling on a piece of paper with a crayon. A pot of tinned soup was bubbling over onto the surface of the cooker.

'Mumma!' said Samantha, swinging her legs rapidly from the edge of the highchair. Mark ran from the sofa, capturing the pot as slimy liquid dribbled angrily from the lip. He placed the hot pan into the sink.

'What's wrong with you? Why aren't you paying attention?'

'Sorry. I—'

'You've been behaving strangely all day.'

Tina so wanted to share this 'news' with him, ask his advice – anything, but they'd begun a row the night before. That's right, she'd asked about Gita and her mum spending the day with them and Mark had said no.

'I've had a weird twenty-four hours,' she said.

'Try not to burn down the house, please,' he said, before returning to the adjoining lounge and his newspaper. Glad of her husband's rejection, Tina made a decision she could actually cope with.

'I'm going out, Mark!' She needed space away from the house. Away from the lies.

'Where to? It's a Saturday.'

'I am aware of that,' she said under her breath.

'Tina!'

She could hear the anger in his voice. Yesterday, that would have intimidated her, but at that moment she could only answer him in one way – and that was by opening the door and releasing herself into the world, away from him, even away from Samantha; away from her life, whatever that was … whatever it *is*.

She inhaled quickly.

The driveway, the trees, the sky, everything around her had now taken on a new air she did not recognise. Her skin swelled with goosebumps. Nothing made sense anymore.

She didn't make sense anymore.

Chapter Thirty-five

Lana was unable to imagine just what she'd uncover behind the door of the large semi-detached house.

Tina's house.

What she looked like and sounded like as an adult remained a mystery. Lana had been unable to glean any clues from a house Tina hadn't even lived in for three years and a woman who appeared quite cold and unwilling to share more of Tina than was necessary. And now she was standing in front of a home her little sister shared with a husband and baby girl.

In all of her fantasies, Lana had never envisaged Tina being a wife and mother.

She felt her knees buckle slightly.

Tina having experienced so much in the time Lana had spent simply pining for her provoked a pang of envy. Her little sister had already experienced adult feats like travelling the world, marriage and giving birth whilst Lana had experienced none of that. But now was not the time to think about regrets.

She reached for the doorbell and paused. In her haste to find a suitable outfit, sensible shoes and a non-distracting hairstyle, she'd forgotten to pack the photographs of Mummy. She would have them for the next visit, should there be a next visit. There was always the possibility that Tina would feel the same way as Eve and want absolutely nothing to do with her.

She slowly exhaled.

Tina would have been given the news from her mother by now. Her whole life would have taken on a new complexion; everything she'd once believed would now be questioned. Perhaps she should have waited before the visit and given her baby sister even more time than Mrs Jennings had suggested. But she'd waited a lifetime to see her again, whilst Tina hadn't even known she'd existed. Lana had been cheated of enough time already. Enough was enough. Time to meet her sister.

As she moved to press the doorbell, the door suddenly swung open and there stood a white lady saying her name.

Multicoloured squiggles from a toddler adorned the fridge along with a picture of a newborn baby wrapped in a red blanket. Lana stood nervously in the space between the kitchen and lounge, watching this woman-child stoop down to an oven. The smell of fresh baking tantalised her senses as Tina placed a large plain sponge onto a cooling tray beside the sink.

'I do rather like baking sometimes, but when I'm nervous I bake a lot!'

Her accent pointed to private schools and a posh upbringing, miles away from what Lana and Eve had experienced – and yet her conception and birth had been the most traumatic.

'I'm sorry, this must all be so confusing to you,' said Tina, leaning down to close the oven.

'No, I'm sorry for you. You've had a shock. Though I guess it doesn't matter who's sorry, does it? We're all victims of circumstance,' said Lana, searching this woman for signs of a shared lineage. What was confusing was Tina's skin complexion. If she didn't know about Tina's history, if she hadn't seen the toddler photos at Mrs Jennings's house, Lana would have assumed there had been a mistake. She would have assumed 'Tina' was indeed white.

Tina wiped her hands on the spotted apron, reminding Lana of a pair of spotted socks she'd once placed on her feet as a baby.

'Let's sit down, shall we?'

They both sat at the table, facing one another and Lana instantly felt a warmth that had been missing with Eve.

Both women placed their arms onto the wooden table that separated them.

'This is so strange,' said Tina.

'I didn't mean to spring all of this on you. I was just so desperate to see you,' said Lana.

'Mother told me. I ... I'm sorry if it's not the reunion you were expecting. It's just that forty-eight hours ago, I didn't know I had a sister.'

'Two sisters!'

'Two sisters! Of course. Wow!'

'It must have been a shock.'

'I thought, is this a joke? So I baked.'

Lana smiled, already captivated by the openness radiating from this woman ... her sister. Hope existed in this room. So much hope.

'You're very pretty,' said Tina. 'And your hair is fantastic.' She traced the outline of a skinny plait, the way white ladies at reception sometimes did without her permission.

'You're pretty too,' said Lana.

Tina stood up and poured water into a glass. 'I'm suddenly very dry.'

'I'll have one too.'

'Things like this don't happen to me,' Tina said.

'You're taking it very well.'

'Did the other one ... Mayo ... not come with you?'

'Her name is Eve now.'

'Now, that I can pronounce.'

'She won't be coming today, no.'

'Wow, wow, wow. I have two sisters!' she said to nobody. 'I still can't believe it. Little old me. Wife, mother ...'

'You have a little girl, right?'

297

'Samantha, yes. She's amazing.'

Lana could not help thinking how un-posh the name sounded.

As if she read her mind, Tina continued. 'When I was a little girl I had a doll I took everywhere. Her name was Samantha. I said that if I were to ever have a little girl, I'd call her Samantha too. Childish, I know, but that's what happens when you get married at nineteen and give birth not long after. Still a child ...' she said wistfully.

Lana wanted to remind her of the Puffalump, the soft toy she took everywhere. Of course Tina wouldn't remember that time, or the soft toy she had once loved so much. Or her sisters.

'Anyway, she's the love of my life and she's a real daddy's girl.'

'That's so lovely,' said Lana, overwhelmed with the effort needed to suppress the joy she felt inside. Tina handed her a framed photograph of a smiling little girl and the recognition was instant.

'You're crying?' said Tina.

'Y ... yes ... I'm sorry,' she sniffed.

Tina handed her sister a tissue.

'She ... she looks so much like our mother. I think it's the nose.'

Tina's shoulders began to heave and her tears were instant.

'Why are you crying?' asked Lana.

'Because I've always wondered where she got such an unusually shaped nose from. I never knew my birth family, of course, and my husband's family don't have it. Actually, I think he believes I had an affair!' The two sisters burst into a fit of snotty, loud giggles, then deep body-shaking guffaws of laughter. Just like sisters. Just like they had never spent the last twenty years apart.

Chapter Thirty-six

One week on and Tina's life was still in a whirl.

Familiar sounds, colours and sensations had become unrecognisable. Her entire life was divided into two halves: Tina before the news and whoever she was now.

Of course, she wasn't a stranger to changes. Quinton's death, getting married and becoming a mother had all been major life shifts, yet somehow this was different. This transition from only child to one of three felt even more life-changing. There were two other women out there in the world that shared her DNA ... shared a mother ... the triangular nose. Two women who were born in Africa – Nigeria, to be exact; a culture and language she knew nothing about.

This was absolutely huge! Not for the first time in her life, she wished for friends she could call up and confide in. But there were no girlfriends, just Mark. And she wasn't quite ready to talk to him about any of it – not before she herself could process it all.

Once or twice as a child, she'd wondered about her biological family and the possibility of siblings. As a teenager, she'd even wondered about this black side of her. But the love of Quinton Jennings had shamed her into burying such thoughts, desperate never to betray him by searching for another 'family'. Even after his death, this resolve only strengthened, with the love of her own child seemingly able to fill the void.

Rex as her biological father would be harder to digest, though.

As would be the knowledge that he had more than likely taken advantage of her mentally ill birth mother, perhaps even raped her. She had not wanted to say the word, just like her mother, who had skirted around this horrifying possibility as she coldly reeled off the events of her 'adoption'. But Tina wasn't about to sugarcoat what went on all those years ago and how she came to be in this world. There would be no fantasising about the loving young couple who'd been forced to give her up for adoption because no one could understand their love. Her conception had come about in a most horrible way.

Tina thought about the mother she would never meet: how she must have felt in the presence of Rex Andersen; having to give up her children. Tina would never give up Samantha; they would have to kill her first. That poor, poor woman, she thought. In the absence of a single memory of Adanya, Tina's empathy could only stem from a place that sympathised with all women who were victims of horrific circumstance. That she could give her: empathy. There just wasn't enough space for much else at the moment. She had a lot to digest.

Her mother – her adoptive mother – called daily, with Tina unable to speak with her for more than five minutes. A latent anger threatened to expose itself at any time. Her mother had lied to her all her life.

What kind of woman did that?

Tina understood why she couldn't have adopted all three children, but the rest was unforgivable. Tina would find it hard to trust her – or anyone – again. Like Mark. The husband who always worked late and who was always so ... distant.

To any outsider who cared enough, Tina's life was continuing on as it always had. Nothing had changed.

Everything had changed.

She now had two sisters.

Sisters.

She had sisters now! Warmth swam across her tummy at the thought of this. The excitement of having two real-life sisters overshadowed all the negativity surrounding her birth and the lies. As a child she'd longed for sisters – or brothers – anyone to take away the loneliness of being shipped from country to country thanks to Daddy Quinton's job.

Tina was grateful his memory had not been tarnished with a lie. He'd always be the man who'd accepted her as his own, insisting she call him Dad within hours of the wedding. He'd been the best father she could ever have hoped for and no one could erase those memories from her mind or her heart. Quinton Jennings was hers forever. Quinton Jennings had known nothing about the deception surrounding her 'adoption'.

The way ahead would be full of kinks and confusing emotions. Yet with two brand-new sisters holding her hand, at least she wouldn't be treading this unknown road alone.

Chapter Thirty-seven

As she stared into the full-length mirror, her focus remained on the contours of her face and the texture of her hair, piled high into a bun. That day, almost a week ago, sitting opposite her sister Lana, it had been instantly clear how different they looked. They even pronounced certain words differently thanks to their upbringings. She had never believed in a class system – that was more her mother's beliefs – but it was clear that she had experienced a life very different to that of her sister: the woman sitting at her kitchen table and with whom she shared a sizable amount of DNA.

Warmed by the disclosure that Samantha looked like Adanya, she longed for something, anything, that could tie her to the woman who gave birth to her.

She ran a hand through her high, blonde bun, overlooked stray strands of dark-brown regrowth betraying its true shade. Lana's jet-black braided concoction was so far removed from any style Tina would ever have considered, yet what she saw reflected back from the mirror was worrisome. Very worrisome.

A framed picture of Rex had sat on the shelf of their busy wooden cabinet ever since the family had moved into the four-bedroom house. Both her mother and stepfather had insisted on some sort of homage to the man who'd 'adopted' her as a baby and who had, at one point in her life, loved her. Now it lay on her bed as she attempted to appraise the image with new eyes. No longer an adoptive father, but her biological sperm donor.

She could now see the contour of his face that resembled her own. Even her eyebrows and the shape of her ears were his.

She closed her eyes and released the bundle of hair from its bind, allowing it to tumble loosely around her shoulders.

For the first time in seven days, she had clarity.

Tina glanced at her reflection in each shop window she walked by, looking at herself questioningly.

Who am I?

This was not about becoming a new person, but perhaps adding to the current one and arming herself with the confidence to sit her daughter down one day and tell her about her grandparents. But how would she explain an ancestral past she herself knew nothing about? Nigeria was a country she'd only ever heard about on the six o'clock news. Didn't they have a military coup a short while ago? She was on the cusp of the biggest ever change in her life and didn't know where to begin this unexpected new journey.

'Take the first step, shall I, Daddy Quinton?' She often 'spoke' to her father, finding comfort in a habit she never wanted to break, recalling his wonderfully comforting energy, which always allowed her to feel safe.

'The first step,' she reiterated.

Tina stiffened as she opened the door of E and A Afro Hair and Beauty Salon. She'd often driven past the shop with Mark on their way to somewhere unimportant, her mind never resting on the possibility she might actually one day walk through its doors. A quick panic ensued, having never set foot in an Afro-Caribbean hair salon before, followed by a pang of shame at that fact.

'Hello,' she said meekly. Her voice was practically inaudible over the harsh sounds of dryers, a radio and animated chatter. The variety of styles stuck on the wall was confusing, as was the stylist's method of using a large needle to sow a weft of hair into a woman's head. Such unfamiliar expressions of style had never been a part of her life. Just another section of her upbringing which had been stolen, she thought.

'Can I help you, love?' said a smartly dressed woman. She was combing a smelly white substance into the hair of a woman engrossed by a magazine. Tina glanced at the wall and at the picture of Janet Jackson in a short crop, a striking blue sea as a backdrop. A tiny radio bellowed a reggae-type Bob Marley-sounding song she was not familiar with. Tina had never been familiar with anything except Wham! and Duran Duran – she liked them, even if her mother and Mark often referred to the music as 'noise'.

'Can I help you, love?' repeated the woman.

The volume on Tina's voice remained jammed at zero as a few of the women turned to look at her.

'I just wanted a ...' She looked to the picture of Janet Jackson again, the only person she actually recognised.

'You all right there?'

'Y ... yes.'

'So, is there any particular style you'd like?'

'What do you do here?'

'There's braiding, relaxing, weaving, bonding, curly perm, Ghana weaves, interlocking, texturising, twists, dreads – loads, really. Depends what you want.'

The lady with the white substance on her head huffed loud enough to be heard over the music.

The hairdresser, picking up on her customer's irritation, said, 'I'm a little busy, love, so if you could let me know what you'd like ... I mean, although we specialise in Afro-Caribbean hair ...'

a faint snigger from a large lady under the dryer '… we can also do European hair.'

'Actually …' Tina began to explain, but thought better of it. The urge to just leave the building was growing more urgent. She apologised profusely and found herself back outside in the cool winter air, hair still in need of something, her pride a little bruised. Although the hairdresser had been courteous, what stung more than anything was her mixed heritage being totally over-looked. It dug into the very core of who she was, or wanted to be.

This was all very confusing.

She could only blame herself for this disconnect, having long since rejected her mixed heritage, happy to live in the bubble her mother had created for her. There had never been any ver-bal denial that she was mixed race – indeed, it was never really spoken about. As they travelled to different countries throughout the course of Daddy Quinton's career, she was never subjected to any questions about her heritage. The 'adopted child' moniker was explanation enough, it would seem.

An hour later, she was in the hands of K, her trusty hairdresser for the last two years.

'I see the roots are showing a little,' he said, pulling at strands of her hair. 'Just in the nick of time, Miss Tina.'

She glanced at the modern chrome and white décor, triangu-lar mirrors and oval styling stools, and the absence of any black faces around her. Not one person looked like her sister.

'Thanks for seeing me at such short notice,' whispered Tina.

'No problem. You know you're my favourite customer.'

'I am, am I?'

'Yes. You have the same style every visit and no complaints.'

Tina glanced at one of the stylists currently adding the finish-ing touches to a rather intriguing hairstyle of ginger hair braided into scores of tiny plaits and interwoven with bright yellow ribbon.

'I don't think that will suit you, Miss Tina.'

Tina knew she wouldn't be returning to her regular hairstyle but was unsure of what to try. Her mind wondered back to the pictures adorning the wall of the previous hair salon.

'I need a change, K.'

He felt the surface of his forehead and sighed. 'I never thought I'd hear those words from your mouth. Dare I get excited?'

'I would like you to give me my natural colour back.'

'Mousey blonde?'

'No, my natural colour please, K.'

'May I ask, what's brought this on?'

'Nothing. I ... I ... just thought I might have a change, that's all.' However long she'd known K, she could never consider telling him her news. Indeed, Mark's reaction the night before had probably made her even more determined never to confide in another soul.

'Wow,' Mark had said rather underwhelmingly, as if he'd known all along and had been waiting for her to merely articulate this news.

'I've just told you my adoptive father was my real father and I have two older sisters and all you can say is wow?' She wanted to feel his arms around her body and for his hands to massage her tense shoulders. She wanted to simply bury her face against his chest and feel his heartbeat – a reassurance that the life she'd known previously still lived and was real.

'What happens now?' her husband asked instead.

'I don't know.'

Mark had shaken his head. 'Your mother has a lot to answer for.'

'Which one?' A surprising yet misplaced attempt at humour.

'She should never have done this to you, Tina. Never.'

At last, she thought, some sympathy.

He moved over to her, his mouth curving into a solemn smile. 'You will get through this, Tina. It's a setback, but you'll get through it.'

And that was it.

She'd turned her back, feeling his eyes on her. Perhaps he had wanted to say more that night – she would never know. Instead she picked up her daughter, buried her face into her soft hair and, holding onto her, sobbed discreetly and privately for the rest of the night.

'You haven't changed your hairstyle in ages, Tina. What's brought this on?' asked K.

'I need to be me again.' She didn't care how corny that might have sounded. 'Although I'm not sure who me is!'

'I'd say you're more ...' He placed a finger to his lips.

'White?'

'Where did that come from?'

'Sorry.'

He shook his head as if to shake off her random comment and began to appraise her hair, as if seeing it for the first time. 'We'll give you your colour and curls back ... actually, no, we'll go for the crimper. Very now!'

'I won't be straightening it for a while.'

K placed his hand to his chest as if being shot. 'That hurts. But you're right, we may as well go all out.'

Hours later, the big reveal was announced to the entire salon and Tina felt a flush of embarrassment.

'Let me look at you,' he said, pulling Tina up out of the chair. 'Yes, that style really brings out your mixed heritage.'

'What ...? You knew I was half African?'

'Well, not sure about all that, but I knew you were half black. I'm a hairdresser, I get to see my clients in their raw natural-ness. And I know my curl patterns. Hairdressing is a science, you know.'

'I can't believe you knew ...'

'I did wonder why you wanted to change yourself so much. But, hey, who am I to judge?' He guided her over to the mirror. 'Make sure your eyes are closed. No peeping.'

She dreaded the sight awaiting her.

'Ta-da!'

She slowly opened her eyes and her smile widened quickly.

The woman in the mirror wasn't her.

The woman in the mirror *was* her.

Her hair, held in place by a band, tumbled down in crimped waves, infused with her natural dark brown. Her fingers rolled over each dark strand and she wondered if she now looked more like Adanya. She hoped so. Lana had promised to provide photos the next time they met, but, for now, she could only imagine.

'What do you think, Tina?'

'I think it's lovely!' For the first time in a week, Tina was immersed in happiness. She'd always felt she was merely accepting what others decided for her and what they wanted for her and how they saw her. Returning to her natural colour was a small step towards regaining part of who she really was. And, for the first time in her life, Tina felt as if she was finally growing up.

Chapter Thirty-eight

Lana hated the term half-sisters.

It felt like a demotion, a suggestion they'd never shared a life, a home, a history – a mother. She would never refer to Tina like that, because she'd forever be her baby sister, her love and her joy, and, now she'd finally found her, she yearned to be around her every single day of the week. She wanted to learn all she could about the last twenty years of her life, to hold her daughter, to give her husband Mark a hug. From a rational standpoint, Lana knew that Tina needed time to come to terms with the news and she would just have to stay away until invited – dial her number and say hello from time to time, but give her the space she needed.

Clearly not all of Lana's plans had worked out as she'd hoped and she could only cling to the possibility that Eve would somehow become more receptive. Lee, her sympathetic assistant, had informed Lana that his boss had flown to America on business for a week. Any planned reunions with the three of them would clearly have to wait, dependent on whether Eve would want to see any of them again anyway.

Lunch with Tina and Samantha was imminent and Lana had yet to find one photo of Adanya and Tina together. She'd blindly promised to look for one while being fairly certain that such a picture did not exist. Daddy had shot all the pictures she owned: Eve and Lana as children and single shots of their mother, smiling beautifully towards the camera. She hoped one of those would be enough for Tina and she would pick up the copies she'd ordered from the chemist on her way to Tina's.

The sound of the doorbell startled her.

'Hello, stranger,' said Clifton, with his arms outstretched.

She opened the door first and then the protective gate. 'It's been a while, old friend. You'd better come in,' she said, playfully shrugging away his hug. 'Feels like ages since I last saw you,' she said, handing him a mug of tea.

'How are you doing, Lana?'

'Brilliant, really great. Tina is really lovely! I'm seeing her later, in fact and meeting her little girl!'

'You're an aunty! I'm so pleased for you. I can't wait to meet them.' He placed the mug to one side. 'I'm really glad you're happy, Lana. I am too. You see, I'm about to do something really amazing.'

'Walk up Machu Picchu? You used to talk about that a lot.'

'I'm going to apply for a loan and open my own mechanics business.'

'That's great!'

'And I'm going to ask Denise to marry me.'

'What?' Her body jolted in surprise.

'Not the reaction I was hoping for!'

'Wow, you're getting married?'

'I haven't asked her yet. And she might say no.'

'She'd be crazy to.'

'Thanks.'

'So, what's brought this on?'

'I love her and, well, I'm into my mid-thirties and I don't want to be an old dad out of breath chasing a ball around.'

'You've always been out of breath chasing a ball around! Seriously, I'm pleased for you.'

310

And she was, genuinely so. Perhaps a month ago, her internal reaction would have been laced with self-pity and the fear of utter loneliness at the thought of her best friend leaving her. But she had her sisters back now. Well, at least one. She'd be OK.

'Clifton Joseph is getting married! What will the world's single women do now?'

'Are you happy for me, then?'

'Yes, Clifton. I am.'

'Great hair!' enthused Lana.

'Why, thank you.' She fingered a few strands as if suddenly remembering she had a new hairstyle. K was right; she wasn't one for change.

'Your niece has been dying to meet her aunty,' said Tina, as Lana followed her into the living room she'd last seen a week ago. 'Although at this age, she's probably just happy to see a new face!'

'You were very intelligent when you were little. You knew so many words and you loved it when I read you a story.' Lana was fishing for memories, for anything.

'I'm so sorry, Lana, but I can't remember a thing about that time. I really wish I could. I know it would mean a lot to you.'

Tina, her wonderful sister, knew that a memory would have pleased her, such was their bond. And this fact alone brought joy.

'Mark's away on a business trip, so it's only the three of us, I'm afraid. I'll go and get Sleeping Beauty.'

Her eyes rested on a row of framed pictures she hadn't noticed during the crazy first visit. Husband, wife and a baby posing awkwardly for the camera. A newborn, a toddler. A toddler holding a dolly with stringy hair.

'Go over into the kitchen!' called Tina.

Lana liked how casual it all sounded, as if she'd been a frequent visitor over the years. Tina walked in, carrying the most beautiful little girl Lana had ever seen.

'Here is her ladyship,' said Tina, securing the child in the red and white highchair. Her little stubby legs were swinging and her hands clapping. She was suddenly excited.

'Meet your Aunty Lana, Samantha, darling!'

Aunty.

Tina switched into baby talk. 'This is my sister and your aunty, yes!'

Lana moved closer, her throat tight.

'Hello, you.' She traced her hand across the child's soft cheek and she was instantly transported to Sir John Adams Children's Home and being she was told her mummy had died and her little sister had been adopted. She now saw Mummy in Samantha's face. She saw hope.

'I'm so sorry,' she said, wiping her eyes with the back of her hand.

'I'll get a tissue. We really need to stop crying … and apologising!'

Tina handed Lana the tissue and she cried into the soft layers. She hoped to one day cuddle the little girl with the adorable chubby legs, but, for now, all she could do was cry.

'It's such a shame Eve had to take a business trip,' said Lana as they sat at the table and tucked into homemade fairy cakes and chamomile tea. Lana was still feeling the euphoric effect of spending time with her niece, who had since fallen asleep and lay dozing in her pram.

'Maybe next time, we'll all be together,' said Tina.

'I hope so.'

'She doesn't want to see me, does she?'

'That's not it!'

'Isn't it?' Tina replied sceptically.

'I'm working on her, trust me.'

'I do feel rather silly because, not long ago, I didn't know either of you existed. Now I want you both in my life so badly. I'm rather impatient!'

Lana changed the conversation. 'I really like your new hairstyle. I don't remember much about our first meeting, because it was all a bit of a haze, but I know you looked a bit different to now.'

'I do?' Tina said with a wry smile.

Lana wasn't sure what that was about, but during their first meeting she hadn't really wanted to focus on how white Tina looked and still did.

'I love it. Very fashion-forward with the crimping. As you can see, I'm a plaits sort of girl. Having plaits keeps me closer to Mummy ... Adanya. It's one of the things I remember vividly about being in Nigeria. Her plaiting my hair in the yard and my ... our grandmother joining us for a chat.'

'That must have been amazing, you know, living in Africa.'

'What I can remember of it, yes. And it was home ... and hot! So very hot!'

Their laughter caused the baby to stir.

'You must be missing your husband.'

'Something like that.'

Lana was aware she'd overstepped a boundary. Of course they weren't ready to talk about personal matters yet!

'I didn't mean to get all personal.'

'Don't be silly! Mark and I are having a few problems, that's all.'

'I hope that's not because of me turning up out of the blue?'

'No, not at all. These problems were there long before. Everything that's happened just highlighted them.'

Conflicting emotions followed: Lana was sad that her sister was experiencing marital difficulties, yet ecstatic that Tina had confided in her. When Tina reached over and placed her hand on top of Lana's, her happiness was complete. 'I'm so glad you found me. I'm so glad you found us.'

Chapter Thirty-nine

Eve's hotel overlooked an expansive New York skyline.

Waking up to such a breathtaking view did nothing to quell the mound of maddening anxiety inside her. She'd spent the last few weeks silently questioning why Lana had assumed she could just waltz back into her life after so many years, expecting a warm hug and cup of cocoa. Initially, she'd assumed Lana wanted money, but that idea had been squashed within minutes.

Eve had been to New York on countless occasions and although a roomful of junior staff would have jumped at the chance to attend this trip, she'd pulled rank and gone herself. Even thousands of miles couldn't erase that updated image of Lana out of her mind. She'd grown into such a pretty woman, as well as an articulate and confident one.

She wondered how she'd come across to Lana.

Rich!

That's right, she was rich. She had everything she could possibly need, a wonderful life filled with everything she would ever want. The first black woman on the board of a British-owned retail company, having smashed through the old boys' network. A self-made woman who'd risen from a children's home – to this. She'd never needed anyone and would certainly never need these women in her life.

Or perhaps Lana had seen through it all and caught a glimpse of the little girl she'd once been, the little girl in a corner reading a tattered book, ignored by a mother who couldn't bear to look at her and missing the father she had loved more than life.

Eve picked up the desk phone and tapped into her home answering machine. Lana's voice echoed through the receiver.

'I know you've been screening my calls ... and that's OK. I just wanted to let you know I ... well, as I said in a previous call, I've met with Tina and, well ... Sorry, I hate talking on machines! I'm going to Tina's again tomorrow to see her and Samantha, her little girl. She's adorable and seems excited about having aunties. Anyway. Bye. Oh, and I hope you're enjoying your trip!'

Beep.

Eve placed the phone back onto the cradle.

She was an aunty.

She turned to the walled window and that 'fantastic' view again. She was attempting to focus on the tall majestic buildings, yet all she saw reflected through the glass was an image of a child. A child named May.

She hated this. She hated to feel. What was the purpose of it, anyway? Many years ago, she'd disposed of the Puffalump, as it too had the power to make her feel every time she looked at it. The first sixteen years of her life were over and had been for a very long time. She no longer needed the feelings attached to a past that only contained loss and pain.

She was Eve Cole. The past, along with May, was dead.

Eve was unable to concentrate at the trade show and found herself sitting outside the venue and in the firing line of an unforgiving New York heat.

'I've been looking for you,' said Phillip, sliding up beside her on the bench. After he'd headhunted her for various positions over the years, they'd remained firm professional friends. At times, it had spilled over into something more.

He took her hand, brushing it with his lips. 'Fancy seeing you here, Eve. This isn't really your thing anymore.'

'I fancied a change of scenery,' she said, pulling her hand away.

'You should have told me you were in town.'

'I didn't think you'd be here,' she lied.

'I'm anywhere where there are people who could use a new job.'

'Well, now I know,' she replied with sarcasm.

Phillip's neediness had always been a turnoff. Ever since their last tryst, he'd complained about not being invited into her home and whined that they never spent a weekend together. Eve had no time for men, especially those like Phillip.

'What are you up to later? A couple of the guys are going to try some good old-fashioned New York strip steaks. Apparently there's a nice spot not far from here. Fancy it?'

'Why do you insist on behaving like a tourist?'

'It's not every day you get to be in the Big Apple.'

'You're like a child.'

'It's called having fun, Eve.'

'I'm tired. I will be at my hotel in about an hour,' she said, aware Phillip understood the hidden meaning and, for all his complaining, would be at her room in exactly one hour like an obedient puppy. She wouldn't generally entertain the thought of him, especially after the last time, but if his presence could in some way squash the collection of weak thoughts running around in her head, a night with him would be worth it.

Predictably, the knock on her door came just as she stepped out of the shower.

'You knew I'd come.' He walked over to her slowly and tugged at the tip of her towel. Her mouth was upon him quickly as she led him to the bed. She just wanted to forget, just for a moment. She needed to forget about them all.

*

The following morning, Phillip behaved just as she knew he would.

'Have breakfast with me!' he said, sitting up in the bed.

'I said I do not want any room service. I'm going for a walk in Central Park.'

'Let me guess, you want me gone when you get back?'

'Yes.'

'I have never met a woman like you and that's not a compliment. I don't understand you. I probably never will.' He stood up and thrust his feet into his trousers. 'I will say this though: you're going to end up one lonely lady if you're not careful.'

'Get out!' she screamed, the tone of her voice surprising even herself.

'I'm going. Have a nice life, Eve Cole!'

As the door finally slammed shut, she collapsed onto the bed. Her fingers went to her face, where instantly she felt the sticky wetness of tears mingling with moisturiser. This was not supposed to happen, she reasoned, desperate to keep the emotion from spilling into her hands and into her heart. But a dam had been broken and the tears flowed freely from her eyes and straight through to the Egyptian cotton sheets. When it was over, she felt better for it. Yet one remaining thought lingered: that of a little girl, another version of her baby sister Tina. Possibly with big eyes and curly hair, too, who simply wanted to meet her aunty.

And she wanted to meet her too.

Chapter Forty

Tina stared at the grainy picture of Adanya.

An unfamiliar pain surfaced as she noticed the remaining three photos did not contain one shot of her as a baby. As her sister had quite reasonably explained, the pictures had been taken by Lana's father before Tina's birth or conception. The facts, of course, were easy to understand, but her feelings didn't care about facts.

Her eyes ached as she continued to assess the picture of Adanya, trying desperately to find a feature that could connect her to the woman who had given birth to her. The shape of her chin, her eyes, her beautiful smile – Samantha did indeed share the triangular nose, but Tina had clearly taken most of her features from her biological father, Rex Andersen. That bastard. Her anger boiled as she replaced the picture and rushed to the bathroom. Her hands shook as she picked up the bottle of cleanser and squirted the cool white liquid onto a cotton wool pad. She started at her forehead and gently wiped away any trace of the foundation she'd been using for the past six years.

Now free of any make-up, her darker pigmentation was more visible. Since her teens, Tina – like many girls she'd known – had preferred the perceived security of make-up, but unlike them, she'd always worn a shade which served to dilute her true self. It was a shade that made her look more like Quinton, the beloved stepfather she had just lost; a shade that wiped away any evidence tying her to Adanya and her sisters.

Her mother Sarah had tacitly encouraged this look by never pulling her aside to discuss it. Indeed, it seemed to please her in some way and recent revelations had made her reasons clear.

Now, her Scandinavian and African heritage would be visible. She was mixed. And Tina was ready to fully acknowledge this important part of her.

Tina admired women like Lana who were unconcerned with foundation, blusher and lipstick colours, but knew she'd never have the strength to live without cosmetics completely. Having spent almost the entire morning searching for make-up catering to 'ethnic' skin tones, a woman in the chemist directed her to The Department Store in town as, apparently, they stocked a range called Flori Roberts.

'I think we can go for this shade,' said the make-up girl from inside her small kiosk, surrounded by glossy pictures of women all with very different skin tones snapped in various poses. 'I tell you what, I'm so glad we sell this range here. One of the previous managers or buyers was a black woman and apparently she fought for this to be stocked.'

'Oh, wow, really?'

'Yes, I don't remember her name, but good on her. It's a nightmare trying to find make-up for our skin. No one seems to think we exist.'

We.

Her ethnic origin had not been questioned. This woman assumed she'd been like this her entire life!

She had been like this her entire life she realised.

'Almost done. Hang on while I try a few lipstick shades on you.'

Tina had been used to pale lipsticks, intent on playing down the definition of her fuller lips. Now they were accentuated with a lip pencil and darker shade.

'You look wonderful, if I do say so myself! I'm sure your hubby will love it!'

Tina glared into the mirror. With her crimped hairstyle, fuller lips and darker shade of foundation, she almost didn't recognise the reflection staring back at her.

'Happy with it?'

'Yes ... yes, I think so.'

Tina bought the recommended products and, with a few hours to spare before collecting Samantha from her mother's (she suddenly wanted to spend more time with her granddaughter these days), she hopped onto a bus headed to Brixton.

'I forbid you to go there, Tina,' Mark had told her, when she'd once planned to go there, complete with an obligatory look of disgust. 'It's a ghetto full of Rastas and riots!'

'Oh, don't be so silly,' she had replied. 'Why would you not want me to go there?'

Well, she was on her way to this 'ghetto' now, along with a hot cauldron of excitement bubbling inside of her.

Despite all the stories of street violence and poverty, Tina felt at ease walking along the colourful, vibrant street, the sounds of Bob Marley-type music (reggae, that's right) wafting from large speakers; red, gold and green T-shirts and posters; the smell of spicy food and the shock of tasting her first Jamaican patty.

She felt even more exhilaration after jumping on a train to Lewisham, determined to tour the parts of London that had previously been closed off to her.

It was in an area named New Cross that Tina finally found what she was looking for.

The strong waft of lemongrass hit her first. The shop was like a grotto, with mini beaded chandeliers and dream catchers hanging from the ceiling. Her eyes happily feasted on multicoloured oblong candles, sparkling triangular crystals and a painting of three bare-breasted tribal ladies. Perhaps this was the closest she would get to Africa for now.

'Well, hello there,' said a woman dressed in a tie-dyed head wrap. Tina placed a set of bangles decorated with flags of several countries back onto the counter. 'I'm Ama.'

'I'm Tina.'

'Feel free to browse and ask me anything about anything, OK?'

'Thanks,' she replied, feeling immediately at ease in her surroundings. She wondered if Ama looked like her own biological grandmother. She almost had the same name as her mother, after all. Her eyes were drawn to a wide book, edged between wooden handcrafted bookends and a white pillar candle.

'That's a good one,' said Ama.

'*I Am Beautiful*,' read Tina. Three little girls on the front cover representing the three continents of Asia, Africa and Europe.

'Yes, you are.'

'I was reading—'

'I know.'

Tina rolled her eyes and scoffed, as if this was the most ridiculous statement she'd ever heard.

'You are,' said Ama. Tina felt a little silly, not quite sure how to reply to this statement. 'I've found over the years that loving yourself has a lot to do with how you feel inside and how you react to certain things, however hard they may be. Your interpretation of your life now, right at this moment, is important.'

'I think I understand,' Tina said, placing the book back onto the shelf. 'I have had a lot of changes lately.'

'When I look outside,' Ama continued, 'sometimes I see sun and sometimes it's rain. You have to roll with the punches, so they say. We don't know why things happen – they just do. My mummy used to tell me: you start out young and then you suddenly get old. And she was right!' Ama laughed, covering the seriousness of what Tina felt she was trying to say. 'I will leave you in peace to browse. Of course, if you need anything, just yell!'

'Isn't it a cliché to say everything happens for a reason?' added Tina, not wanting Ama to leave.

'There's a plan, Tina. There's always a plan.'

Tina smiled warmly. This wonderful stranger who might just look like her grandmother back in Nigeria, had remembered her name. And those words – Ama's words – had merely supported what Tina had already decided to do. She had no choice but to acknowledge the legacy her parents – all four of them – had left her, yet, at the same time, it was up to Tina to decide how.

I choose joy, she whispered to herself.

I choose joy.

Mark returned from his business trip and, as usual, placed his briefcase in the hallway. The tapping of his shoes on the laminate flooring as he headed towards the kitchen – lounge only made her anxious.

'Hello, darling,' he said. Her back was to him as her fingers swished about in the kitchen sink. His voice had sounded cheery, alerting her to the possibility he'd had a productive business trip. He placed both hands gently onto her shoulders and spun her round to face him. His expression flicked from slight surprise to horror in quick succession.

'What the—?' He fingered strands of her dark hair. 'Have you been experimenting?'

Her gaze dropped to the floor. 'You don't like it, then?'

'Not really. Maybe you should put this down to an experiment gone wrong.' He placed a cold kiss onto her cheek. 'How has everything been? How's Samantha?'

'I like it and I ... I don't think I will be changing it,' she said.

He slowly placed his hands by his side. 'You look so different, though!'

'You'll get used to it ... Just give it time, Mark.'

He wrinkled his nose and Tina's earlier resolve began to diminish. Her mind flashed back to K marvelling over her new look. Her sister remarking just how much she looked like the Tina she'd last seen as a baby. Ama's words.

'I'm keeping it, Mark.'

A moment of silence, which spoke a thousand words.

'Let me know when I should come down for dinner,' he said, turning away from her.

Tina knew what had just happened. The way he'd stared at her new shade of make-up, the accentuated lips and darkened hair and his sudden lack of words. They had fallen into their pattern again.

Predictably, dinner was a silent affair with Samantha asleep and the television on mute.

The following morning was much the same. Her 'Good morning' was met with a terse glance; there was a kiss for Samantha but nothing for Tina. Mark would continue this tactic of freezing her out until she backed down, which would generally follow a restless night's sleep shot through with the worry that he would leave her.

Not this time.

The following morning and en route to pick up Mark's dry-cleaning, Tina made a detour.

'Back so soon?' said K, as she tentatively shut the door of the salon behind her. He spoke to a head of fuzzy hair he'd been working on. 'Excuse me, love? Won't be a minute.'

'Do you have any spaces?' she asked.

'Why would you want an appointment? Your hair has only been in five minutes!'

Tina fingered a few strands as if feeling the texture for the last time.

She gazed towards the floor. 'I ... I just think it's a bit too brave for me. You know what I'm like.'

'Yes, a beautiful bud finally coming into blossom.'

She forced a smile. 'That is rather corny.'

'It is, but it's all I have. Hairstyles take a bit of getting used to, Tina.'

'Perhaps it was a bit too brave,' she repeated, unsure of herself.

'Listen, my wife wore a hat for the first week of her short crop and now she loves it! Tina, this is a huge change for you and I understand it's more than just a hairstyle.'

'What do you mean?'

'You know what I mean,' he said with a wink. 'Now you go out there and show the world who you are. We only get one life, Tina, so why live it being something or someone you're not comfortable with anymore? This isn't about them, it's about you! Now get out of here before I give you a Mohican!'

A feeling of shame washed over her, followed by Ama's words floating back into her head. She left the salon with a new vigour and increased purpose, along with a fresh crimp. It wasn't just Mark who needed to get used to the new Tina – she also needed to. So many changes were ahead – both inside and out – and she couldn't wait to meet each and every one of them.

Mark continued behind his wall of silence. The difference this time was that Tina no longer felt she needed to break that silence. Unlike before, she no longer had to rely on her husband for company, because she now had a sister whose daily calls she looked forward to.

When Lana revealed that Eve would be accompanying her on the next visit, Tina wished she could share this major development with her husband. However, as he was still refusing to utter a single word to her, telling him would be mistaken for giving in and making that first move.

And she wasn't going to be doing that any more.

When Mark was officially an hour late home, dread invaded her body. He was punishing her; she knew it. He'd done this before. When he finally rolled in close to midnight, she could smell the alcohol on his breath.

'You couldn't call?' she asked. 'I was worried!'

'Why?'

'I'm your wife!'

'Oh, really? You see, I do have my doubts sometimes!' His words were slurred but she had no doubt he meant them.

'You're right. I am not the same naive young girl you married. I've changed. I change every day, but do you know what the biggest change has been for me?'

He sat on the kitchen chair and loosened his tie. 'What?'

'When my sister walked through the door and found me. She found me, Mark!'

He appraised her like a stranger.

'She not only found the sister she'd been looking for, but she also allowed me to get to know the girl I was truly meant to be.'

'I have no idea what you're talking about.'

She exhaled slowly and sat down. 'I have a family.'

'Yes, me and Samantha. Our daughter.'

'I have a family I knew nothing about. People who care about me. The woman, the girl you met and married, did not know she had two sisters and an aunty Ginny who loved her. A whole set of grandparents and family in Nigeria who exist ... Oh Mark, it's so overwhelming. There's so much more to uncover ... and right now, I love who I am becoming. I love me! I haven't been able to say that for so long. Maybe not since Daddy Quinton died. So when you say I have changed, you're right! And that's a good thing!'

'I'm not talking about all that psychobabble. I'm concerned with the way you look. You look so fucking different!'

She scrunched her eyebrows, annoyed at the superficiality of his concerns.

'You've changed your hair and make-up – everything. When I married you, you looked one way and now ... I just don't know who you are. I feel a bit ... cheated.'

'You wanted me blonde!' she spat.

'That was all your idea, Tina. That's how it was when I met you!'

A radical thought popped into her head. Had she really been the one to suggest going blonde all those years ago, or had she merely been following orders from her husband? Didn't a lot of men prefer blondes anyway? But what about his long-held political views concerning 'bloody foreigners' and his staunch refusal to let Gita and her mother spend time with them? Not once had he ever shown any interest in Tina's possible background.

'If I had dyed my hair ginger, would it have made a difference?'

'What are you talking about, Tina?'

She turned away from her husband, ugly thoughts permeating the air. Perhaps she'd never known him. Perhaps …

'Tina, what's happening to us?'

'I don't know.'

He dragged another of the chairs closer to him and patted the seat. She sat down beside him.

'Have … have they turned you against me?'

They? Did he mean the black people?

'I just want my wife back. Is that too much to ask?' The pleading in his voice moved her away from such hateful questions and towards guilt. She had no black friends of her own (although she didn't really have any friends), she'd enjoyed being a blonde and she had never made an effort to research the origin of her background. Confronting Mark with 'crazy' theories was just a deflection of the part she'd played in this deception. She could blame a lot of it on not wanting to upset Daddy Quinton, but he'd been dead for seven years now.

Mark continued. 'You know how messed up my childhood was, Tina. Remember what I told you when we first met?'

She nodded her head. 'Yes, yes, I do.' A few days after their first date, Mark had spilled out details of a childhood that had included neglect at the hands of a mother who appeared to hate him. Tina had lovingly held him in her arms, wracked with guilt at her own perfect childhood, promising to always be there for him. It was so soon into their relationship and yet this statement had felt necessary for the both of them. It was at that moment she'd known she would become his wife and be the one to rescue him from a loveless past.

They had needed one another.

'When I met you, Tina, with your private school education, your almost-perfect family, your clean background … these things attracted me to you. I wanted to erase everything bad that had happened to me by marrying someone—'

'Pure?' she said with disgust.

'If you like. Untainted by circumstances. I knew you were adopted, yes, but as far as I imagined some young mum gave you to a lovely family to raise and that was the end of it. Now I find out all of this and it changes how—'

'How you see me?' Tina would not let his words sting. She'd experienced enough of his hurt during their time together and refused to ever allow his words to sting her ever again.

'I now find out you come from almost as fucked up a background as I did. And I'm hurt. I'm hurt for you, for our daughter—'

'Samantha is fine!'

'You don't understand what I am trying to say.'

'No, you're right, I don't. Perhaps I have never understood you at all.'

That night, they talked a table tennis of words until two in the morning. She shed tears. They'd even attempted to make love, but she hadn't been able to let go.

There was only one thing left to say: 'I do love you, Mark … I think I do. But the fact is I haven't loved myself for so long. You make me sad and I am just so tired of being sad. It's draining and I was becoming more and more sad until my sister found me.'

'What are you saying?'

'I'm leaving.'

He didn't try to stop her as she crushed a small amount of clothing and toiletries into a tiny case. She looked in on a sleeping Samantha and simply informed Mark she would be coming back for her in the morning. One hour later, she found herself sat in a cab inside the graffiti-laden underground car park belonging to a large South London estate.

'You sure this is where you want, love?' said the cab driver as she handed over the money.

'This is the right address, yes.'

'Be careful. This is a really rough estate. Not for a woman like you.'

'I'll be fine. I'll be with my sister.'

Chapter Forty-one

Tina's arrival on Lana's doorstep had been both thrilling and surprising.

'This is nice!' her little sister had said, sounding almost relieved the inside of her flat did not reflect the outside.

Lana had tentatively led her into the living room, having always imagined the first sister to see her home would have been Eve all those years ago.

They chatted over spaghetti shapes and watched the sun come up to the sound of morning television, acts remarkable in their simplicity, yet wonderfully joyous to experience. Tina was real. Tina was sitting on her bed drinking coffee and scrunching her face at the bitterness.

'I'm not really a coffee drinker. I'm more of a fruit tea fanatic.'

'I'll make sure I get some in. You know ... for next time.' Lana smiled cautiously towards her sister.

'You'd better get a lot in, then, because you'll be seeing a lot more of me. And of course my daughter. I would have brought her last night but didn't want to wake her ... the disruption you know ...'

'And you didn't know what to expect from a rough estate!'

'No, not really ...'

An unapologetic, beaming smile appeared on Lana's face. 'It's OK. I just hope you can sort things out with your husband.' Lana wasn't even sure she meant this, once again torn between wanting her sister to be happy and being glad to spend time with her.

'It got to the point where I couldn't even look at him any more. Is it OK if we stay a few days? I've never been away from Samantha for more than a night and I doubt if Mark could even cope with keeping her fed!'

'I would like nothing more.'

'I'm quite happy to sleep on the floor. Mark tells me I like to hog the covers!'

'You haven't changed, then?'

'You mean—?'

'Yes, even as a toddler!'

Waiting in a cab outside Tina's house, Lana could not believe the rapid turn of events. Her insides bubbled with excitement each time she thought about how far her relationship with Tina had progressed. She peered through the window. Tina and her husband were clearly engaged in a tense but dignified set of words as Samantha wriggled in Tina's arms. She was glad her first meeting with Mark would not take place under such circumstances and was utterly relieved when he did not follow his wife and child to the taxi.

The trio took a detour to the toyshop where Aunty Lana was happy to fully indulge in the joy of gift-giving.

Later, they sat inside a small Italian cafe laughing about Lana's travels to Barcelona and the fact they had missed one another by a few good years! In the cab, laden with bags and a new foldaway buggy, the tired toddler gleefully clutched her new teddy bear and slept in her auntie's arms, evoking a memory of a snoozing baby attached to a multicoloured elephant called the Puffalump.

'Are you OK?' asked Tina.

'Sure. Yes, I'm fine.' She sniffed into her hand, once again astonished at Tina's perception; proof of their sisterly bond.

'Thank you for being there when I picked up Samantha. I don't think I would have had the courage to do it alone.'

'I'm sorry I saw your husband for the first time under such circumstances.'

'And I'm sorry for his rudeness.'

'He didn't actually say anything.'

'That's my point. It's like nothing about me is important to him.' She stared out of the car window and it was Lana's turn to ache for her.

'At least he didn't try and stop me taking my child. I could never be without Samantha.

'That must be the worst pain.'

'You're thinking about Adanya, aren't you?' asked Tina.

'How did you know?'

'Because I was thinking about her too.'

'My niece is way too heavy and I'm not as fit as I'd thought!' said Lana as she followed Tina up the stairs leading to the flat.

'Lana, there's someone here to see you,' said Tina, suspiciously.

'Clifton?'

'Erm … I don't think so.'

'Hello,' said Eve.

'I didn't expect you all to be here …' said Eve awkwardly as Lana laid a sleeping Sam onto her bed. 'I can come back, if you like?'

'No way,' said Tina, moving closer and leaning into her space. 'It's so good to see you. Finally.'

'About that. I'm sorry, it just took me a while to sort things out at work. I had some leave owing, so I wanted to wait until then. It can get a bit hectic. And what with the urgent business trip—'

'You're here now and that's all that matters,' said Tina, looking like the young woman she was. Her eyes were wide with excitement. Eve's shoulders, however, remained stiff and upright. This was clearly hard for her; Lana recalled how much easier it had been for Eve to assert herself more confidently in the office.

'Tea?' asked Lana.

'Do you have any peppermint tea?'

'No, sorry.'

'Do you have an upset tummy?' asked Tina. 'I always use that if my tummy is in a bad way.'

'You could say that. I have not been looking forward to this meeting. No offence.'

'None taken. Unlike poor old me, at least you had a choice!' Tina laughed.

Eve did not jolt.

Lana sat on the arm of the chesterfield sofa. Tina sat at the opposite end with Eve placing herself awkwardly in the middle.

'There's no need to be so nervous. We're quite friendly, really,' said Tina.

'I'm not really used to this sort of thing.'

'None of us are. It's OK,' soothed Lana.

Lana and Tina aimed a barrage of innocent questions at Eve, who remained aloof with her answers. She appeared most comfortable when probed about work, her many achievements and the numerous challenges faced as a black woman in the industry. Not once did she delve into her time at John Adams after Lana's departure or the period after she'd run away. Her responses were PR-perfect.

'It's getting late,' said Eve eventually.

'Why don't you stay?' Lana was desperate to keep her two sisters together with her for as long as possible.

'Stay here?'

'I know it's not what you're used to, but it's … home … and it would be nice to catch up some more.'

'No, I didn't mean ... Your home is very nice.'

Lana smiled. 'Stay. Please. I'd love it and I'm sure Samantha would like to meet her new aunty when she wakes up.'

'OK,' she said, surprisingly. Lana hadn't allowed herself to believe Eve would actually agree!

'Where will I sleep?'

'I have a blow-up bed. Ironically, I started buying them for you when I thought you were coming to stay all those years ago.'

'Oh, I see ...'

'Clifton sometimes uses one when he can be bothered to pump it up, so I end up buying a new one every couple of years, you know, because they don't last. I wanted to make sure there was always a spare bed in case you ever came to stay ...'

She'd no idea that such a statement would lead to anything significant.

But it led to everything.

That night, with Lana, Samantha and Tina in one bed and Eve on the blow-up mattress, all three sisters were finally back together under one roof, yet no one felt like celebrating. All three were cocooned by thoughts of the words spoken just one hour ago when Eve had poured out the entire contents of a memory box that had existed in her head for so many years.

The extent of Stan's incessant bullying, the racial abuse, her time spent homeless on the streets of London with no one to turn to ... both Lana and Tina had wept as Eve reeled off each tale with a detachment Lana could not judge. Anger flooded her own mind; anger at a system that allowed this to happen to so many vulnerable children and anger at herself for not taking more notice of what her sister had clearly been going through, even when she was still a resident at the home. Tina had intervened at this point, asking just how a child of Lana's age could have noticed.

'I should have seen something.'

'Lana, it wasn't your fault.'

'I can't help how I feel,' she sniffed.

'I know, but we have to let her finish ... we have to let Eve tell her story.'

When Eve had finished, a look of surprised relief was evident upon her face. Lana suspected Eve had never confided in anyone before, but she also believed there was a lot more to the story that Eve was holding back. The woman at social services had spoken of investigations ... abuse. She believed there had to be more, whilst hoping, praying and wishing there wasn't.

As she closed her eyes and welcomed what would be a short sleep, Lana was so very thankful for Clifton's constant presence in her early life. She, too, could have been in the same predicament.

If only she had also protected her sister.

She understood that Eve needed time. Time she hoped they still had.

'Meet your niece!' said Tina, placing the child into Eve's stiffened arms. The morning sun covered the side of her rather startled face.

'How do you do?' Eve said awkwardly as Samantha appeared more concerned with Eve's perfectly manicured red nails.

Eve turned to Lana, who simply shrugged her shoulders and said, 'She can be a talker, so watch out!'

'I see,' she said, patting the child's head.

'Are you coming with us to the park?' asked Tina.

'I ... I have to get home and change.'

'That's OK, you can borrow Lana's clothes!'

So that afternoon, they went to the park.

'I think Samantha has a new fan,' commented Tina, as they sat on the park bench and watched Eve assist her niece with feeding the ducks.

'Finish!' said Samantha, running up to the bench. Tina reached around the little girl and pulled her onto her lap.

'And I thought running a department store was hard work!' said Eve.

'About last night,' said Lana.

'What about it?' asked Eve, embarrassment clouding her face.

'I feel so bad about what happened. To you.'

'It's over. We've discussed it. Now, let's move on and, as Tina said, forget it!'

'I didn't say we should forget it. We couldn't even if we wanted to. I sometimes think that what we go through shapes us into who we are today. Do you know that how we react to things determines a lot of . . . oh, I've forgotten what Ama said now!'

'Who's Ama?' said Lana with amusement.

'A lovely lady I recently met.'

'Sounds intriguing,' said Lana.

'Let's just say, we did not meet by accident. And I promise I'll tell you all about her one day. Anyway, she also gave me a book to read. *I Know Why the Caged Bird Sings*.

'By Maya Angelou,' said Eve.

'You know it?'

'I read that a very long time ago!' said Eve excitedly.

'I remember when your head was constantly stuck in a book, Eve,' said Lana. 'So you both have that in common.'

'Books got me through a lot,' said Eve.

'Yes, I remember.'

'You'll also be pleased to know that you and I have the same taste in sofas. I own a leather chesterfield,' added Eve.

Lana allowed her to change the subject. For now. 'That's amazing. Although mine's cloth!'

'I also have a gate to my apartment.'

'It's hardly the same, Eve. Mine is to keep the undesirables out!' said Lana, recalling the name they'd both been called at one time in their lives.

'So's mine!'

They both smiled and Lana saw Daddy's curled lip reflected in her sister's face. Eve should certainly smile more.

'You both lived behind iron gates at Sir John Adams and still do ...?' said Tina tentatively.

Perhaps there was more to Tina's statement, because Eve had certainly erected a tall set of psychological bars Lana wasn't certain she could climb. Lightening the mood, Tina then added, 'So, can we all agree that my life has changed the most out of all of us?'

'I'll let you have that one,' replied Eve.

'And because of that, I've done a lot of soul-searching. Met some fantastic people – present company included – and I have changed so much in the last few weeks. Did you know this never used to be my foundation colour?'

Eve look surprised. 'What's make-up got to do with anything?'

'You'd be surprised. What I'm trying to say is, Eve, with you ... if you hadn't gone through what you did, perhaps you wouldn't be the success you are today.'

'Define success,' said Lana. Her sister had all the money she could possibly need, yet where was the love? She suspected her initial awkwardness had more to do with hardly speaking to people outside of work. And at thirty-one, that was sad.

'Mummy, Mummy, look!' shouted Samantha, pointing to a lone duck.

'Lovely, darling!'

Lana gazed at her two wonderful sisters. Both were weighed down by suitcases full of issues, yet were doing their best to carry them without injury. They were her precious baby girls and she would always love and protect them. This felt like a second chance.

It was shaping up to be a day full of surprise revelations with the feeling there was more to come. Back at Lana's flat, Tina scanned the local Chinese takeaway menu, whilst Eve checked in with work. Force of habit, she claimed.

The shrill ringing of the phone interrupted the moment.

'Hello?' said Lana.

'Hello, is this a Miss Lana Cole?'

'Yes.'

'I was told you were looking for Ginny Jones.'

'Who are you?'

'Her son.'

When Lana hung up the phone two minutes later, she turned to her sisters.

'She's alive!'

'Ginny?' asked Eve.

'Aunty Ginny's alive!' she sang, her voice full of relief and absolute joy. Without realising it, Aunty Ginny had always been a part of this puzzle. Searching for her sisters had also meant looking for Aunty Ginny, because then and only then would she have truly found her family.

Chapter Forty-two

Tina heard the door close as she spooned cold chilli con carne into a Tupperware dish.

'Mark, I've made you enough food to last a few days, so you won't starve.'

'You're not coming home?' He hadn't shaved for days and his shirt obviously needed ironing.

Cooking was one thing – perhaps born out of habit, concern or both – but she certainly wasn't doing the ironing, she thought to herself.

'What about Samantha?'

'I'll need you to have her this weekend while I go away. I'll call every day.'

'Of course I'll take care of her, she's my daughter. What do you take me for?'

She wasn't about to remind him of the various times she'd pleaded with him to babysit his own child and how he'd question why she was going out without him anyway and weren't they supposed to do things together?

'How long is this going to go on for, Tina?'

'Until I'm ready, Mark. Please don't push me.' She would not catch his gaze. She needed to keep her resolve; she couldn't return home, not until she truly felt strong enough. Her positive outlook and demeanour might have worked with sisters who didn't really know her and demanded nothing of her, but Mark still had the power to break down this new strength. She couldn't let him do that to her, not this time.

Spending the entire weekend with her sisters and visiting Aunty Ginny was just what she needed.

The final piece of the puzzle.

As Eve prepared for the trip, she stopped for a moment to reflect on a most extraordinary week.

She'd fed ducks with a beautiful toddler who, by some genetic marvel, was related to her. She'd slept on a very uncomfortable blow-up mattress on a very rough council estate in a flat surrounded by iron bars. She'd slotted herself neatly into the middle of three sisters without breaking a sweat and she had to admit to herself it felt … OK.

She could do this.

What she'd thought would be the hardest thing in the world to achieve was actually coming together. There'd be no holding hands or skipping down a hill together, but she could envisage a time when they'd be able to exist in each other's worlds again as … sisters. Real-life sisters. And this felt good.

As for seeing Ginny again, Eve wasn't quite sure if she wanted any part of that. Of course there'd be some pleasure in showing off her achievements, to show that, despite what happened all those years ago, her life had turned out more than fine. Amazing in fact. She'd never forgotten Ginny's weak excuses for not taking the girls in all those years ago or that fateful trip to Brighton where she'd been shooed away by Ginny's ignoramus son.

She didn't quite know what to expect, but after the week she'd had, Eve felt ready for anything.

Lana enjoyed the joviality of the train ride, but fell into seriousness as the three women stood before a little cottage-style house on the edge of a road in Essex.

'Hello,' said the woman who answered the door. She was about the same age as Lana, dressed in baggy high-waisted jeans, with mousy blonde hair bundled into a high ponytail.

'We're here to see—'

'Ginny. Yes, she's waiting for you.'

They followed the woman through to the kitchen and into a garden bursting with flowers of every imaginable variety. Lana could only recognise the pink roses and white carnations, whilst Tina smiled at the rose-like flowers she referred to as pretty peonies that were alive with flowery aromas.

'Just through here,' the woman said, pointing to a smaller building nestled among large hanging pot plants and decorative moss. The sudden sound of a dog barking shook her, as did the tiny stooped figure with grey, almost white, hair who appeared at the door of the building. A small white dog rushed up to the three women, its barking far from threatening. Now in her late sixties and wearing a pair of mauve elasticated-waist trousers, this was undoubtedly Aunty Ginny.

'Girls,' she said quietly. Eve and Tina remained where they stood, but Lana rushed towards her and into an embrace that seemed to last forever. She breathed in the smell of Chanel No 5 and a stream of warm memories followed.

'Let me look at you,' said Aunty Ginny. The dog ceased barking, satisfied with the lack of threat.

'Wow, just like Addy! It's uncanny,' she said, a tear welling up in the corner of her eye. The sound of Mummy's nickname almost brought on a similar response in Lana and, sniffing, she remembered her sisters.

'This is Tina, the little one.'

Tina moved tentatively towards the older woman.

'Oh, Tina, I can't believe it's you. Come here,' she said. Tina gently wrapped her hands around Aunty Ginny's rounded waist and placed a short kiss onto her cheek.

'I named you, you know.'

Tina gaped. 'I ... I had no idea ...'

'I always wanted a little girl called Tina. When they asked your mum to name you, well, she couldn't. So I called you Tina. I can't believe you're stood here in front of me now!'

'I did wonder why I didn't have a Nigerian name. It all makes sense now,' Tina replied solemnly.

'And this is—'

'May – I mean, Mayo-wa,' said Aunty Ginny in that very British way Lana remembered and loved.

'My name's Eve now,' she said curtly.

'I'm not surprised. It was always a bit of a tongue-twister!' Aunty Ginny laughed. Eve smiled falsely, making no attempt to move closer.

'Please come into my little granny flat and we'll have a chat,' she said.

Although disappointed at Eve's reaction, Lana hoped that as time went on her sister would begin to thaw again. The expensive haircut and designer clothing had done nothing to diminish the teenager Lana remembered, so introverted, yet so quick to voice an opinion when she felt attacked. She had no doubt that these traits could reappear intermittently during a sunny afternoon in Essex, drinking tea from china teacups, eating Jammie Dodgers and laughing at a small white dog chasing its own tail.

With Aunty Ginny's vivid and loving descriptions of her grandchildren, Lana watched Eve's emotions simmer. Tina was not a problem; she was lapping up the conversation, offering her own contributions with pictures of Samantha.

'This is such a lovely house, Aunty Ginny,' enthused Tina.

'That's thanks to my son. When they were growing up they were such a couple of tearaways, but they clubbed together and built me this place in the garden. My oldest wanted me to stay inside, but I wasn't having any of that nonsense. I need to be free. I've always been that way.'

Lana caught the eye-roll from Eve.

'They got the planning permission and here I am. It suits me down to the ground.' Her eyes rested on the silent Eve.

'Eve, tell me more about this job of yours. Lana says you were in the paper.'

'Yes,' she replied coldly. 'Well, it was an in-flight magazine.'

'Still, fancy! That's really lovely.'

'Yes.'

Thankfully, Aunty Ginny's daughter-in-law arrived with more biscuits as Lana noticed the incessant tapping of Eve's right foot. She feared an explosion of some sort and could only hope it would be the type she – as the big sister – could contain.

'We'd better be getting back soon,' said Lana.

'Thank you so much for coming down. I hope you'll all be back. Maybe bring Samantha?' Ginny turned hopefully to Tina.

'Of course I will! I want to know more about Adanya too. You're the only living person who can tell me all about her as a woman. As a mother. I can't wait to hear more stories,' gushed Tina.

'And you, Eve, will you visit again?'

'I think this will be enough, thank you,' Eve said, smiling very faintly. But this did not remove the sting of her words.

'Eve!' chastised Tina.

'Tina, please, no wishy-washy comments about self-awareness. There are things you know nothing about.'

'Like what? Aunty Ginny has been perfectly nice. Remember what she meant to our mum, Adanya.'

'She meant so much to her, Aunty Ginny stopped writing to us at John Adams.'

An uncomfortable silence ensued as each woman sat back in her seat. No one was leaving yet.

Aunty Ginny cleared her throat. 'You're right, Eve. That was very wrong of me, but it was just so hard for me knowing I was letting you all down. I did mean—'

'Oh, that's not even the big one. How about refusing to take on Adanya's children when they needed you the most? Three little girls with nowhere to go. How about that?'

'Eve, let me tell you something. I may be an old woman, but I'm not taking that kind of talk from anyone. Even my boys know that.'

Eve rolled her eyes and sighed.

'I was potless with two big boys to support. I couldn't take you all on. You have to understand that. I know Addy would have—'

'Don't say that! You don't know what she would have wanted!' shouted Eve, the anger in her voice echoing throughout the room.

'Eve, please—' said Lana.

'No, let the child finish,' said Aunty Ginny.

'I came to you, Ginny. I came to you when I was a kid. When I ran away from that cesspit John Adams. I came to you and you turned your back on me!'

Aunty Ginny's forehead tightened as she spoke. 'When, Eve? When did you come? I don't remember.'

'I was sixteen years old and on the streets. I left you a note and a message with that son of yours, to meet me later. You never showed. I waited and waited for you at the fish and chip shop and you never came. Are you going to tell me you never got the message?'

'Maybe she didn't get the message,' added Tina, softly.

'Well?' spat Eve.

'I did get the message,' said Aunty Ginny.

Tina's eyes widened in surprise. 'Then why didn't you meet her?'

'I wanted to. I so wanted to.'

'I get it, another excuse. This time you didn't even have the guts to face me and tell me you weren't interested.' Eve stood to leave. 'I'm not waiting around here. You guys enjoy your little reunion, but I'm going back to London. Back to the one life that has never let me down.'

'Eve, wait!' said Lana.

'What for? I've heard enough. Ginny hasn't changed a bit – always making some excuse or other! I will never forgive you for pretending to be our mother's friend and I will never forgive you for turning us away. Turning me away, twice!'

'I was ill.'

'What?' said Lana.

'When you came to me in 1969, I had just had a heart attack. My head was all over the place. My boys were a mess. Men are no good at all that, you see. I was so wiped out and I looked a bloody state, too, like I was already dead.'

Lana breathed into her hand, Tina closed her eyes, and Eve stared towards her feet.

'Luckily I got better, but my boys were so concerned about me they packed me up and we drove down here. Got me sorted with the local hospital to be monitored, you know, just in case I had another one. I think when you came to the door … it probably didn't occur to me you were underage and had most likely run away. I just thought you were visiting and I didn't want you to see me like that, especially after what happened to Tayo and Addy. Especially as I wasn't even sure I'd make it.'

'I came a day later and the next-door neighbour told me you'd gone somewhere with suitcases,' added Lana.

'That would be when we drove up here. I didn't have this place yet, but we lived down the road for a bit. My boys just wanted to look after me.'

'I don't know what to say,' whispered Eve.

'You don't have to say anything, darling. If you'd come a few weeks before or months afterwards, I would have gladly taken you in. Just bad timing, I suppose. Bloody heart attack!'

'How are you now? Are you—?' asked Tina, moving closer to Aunty Ginny.

'I take it easy. That bugger didn't get me after all. But I get my checks and I have to be careful with this ticker of mine.

All those wonderful doctors and nurses at the hospital know me now. They call me a walking miracle. Every day is a blessing. Seeing you girls is a blessing and a miracle, if you ask me!'

'I can't believe it,' said Lana.

The four women sat in their own contemplation of the misunderstandings that had plagued their lives for many years.

'I hope one day you will find it in your heart to forgive me, Eve ... all of you. There hasn't been a day gone by that I didn't think of Tayo and Addy and you three kids. I failed you and that's something I've had to live with all these years.'

Lana took Aunty Ginny's hand in hers, squeezing softly. 'We're here for you now.'

'And I still can't believe it. You all sitting here with me in my granny flat, eating biscuits. Three beautiful young kids; a mixture of your lovely parents. I can't make up for the past but I can bloody well be here for you now. As of today, I'm going to try my best, girls.'

Tina placed her hands over Aunty Ginny's remaining free hand as Eve looked on with a stiff smile.

A light lunch followed, as did a calmer atmosphere.

Aunty Ginny moved slowly out of the chair. 'Girls, there's something you need to see.'

She returned a moment later, clutching a small circular leather case.

'That's very elegant,' commented Tina.

'It was our mother's vanity case,' said Eve, nodding her head slowly.

'I have one at home ... the one you gave me,' added Lana.

'Your father was always buying her things. She had more than one, you know. And I kept this one for myself, you know, just to have something of my best friend.' Aunty Ginny closed and opened her eyes with a sigh. 'Now, how do you open this thing?'

The three women edged closer as Aunty Ginny struggled with the silver lock.

'Looks like it hasn't been opened in years,' said Tina.

'It hasn't. I may have opened it once when she first died but since then I couldn't bring myself to do it again. I think twenty-one years is time enough.'

'Wow!' said Tina.

'What? I must have been waiting for you lot to get your arses in gear and come and visit me!'

Lana gave an impatient chuckle, unable to override the anticipation she felt at the arrival of this second vanity case. It could contain anything from knitting needles to cotton reels. Yet it almost wouldn't matter what was inside – the fact it had been touched by Mummy was enough.

Aunty Ginny carefully opened the lid and placed her hand inside. 'Now, what do we have here? Oh …'

'What is it?' asked Tina.

Aunty Ginny pulled out a symmetrically folded piece of paper with Adanya written on the front.

'I'd recognise that handwriting anywhere. So neat.'

'Daddy?' said Eve.

Aunty Ginny handed the letter to Eve. 'I'm not sure what it says. Could be a shopping list. But it's something.'

Eve could only stare at the paper in her hand. Her daddy's handwriting.

'This is amazing!' said Lana, heartbeat pounding against the fabric of her blouse. 'Just amazing.'

Eve held the letter closely to her chest.

'You can all sit together at home and have a read. I can't, though … it seems wrong to – you know. It's private stuff. Wow, did those two love each other. True love. And that's more than some of us ever get,' said Aunty Ginny mournfully. She placed her hands back into the case and once again the sisters' stood by in anticipation.

'Pictures!' Aunty Ginny handed each sister a handful of images. A mixture of monochrome and colour, some still intact and others grainy with age.

'These are just some of the pictures your father took of the two of you after he got that fancy new camera. I think he had this idea about showing all these pictures to your grandparents back in Nigeria. Shame he never got to do that.'

'This one is so funny. Eve in a sailor's suit,' said Lana.

'I look like a little boy!'

'The image of your father, even then. You still are now ... but in a womanly sort of way ... you know. I mean, you are very stylish, Eve.'

'I'm in the fashion industry, so I should hope so!' A rare joke from Eve to balance an atmosphere clogged with sadness.

Aunty Ginny scattered more photos onto the coffee table. 'These were taken in the park around the back of where you lived. Your dad would take the two of you there for picnics and to feed the ducks every Saturday to give your mum a rest. Sometimes she would join you.'

'I remember that,' said Lana.

'Me too. A little bit, anyway. Unfortunately, I don't recall a lot about my father,' said Eve sadly. 'I'm not sure if I just blocked it all out.'

'You and Lana were his angels. He always called you that.'

Eve smiled Daddy's smile, her top lip curling just like his had. 'I like that.'

'Oh, bloody heck, look at how slim I look!' said Aunty Ginny, pointing to the black and white picture of her standing beside Mummy. Two beautiful women from opposite worlds who had forged a love that would remain long after death and transcend into the lives of three little girls.

'Look at me here. I look so weird!' said Lana towards the picture of her with ice cream all over her cheeks.

Lana felt privileged to be transported to a time when both her mother and father were alive. She could remember the love, the closeness, the sense of family she hoped would be recreated now she'd found Aunty Ginny and her sisters.

'Is there anything left in the case? Anything there of me?' said Tina, her voice heavy with sorrow. Lana had already learned her baby sister's nuances, her little facial expressions and hand gestures, and right now she was in pain.

'It's empty, love.'

'I see ...'

'This was all a bit before your time,' said Aunty Ginny.

'I know ... it just would have been nice to see something. At the moment I don't have much tying me to you – just a birth certificate that says 'Father: unknown'.'

Lana leaned over and squeezed the hand of her little sister. She recalled lulling her to sleep most nights as they lay on one of the twin beds at John Adams Children's Home, unable to work out if her tears were born of frustration or if the little girl just missed her mummy. Lana's only concern then was to help her to feel better, like now.

Aunty Ginny eased herself out of her chair. 'Just off to the little girls' room,' she said.

They continued to scour through the pictures, attempting to decipher stories attached to each old photograph. Their mother in various poses on the couch, sitting on the grass, standing by the front door in a black coat. She was easily the most beautiful woman Lana had ever seen.

Engrossed in these images from the past, Lana did not notice Aunty Ginny return.

'I should have remembered, silly me! Must be old age!' said Aunty Ginny. 'The camera wasn't as snazzy as Tayo's, but it did the trick. I took it when you were both in hospital. I knew when she got better she'd want to see something of her little girl, you know.' Aunty Ginny handed Tina a faded black and white photo.

'Is that—?'

'Yes, it's you, Tina. A few hours old. I'm sorry it's a bit faded, but it's all I've got.'

Lana's emotion bubbled to the surface as she watched her little sister sob with absolute and complete happiness.

'It's perfect ... thank you, Aunty Ginny!' The gritty surface of the black and white photograph did nothing to reduce its importance. A picture of a tiny baby nestled in the arms of a vacant mother. The sparkle was gone from her eyes and she was clearly unaware of the little girl asleep on her chest – but this one photo was a special gift that legitimised Tina's ranking as the youngest daughter of Adanya Cole and little sister to Lanre and Mayowa Cole.

Tina kissed the surface of the photo and pressed it against her cheek.

'I can't believe you kept all these,' said Eve, clutching an image of her father.

'I never stopped thinking of you three. You were always in my heart, always. You were the daughters I never had.'

'Well, we are your daughters.' Lana smiled, resting her head onto Tina's shoulder.

'Really?' A tear trickled down her face as Eve leaned over and placed a hand onto Aunty Ginny's knee. 'Addy was my best friend and a sister. She'd be so happy to know we're all here together.'

'I'm sure she knows,' said Tina.

'Your mother taught me so, so much and I will never forget her. To have you three beside me today and say you're my daughters ... this is one of the happiest days of my life. Thank you so much, girls, for making old Ginny Jones a very happy woman. And Lana, forget about returning to work as a receptionist ... you need to become a blimming detective!'

A round of laughter followed.

'It was all in the clues.'

'Then again, I always knew you'd be in the health service. I just thought you'd be more on the medical side.'

'I have always wanted to help people ... maybe become a nurse. But the thought of all that studying ... I don't know. I haven't really thought about it much. Everything was about finding these two girls!'

'Well, you've found them now, no more excuses!' said Aunty Ginny.

'Perhaps I'll look into it.'

'It doesn't really matter. I know that Tayo and Addy would be so proud of how you've all turned out. So very proud.'

For Eve, hearing that her parents would actually be proud of her almost brought her to tears. But that was something she could do in private. Later. And possibly after reading her father's precious letter.

As the three of them walked Scottie the dog, Aunty Ginny and Tina chattered away in front as Eve thought about how little all the accolades, fast cars and beautiful apartments meant without someone there to share them with, someone who could be proud of her. She couldn't see her parents any more, but she now had two sisters, a niece and an aunty who seemed, despite her own reluctance, ready to take her in. Perhaps the concept of family was not so awful after all. Perhaps it had been wrong to base her beliefs on a set of circumstances she'd no control over.

Eve couldn't remember most of the events depicted in the photos – she could not even remember her mother holding her – but it all must have happened at some point, as the pictures seemed to prove. Her father Tayo – her twin in looks – had also loved and cared for her before his death. Eyewitness reports from Aunty Ginny and the masses of photographs confirmed it. Eve pondered what her life might have been like if death hadn't claimed him. No. As Tina had mentioned earlier, this was not the way to be thinking. She needed to be concerned with the importance of now.

The day had taken such an unexpected turn for Eve. She'd started out wanting to reveal the hurt and lies she'd painted around Aunty Ginny, yet instead was leaving the granny flat perhaps not a changed woman, but one well on her way to true, true healing.

Chapter Forty-three

'Should I have brought along some armour?' asked Phillip as Eve joined him at the table.

'No,' she replied with a smile.

'A mineral water, please,' said Eve as the waiter appeared.

'Same,' Phillip said.

'This is nice.' Her words felt clumsy and unnatural. This and so many new scenarios still felt very alien to Eve, but she would 'go with it', as Tina had suggested, and try to embrace the unfamiliarity currently invading her life. Two sisters she'd fooled herself into thinking she hadn't missed, a niece and even a brother-in-law were now a part of her everyday life. Nothing would be the same again. And that was OK.

'To what do I owe this pleasure?' asked Phillip, his voice tainted with suspicion. Eve looked at him questioningly. 'It's not every day you ask to meet me in a restaurant, unless it's to discuss work or a prelude to—'

'I just wanted to see how you are.'

'Finally come to your senses about us, huh?'

Eve made an exaggeratedly horrified face, wondering if this was a bad idea. Her rigid beliefs about romantic relationships hadn't suddenly shifted. That would take time, and a lot of trust. But outside of her sisters, Phillip remained the only human being who'd witnessed her away from the protection of a boardroom and desk. She was changing and Phillip, by default, would be the first non-family member privy to this transformation.

'I asked you here to get to know you.'

'Excuse me?'

'I don't know much about you, Phillip … and I suppose I would like to – you know – get to know you more.' Again the words sounded unnatural coming from her mouth, yet she hoped they appeared sincere.

'You. Want. To. Get. To. Know. Me?'

'Why not?'

'Is this a joke?'

She sighed. Clearly, this would be harder than she'd envisaged. Eve would never be as emotional as Lana or as airy-fairy as Tina, but they shared DNA and a past, and these had to count for something.

The waiter placed their drinks onto the table.

'If you want to know more about me, I will tell you about me,' he began.

Fifteen minutes later, Eve had found out the man she'd 'known' for years actually grew up on a farm and disgraced the family name when revealing a passion for headhunting in the city!

'My parents were distraught.'

'They must have come around by now.'

'Yes. When I bought them a silver Mercedes!'

Eve allowed her shoulders to relax, determined that the evening would not turn out so bad after all.

'So, what about you, Eve?'

'Don't push it!' she said passionately, hiding her fears. She cleared her throat. 'OK … me …'

'Who is Eve Cole?'

'Don't be so dramatic, Phillip,' she said sternly.

'And she's back.'

She ignored him. 'Me, I'm one of three girls.'
'Wow! I had no idea you had sisters!'
And that was all she would be willing to share.
For now.

Chapter Forty-four

'Seen anything you like?' Ama asked. The smooth flow of Indian music had been replaced with 'Freedom' by Wham!, which didn't fuse as effortlessly with the smell of lemongrass as Tina browsed the cluttered shelves of Ama's tiny shop.

'I fancied a change,' Ama said, noticing Tina's amusement. 'I do like current music as well!'

'Every time I'm in here, I realise I haven't seen or heard everything!' replied Tina, marvelling at the crystal heart-shaped earring box.

'A bit like us humans,' said Ama. 'What you see isn't always the big picture. There are so many layers.'

Tina knew she was referring to her. She'd confided in Ama about the tidal wave that had risen up in her life. One she was still riding.

'Do not feel obligated to buy anything, Tina. I think you've bought my entire inventory of books anyway!'

'They were for my sister, Eve.'

'It does appear you have yet to find what it is you are looking for.'

'What do you mean, Ama?'

'Despite what you have said, I do not believe it was fate that brought you into my shop. A part of you may like to think I am this magical African woman who was thrust into your path to help you find out about your culture. But that's just not the case.'

'It isn't?' Tina replied wearily.

'No. You searched until you found a shop that looked remotely ethnic enough, saw me with a kaftan and my African name, and thought you had found what you'd been looking for. I bet you even tried Brixton first, am I right?'

'Maybe,' Tina admitted, with an embarrassed smile.

'Well, I was born in Basildon to Bajan parents and only recently changed my name to Ama from Amelia. I wanted to hold onto my ancestral past in any way I could, just like you.'

Tina gazed around the warm, inviting grotto-like space.

'This shop covers a lot of continents, a lot of people. What you find here will give you something of what you need to know, but not enough.'

'So where can I get information? A library?'

'You've had it all along, Tina. Everything you need to know about your culture, about Nigeria, you have in your two sisters. They're there. Talk to them, quiz them!'

'I sometimes feel so guilty talking to them about the past. I had a wonderful life whilst they were stuck in that dreadful place. But you're right, of course.'

'Maybe I am magical after all.' She smiled. 'I enjoy your visits, Tina, but they must lessen as you get to know your sisters, your culture, and *you*!'

'Thank you, Ama.' Tina reluctantly turned to the door.

'And one last thing,' said Ama. 'Talk to Sarah. Your mother. Eventually you must forgive her.'

Tina used her key to let herself into the house.

'You came back!'

'I'm here, aren't I?' she said. Oh, how she wanted her words to come out harsher, to place just some of the hurt and anguish onto her mother. But what would it accomplish?

Her mother stood under the ridiculously grand chandelier as Susan hovered on the spiral staircase in that dreadful uniform her mother made her wear.

'Hi, Susan,' called Tina with a wave.

'Hello! Do you need anything?'

'No, I just want a word with my mother. I'll come and have a chat after.' Tina had always liked Susan and at times wished her mother was more like her: warm, open and not the stiff, enclosed woman who'd brought her up. Of course, it all made sense now. How else could she behave towards the child of a woman who had slept with her husband?

After telling her mother for the second time that she didn't want any tea, Tina was finally able to say the words which had been sitting on her tongue for weeks.

'You should have told me.'

'I know.'

'I don't just mean about Rex being my real father, but about everything. What you did was despicable. You can't play God like that.'

'I know. You're right.'

She hated her mother just a little bit more for agreeing with everything she said. How was she supposed to chastise this woman who had suddenly aged ten years overnight? Once a sprightly and still handsome woman, she was now reduced to being a hunched-over pensioner in floods of tears. How would Tina look? What would Susan say? She'd probably escort Tina out of the house, mumbling how disappointed she was in her.

'I am so sorry, Tina. You mean the world to me, you're all I ever cared about,' she said, in between sobs.

'I find that hard to believe right now. I think you were just saving yourself, worried about what your well-heeled friends would feel. Daddy Quinton was your leg-up on the social ladder. Finally, you had married the man you thought you had deserved

all along. You told me enough times how important that was –
especially when you were selling Mark to me.'

Her mother closed her eyes and slowly opened them.

'You told me often enough that Rex, my real father, was just
a jumped-up businessman who struck it rich with property but
had no real class! So, you weren't going to jeopardise your new
and better life by telling me the truth, Mother. This was all about
you. All about you.'

'I am so sorry.' Her mother placed a bony hand onto Tina's
arm. 'I'm sorry.'

Tina pulled her arm away. 'I can't forgive you, Mother. Not
yet. It's too much.'

Her mother nodded her head rapidly as, thankfully, the tears
began to subside. 'I understand.'

'It's too much,' Tina repeated.

Tina returned home that very night.

'I'm so glad you're back … you are back, aren't you?' said
Mark. The dark circles around his eyes suggested he'd not been
sleeping much lately.

'I am,' she replied. 'But things are going to have to change.
I don't want what we had before. I need more. So much more.'

'I will try. I can only try, Tina. I was never the most romantic
man when you met me. That's just not me.'

She rolled her eyes. 'It's a bit more than that, Mark.'

'I will try my best to do what I can. Whatever you need.'

'Well, that you're willing to try is a start. But I can't promise
you anything. We'll have to take it day by day.'

'Tina, I am willing to try anything, whatever you want,
because I will do anything to keep you. I love you, Tina. I'm
nothing without you.'

'Don't say that, Mark. That's how I used to think – that I was
nothing without you. All my life I've been looked after. First
by my sisters, then Mother and Daddy Quinton … and then

you. I've remained this little girl, but at twenty-two I'm ready to become a woman, with all my nuances and flaws. I'm ready. And you will have to accept that side of me, too.'

'Anything. Anything you want, Tina.' He still wasn't getting it, but that was OK. This was about Tina and no one else.

Chapter Forty-five

For Lana, having found her sisters months earlier than anticipated meant she had plenty of time to spend with them before her sabbatical was over. She would harass Eve into taking a break and treat her to a modest noodle lunch, or just rediscover the joys of walking aimlessly with Tina on a Tuesday afternoon, enjoying the mild weather. It was during such a walk that a huge gym bag appeared from nowhere, swiping her across the shoulder.

'Oops, sorry!' said the woman as she lowered the bag onto the floor.

'That's OK—' she said, immediately locking eyes with Denise. 'Denise!'

'Lana. Hi,' she said awkwardly.

The three women moved away from the crowds.

'Just left the gym,' said Denise.

'This is my sister, Tina.'

'I didn't know you had a sister.'

'Neither did I!' said Tina, her smile lost on Denise. She quickly focused on the children's clothing displayed in a shop window.

'I thought Clifton would have mentioned it,' said Lana, suddenly feeling uncomfortable. 'How are you?'

'Busy, busy, busy,' said Denise, with what sounded like exaggeration.

'I hope everything's OK, you know, with us?'

'Why wouldn't it be?'

'I don't want you to stay away from me because of the whole answering-the-phone incident.'

'Clifton explained all of that. Ancient history.'

'Good, because, well, you're going to be around for a very long time and we really need to get along. Maybe we can even go out sometime, just the two of us. What do you say?'

'No, I think I'll pass on that, if you don't mind.'

'I thought you and I were OK?'

'We are. Me and Clifton on the other hand ...'

'I don't understand, Denise.'

'He didn't tell you, did he?'

'Tell me what?'

'Clifton and I broke up over a month ago.'

Clifton had almost finished the seafood sandwich by the time Lana slid up beside him on the park bench.

'I thought we were having lunch together?' asked Lana.

Clifton placed a bulky plastic bag onto her lap. 'I didn't forget your sandwich, if that's what you're asking!'

She carefully unwrapped the sandwich. 'Tell me the truth, Clifton. Are you and Denise still together?'

'Nope.'

'Why didn't you tell me?'

'You didn't ask.'

'That's pathetic.'

'You've had a lot on. I didn't feel I should say anything.'

'You split up with probably the only girl you've ever loved – the girl you were going to marry – and you think I wouldn't have time for you? What kind of friend do you think I am?' She turned to him. 'Seriously, you've always been there for me, so I'm not sure why you'd ever think I wouldn't do the same for you.'

'Lana, let it drop, it's no big deal.'

'Clifton!'

'What do you want me to say? It's over. It has been for ages and long before we split up.'

Lana bit into the sandwich. 'Why did you split up anyway?'

'I liked someone else. More than liked.'

'Oh, I see!'

'Don't worry. She doesn't want anything to do with me.'

Lana rewrapped the remainder of the sandwich, suddenly not that hungry. 'Tell me more about her … you know, if you want. I'm not here to judge you.'

'She's kind, funny, really generous. Talks a lot, but that's OK and she's highly emotional, cries at the drop of a hat.'

Clifton slowly wiped a stray crumb from Lana's cheek and her throat suddenly felt dry.

'I see …' she said hoarsely.

'She's gorgeous … but there's so much more to her than that. She's … she's home.'

'Wow, OK,' she said, shrugging him away, her voice suddenly higher-pitched. 'This girl sounds great!' She couldn't decide where to look, because if she looked into his eyes …

'We liked each other once, but the timing was off, so I waited. Then, just when the both of us were finally free, she gets caught up again.' His gaze became a little intense. His eyes bored into her, exposing a truth she was trying to ignore.

'Clifton?' she whispered, feeling clumsy, unsure if they were actually back at Grassy Green as teenagers, when they had confessed their feelings only to be torn apart by a parent who wanted her son back. Nights spent dreaming of kissing him again, fading into a reality involving a friendship with no trimmings – the best of friends and a bond no one, not even a girlfriend, could ever break.

'Don't say I'm like a brother to you! I know we've missed our time, but just don't say that!' He stood up. 'I'm going to go now. I hope you enjoy the sandwich.'

'Clifton, I don't want to ruin what we have because your friendship means everything to me. You've always been there. I can't do this.'

'I know.'

As she watched him turn and walk away, Lana wondered if their friendship had now been severed beyond repair. They'd been 'Lana and Clifton' for so long she had no idea where he ended and she began. The last few months for her had been so wondrously life-changing. She'd never envisaged losing Clifton in the process.

Was losing Clifton the payback for gaining her sisters?

Was she about to lose the one person who had never left?

'Wait!' she called out. Clifton's long legs had already reached the gates of the park. She ran as fast as she could, catching up with him.

Her breath caught in her throat as she spoke. 'Don't go yet.'

'What are you doing?' he asked with amusement.

'I'm not prepared to lose you. That's not happening.' She placed her hands on her knees, doubling over and breathing rather heavily.

'You would never lose me. I'm not going anywhere.'

Lana looked up at the boy she'd known since the age of twelve. They'd always related to each other in a special way. Clifton was her friend, her protector. And, at that moment, slightly out of breath through lack of fitness, she'd no idea if her relationship with him had survived merely because of their upbringing, or because there was a chance they'd be able to rekindle their teenage romance.

Anything was possible, though.

The last few months had taught her that.

Chapter Forty-six

The last time Tina had been to a graveside, she'd been fifteen. That day, she'd helplessly watched those around her fall apart and with her mother unable to reach out to anyone, Tina had been left to grieve alone. She'd dressed all in black then, but this time she would wear a purple jumper and black skirt as, apparently, purple had been her favourite colour.

'Would you like me to come with you?' asked Mark. Her husband had been trying his best to morph into the man he thought she wanted, washing the dishes and reading Samantha a bedtime story every night. Although she'd accepted Mark's flaws a long time ago, she was enjoying this change and as long as he accepted her changes, they would have a good chance of making it. Of that she was sure.

'I'll be OK, Mark. Spend some time with our girl. She'll love that.'

*

Eve could barely remember the girl she'd once been, standing beside her mother's grave and refusing to look at it. She could recall a howling wind blowing in the distance and her numb refusal to feel. The temptation was there to shut down yet again and to reject her heightened emotions, but at least this time she could turn to her sisters for support.

This time would be different.

Eve slipped each arm into her black Claude Montana wide-collared jacket, covering the purple blouse Aunty Ginny had told her to wear. It was her favourite colour, apparently, and yet another titbit she'd never known about her mother. Eve looked forward to the masses of information Aunty Ginny would divulge over the years. She had so much more to learn about her mother and father, about Tayo and Adanya Cole.

Eve smiled as she recalled her assistant Lee's astonishment when she'd announced a three-week break for next month – similar to how he'd looked when she'd handed him a birthday present (a regift from a grateful client, but a gift nevertheless).

Eve planned to spend the bulk of the break on a well-earned holiday with her sisters. The three women had playfully argued on where they would stay. Eve insisted on a five-star hotel, Tina was fixed on a weird yoga retreat and Lana preferred a B & B. Of course, Eve had no intention of staying in a B & B. She'd had her fill of those!

Eve and her sisters were so different, yet the same. She'd never be able to explain this concept to anyone, but they knew. Deep down, each sister was deeply aware that such differences merely strengthened the bond between them.

They were sisters. They would always be sisters.

*

Lana admired her purple slingbacks in the mirror, thrilled to find out Mummy adored purple. So did she. It was another confirmation of the bond she'd always felt with her mother.

'You look lovely,' said Clifton.

'Thank you.'

'You sure you don't want a lift?'

'That's OK. I don't know how long we'll be and I don't want to think about you waiting around. Besides, you have a business to run!'

'My garage can survive without me for a couple of hours.'

'This will probably take a bit longer than that.'

'True. I know how you three can get.'

'As I always say, you can't blame us – we've got a lot to catch up on!'

Lana was second to arrive as Eve waited by the pillar as instructed. Two bouquets of purple roses flared against the blackness of her jacket. Tina arrived a minute later with a simple yet elegant tall-stemmed purple orchid.

'There she is,' said Eve, as Aunty Ginny slowly climbed out of her son's blue Ford.

She headed towards them. 'Addy's girls.' Lana always felt a rush of warmth whenever Aunty Ginny referred to them this way.

'Ready?' asked Aunty Ginny. With Tina beside her and holding hands with Aunty Ginny, Eve trailing slightly behind, the four women walked towards their parents and best friend.

The sun was radiant as each sister stared down at the two plaques depicting their parents' names.

'I haven't been in a while. Many years, in fact. I just couldn't, not with you girls still out there,' said Lana, as Tina removed the older flowers and placed them into a plastic bag.

'I've never even been. If I had known—' said Tina.

'That wasn't your fault.'

'I know, but it still hurts. That's my mum!'

'You're here now,' said Aunty Ginny.

Lana noticed the rigidity in Eve's body. She hadn't said much since they'd arrived, merely clutching the two large bunches of purple roses as if letting go would be the hardest thing to do.

'Have you ever thought about finding the rest of your family?' asked Aunty Ginny.

'I wouldn't know where to start,' admitted Lana. 'The authorities didn't do a very good job in looking for them the first time around.'

'Those useless idiots wouldn't know their arse from their elbows!' said Aunty Ginny.

'She's right about that. You found us, so I know you can find our grandparents, if they're still alive,' said Tina.

'And you chased Tina all around a foreign country!' added Aunty Ginny. 'Seriously girls, you have a whole family out there. Not sure about Tayo's parents ... that was a sore point ... and I don't know if that was Addy's illness talking or if it was real. But she talked a lot about her mum and dad, and four or five brothers. They must be out there wondering what happened to you lot!'

'Four,' corrected Lana.

'You see? You remember more than you think. If we look in her diary, we can get addresses and see if they match up to what you remember when you lived there.'

'There's so many pages that have torn out and only one address that looks remotely Nigerian in the book,' said Lana.

'It's a start,' said Aunty Ginny.

'Then there's the address on the fan.'

'What fan?'

'The one you gave me, Aunty Ginny. Just after the funeral. It was in the vanity case. I haven't looked at it in a while, but I remember a faded address of some sort. It's probably nothing, but maybe not.'

'There you go, then. I can hear the cogs of your mind working already.'

'To think we have all those family members living five thousand or so miles away! What do you think Eve?' asked Tina.

Eve remained with her back to the group, staring down at Mummy's grave.

'Eve?' asked Lana, moving over to where she stood, and immediately seeing the single tear rolling down her sister's cheek.

Lana edged away.

The sun had all but set and it felt like it was time to go.

Aunty Ginny whispered a prayer to her best friend and warned Tayo to 'look after my Addy'.

'Bye Mummy, bye Daddy,' said Lana.

Tina blew a kiss at her mother's gravestone, closing her eyes solemnly. She turned to Tayo's plot and said, 'Look after my mum.'

'I'll probably see you soon, you two,' said Aunty Ginny, pointing to each of the graves.

'Don't say that! You're going to be around for a long while yet!' said Tina. They turned to leave. All except Eve. Lana looked back to see her sister stoop and finally place the bouquets she had been clutching onto each of the graves.

'We'll give Eve a bit of privacy,' suggested Aunty Ginny.

Lana felt her heart break all over again at the sight of her sister placing herself on the ground, between the graves of their parents. At that moment, Eve was not the first black woman ever to be voted onto the board of a UK retail company, but a little girl who was lost and confused. Only this time, she was not alone. Lana would make sure that Eve Cole would never be alone again.

Despite the tears and the sadness, the day had been a joyous one for Lana. She had so much more to share with her family, including the news that she would be honouring her mummy, daddy and her Nigerian culture by switching her name back to Lanre – and that Lanre Cole was about to embark on training to become a nurse.

As a family they had so much to look forward to and a lifetime of wishes to fulfil. And, with her life still on its wonderfully eventful journey, she was now ready to fully embrace the sensation of love with those around her. Lanre couldn't wait to continue learning from three people with whom she had shared a deep and remarkable bond all those years ago.

Adanya and Tayo would always live on inside of Lanre, Eve, Tina and Aunty Ginny. Their love affair, although brief in time, would remain in the hearts of those left behind forever.

Epilogue

My beautiful Adanya,

I am writing this as I wait for you and my children to arrive at the airport. My three beautiful girls will soon be reunited with me, and I can't believe this is real. Tonight I will get to sleep in the same house as my family! But more than that, I will be allowed to give these girls a start in life my own father could only dream of, and I will be able to treat you like the queen you are.

I know that coming to England has always been important to you and I live to make you happy. I will always remember the days after you gave birth to Lanre. Your smiles were not plentiful like before. I could not do anything to please you, and I felt helpless. You kept saying that England was the answer. It was then that I knew I would do everything in my power to make it happen.

So as I wait for you, Lanre and Mayowa to appear through the door, I know that I have not failed you, Adanya. Everything will be wonderful once you arrive.

We are about to live the life we have always dreamed of!

Forever yours,
Tayo Cole

Acknowledgements

I'd like to give thanks to: God, for everything; also to Judith Murdoch, for always sticking by me – even when what I wrote wasn't 'all that' – and always managing to see the bigger picture; Gillian Green, for seeing something in my writing many moons ago and being that silent cheerleader over the years (was a bit like a 'will they, won't they?' film, and here we are!); my family and friends in the UK and USA – especially those who would simply ask, 'How's the writing going?' on days when I preferred the company of my TV!

A special mention also to those who, whilst I was numb with grief, kept me propped up during the editing of this book: Zeeshan Mallick, Pearl Yamoah, Nike Buli, Belen De Paz, Carmen Munoz, Julia Blues, Joy Kenyon and Zalika and Aaliyah Akinsete. You are the best!

Lastly, those encouraging voices, which suddenly became silent, remain in my heart. Rest in paradise: Grace Akinwunmi (Mum), Tunde Abdullah Akinsete (bro) and Mrs Sheila Graham (Mum, too); you are missed every single day.

Also available from Ebury Press:

An Orphan's Secret

MAGGIE HOPE

Life is a long, tough struggle for Meg Maddison . . .

Growing up caring for her brothers after the death of their
mother, it is only her indomitable spirit that gets her through
the hard times. And when she marries and starts a family
of her own, it seems as if the hardships are over.

But the return of a darkly menacing figure from her past
threatens to destroy all she has fought for . . .

Also available from Ebury Press:

War Orphans

LIZZIE LANE

"If at all possible, send or take your household animals into the country in advance of an emergency. If you cannot place them in the care of neighbours, it really is kindest to have them destroyed."

Joanna Ryan's father has gone off to war, leaving
her in the care of her step-mother, a woman more
concerned with having a good time than being
any sort of parent to her.

But then she finds a puppy, left for dead, and Joanna becomes
determined to save him, sharing her meagre rations with him.
But, in a time of war, pets are only seen as an unnecessary
burden and she is forced to hide her new friend, Harry, from
her step-mother and the authorities. With bombs falling over
Bristol and with the prospect of evacuation on the horizon,
can they stay together and keep each other safe?

Also available from Ebury Press:

Flora's War

AUDREY REIMANN

Dare she risk her reputation?

When the orphaned Flora MacDonald escapes from
a harsh reform school she falls – literally – into the arms
of Andrew Stewart, a handsome sailor on shore leave. But
their blossoming love is interrupted by the outbreak of the
Second World War.

With Andrew away fighting, Flora finds herself in an
impossible situation: alone and pregnant. Out of desperation,
she travels to Andrew's country estate, but she doesn't
know how kindly his well-to-do family will welcome her in.
Will she find a home where she can raise a child?

Also available from Ebury Press:

Maggie's Kitchen

CAROLINE BEECHAM

A young girl trying to do her best for her country . . .

When the British Ministry of Food urgently calls for the opening of restaurants to feed tired and hungry Londoners during WWII, Maggie Johnson seems close to realising a long-held dream. After overcoming a tangle of red tape, Maggie's Kitchen finally opens its doors to the public and Maggie finds that she has an unexpected problem – her restaurant is too popular, and there's not enough food to go round.

Then Maggie takes twelve-year-old street urchin Robbie under her wing and, through him, is introduced to a dashing Polish refugee, digging for victory on London's allotments. Between them they will have to break the rules in order to put food on the table . . .

Coming soon from Ebury Press:

A Wartime Friend

LIZZIE LANE

Will an unlikely friendship be enough to save them?

After escaping a train bound for a death camp with a trusty
German Shepherd dog, a girl wakes to find that she has no
memory of her former life.

Lily is fostered by the kind RAF pilot who found her and
his wife, Meg. It is not long before their lives are disrupted
once again by the war and, with their home in ruins, they
are forced to flee to the country.

In the Somerset countryside, Lily is reunited with Rudy,
the heroic German Shepherd. However it soon becomes clear
that Rudy is not just her companion, he is protecting her too,
and someone wants him out of the way ...

Coming soon from Ebury Press:

Workhouse Angel

HOLLY GREEN

Angelina was abandoned on the doorsteps of Brownlee
Workhouse when she was just a baby. The only clues to
her parentage are her golden curls and the rag doll she
held in her arms.

Nicknamed 'Angel', she finds a friend in the little orphan
girl, May, who protects her from the harshness of workhouse
life as best she can. When Angel is adopted by the McBrides,
she thinks at first that she has found a family to call her own.
However, her new parents are not the pillars of society they
seem. They treat Angelina harshly and are terrified of people
discovering their daughter's humble origins.

But then a man comes to the workhouse, looking for the
little girl he was forced to give up. A girl with golden hair
and a ragdoll who isn't an orphan after all …

The Runaway

AUDREY REIMANN

Oliver Wainwright is still a boy when he first sets eyes on the fair, delicate Florence – the aristocratic granddaughter of Sir Philip Oldfield. And, determined never to be a servant or follow in his father's footsteps as a quarry worker on the Oldfield estate, he runs away to Middlefield, that very day.

Slowly but surely, he sets about becoming a man of property and a cotton industry king. He works single-mindedly to achieve his ambition – until he meets Rosie, a married mill hand who distracts him with her dark, warm beauty. Has Oliver finally found what he really wanted all along?

Set against a background of the Lancashire cotton industry, *The Runaway* is a magnificent saga of a young man's rise to power, his passion and poverty, feuds and triumphs and the two very different women who shape his life.